REBEL CAMP

"On the left," Jaybird chirped. "Looks like six men. Yes. A small puff of smoke, had to be a rifle shot."

At once the pilot wheeled away from the river and dove to get out of the line of fire.

"Stay close enough so we can see the river," Murdock shouted. "Go up another five thousand feet. Then get back to the river."

"Too dangerous," the pilot said.

Murdock put his KA-BAR blade against the young pilot's throat. "For now, I'll tell you when it's too dangerous. Now take us up to five thousand feet and get us back so we can see the river."

The pilot's forehead beaded with sweat and he swallowed twice. "Yes, sir. Will do."

In the distance, about a half mile from the river, they spotted a large clearing, and could see tents, many fires, and as they came closer, dozens of men.

"Get out of here," Murdock told the pilot when he saw some riflemen on the ground and figured they were about to fire. The bird pivoted to the left and dove a thousand feet, then leveled off.

SEAL TEAM SEVEN
DEADLY FORCE

KEITH DOUGLASS

BERKLEY BOOKS, NEW YORK

This is a work of fiction. Names, characters, places, and incidents either are the product of the author's imagination or are used fictitiously, and any resemblance to actual persons, living or dead, business establishments, events, or locales is entirely coincidental.

Special thanks to Chet Cunningham for his contributions to this book.

SEAL TEAM SEVEN: DEADLY FORCE

A Berkley Book / published by arrangement with the author

PRINTING HISTORY
Berkley edition / December 2002

Copyright © 2002 by The Berkley Publishing Group.
SEAL TEAM SEVEN logo illustration by Michael Racz.
Cover art by Cliff Miller.

Visit our website at
www.penguinputnam.com

ISBN: 0-425-18634-2

BERKLEY®
Berkley Books are published by The Berkley Publishing Group, a division of Penguin Putnam Inc., 375 Hudson Street, New York, New York 10014. BERKLEY and the "B" design are trademarks belonging to Penguin Putnam Inc.

PRINTED IN THE UNITED STATES OF AMERICA

10 9 8 7 6 5 4 3 2 1

*This novel
about the fictional
SEAL Team Seven is gratefully
dedicated to the real SEALs based
at Coronado, California: Teams
One, Three, and Five
of the Naval Special
Warfare Command.
These real SEALs
do the dirty
little jobs
that
keep America free!*

SEAL TEAM SEVEN
DEADLY FORCE

SEAL TEAM SEVEN

Rear Admiral (L) Richard Kenner. Commander of all SEALs.

Commander Dean Masciareli. 47, 5' 11", 220 pounds. Annapolis graduate. Commanding officer of Naval Special Warfare Group One in Coronado, including SEAL Teams One, Three, Five, and Seven and the 978 men.

Master Chief Petty Officer Gordon MacKenzie. 47, 5' 10", 180 pounds. Administrator and head enlisted man of all NAVSPECWARGRUP-ONE in Coronado.

Lieutenant Commander Blake Murdock. Platoon Leader, Third Platoon. 32, 6' 2", 210 pounds. Annapolis graduate. Six years in SEALs. Father important congressman from Virginia. Apartment in Coronado. Single. Has a car and a motorcycle, loves to fish. Weapon: Alliant Bull Pup duo 5.56mm & 20mm explosive round.

ALPHA SQUAD

Timothy F. Sadler. Senior Chief Petty Officer. Top EM in Third Platoon. Third in command. 32, 6' 2", 220 pounds. Married to Sylvia, no children. Been in the Navy for fifteen years, a SEAL for last eight. Expert fisherman. Plays trumpet in any Dixieland combo he can find. Weapon: Alliant Bull Pup duo 5.56mm & 20mm explosive round. Good with the men.

David "Jaybird" Sterling. Machinist's Mate First Class. Lead petty officer. 24, 5' 10", 170 pounds. Quick mind, fine tac-

---

*Third Platoon assigned exclusively to the Central Intelligence Agency to perform any needed tasks on a covert basis anywhere in the world. All are top-secret assignments. Goes around Navy chain of command. Direct orders from the CIA.

tician. Single. Drinks too much sometimes. Crack shot with all arms. Grew up in Oregon. Helps plan attack operations. Weapon: H & K MP-5SD submachine gun.

Luke "Mountain" Howard. Gunner's Mate Second Class. 28, 6' 4", 250 pounds. Black man. Football at Oregon State. Tryout with Oakland Raiders six years ago. In Navy six years. SEAL for four. Single. Rides a motorcycle. A skiing and windsurfing nut. Squad sniper. Weapon: H & K PSG1 7.62 NATO sniper rifle.

Bill Bradford. Quartermaster First Class. 24, 6' 2", 215 pounds. An artist in his spare time. Paints oils. He sells his marine paintings. Single. Quiet. Reads a lot. Has two years of college. Platoon radio operator. Carries a SATCOM on most missions. Weapon: Alliant Bull Pup duo 5.56mm & 20mm explosive round.

Joe "Ricochet" Lampedusa. Operations Specialist First Class. 21, 5' 11", 175 pounds. Good tracker, quick thinker. Had a year of college. Loves motorcycles. Wants a Hog. Pot smoker on the sly. Picks up plain girls. Platoon scout. Weapon: H & K MP-5SD submachine gun.

Kenneth Ching. Quartermaster First Class. 25, 6' even, 180 pounds. Full-blooded Chinese. Platoon translator. Speaks Mandarin Chinese, Japanese, Russian, and Spanish. Bicycling nut. Paid $1,200 for off-road bike. Is trying for Officer Candidate School. Weapon: H & K MP-5SD submachine gun.

Vincent "Vinnie" Van Dyke. Electrician's Mate Second Class. 24, 6' 2", 220 pounds. Enlisted out of high school. Played varsity basketball. Wants to be a commercial fisherman after his current hitch. Good with his hands. Squad machine gunner. Weapon: H & K 21-E 7.62 NATO round machine gun.

Bravo Squad

Lieutenant (j.g.) Christopher "Chris" Gardner. Leader Bravo Squad. Second in command of Third Platoon. 28, 6' 4", 240 pounds. Four years in SEALs. Hang-glider nut. Married to

Wanda, who designs clothes. Father is a Navy admiral. Grew up in ten different states. Annapolis graduate. Weapon: Alliant Bull Pup duo 5.56mm & 20mm explosive round.

George "Petard" Canzoneri. Torpedoman's Mate First Class. 27, 5' 11", 190 pounds. Married to Phyllis. No kids. Nine years in Navy. Expert on explosives. Nicknamed "Petard" for almost hoisting himself one time. Top pick in platoon for explosives work. Weapon: Alliant Bull Pup duo 5.56mm & 20mm explosive round.

Miguel Fernandez. Gunner's Mate First Class. 26, 6' 1", 180 pounds. Wife, Maria; daughter, Linda, 7, in Coronado. Spends his off time with them. Highly family oriented. He has many relatives in San Diego. Speaks Spanish and Portuguese. Squad sniper. Weapon: H & K PSG1 7.62 NATO sniper rifle.

Omar "Ollie" Rafii. Yeoman Second Class. 24, 6' even, 180 pounds. From Saudi Arabia. In U.S. since he was four. Loves horses, has two. Married, two children. Speaks Farsi and Arabic. Expert with all knives. Throws killing knives with deadly accuracy. Weapon: H & K MP-5SD submachine gun.

Tracy Donegan. Signalman Second Class. 24, 6' even, 185 pounds. Former Navy boxer. Tough. Single. Expert tracker and expert on camouflage and ground warfare. Expert marksman. Platoon driver, mechanic. Frantic Chargers football fan. Speaks Italian and Swahili. Weapon: H & K 21-E 7.62 NATO round machine gun.

Jack Mahanani. Hospital Corpsman First Class. 25, 6' 4", 240 pounds. Platoon medic. Tahitian/Hawaiian. Expert swimmer. Bench-presses four hundred pounds. Divorced. Top surfer. Weapon: Alliant Bull Pup duo 5.56mm & 20mm explosive round.

Frank Victor. Gunner's Mate Second Class. 23, 6' even, 185 pounds. Two years in SEALs. Radio, computer expert. Can program, repair, and build computers. Shoots small-bore rifle competitively. Married. Wife, June, a computer programmer/

specialist. No children. Lives in Coronado. Weapon: Alliant Bull Pup duo 5.56mm & 20mm explosive round.

Paul "Jeff" Jefferson. Engineman Second Class. 23, 6' 1", 200 pounds. Black man. Expert in small arms. Can tear apart most weapons and reassemble, repair, and innovate them. A chess player. Weapon: H & K MP-5SD submachine gun.

1

Gaslamp Quarter
San Diego, California

Senior Chief Petty Officer Timothy Sadler stared up at
Shortchops Jackson where he was taking a solo on his bass
fiddle in the middle of a wailing rendition of "When the
Saints Go Marching In." He was good, had played with a
lot of great jazz groups, but everyone knew he was over
the top of the curve and well on his way down the other
side. Even so, Shortchops simply blew away the knowl-
edgeable crowd there at the Basic Jazz Club in the Gaslamp
Quarter.

Shortchops finished the riff with a flourish and a wide-
mouthed grin as he shouted, "Oh, yeah," and everyone in
the room clapped and cheered.

The rest of the Gaslamp Quarter Dixieland Band came
in and raced through to the last notes on the old standard
tune. Sadler took a short blast in the middle of the last
phrase, and squealed his golden trumpet up to high C and
down again as they all came to a big finish.

Sadler knew that this was his pressure-relief valve. His
wild ride, a great way to relax after his high-powered, strict,
and often strident life as the top EM in Third Platoon of
SEAL Team Seven. It was a relief after the violent and
deadly games they played as the best and most active combat specialists in the whole SEAL contingent. They were
on direct call to the CNO, Chief of Naval Operations, who
set the wheels in motion when the President, the head of
the CIA, the State Department, or the National Security
Advisor needed some dirty little covert job done anywhere
in the world.

"Oh, yeah, Tim, you hit some good ones there," Short-chops said as they put their instruments on stands and headed for the back room where they could take a twenty-minute break.

"I try to keep up with you, Shortchops," Sadler said. "You were really wailing and flailing out there tonight."

"I'm getting it on, brother, getting it on. Almost felt like old days there for a few minutes." He closed his eyes, lifted his head, and shook it gently. "Oh, yeah, there were some great times back there twenty years ago. Memories, yeah, I have some great memories."

Sadler knew that Shortchops was on something. He didn't know what and he didn't want to know. The five of them were making good music together. It was a traditional Dixieland group: trumpet, clarinet, bass, trombone, and banjo. Sometimes they doubled with drums, piano, even a saxophone, and a tuba.

Sadler was thirty-two years old, young for a Dixieland man, but the oldest man in his SEAL platoon. He was a tough six feet two, married to Sylvia, and had no children. He had a thin face, heavy brows, a muscled body, and a whiteside, flattop brown haircut reminiscent of the 1940s. His blue eyes took in everything he saw like a camera.

Sadler gave Shortchops a high five, and they went into the back room. The place smelled of stale tobacco smoke, the sweat of dozens of musicians over the years, and a whiff of Lysol. Sadler watched Shortchops. He was the only black in their group. Six months ago he had been a patron of the club, sitting in with them from time to time. Then the U.S. Navy had transferred their bass player to Norfolk. They'd asked Shortchops to become a regular, and he'd fit like the middle finger of a glove. Sadler had no idea how old he was, maybe seventy-five. He was so thin, it looked like his white shirt would fall off his shoulders. They all wore identical ties, blue vertical-striped jackets, and flat white straw hats. Sadler was sure that the jacket sleeves of Shortchops covered up needle marks, but as long as he played the way he did tonight, nobody was going to ask him about drugs. The rest of them were clean.

Steve Rawlings was fifty-five, and hit the bottle a little hard now and then, but he could play his trombone as well drunk as he could sober. He worked in the post office, and had a beer gut that hung over his belt. He still wore a crew cut from his Navy days, and had two kids he put through college.

Dick Andrews, on clarinet, was fifty-one, and a lay preacher at his church. He had slicked-back black hair, a full beard, and was a singer for the group. He could have been great if he'd started his music earlier. Now he played for the love of it.

Tom Peterson, on banjo, was fifty-five, the band's leader and business manager. He worked as a stockbroker by day. He was a large man, just over six-five, and built like a concrete block. He had a grin you remembered all day.

It was their midnight break, and Sadler checked out the tray of sandwiches the kitchen always provided. They specialized in triangular white-bread tuna fish that was the best Sadler had ever had. They put chopped-up nuts in the mix.

"We was rollin' tonight," Shortchops said. He grabbed a sandwich and ignored the bottles of beer. "Got to hit the head," he said. Sadler watched him go. He'd come back a little higher and ready to wail. He must have his drugs stashed somewhere in the bathroom, or maybe just in his pocket.

Sadler grinned as Shortchops came back five minutes later with a black woman. She was maybe twenty, Sadler figured. Had on a skirt that barely covered her panties, fishnet stockings, and a blouse that showed half of one breast. He could smell her perfume from across the room. Poison maybe, or Obsession.

"One of my ladies," Shortchops said. "Wanted to see you'all, a real live Dixie-shit band. Now you seen them, baby, let's move."

She turned and one bare breast popped out of her blouse. She looked down and giggled. "Well, look at that. Miss Boob here wants to say hi, too."

Shortchops turned her around. "Baby, this ain't no tit show. Let's get to the important stuff." He looked back, grinned at them, and angled her out the door.

After their twenty-minute break, the band was halfway through "Too Tired in New Orleans" when Shortchops came in late and grabbed his bass. His face was bright, his grin wide, and he latched onto the next sixteen with a crazy and wild beat that went beyond syncopation. That run proved to Sadler again that each jazz musician, and especially each Dixieland cat, became his own composer. Their group never played the same number the same way twice. Each man had a turn at a wailing solo, and the true fans of Dixieland gloried in the variety and diversity that these improvised riffs brought to their music.

The Gaslamp Dixieland Band played for another hour, and Sadler noticed that Shortchops was not looking good. He missed his solo twice, and had trouble giving them a solid beat with his whanging on the long strings. He seemed distracted or worried about something. Sadler saw Shortchops watching the side door that led off the small stage they played on. Then he looked at the front door. A half hour before they were due to stop playing, Shortchops picked up his bass and left the stage. Sadler thought the bass player looked angry. The tall black man had never bugged out early before.

They played through to the two o'clock closing hour, and finished with their theme song, "It's Been a Long Night Coming."

Before the band members had their instruments put away, two men in suits came in. Sadler figured they could only be cops. Sure enough, they flashed San Diego Police Department badges and said they wanted to talk to the band.

"Talk? What about?" Sadler asked.

"We ask the questions," the tall detective said. He told them his name was Petroff. He had a thin, angular face with deep sunken eyes that were almost black. "Were any of you in the alley behind the club tonight?"

Dick Andrews, the clarinet player, nodded. "Yeah, I parked out there tonight, way down at the end. Hope my car hasn't been trashed."

"Wouldn't know about that," Petroff said. "You go into the alley between parking it and now?"

"No."

"Anybody else been back there?"

The other three shook their heads.

"We've got a problem. A young black woman dressed like a prostitute. A friend with her said the girl came into the club by the back door. Said she knew one of the musicians. She came back and said she had taken a pop of heroin, and then she sat down in the alley. They talked, and five minutes later the girl was dead on an OD. We want to know who gave her the stuff."

The second detective frowned. He was short, and as he took off his jacket, his white shirt showed wet spots under his arms. His tie had been loosened and he was fifty pounds overweight. He didn't tell them his name. Sweat moistened his face and fought with a heavy dash of mint-smelling aftershave.

"Where the hell is the fifth guy?" he asked. "I was in here last week and five of you played. Yeah, a black guy, older than most of you. Where's the cat who banged on the bass?"

"He went home early," Anderson said.

"Yeah?" the fat detective asked. "Was he wasted? Was he on drugs?"

"I never saw him do any drugs," Sadler said.

The cop looked at the rest of them. They all said the same thing.

"Did you see a black girl in a short skirt come into the club tonight?" Petroff asked.

"Oh, damn," Tom Peterson said. "Yeah, we all saw her. Short plastic skirt that barely covered her and a yellow blouse."

The detectives looked at each other. Petroff took over. "All right, just relax, everyone. This could take some time. We're going to take statements from all of you. One at a time. You, sir, will be first." He pointed at Steve. "The rest of you go out into the club with Detective Lasiter. I know it's late, so we'll do this as quickly as possible." He took out a small notebook and looked at Steve.

"Now, give me your name, address, work and home

phone numbers, and then tell me exactly what happened
when the black girl came in."

Sadler and the other two musicians went into the club.
It was a half hour after closing. A waitress brought them
coffee on the house. She looked frightened. This little club
always smelled like beer. He didn't know why. It wasn't a
grungy beer bar. But the hops-and-malt scent hung heavy
in the air. At least there was no smoking allowed.

"They said they want to talk to all of us," the waitress,
with the name tag of Bunny, shrilled, not able to keep her
voice down. "Christ, we'll be here all night."

Sadler sipped his coffee and tried to think what the SEAL
training sked was for tomorrow. No, it was for today now.
Damn. They had only been back to duty for two weeks
since they got home from the last mission in the Philippines. They'd all taken three-day leaves and come back
rested and ready. He grinned. Murdock and DeWitt had
both been on local television. That mission had not been
covert, and the press was all over it from the start. The
story was picked up nationally, and the two officers had
their fifteen minutes of fame.

Yesterday DeWitt had been officially transferred to another platoon as the commander. Good. He deserved it.
They still had to find a replacement for Franklin, who got
himself shot dead in the Philippines. Also, they needed a
new officer to lead Bravo. Both officers had wounds from
the mission. Murdock had had a bullet tear through his left
arm, but it wasn't serious. DeWitt had had a slug dig into
his right leg. Both would stay on duty.

Canzoneri was the worst hit, with a bad wound high in
his shoulder. He had been in Balboa Naval Hospital in San
Diego, and would be barred from any serious training for
another week.

Then it was Sadler's turn to be questioned. This was a
new experience for him. He wasn't sure he liked it.

"Your name?" Petroff asked.

Sadler told him: name, rank, and serial number.

"Navy. I did one hitch. What unit?"

"Third Platoon, SEAL Team Seven, Coronado, sir."

"A SEAL. A good outfit. Now tell me about the girl."

"What's all this flap about a hooker? Don't they cash in quite often?"

The detective frowned. "Yeah, but this one is different. I recognized her right away. She's famous, at least her father was. It was in the papers. She's the only whore I know who inherited three and a half million dollars."

"So why is she still whoring? If she's a junkie, she could be in dreamland for the rest of her life." Sadler scowled. "About the girl, yeah, she came in with Shortchops. I figured she was a hooker. One of her breasts popped out of her blouse and she laughed it off. Shortchops ushered her out and that's the last time I saw her."

"In your opinion, was Shortchops on drugs?"

"I'm no expert. But I'd say he was on something."

"Did you see him take pills, snort, or shoot up with a hypodermic needle?"

"No, sir."

"Not tonight?"

"Not tonight, not ever."

"Is Shortchops a violent man?"

"No, sir. He's soft, mellow. If he were drunk he'd be slobbering and crying. With drugs, I don't know. He's always been gentle and easy around me."

"How often do you see Shortchops?"

"Once a week. But I miss some of our gigs. I do some traveling with the SEALs."

"You were in the Philippines recently?"

"Yes. That one the papers went wild with."

"You men did a great job over there. Thanks, Senior Chief. You're free to go. I may want to talk to you again."

The other three members of the band were on the sidewalk outside the club.

"Damn, looks like we're going to need a new bass player," Dick Andrews said.

"You think Shortchops is involved with that girl?" Sadler asked. "They never said she must have taken an overdose. Petroff said she was rich, just inherited three and a half million dollars."

"No wonder they were spending time worrying about a hooker. This will be all over the papers tomorrow."

"Probably," Steve Rawlings, the trombone player, said. "I wonder if Shortchops had any part in what happened."

"He does do drugs," Peterson said. "Hell, I don't know much about drugs. Just enough to stay the hell away from them."

"Me, too," Rawlings said. "We're the wrong generation."

Peterson looked at Sadler. "Hey, Sailor, you going to be in town Friday? We got promoted to the weekend. And a small pop in pay to $125 each a night."

"Great, I'll get here whenever we're in town. Sometimes I don't have time to call you."

"Yeah, we play when you show," Peterson said. "Always glad to have your trumpet. Look at the time. I'm heading for home."

Sadler waved at them and angled across the street for his well-worn Buick. Sylvia would be worried. Usually he was home by this time. He always told her to go to sleep, but she never did. A few times she came to the club and had a sandwich and three or four Cokes. But that got old after a while. Great lady, but not much of a Dixieland buff. The Buick started on the first crank, and he drove toward the Coronado Bay Bridge and their condo.

A block down from the Basic Jazz Club, Shortchops Jackson watched from the front seat of his car as the police boiled around the front door and the alley. Suits all over the place. The ambulance rolled out of the alley with no lights and no siren. So she was dead. He'd been afraid of that. No rush now to get the body to the morgue.

Shortchops rubbed his hand across his face. She had been one fine lady. At eighteen Joisette Brown had been a knock-out. Then some asshole boyfriend got her hooked on shit and she never came out of it. She moved in with him. He pimped for her and six other girls. Six months ago Shortchops had paid off the pimp with the quick thrust of a thin-bladed knife through his fancy red vest, through his two-hundred-dollar sport shirt, and halfway into his heart before Shortchops turned the blade and sliced it outward. The pimp had died in that alley within seconds. Shortchops

had left the knife in the body. He had sauntered out of the
darkness into the light and gone a half mile over to play
his bass at the Basic Jazz Club.

After that, he had to take care of Joisette again. Her
father never knew what happened to his beautiful daughter
after she'd dropped out of San Diego State University a
year ago. He couldn't find her. She'd just vanished. Not
the cops, the private eyes her father hired, nor her friends
could find her.

She had stayed in Shortchops's one-bedroom apartment
in the worst part of town. Twice he had weaned her off
heroin. Twice she'd gone back on it, and into the streets at
night to make a few dollars to buy shit with. Then her father
died, unexpectedly. The music world mourned his passing.
There was a special on TV. Nobody spoke of his daughter,
but his entire estate, valued at something like 3.5 million
dollars, was left to Joisette Brown in his will. A close friend
said he'd talked about changing his will, but never had.
Shortchops read the story in the paper about the millionaire
daughter who couldn't be found. He dried out Joisette
again, got her off drugs for a week, then told her about the
money.

"Dad didn't love me or he wouldn't let me live like this,"
she'd said in one of her more lucid moments. "Hell, I don't
know if I want his money or not. I want to make it on my
own. I'm going to be a porn queen star. I could use that
money to produce some porn videos on my own." She had
frowned. "Hell, no, too complicated. I'd blow it in week,
give it away, gamble it. You get a lawyer and I'll make out
a will leaving everything to you. Then you keep me straight
for a month and we'll go to a lawyer and claim my money.
As soon as the estate gets settled, I'll give you a million
dollars. After that you keep me with all the shit I want and
a nice apartment where I can have friends in." Shortchops
had watched her. For a few minutes she had seemed almost
happy.

They had the will made up by a lawyer, had it notarized,
and it was legal and ironclad. Shortchops Jackson was the
major heir to Joisette's 3.5-million-dollar estate. That was

a month ago. Her dad's estate was still in probate, so he hadn't seen any money.

The next day after the money was claimed by Joisette, the story broke in the papers that Joisette Brown, daughter of jazz great and recording superstar Billy Ben Brown, had turned up in San Diego. The notary had talked to the newspapers.

Shortchops drove away from the club slowly. The cops would come hunting him. The other guys in the band had seen him go out with Joisette, and the cops must figure he shot up with her. No way did he kill her. He had never provided her with that shit, and he never would. He loved her in a strange, weird way. The 3.5 million dollars wasn't bad either. He'd need a good lawyer who would wait for his money. Shortchops knew that before he saw a lawyer, he needed to dry out and clean up and get straight again. When the cops found him, there was gonna be hell to pay. Until then he would vanish for a while. He had more than five hundred dollars in his shoe. Hell, he could get a high-roller suite at one of the Vegas hotels and last for at least a week. Oh, yeah. He'd drive over. He'd done it before. Just as he put his foot to the throttle to dodge down to the freeway, a blinking red light zeroed in on his rear bumper and the police siren gave one small wail. Shortchops swore at the rearview mirror as he pulled over to the curb and stopped his two-year-old Cadillac. Damn. If he'd been white, the cop never would have stopped him. Here it was almost three A.M. and a black dude was driving a good-looking car. A must stop. Shortchops rolled down the window and waited for The Man to come up to him.

2

West Coast of Africa
Sierra City, Sierra Bijimi

Twenty men in jungle cammies and floppy hats slid into positions near the Sierra City Central Police Station. All were armed with AK-47 rifles or H & K submachine guns. Their leader, Mojombo Washington, motioned one man ahead. A sentry walked his post outside the four-story building. He moved twenty feet beyond the main door, turned, and came back twenty feet this side of the door. As he turned on the near end of his post, a cammy-clad figure rose out of the shadows, rushed forward, and drove a fighting knife into the sentry's back. The guard didn't have time to scream before he died. The attacker caught him as he fell and pulled the AK-47 from his shoulder. Two more men dragged the dead policeman into deep shadows where the floodlight over the main door did not penetrate.

Six of Mojombo's fighters raced to the police headquarters' door from each side. Two men pulled the twin panels open and the twelve men charged inside. Mojombo led the troops, swinging his submachine gun to the left side he fired a three-round burst, dumping a police sergeant off his chair behind a desk, and then laced three rounds up the chest of a second cop who had been talking to his sergeant. The man on Mojombo's right dispatched a policeman who had lifted a pistol. The firing inside the building billowed into a roaring sound like a dozen thunderclaps all at once. With only half their usual hearing, the men communicated with hand signals. Mojombo had briefed them before the raid and each of the men knew his job.

Mojombo sent four men up steps to the second floor. He and six attackers drove into the hallway that led to the police headquarters supply rooms. They shot locks off doors, found the armory, and soon staggered from the room loaded with new AK-47's, boxes of ammunition, and pistols. They rushed them to the back door of the building, where a stolen truck waited. The men on the second floor fired down the hallway, keeping anyone in the rooms bottled up. Two blasts of a whistle sent those men dashing back down the stairs.

By that time some opposition had arrived. Four policemen tried to rush in the front door, but were met with a withering fire of submachine-gun rounds. The two still alive stumbled back outside and hid.

Mojombo and three of his men rushed into the central radio room and found two men on duty with earphones on. He guessed they were listening to music. Both died of multiple gunshot wounds before they knew anyone was there. Mojombo and his men searched the area until they found what they wanted: a box with six handheld radios in it, fresh from the factory. They had batteries with them and were ready to use. The attackers took the prize with them.

Down the hall in the records section, they dumped out files and tipped over desks and poured a gallon of gasoline on the pile, then threw a match into the mix and jumped out of the way of the whoosh of fire that the gas fumes ignited. They watched it burn for a moment, then rushed out. Four attackers stood guard in the hall. They were done except for one more stop. At the back of the building they found the storeroom for the kitchen. The police headquarters had a cafeteria for employees.

Mojombo and his men looted the storage area of dozens of boxes of canned food and baked bread, and from the freezer took two quarters of frozen beef. All went onto the truck that waited at the back door.

Mojombo blew the whistle again, and the nineteen men in his force charged through the first-floor hall and out the back door. They climbed on the open truck and Mojombo jumped in the cab. The driver gunned the rig down the narrow street and away.

Mojombo looked over at his driver and trusted lieutenant. "Gabu. Any casualties?"

"Two wounded, not seriously. We go to the old Army fort now?"

Mojombo smiled. Gabu had been his friend for many years, and was always eager for action, ready to strike back for the people. "Yes, Gabu. We know that half of the force there is on vacation for the holiday. Many of those left on the post will be drunk by now. We will go in the south gate, take out the guard, and charge to the supply depot on the far side. We may get there without any opposition." He grinned. "After all, this is an Army truck."

Mojombo Washington relaxed for a moment. This day had been a long time coming. He had gone away to school in America, and come back home to use his knowledge and skills in helping to govern his nation. But he'd found only corruption and graft and murder at almost all levels of government. He had tried to right small wrongs, and had been thrown in jail for a year. When he got out he had started his campaign to free his nation. He left his parents' modern home in Sierra City and took to the jungle, where government troops and police couldn't find him. Slowly he began to gain followers, men and women who thought the way he did and were willing to fight and die to make their country free from the thieves and murders who held it captive. He had made progress, but his people still had a long way to go. He called their movement the Bijimi Loyalist Party.

They drove down a street in the business section of Sierra City. Mojombo marveled at how the place had grown in the two years he'd been away. There were new buildings, owned and operated by President Kolda, no doubt financed with money he'd stolen from the federal treasury. Mojombo had heard there were more than 200,000 people living in his hometown now.

"Roadblock," Gabu said.

"They have put up a few lately to try to control the street traffic," Mojombo said. "I didn't think they would be manned this late at night. Slide up to it and stop. If the guard gives you any trouble, we'll have to shoot him and move on. Looks like he's Army."

The Sierra Bijimi soldier on duty at the roadblock saw the military truck coming, and quickly lifted the swing-down bar and gave a snappy salute. Then they were through.

Another five miles and they were at the edge of the city and coming up to the sprawling Sierra Bijimi Army base, Fort Sierra. It wasn't a real fort, just a collection of buildings, training grounds, a parade ground, and about three thousand troops. They slowed as they came to the south gate. The guard there, in a clean and pressed uniform, noted the number of the Army unit painted plainly on the bumper and waved them through.

"That hasn't changed since we were stationed here," Mojombo said. "No security at all. Not even a good try. Swing past the motor pool. We need a second truck. Two men will drop off the tailgate and negotiate with the guard on duty for a six-by-six."

"So far, so good, Captain," Gabu said. "We'll have supplies to keep us rolling for six months."

"Let's hope we can get our revolution going long before that, Gabu. It all depends on how much the people of our country support us, and help supply us. We have a lot of work to do yet."

The truck stopped at the motor pool, and two men in cammies and with sub guns dropped off the truck, which moved away to Building 426, marked "Supply Depot."

Gabu backed the truck up to a side door, and Mojombo and two men went to the front door. The guard saluted when he saw the captain's bars on Mojombo's shoulders.

"I'm here to see the officer in charge," Mojombo said.

The guard frowned. "Sorry, sir, he isn't here tonight. He reports to duty at 0800."

"Soldier, I'm on a special night-training exercise and I need to pick up supplies for the troops. I guess you'll have to sign the order form."

"Not allowed to do that, sir." The soldier had just got the words out when one of Mojombo's men stepped in behind him, caught his hair, and pulled his head back, then slit his throat from one carotid artery to the other. The soldier's eyes went wide, his voice coming out in a whisper as rich red blood spurted four feet into the air from both carotids with every beat of his heart.

The soldier dropped his rifle and put his hands up to his throat trying to hold in the blood. He slumped to the ground as the vital blood supply to his brain dropped lower and lower. He would be dead in a minute and a half, Mojombo knew. They dragged the body into some shadows and slid inside the unlocked front door. One man ran to the loading dock area and lifted the truck door. There were now two trucks at the dock waiting for supplies. Ten men stormed inside and went to selected sections of the huge warehouse where they picked out the designated supplies. Mostly they took dozens of cases of canned and packaged food, sacks and boxes of sugar, flour, cornmeal, and other staples.

In another section they found submachine guns and ammo. They piled them in boxes and took loads of RPGs, flares, armloads of uniforms, boots, and another case of handheld radios.

"Let's move," Mojombo shouted. "We could have company at any time."

A minute later a jeep rounded the corner of the huge warehouse, its lights picking up the truck at the loading dock. Mojombo walked out to the front of the truck and waited for the jeep. It stopped a dozen feet away and a man stepped out. He wore the dress uniform of an officer in the Sierra Bijimi Army. He walked up and saluted smartly.

"Sir, Officer of the Guard on rounds. I don't recall any orders for loading trucks tonight."

"At ease, Lieutenant. Special orders on a night-training exercise. It has to be realistic or training is no good. We load here, drive to another warehouse, get it checked out by the umpire on duty there, and then drive it back here and unload. From a practical standpoint it's absolutely useless, but then it's training."

"Yes, sir, I understand. I'll need your unit number and name for my report."

Mojombo saw one of his men approach the jeep from the driver's side. Mojombo drew his 9mm Glock from his holster and shot the officer twice in the chest before the man sensed any danger. Two more rounds sounded at the jeep, and the driver crumpled over the wheel.

The men were finished at the trucks. They pulled the canvas down over the backs and the rest of the men jumped on board.

"Let's get out of here," Mojombo said, and stepped into the cab of the first truck. At the south gate, the guard flagged them down.

"Been a little trouble on base, sir," the guard said. "I'll need to see your transit papers and orders."

Gabu shot the guard twice in the throat, and stormed the truck out the gate and down the road. The second truck followed closely behind them.

Mojombo looked at his watch in the truck's faint dash lights. "Almost three A.M. Time we head for the river. No chance that we can get to the President tonight. Maybe on the next trip."

"A good night's work," Gabu said.

"Yes, we did well."

Gabu looked at the blackness of the roadway. They were outside the town now and well into the countryside. There was only one road north, so they had to take it. "We expecting any trouble up the road?" Gabu asked.

"Probably. We didn't cut any telephone wires. Somebody will report our raid. They know we always go north."

"Probably around Tambacounda. They still have an Army post there?"

"They've rebuilt it since we burned it down a month ago," Mojombo said. "Yes, my guess is they'll have every man on the post out to the road to stop us. They for sure will get a telephone warning."

"So how do we surprise them?" Gabu asked.

"They know we'll be coming in by truck. So, we stop a half mile from their roadblock and take them on the ground. We get behind them if we can so they won't have any protection, and we take them out. Then we can clean out their supply room as well and be gone."

Gabu smiled. "How about my taking half the men to go around them and hit them from behind while you're engaging them from the front?"

"Yes, Gabu, yes. How much farther to Tambacounda?"

The driver checked out the window. "Maybe six or seven miles."

Mojombo settled back in the seat, his submachine gun over his knees. Yes, he remembered the small village well. Maybe three hundred souls. Extremely poor. Only one road through the town. At this side the road went over a small river. The attack would come at the bridge. Yes. They would stop a mile from the bridge and advance on foot, half on each side of the road.

Twenty minutes later the cammy-clad men with their submachine guns and AK-47's moved cautiously up the road toward the bridge. When they were a half mile away, they angled into the light brush and trees at the side of the blacktopped road and moved slower. A scout out in front came back quickly.

"Yes, there are soldiers at the bridge. On both sides of the road."

Mojombo nodded. Soon he and his men would have the radios operating and would be able to coordinate their efforts better. He sent a runner to the other side and told Gabu to continue. They would both attack when fifty yards away. A call of the nighthawk would be the signal to open fire. Mojombo had heard about night-vision goggles. He wished he had some. Then he could see where to shoot.

They moved up slower now. Soon their scout dropped down, and the rest of them went to ground. He crawled back. "I can see them. Most of them are smoking and talking. Maybe ten or fifteen on this side."

Mojombo thanked him and went up to look himself. They were thirty-five yards from the bridge. He brought his men up to form a rough skirmish line five yards apart, and cupped his hands and made the eerie sound of the nighthawk's call.

Then he lifted his weapon and opened fire. The twenty guns caught the defenders in total surprise. Half of them dove behind protection and fired back at the muzzle flashes. The attackers had the benefit of selecting cover first, and now kept up the firing at the few muzzle flashes they could see.

The firefight lasted for only forty-five seconds. "Cease

fire," Mojombo bellowed, and his weapons went silent. He saw two Army men lift up and race for the bridge. He brought them down with two three-round bursts from his sub gun. Nobody else moved. He waited five minutes. He knew that sometimes the man with the most patience in combat was the winner.

Another Army man tried to get across the bridge. He didn't make it. Then Mojombo heard splashing. Some of the defenders were wading across the small river.

"Forward," Mojombo bellowed. "Let's clean them out." By the time the twenty men got to the edge of the river on both sides of the bridge, they found only the dead and two seriously wounded Army soldiers. Mojombo dispatched them both with head shots. He counted fourteen bodies.

"Dagana," Mojombo called. The man who could run the fastest in his camp hurried up. "Run back and bring up the trucks. They should have crept up to within a quarter of a mile. Go."

His men picked up all the Army weapons they could find, mostly older AK-47's. They stripped all the ammunition from the bodies and took it with them. When the trucks arrived, they climbed on board.

"We won't hit the Army building," Mojombo said. "We're this close and we need to get to the river. Any casualties?" One man had a bullet in his arm. Another had what looked like a broken arm.

Mojombo smiled as the trucks raced through the small village and out the other side with no opposition from the Army. Now it was only five miles to the end of the road, and the dock where their boat should be waiting for them. He had left six men with a machine gun and five AK-47's to defend it. He didn't think that the Army would try to capture it. He nodded. Yes. He had struck another blow for freedom of his country. Not many of the people knew about his movement, but they would. When he had enough arms and enough men, he would blow the President right out of his corrupt Administration. He looked forward to that day. But he would need some help. He knew how he could get that help, how he could get the ear of the world so everyone would know about the corrupt and murderous President Thom Kolda.

At the end of the road, the two trucks crept through the tiny village of Abuja. About fifty people lived there, and they all were supporters of Mojombo. He could see no Army trap. Then the trucks drove up near the boat. All appeared normal. He sent Dagana running toward the boat. Soon the runner blinked a small flashlight twice at the trucks. All was well.

It took them a forty minutes to load all of the matériel and food they had brought on the trucks into the boat. Then they drove the rigs into the dense jungle as far as they could and camouflaged them with cut branches and limbs. With any luck the six-by-six trucks would be there when they needed them again.

Mojombo watched their only man who had any medical training treat the man's bullet wound, and put the other man's broken arm in a splint and a sling. The forty-foot wooden-hulled boat pushed off from the dock and angled into the current, heading upstream. The ancient diesel engine in the hold could move them against the flow at eight knots, so it would be a long run up the Amunbo River to their camp.

Mojombo welcomed his skipper, an old sailor with many sea voyages in his log. Tansarga had been one of Mojombo's first recruits. Mojombo eased back against the wall of the small cabin and watched out the windows as they hugged the shore to keep in the slower part of the current. Yes, he had made another successful raid. President Kolda would soon be paying more attention to him. Once, he had sent soldiers upstream to destroy Mojombo and his camp. The Army had found only an empty camp and an ambush, which resulted in fourteen Sierra Bijimi Army dead and twenty wounded from the accurate sniper fire of the hidden marksmen around the camp. The government soldiers had withdrawn at once in what turned out to be a rout.

Yes, President Kolda would send troops again, but with more caution. What Mojombo needed now was some help. Some outside assistance and plenty of worldwide publicity about his patriotic cause to free his nation from the pack of thieves, robbers, and murders who made up President Kolda's Administration. Now his job was to get that help.

3

NAVSPECWARGRUP-ONE
Coronado, California

Lieutenant Commander Blake Murdock sat at the desk in his small Third Platoon office and studied the files on three officers. He needed a new second in command for the platoon. Lieutenant Ed DeWitt's transfer had come through, moving him into command of the Second Platoon in SEAL Team Five, based right there in Coronado.

Master Chief MacKenzie had narrowed down a stack of volunteers for the position after word had gone out last week. Now Murdock read through the three. All were qualified. All had the needed rank of lieutenant (j.g.). All had good records in the black-shoe Navy and as SEALs. It would come down to the personal interviews. Two of the men were from there in Coronado. One was flying in today from NAVSPECWARGRUP-TWO in Little Creek, Virginia. He was due at the Quarterdeck at 0900. Murdock checked his watch: 0745.

He flexed his left arm. The bullet hole there still throbbed, and he wasn't up to speed on the O course. He grabbed three ibuprofen, tossed them into his mouth, and swallowed them. It had always been easy for him to down pills.

He checked the file on the man coming in from Virginia. JG Harry Belmer, twenty-six, six-two, 205 pounds, four years as a JG. Seemed like too long. He'd been a SEAL for three years. Yeah, tougher to get promoted inside. He scanned the man's records, including a recommendation by his current platoon leader:

"Personable, good with the men, commands respect, high leadership qualities, second-string all-American collegiate linebacker. Can follow orders, can evaluate situations well and lead his men in difficult situations. No combat experience. Has not been blooded."

Murdock nodded. Not many SEALs did get blooded these days. With no war on, and no police action, there were few calls on the SEALs to get down and dirty. Except for Third Platoon of Seven. He leaned back, laced his fingers together behind his head, and thought about his situation. Unique. None like it in the service. Even in any of the quick-response Special Forces. His platoon was one of a kind. Direct control from the CNO. The Chief of Naval Operations had battered down the complaints from Commander Masciareli, who headed the Coronado NAVSPECWARGRUP-ONE, and probably Admiral Kenner, boss of all the special war groups and the SEALs. Yeah, Murdock and his platoon were on call like a five-hundred-dollar whore, waiting to get into the field and take care of those dirty little jobs that the public could never know about but that helped to keep the good old Stars and Stripes flying.

"Morning, Skipper," Senior Chief Sadler said.

Murdock straightened up in the chair and brought his hands down. "Senior Chief, you look like roadkill that some big dog dragged in off the highway. Are you all right?"

"Been better. The Dixieland gig lasted a little longer than usual last night. Hell, ten years ago I wouldn't even have noticed."

"You're the old-timer of the platoon, Senior Chief. You have to learn to slow down a little." Murdock chuckled. It was a running and friendly joke between them.

"This morning I could almost believe you. You and Lieutenant DeWitt going to be interviewing today as I remember. I'll take the platoon for some training."

"Right. Here's the sked. The O course, then a soft-sand run down to the Kill House, and put everyone through there twice and bring me the scores. Then a swim back without fins. Should keep you busy all morning."

"I was hoping we could get back to some basic push-pull-sit work, Commander."

"Schedule it for the afternoon with a twelve-mile run to the antennas and back." He peered at the senior chief. "Sure you don't want to let Jaybird do the drill and you flake out with us here to evaluate the new JG?"

Sadler hesitated just long enough to give Murdock doubts.

"Sir, I better stay with the men. This choosing stuff is Officer Country. I'll do what I'm best at. Just a little fog across my bow. It'll clear and I'll be leading the pack. Good to be back in the saddle again here, sir." He did a snappy about-face and went into the squad room.

Ed DeWitt came in; his grin was still ear-to-ear, Murdock saw.

"Sit down, sad boy, and tell me your woes."

Ed laughed and sat. "Oh, yeah, it's going good. I talked with the JG in Second of Fifth and I like him. He's shouldering it for the time being. They do lots of training. Yeah. Your new man show up here for a look-see yet?"

"If he is, he's hiding."

The phone rang.

"Yeah, Third-Seventh."

"Commander Murdock, sir," Master Chief MacKenzie said. "I'm sending JG Belmer to your office with a guide. Should be there shortly."

"Thanks, Master Chief. You do good work."

They hung up. "He's coming."

Ed had picked up the file on Belmer, and read through it quickly. "Wow, second-string all-American in football. Not bad. At least he won't have any trouble hitting the dirt."

The two old friends talked about the last mission. Ed's leg wound was healing, but it would be three weeks before he was back a hundred percent.

Then a knock sounded on the door, and a large man in desert cammies filled it. His floppy hat scraped the top of the doorjamb.

"Sir, Lieutenant (j.g.) Belmer, reporting as ordered."

"At ease, Lieutenant, come in, sit down. Ed was just ready to stand up. Ever been to California before?"

"No, sir."

"Lieutenant, this is Ed DeWitt, who is leaving the platoon. He'll be on hand to help the new man merge into our operation here. Tell me, why do you want to join us?"

"Because you're the top-rated platoon and you get all the action. We keep hearing that you go on missions on average of one a month. I want to get in on the action."

"Lieutenant, did you know that over the past three years we've had twelve men killed during our missions?"

Belmer's eyes widened. He swallowed, then looked at Murdock. "No, sir, I didn't know that. I'd heard that your men do get wounded now and then."

"We average about four wounds a mission, Belmer," Ed said. "Last week we sent a KIA home in a coffin, and took three more wounds. Both Commander Murdock and I were shot last week."

"Wow. I didn't know."

"Does that change your mind about wanting to join us?" Murdock asked.

"No, sir. Not one bit. It's what I've been trained for, and so far I haven't had one single mission. A guy could go stale that way."

"Where are you from, Belmer, and how long have you been in the Navy?"

Ed sat back and listened. Murdock took notes. Early on Ed had had reservations about this young man. It was a gut feeling. There were two more to go. He knew long before the hour interview was over that Belmer would get a B rating, right in the middle. The other men would go above or below him. He'd have to wait and see.

After Belmer left the two friends talked it over.

"I wouldn't want him protecting my back in a firefight," DeWitt said. "Nothing concrete, just my overall impression. He seemed to be more interested in telling his friends he was in Third than being here to help us run the outfit."

"Grade him, with A the highest, C the lowest," Murdock said.

Ed slid out in the chair, massaged his wounded leg, and scowled. "Is this part of my job here?"

"It is. Give me a grade."

"Okay, I'd put him at a B. Depends on who else we get. When's the next one?"

"At 1100. A JG from SEAL First, First Platoon."

"I've heard they're plenty sharp," Ed said. "Hope their JG is a good one."

Senior Chief Sadler led the platoon on the run to the Navy antennas just six miles down the Coronado Strand toward the outskirts of the town of Imperial Beach.

"Hey Senior Chief, this dry sand is a bitch to run in," Jaybird squawked.

"Keep it up, Jaybird, and we'll run back the same way, only twenty percent faster."

At the Kill House, dug into the sand near the far end of the strand, they went through the routine of quick-firing at the pop-up targets. With fifty thousand variables on the computer-programmed targets, there was little chance they would ever see the same ones again.

"We're keeping scores and reporting them to the CO," Sadler said. "Top score gets my personal six-pack of your choice of beer. Now let's do some good numbers."

The Kill House was also known as a CQB, Close Quarters Battle house. It had been dug into the sand and had bullet-proof sides on all walls. There were three rooms with ceilings and all sorts of furniture. There were also terrorist figures and terrorists with hostages that popped up the moment SEAL boots hit the floor activators. The computer registered the hits and misses, and any time enough seconds passed without a SEAL response, the computer determined that the terrorist had killed the SEAL.

A pair of SEALs attacked the house, one taking the right-hand side of the first room, the other the left. When it was clear, they said so and moved to the next room and new problems.

Jaybird and Sadler were the first ones into the house. Jaybird took the left. Just inside the door he saw three terrorists pop up with a hooded hostage between them. He cut down the two on the right and shifted to the left, but the target had vanished.

Sadler had one target on the right, drilled it with a three-round burst, then at once two more terrs jolted upright almost in the center of the room holding sub guns. Sadler slapped down both of them with swinging bursts from his Bull Pup rifle set on 5.56mm.

The next room proved tougher, with one after another terrorist popping up after the SEALs thought the room was clear. They missed three of them.

"Damnit, I just shot a hostage," Jaybird wailed.

When they came out of the last room, Sadler went to the side of the building to a weatherproof hutch and punched the button to get a printout of their score.

"Seventy-four," Jaybird screeched. "We did better than that."

"We could have," Sadler said. "But they fined us fifteen points for that hostage you shot. The setups on the targets are tough today."

After the last pair went through the Kill House, Sadler checked his watch. No time to make a second pass. He brought the men back to the beach, looked over the printouts, and yelled, "Look at this, you slackers. Van Dyke and Fernandez came up with the winning score. Eighty-nine. I bet they didn't gun down any hostages like some people I know did. Okay, back to the compound. We have thirty-seven minutes for the trip. That's a little over seven minutes to the mile. Who can set the pace?"

"Hell, Senior Chief," a disguised voice yelped. "You know SEALs don't fucking never volunteer for goddamned nothing."

There were a dozen hoorahs, and then Lam moved out front of the pack. "I'm not volunteering, I'm just trying for a personal best. If any of you want to try to keep up with me, be my guests."

He took off down the wet sand, where footing was sure and easier. The SEALs fell in behind him in a column of ducks, and Sadler brought up the rear.

By the time they hit the sand in back of the O course, they were puffing. Sadler knew that a seven-minute mile with their combat vests, packs, and combat weapons was a strain. He figured most of the men had about forty pounds on their backs.

The men stopped and blew hard. Some of them had hands on knees, bent double. Some sat on the sand. Others kept walking in tight circles to keep their hearts pumping as they oxygenated their spent blood.

"Oh, shit," Senior Chief Sadler said. "We were supposed to swim back. Now we'll have to swim out four miles and back four miles."

All twelve of the SEALs threw their floppy hats at Sadler, who grinned at them and threw the hats back.

At 1100, Lieutenant (j.g.) Christopher Gardner knocked on the door and was invited into the Third Platoon office.

"I'm Chris Gardner from First Platoon of SEAL Team One."

"Chris, come in," Murdock said. The man was six-four, maybe 240 pounds, and grinned like a big teddy bear. He had a whiteside haircut with brown hair almost long enough to comb. His face was square-cut, and he'd have a five o'clock shadow by noon. His clear green eyes took in the office in a glance. "Take the hot seat there and we'll have a talk," Murdock said. "How are things over at the First Platoon? That would be Charlie Brashears as the CO?"

"Right. He said to say hello. You two go way back, he said."

"Known Charlie a long time. Chris, I'm Murdock and this is Ed DeWitt, recently promoted and moving up to a platoon of his own. His feet aren't too big, but when it comes to filling his shoes, it's going to take a damned good man."

"Lieutenant," Chris said, nodding at Ed. "I've heard about what you guys do over here and I'm amazed. Your platoon gets twenty missions to our one. And then we usually dig out some harbor mines or maybe help train some recruits in Africa. Truth is, nobody has shot at me since BUD/S. Not that I'm anxious to get some lead in my hide. Just a fact you need to know."

"So, why do you want to be in the Third?"

"I figure I trained to do certain things, and I'm not doing

them. No fire missions, no rescues, no work like you guys did on the Chinese invasion and on the Philippine kidnappings. Those two we know about. That's what I trained to do, and I feel like a slacker when I'm not in the mix on them."

Murdock looked at Ed and nodded. "Chris, we've been over your file, and frankly, we like what we see there. You're Annapolis. But you must know that SEALs is not an outfit that will give you a good career path to admiral."

"Yep, I know that."

"Did your father tell you that?" Ed asked.

"The admiral has strong feelings about almost everything. He loves the SEALs. Actually they pulled his ass out of the fire once. But he didn't want me involved because it isn't blue-water sailing, and as you said, not a fast track to admiral."

"Is your father still on active duty?"

"Yes, sir. He was Navy air, and now he's captain of a carrier."

"I understand that you're married, Chris."

"Right. Been married now for almost three years."

"SEAL scheduling and sea tours haven't hurt your marriage?" Ed asked.

"Sure, some, but Wanda is an understanding woman with a career of her own. No kids yet. Waiting a few more years."

"What does she do?" Murdock asked.

"She has her own small sport clothes design and manufacturing firm here in town. Fabricates the clothes in Tijuana, part of that new across-the-border deal with Mexico."

"Successful?" Ed asked.

Chris laughed. "Oh, yes, sir. Last year her gross income for the business was a little over twelve million dollars."

"Just about as much as a JG makes," Murdock said. They laughed.

"It doesn't bother me that she makes a lot more money than I do. She earns it. She's excellent at designing and has a great head for business."

They talked for another half hour. Murdock sensed it

quickly, an immediate bonding with the young man. A
meshing of purpose, ideals, and style. It had happened a
few times before. An immediate rapport, both on the same
wavelength.

Murdock looked at DeWitt and gave a small nod. DeWitt
grinned. "About what I was going to say, Commander."

Murdock stood and held out his hand. "Chris, you're our
man. I'll have the master chief put through the paper today.
He'll tell you when to report, but probably tomorrow morning. You better get your desk cleaned out and your gear
turned in."

"Hey, good, great." Chris seemed a little confused. "But
the master chief told me there were three men to be interviewed."

"True, Chris," Murdock said. "I know the other one and
he doesn't stand a chance after we've talked with you. Now
get out of here and get your papers put through."

Chris grinned. "Hey, absolutely right. I can do that, Commander." He shook his head. "Damn, I'm really gonna be
here with the Third. Wait until I tell Wanda. We're going
to celebrate tonight." He stood, came to a braced attention,
and snapped a salute. "Request permission to leave the
Third Platoon area, sir."

Murdock grinned and returned the salute. "Permission
granted, Sailor. Get back here as soon as you can."

When Chris left, Ed DeWitt dropped into the chair he
had sat in so often and stretched out his feet. He rubbed
his wounded leg and nodded. "Oh, yes, Murdock. I think
that you've caught yourself a good one."

Murdock frowned. "Yeah, but not as good as the one I'm
losing. What do we do to integrate him into the squad as
fast as possible? Like we needed him here yesterday?"

DeWitt rubbed his nose, as he often did when he was
thinking. "Okay, I'm with you here for two weeks yet. Let's
go to the desert for four days, see what this young man is
made of. It'll also sharpen up the men and get them back
in fighting trim. We also need a new man for Chris's squad.
Do you have some candidates?"

"Master Chief sent me over ten who had requests on file.
I looked them over and cut out three. First order of business

tomorrow morning when Chris comes back will be to help him pick a new man for his squad. Introduce him to the men in Bravo. Let him see physically who he has to work with. Then we'll see where we go from there."

"Sounds good from here, oh, wise leader of men," Ed said, cracking a grin.

"How does your new outfit look?"

"Good old Second Platoon of Five. Yeah, I've met them. Don't know squat about them yet. I like the JG there, so that's a plus. Just have to see how it works out. I won't transfer anyone out unless I absolutely have to. I have the option, if I'm sure I can't work with any of the men I inherit."

Murdock laughed and put his feet up on the desk, then leaned back in the chair. "DeWitt, you're used to a bunch of oddballs here in the Third. You'll be able to work with almost anybody. They all are SEALs, so you know they've been through a lot just to get into the Team."

"Yeah, yeah, I keep telling myself that. Just have to wait and see. What do you think about the four-day trip to the desert?"

"Sounds like a lot of work, sleeping on those sandy rocks and getting up double-dog-tired. I love it. We'll work out a training sked that will put Chris in the driver's seat all the way. See how he does."

The next morning Lieutenant (j.g.) Chris Gardner leaned against the office door to Third Platoon when Murdock arrived at 0730.

"Couldn't sleep, Lieutenant?"

"Like a billy goat, Commander. Didn't want to be late my first day on the job."

Murdock shook his hand. "Good to have you on board. This time of day we have to make our own coffee. You any good at it?"

"Not the best, sir."

"Tough. I'll do it." As he made the coffee, Murdock told Chris about the work for the day.

"So, I've got seven personnel folders over there on my desk. Look through them and see if you want one of them for your squad. Pick three to interview. As soon as the men get here, you'll meet the rest of Bravo Squad to see what you have to work with."

"Aye, aye, Commander."

Ed DeWitt came in about 0800, and the three of them interviewed three men that morning. All had volunteered for Third Platoon and all were from other platoons on the base.

"So, which man do you like?" Murdock asked. "It's up to you. He'll be your responsibility, your input to the squad."

"I'm going with the little guy, Rafii. I just like the way he comes across. He's from Saudi Arabia, speaks Arabic and Farsi like a native. Came here when he was four with his parents. Omar Rafii. He's a knife man. I bet you've had times when a silent kill with a knife from fifteen feet would be a bonus. If there are no objections, I'll tell the master chief to get Rafii's tail over here."

"Done," Murdock said. "You're right about the knife work. Ed here is pretty good, but I wouldn't want to bet my life on his getting a kill from even ten feet."

"Amen to that," DeWitt said with a grin.

"Now, Chris, I want you to help us lay out a four-day training sked for the desert. Tell us what elements you want included, and what you think will work best for you to get to know your squad members and to start the bonding process."

4

Nouakchott, Mauritania

Vice President Marshall Adams slumped in the seat of the big Mercedes on the way from Air Force Two to the hotel and another welcoming ceremony, reception, and state dinner. His eyes drifted shut and his head fell almost to his chest. He could never remember being this tired before. Twelve African nations in fourteen days. For a while before landing, he'd been seeing double. He'd give a thousand dollars for a good twenty-four-hour break in which he had nothing to do but eat and sleep.

The limousine hit a pothole in the best highway in town and jolted the VP out of his reverie. Yes, duty, friends to make, cash money to give away in the form of foreign aid, new people to meet, new nations to honor. He loved his job as ambassador extraordinaire for the President, but this was almost too much. His usually immaculate appearance had been reduced to a slightly wrinkled and sat-in suit, he knew, but there wouldn't be time to put on a fresh one before they got to the welcoming. Maybe before the reception. It had been a two-hour flight from the last country, whatever it was. The VP looked over at the man who sat in the limo with him.

"Wally, a thumbnail of this country again?"

Wally looked over at the VP. A moment ago he had been sleeping. "Yes, sir. Mauritania, an Islamic republic. The President is Maaouya Ould Sidi Ahmed Taya. He's sixty-nine years old, in office since 1992. Population two and a half million. In size it's larger than the state of Texas, but not as large as Alaska. Mostly arid except one sizeable river valley. Most of the nation extends into the Sahara Desert. Literacy rate is thirty-eight percent."

"Thanks, Wally. More than I need to know. I understand we're here for only six hours, then fly out just before dark. Where is the next stop?"

"Next we go to the relatively new nation of Sierra Bijimi, only a half-hour flight to the south."

"Any big hoorah there tonight?"

"Nothing but a short welcome, then a whole evening and night of rest and regrouping."

"Damn good, Wally. I could use a lot of both."

Sierra City, Sierra Bijimi

It was just after nine P.M. that same day when Air Force Two, with Vice President of the United States Marshall Adams, settled onto the almost-too-short runway at Sierra City, and came to a stop next to a rolled-out red carpet.

"Wally?" the Vice President asked as he headed for the door.

"Sierra Bijimi, broke away from Central Bijimi in 1990. A republic, just below most of the Islamic nations. Ninety-seven percent African. Four million people. A small land-locked country. It has thirty-five-percent tillable land. The rest is dense jungle. Thom Kolda is President of a shaky democracy. A small country of four thousand, two hundred square miles. About twice the size of Delaware. Literacy rate is forty-seven percent."

The aircraft door opened and Vice President Adams walked out on the steps to be greeted with a blaring band, a dozen floodlights, and a smiling group of black faces at the foot of the aluminum aircraft-access steps. "Here we go again," he told himself. He waved and walked down the steps to be introduced to President Kolda.

Adams beat back a frown when he saw the nation's President. He was short, fat, had a seriously large nose and pig eyes. His suit was rumpled and had stains on the front. The hand that came out to greet the Vice President felt soft and flabby.

"Good evening, Mr. President," Adams said. "It's good to visit your nation."

Kolda said something in the strange Wolof language. An interpreter at his side responded immediately.

"President Kolda is delighted to meet you, Mr. Vice President Adams, and welcomes you to our nation. We have some entertainment for you and your security men."

"Tell the President that's wonderful, but I'm near exhaustion and need to get to my hotel."

The interpreter shook his head. "I can't tell him that. He insists that you come with him for the entertainment or he will be tremendously insulted."

The Vice President sighed and looked at Wally, who nodded.

"Tell the President that I will enjoy going with him for the entertainment."

Twenty minutes later a limo deposited Vice President Adams, Wally, and two Secret Service men at a small nightclub with a guard outside the door. There were fifty people waiting to get in. They hooted and yelled when the Sierra Bijimi President and his party and Vice President Adams and his three men walked in the door. They were taken at once around the side of the club, which had a band on the stage and tables filled with people.

They went through two doors and then up steps into a small amphitheater. It was nearly filled with men of all ages. Adams guessed there were about two hundred men there. He didn't see a single woman in the audience. An usher took them down to the front row, where seats had been saved for them.

"What kind of a show goes on here?" Adams asked the interpreter, who sat between President Kolda and the Vice President.

"Show? Yes, a show. You will see shortly. It does not last long."

A girl with large breasts bulging from a small bra top and wearing a short skirt served them drinks. There was no charge to the President's party. President Kolda took three of the drinks and then fondled the girl's breasts. She smiled as he did it. A moment later one of the President's aides tucked a wad of bills inside the girl's bra and she left quickly.

The Vice President looked around the area and realized that there was some kind of betting going on. Men moved up and down the aisles taking bets and giving out slips of paper, red or green. He asked Wally what it was.

"Got me, Mr. Vice President. Not a clue." Wally asked the interpreter.

The man frowned and leaned away from Adams a moment. Then, with more resolve, he nodded. "Yes, they are gambling. I can arrange for you to make a bet if you wish."

"What are they gambling on?" Adams asked.

The interpreter frowned and glanced at President Kolda. "You were not told?"

"Not a clue. What's going on?"

"You bet red or green," the interpreter said. "Red is the more risky bet, but odds are five to one. Green is safer, but only two to one."

"That I understand," the Vice President said. "But what are they betting on?"

Just then trumpets sounded, and everyone turned to stare at a runway with a red carpet on it that came down one side of the arena and ended at a golden chair that sat in the twenty-foot-wide circle stage.

A girl in a flowing robe of pure silk and wearing a crown of diamonds appeared at the top of the red carpet. She posed for the patrons for a moment. If the diamonds were real, they must be worth half a million dollars, Adams figured. He watched as the girl came down the red carpet to the cheers and applause of the group. The men were standing now, so Adams and his men stood as well. They watched the girl come to the stage, go around it once, smiling and waving at the men. Then she strutted to the golden chair. She looked at the men, who cheered more and more. At last she nodded, loosened a tie at her throat, and whipped off the robe. Under it she was naked.

She stood, posed as a model might. She was slender, well formed and not at all self-conscious about displaying her naked body. The music, which had been low-key during the entry, now picked up. The girl sat down in the chair and the stage began to rotate, giving every man there a good view of the woman. The betting along the aisles surged as men waved money at the bet takers. By that time the betting was at a frenzy pitch. Men shoved others aside to get to the bet takers. Money flowed. A fight broke out, which was quickly stopped. Men were shouting and screaming to get to the betting places. The music built again, then stopped suddenly. When the music ceased the betting evidently was over, Adams decided. The men in the aisles with the betting slips and the money vanished through doors that went under the stands.

Now two men marched down the red carpet to the stage as the music began again. A murmur of interest rushed through the crowd. One man wore a bright red suit and he carried a thin wooden box of highly polished wood. The man dressed all in green carried a smaller box. They showed the boxes to the men as the stage continued to rotate. Then a blast of trumpets ended the new music. The shouting and screaming from the men in the audience shut off at once, and in the sudden stillness Vice President Adams could hear the click of the latch as the red man opened the box he carried.

He lifted from the container a pearl-handled six-gun with a regular-looking barrel. There was a burst of trumpets and then silence again as the second man opened his box and took out a single silver bullet.

"Oh, no," Adams moaned. The interpreter heard him and scowled.

"Mr. Vice President Adams. You agreed to come. It would be an insult beyond measure if you tried to walk out now. You must stay."

The trumpets blared again, and the green man opened the weapon and inserted one round into the cylinder. Then he held the six-gun by the barrel and pushed the cylinder back in place. There was no way he could have put another bullet into the gun.

The hushed silence broke with applause and cheers as the red-dressed man handed the firearm to the woman on the stage. All this had happened Adams realized as the stage kept turning and turning.

"They wouldn't do this for real," Wally whispered into

the Vice President's ear. "It has to be a stunt. It will be all right, I'm sure."

Adams shook his head. "I know this sort of thing happens in the Orient. I've never heard of it here. Oh, it's going to happen, all right. With all that betting there would be a bloody riot if the event wasn't concluded."

The music blared again, and the girl took the revolver and spun the cylinder. She kept spinning it for a complete rotation of the stage. Again the music stopped. A gentle, sympathetic voice came over speakers, and the girl turned toward the red carpet listening. The voice crooned stronger and more hypnotic, and Adams wished desperately that he could understand the Wolof words.

Slowly the naked girl lifted the weapon and put the muzzle over her heart. Screams and yells erupted from the audience, then trailed off when she moved the gun. She held it easily in her right hand, lifted it, and put the muzzle against the side of her head. The voice continued as if directing her. The screams came from the audience. She moved the weapon again, staring hard at the black hole of the muzzle. Then she opened her mouth and pushed the barrel two inches inside.

Silence throbbed through the arena. The girl reached up with her left hand and spun the cylinder again. Then she closed her eyes. The voice came strongly, ending in a scream.

Adams couldn't see the girl pull the trigger, but she must have. A second after the scream the weapon went off and the bullet exploded out of the back of the naked girl's skull. Her head flopped over the back of the chair and the audience stared in agonizing silence. Then the screaming exploded in earnest as the bettors who had won charged the clerks, who had appeared around the stage, which had stopped rotating.

"We leave now," the interpreter said. They stood, and were escorted quickly out a side stage-level door they hadn't seen. Two men had to help President Kolda. Adams saw that the man was so drunk he couldn't walk.

Wally touched the interpreter's shoulder. "Take us to our

hotel at once. The Vice President isn't feeling well. Can you get us back to the hotel quickly?"

The interpreter smiled. "Is he ill, or is it just his soft-hearted feelings for the girl? Those girls get paid well. One pulled the trigger fifteen times and was never scratched. She retired with more than four million of your dollars. Some like the girl tonight lose the bet on their first try." He nodded. "It is show business. Entertainment, no? Now I will get you back to your hotel."

Twenty minutes later Vice President Adams sat heavily on the bed in the Presidential Suite in the Engaffe Hotel, the best in Sierra City, and tried to relax.

"I still can't believe it. Those men bet whether she would live or die. She killed herself, and it was sanctioned by the highest elected official in this backward nation. There must have been three hundred people there screaming at the spectacle. That their President could know about such a terrible event is criminal. That he was there slopping down drink after drink and enjoying the thrill of seeing a young girl in a life-or-death exhibition is totally disgusting. How can we ever deal with these people again?"

Wally held a sheaf of papers he had picked up when they arrived at the hotel. He had started to speak, but let the Vice President have his say. Now he took his turn. "Some more bad news about President Kolda and his regime here. Our ambassador says that the country is in a shambles. That the President and every official the ambassador has investigated is hip deep in graft, corruption, and shows a cavalier abuse of power. One small item. Earlier this year we sent them twelve million dollars of hard currency, which was to be used to build houses and upgrade the buildings and farming technique in one area a half hour outside the capital with rich fertile land.

"The ambassador tells me that only one small building has been constructed and that the Farm Fund, as it was called, is down to a seven-thousand-dollar balance. Everyone is pointing fingers at everyone else."

Vice President Adams shook his head. "Did you see how those animals were screaming for the girl to pull the trigger? They were death merchants, most hoping that she would live since it was a safer bet, but the rest were bellowing and braying for her blood." He shook his head and washed his hands over his face. "Sweet Mother of God, I'll never forget the expression on that girl's face just before she pulled the trigger. I'll never get it blasted out of my memory for as long as I live."

He took another deep breath. "What more do we have to do with these people? I'd like to cut out right now and fly to the next stop, but I know we can't do that."

"We have that tour tomorrow. We should see where they didn't spend the money on the farming area."

"So we cut them off at the pockets," the Vice President said.

"There's not much we can do, Mr. Vice President, about getting the lost money back. It's probably in some Swiss bank account. We can make them aware that we know they stole the money and that there won't be a cent more coming their way until they do what they promised they would."

"Sounds good to me, Wally. I've got to have a long hot shower and see if I can wash some of that filth off my back. I'll never forget that poor girl's face. She must have been on drugs. High on coke probably. Did that interpreter say one girl survived fifteen sessions like that? What a mental nightmare that must be, knowing that your odds are one out of six that you're dead. Damn, how do they find women to do that? Maybe they get druggers who are down and out and almost dead on the streets. Yeah, that must be where they get the girls." He looked at his watch. "Is it eleven o'clock already? What's for tomorrow? That tour?"

"The ambassador has arranged for us to visit several centers here. A ballet school, an industrial arts complex, something else, and the farm center where our foreign aid money was squandered. The head man of the army, General Kiffa Assaba, warned me that there could be trouble in that outlying area. It's only twenty miles from the edge of town, but he said there had been vicious rebel murderers in that section from time to time. He suggested another place to visit in town. I told him we have been given specific instructions to visit that farmland. If he's worried about our safety, he should send trucks filled with armed troops ahead and behind our two-car convoy. There will be one car filled with newspaper and media people right behind our limo."

"Good, Wally. I want to see where this twelve million was not spent. Later I'll throw it up at him by asking President Kolda where our foreign aid money went and demand an answer. If he's sobered up by then. I smelled alcohol on his breath when he first shook my hand at the airport. Man, was he sloshed tonight."

The Vice President pulled off his shirt and stared at Wally. "Do you think there's any real danger out there in the farming country, or is President Kolda just trying to protect his rear end?"

"Oh, a protection ploy for damn sure. He might find some way to detour us around the farm place yet. Danger? I'd bet there's not a bad guy within fifty miles. It's just his story to scare us off so we don't find out for sure that he stole the aid money."

The next morning an armed "honor" guard escorted the Vice President, the ambassador, and their party of six to the three venues they were set to visit. Adams showed the proper admiration and pleasure at the displays, and then settled into the backseat of the heavy Lincoln stretch limo for the ride out to the farm area.

General Assaba came just before they started. Vice President Adams saw that he was a small man, maybe five-five, slender, with a wolfish face and thick black hair. His large eyes seemed to bulge from his head over a short, sturdy nose. His body was in constant motion, and he often raised upward, standing on his toes for ten or fifteen seconds at a time. Adams guessed it was a nervous movement that the small man did unconsciously to give him a taller stature.

Like the President, General Assaba said he spoke no English, and a student interpreted for him.

"The general says he is seriously considering preventing you from making this trip to the Estalante farming area. He reminds you that it is highly dangerous."

The Vice President nodded. "Ask the general how many

men or women have been killed there in the past six months."

The general frowned when the student asked the question in his native Wolof language. Assaba began calmly, but before he finished he shouted in anger, then turned and walked away.

"The general says that he is displeased that you want to take this trip. Diplomatically he can't stop you, but at the same time that releases him from any responsibility for the safety of your party. He will send soldiers with you, but you are being foolish going into this dangerous area."

Vice President Adams grinned. "Yeah, the old boy got his dander up, I'd say. We're going, so let's get moving."

The honor guard changed now. The six soldiers in the jeep in front of the limo were combat-ready, with rifles, web belts, and jungle-print cammies. Six more men similarly outfitted rode in another vehicle behind the second civilian car, which held six members of the press who had been traveling with the Vice President.

The first few miles led them through the city of more than 200,000. Soon the buildings gave way to the strip of farmland along the river and its valley. Then the black-topped highway ended and they rolled along a gravel road.

Vice President Adams wanted to lower the window to have a better look, but he knew it was an armored limo and the windows wouldn't budge. He saw more signs of cultivation and an occasional group of buildings.

Another five miles and the convoy stopped. The driver, who had been with the Vice President since his days as governor of Michigan, turned.

"Mr. Vice President, there's a problem ahead. Looks like a tree has fallen across the road."

Almost at once the Vice President heard rifle fire jolt into the calm afternoon. The five people in the limo could see the soldiers leaping out of the jeep ahead of them. Two died before they made it. The other four died at the side of the road before they could find cover.

In the limo, they heard more fire coming from behind. Then there was an ominous silence. The two Secret Service men inside the limo had their Ingram submachine guns lifted from where they hung by cords around their necks.

"Easy, take it easy," the Vice President said. "No rounds hit our vehicle. They seem to be targeting only the military."

They waited a few minutes more. Then a figure appeared outside the door. The black man in civilian clothes held up both hands to show he was unarmed. He motioned for the door to be opened.

"Don't go out there," the lead Secret Service man said. "We're safe in here, Mr. Vice President. The limo protects us."

"He has no weapon," Adams said. "He looks friendly. I'm going out."

The second Secret Service man grabbed his arm. "No, sir. I'll go see what he wants." The man slid to the near door, opened it, and stepped out. His Ingram was hidden under his jacket. He left quickly and closed the door, which automatically locked.

Adams watched the two men through the window. Both looked calm, talking with no hand gestures. A minute later the Secret Service man signaled, and his partner inside the limo opened the door and the outside man stepped inside and closed the door.

"The man says his name is Mojombo Washington. He says he's the leader of the Bijimi Loyalist Party fighting the corrupt central government. He wants to show you how they squandered and stole the money due to these poor farmers. He has no weapons. He said his men were careful to attack only the federal soldiers. No one in either our car or the press car was hurt in any way. He says he has no wish to harm any of our party. He just wants to plead his case against the government."

Adams rubbed his jaw, then looked at his top advisor. Wally lifted his brows. "Sir, that's what we came here to find out. This man sounds like he knows the facts we need to uncover."

Vice President Adams nodded. "Seems to be the way to go. Let's get out. Keep your weapons ready if we need them." He hesitated, then waved at the Secret Service men. "Let's get out of here and do some investigating."

One Secret Service man went out first, followed by the Vice President and the other Secret Service man.

Mojombo Washington stood outside the limo. The Vice President saw that he was a medium-sized man, a head shorter than the VP, with curly black hair, wide-set eyes, and a flat nose. His smile lit up the landscape.

"Mr. Vice President Adams, so good to meet you. First a bit of business. Secret Service men, please lift your hands away from your Ingram submachine guns. I have expert marksmen who have you sighted in with three rifles on each of you. Any move toward your weapons and you will die instantly. I want no violence here. Lift your hands at once."

The men dedicated to protecting their Vice President hesitated, then looked at the bodies of the soldiers dead on the roadway. A rifle snarled some distance away, and a bullet tore into the ground three feet from one of the Secret Service men. They both flinched, then looked at each other and slowly lifted their hands. Two armed men in cammies darted around the limo and checked inside. Then the driver was pulled out.

Mojombo smiled. "Yes, this is good. I wish to hurt no one from your nation, or the press. Now it's time to leave. Mr. Vice President Adams, please step into the limo. We will be leaving, and the rest of your party will be taken back to the city. Don't worry. We have no wish to harm you or your people in any way. Please, inside."

Adams looked at his Secret Service men for advice, but they stared straight ahead. They had been outguessed, outmaneuvered, and outgunned.

The Vice President stepped into the limo, followed by Mojombo Washington. An African driver moved in behind the wheel, and he drove the big limo smoothly around the stalled jeep and past three bodies before it came back on the road and rolled forward.

The Vice President leaned back in the seat and studied the man next to him. An African who spoke English as well as he did. Obviously educated, a leader of some group. Highly selective in the violence he used, killing only the Army escort. No one in his group or any of the journalists was harmed. That spoke well for the young man. Young.

The Vice President decided that this Mojombo Washington must be about thirty years old.

He turned to his captor. "Now, Mr. Washington, that you have kidnapped me, what ransom are you going to demand for my freedom?"

Mojombo looked at the man beside him and smiled. "Mr. Vice President Marshall Adams. You will learn that in time. But I assure you it is going to be a tremendously stiff price indeed."

5

The Amunbo River

Vice President Marshall Adams settled back in the cushioned chair in the sleek twenty-four-foot cabin cruiser's small cabin and watched the man who called himself Mojombo Washington.

The well-built young man watched the Vice President. He smiled. "As I have told you several times, you have nothing to fear from us. We are the good guys here. We are the Bijimi Loyalist Party, dedicated to throwing out the criminal government of Sierra Bijimi and replacing it with a freely elected democratic government. First my name. You reacted when I said my last name is Washington. Most people do. Actually I renamed myself after the father of your great country, George Washington."

Adams smiled. "That's a good start, young man. Now I hope you will follow through and be the great leader and patriot for your nation that old George was for ours."

"That's my intention, Mr. Vice President Adams, and I hope that after you hear my story, you will help my country." He waved around at the boat. His ten soldiers were sitting around wherever they found space. "This boat was a gift of a generous official in Sierra City. He didn't know he was giving it to us, but we appreciate it just as much. Yes, at times we must take what we want and what we need. It is for the eventual good of our nation. After all, George Washington did do serious damage to that cherry tree." They both laughed.

"How big an army do you have?" Adams asked.

"Not large, and not well equipped yet. We feel somewhat

the way George must have felt that winter in Valley Forge. At least we don't have the snow or the bitter cold to contend with. To answer your question, I have roughly a hundred and fifty men I can put into a pitched battle. Which is why I will avoid that type of combat at all costs. We are a strike-and-vanish guerrilla operation, and we can be tremendously effective."

"I'm sure you are. My main concern now is that my government in Washington, D.C., will be worried. Perhaps worried to the extent of sending in an overwhelmingly large, deadly task force to rescue me."

"We'll take care of that as soon as we come to our camp. I brought along the SATCOM from your limousine. You'll be free to contact anyone you wish with the radio and talk as long as you want to. I won't guide you or insist on what you say. I want you to be a friend by that time, not a captive, but a friend."

"That could take some doing, Mojombo. I was impressed by the way you stopped our cars and did not harm any of our people or the correspondents."

"Mr. Vice President Adams. I know the value of the press. We use them whenever we can, but the government controls the only large newspaper in the country. You were surprised how well I speak your language. I've had lots of practice. I took my B.A. degree at Manley University in Washington, D.C., and my master's in political science at Georgetown, also there in the district. I know about the Beltway politics. I studied intently your Constitution and Declaration of Independence and the three branches of government. The new constitution of Sierra Bijimi will be much like your own. I returned to my homeland to help dig it out of the maze of graft, corruption, misuse of power, and official murder that it has degenerated into."

Adams nodded slowly. "Yes, I can see how your ideals would be shattered returning to this kind of a situation. But couldn't you do it by the ballot?"

Mojombo laughed softly. "You must remember that the government here has absolute power. We have little personal freedom. The criminals run the elections. They count the ballots they wish to count and burn the rest. They adjust the vote count the way they want it to be and if anyone complains or challenges them, that person or persons suffer fatal accidents within a day of their protest. This has been going on in every election for almost ten years, and there is no one who can solve the problem, except a number of men with submachine guns, rifles, and RPGs."

"Would the people support you? Could you foster a general uprising?"

"We have major support for our cause in the outlands, along the river communities. The farther away from Sierra City, the stronger our support. But out here the government has little control. Few of the four thousand soldiers seldom get far from Sierra City. Still, the very number of them is a problem for us."

"One thing I know, I'm not used to this humid weather," Adams said. "Would you have anything cold to drink on board?"

"Oh, damn. My responsibility as a host is plainly deficient. Yes, of course, we have three brands of American beer, Coke, and four other soft drinks for your enjoyment."

"A cold Coke would be delightful. But we need to keep talking. I have to decide how I evaluate you by the time we get to your camp. You used the term camp, so I assume you are in the jungle somewhere up a tributary off this main river?"

"Quite right, Mr. Vice President. Nothing as primitive as you had to endure in Vietnam, but not the Hilton Hotel either."

"You know I was in Nam?"

"Yes. When I heard you were coming to my country, I learned everything I could. A friend in Sierra City has the Web, and she brings reports to me at regular intervals that she downloads and prints out. It's amazing what you can learn there. I just hope that your wife and two girls are not traumatized by this side trip of yours. That's partly why I want you to talk to your office as quickly as you can. I would imagine that your aide has reported your detour to the White House already via the SATCOM they have at the embassy."

Adams chuckled. "Mojombo, you are a highly organized

man who thoroughly researches his projects. Sierra Bijimi was added to my agenda only a week before we left. And that was less than a month ago."

"The Internet and the Web are amazingly fast," Mojombo said. "I also have several friends in Washington who e-mail me reports and will answer any questions I ask them."

"Amazing. You are truly a talented young man, Mojombo Washington. It's taken me some time, but now I'm one jump ahead of you. I'm to be your pawn, your chip of great price that you can use to bargain with the United States for help in your crusade down here."

Mojombo smiled, his dark eyes glistening with a sudden surge of emotion.

"Exactly right, Mr. Vice President. No President or Vice President of the United States has ever been, let's say, detained in a foreign nation before. It's historic. And it should be worth a lot of help from your Air Force, your Navy, and even your Marines. What do you think? Do I have a chance to get some military help down here to aid in my revolution?"

The Vice President smiled. "Mojombo, it's far better if the mouse does not know that he's the mouse in a cat-and-mouse game. I know. So how things go from here on will depend to a great degree what I say and how I say it on the SATCOM when we get to your camp. Are you going to tell me what to say with a .45 at my head?"

"Absolutely not."

"Are you going to make a number of demands from the United States that must be met before I am returned?"

"Absolutely not at this time."

"Do you think that the force of your personality is so great that you can convince me of your sincerity and your plans for your nation and that you can win me over to be a proponent of your cause during the rest of this short trip?"

"I believe that when you see my camp, and my army, and the people we are fighting for, that you will understand our cause and that you will soon be on our side. I understand that you were not pleased with your meeting with our illustrious President last night."

"Not at all. He seems to be a drunk who enjoys watching young girls blow their brains out in a betting arena."

A look of surprise and then disgust washed over Mojombo's face. "He took you there?"

"He did, and two men had to carry him out after the girl died. He wasn't faint with pity or remorse. He was stone-dead sloppy drunk and couldn't stand up or walk."

"That's our boy, our glorious President. I also know that you were upset by the twelve million dollars his regime squandered and stole from the Farm Project."

The Vice President chuckled again. "Mojombo, you don't miss much, do you? Yes, I'm still angry about that. Not a lot of money in terms of some of the massive foreign assistance programs we have, but to have him simply steal it is unforgivable."

"Do you know that we no longer have a national school system? Each province is supposed to have an elected school board and to build and run schools. Six years ago, President Kolda withdrew all of the federal money from the school system. The entire education system failed and over two thousand schools closed."

"Switzerland?"

"Probably that's where most of the stolen money goes. Or a half-dozen other safe-money countries."

"Taxes. I'll bet Kolda's Administration is remarkably brilliant about levying and collecting taxes."

This time it was Mojombo's turn to laugh, but it had a bitter edge to it. "Absolutely right, Mr. Vice President Adams. He bleeds every bit of money he can from the people, and rewards them by raising the tax rates again. Nobody has any idea how many millions of dollars this man and his cohorts have stolen from my country. We probably never will know."

Mojombo went forward and spoke with the captain at the wheel a moment, then came back. He brought with him the SATCOM that had been in the limousine. "I bet you know how to work this, Mr. Vice President."

"I've seen it done."

"We have detailed and complete operating instructions on working the SATCOM. We got it off the Web straight from the maker of the radio." He grinned, clean white teeth flashing in his dark smile. "We try to be as efficient as possible."

"I'm starting to believe you. We had a report that some terrorists attacked the city two days before we arrived. Stormed the Central Police Station and raided it for weapons, and then proceeded to slip into a large military post on the outskirts of town, where they stole two truckloads of weapons, ammunition, and food supplies."

"You're correct, Mr. Vice President, with the exception that the raiders were not terrorists, they were Loyalists. We were highly efficient on that raid, and lucky at the same time. They still haven't realized that we are a solid military organization that won't go away. Those supplies are part of our lifeline."

"Why hasn't that little general we met loaded up fifty boats and stormed up the river and wiped out everything that moved? He could do it with his twelve thousand troops."

"General Assaba tried it two weeks ago, but he only brought fifty men in three boats. We had advance warning that he was coming. Our men were hiding in the trees along the river waiting for him. Fish in a barrel, Mr. Vice President. He tried to attack us, but we routed him with at least fifty-percent casualties. We had one man wounded in the leg, and no KIAs. He must have learned a lesson."

"But could he come with a huge force?"

"Not with the boats he has now. He has no real Navy, and only six river patrol boats. He might move three hundred men if he was lucky. We could handle them, probably sink most of the boats with RPGs before he got within fifteen miles of our camp."

"He knows that?"

"He should."

Adams watched out the window, and saw that the boat turned into a tributary of the larger river. This one was much smaller, and the dense jungle grew down almost to the water's edge on both sides.

"In a setting like this you might recall the missions you ran for the Navy on the Nam rivers," Mojombo said.

For a moment Commander Marshall Adams was back on a Black Navy killer boat on a Nam river and the rifle fire coming at them from the dense growth was murderous. Not even their .50-caliber cutting swaths through the jungle with the large-caliber bullets could slow down the Vietcong firing. More than once they had to turn downstream and race away from sudden death.

Adams looked at Mojombo Washington. "You won't tell me what to say on the SATCOM when I talk to the White House? You won't advise or pressure me in any way?"

"Absolutely not."

"Good. How much farther to your camp?"

"Another hour, almost seven miles up this river."

"It doesn't look that deep out there."

"This is a water-jet-powered boat," Mojombo said. "It can keep moving in less than a foot of water. No propeller to worry about, just a powerful jet of water rushing out the tubes in back."

Adams watched the young man. He was confident, he was intelligent, and he evidently had some military training. But could he lead a ragtag bunch of citizen soldiers in a virtual revolution against the entrenched and powerful current government?

"You must have had some military training."

Mojombo nodded. "Yes. Since I wasn't a citizen, I couldn't enroll in ROTC at college, but they allowed me to audit any courses that I wanted to. I took them all, so theoretically I'm at least a first lieutenant by now."

"You do plan ahead, don't you?"

Vice President Adams heard shouting from the shore, and he looked out the window. There was a rickety dock along a strip of open land. He saw many fires and huts and one frame building.

The boat eased up to the dock. Mojombo went out of the cabin and shouted at the people. They shouted back and chanted something over and over again.

Adams went aft to see better. Quickly the people on shore brought baskets of goods to the boat and handed them on board. Mojombo spoke to the thirty people who had gathered at the landing. Most were men, but there were a few women and children. Adams had a feeling that the whole village had turned out for the event.

After Mojombo spoke, he moved back a step on the boat and waved. Men on the dock cast off the lines and the engine revved up, and the boat edged back into the current, then powered upstream.

Mojombo came back into the cabin smiling. He carried two cold Cokes with him, and handed one to the Vice President.

"Those are some of my supporters. Whenever we pass going upstream they give us food and any supplies they think we might need. There are a dozen or so groups like this along this river and the larger one downstream. You asked if the people would support a revolution. What do you think?"

"Impressive, Mr. Washington. It couldn't have gone better if you had staged it for my benefit."

"Do you think I staged it?"

Adams watched the black man. He had never grown up around African Americans. Over the years he had made some contact with the black caucuses and other black groups in his political dealings, but he'd never had a good black friend. He knew he had a lot to learn, and a lot of prejudices to unfetter that had been foisted on him by his parents. He tried hard to evaluate this situation.

"No, Mojombo, I don't think you staged that little rally. It seemed to come from the heart. It was impressive."

"I'm pleased. Enjoy your Coke before it gets warm."

Ten minutes later, the jet-propelled craft skidded over two sandbars. The engine powered up, and Adams could feel the flat hull of the boat nudge the bars and the bottom slide over the sand, scraping it all the way.

Mojombo grinned at the sound. "That is the noise of a perfect defense," he said. "No boat with a propeller could possibly get over those sandbars or another one upstream."

Vice President Adams nodded slowly. He was becoming more and more impressed with this young revolutionary, this Loyalist Party leader.

Twenty minutes later the boat eased up to a sturdy dock at the edge of the stream. It was only ten feet long, but built well, and would last for years even though it was made of poles and wooden decking.

Ten men dressed in jungle-print cammies ran to the boat, unloaded the food and supplies the villagers had provided, and hurried with the baskets up a trail into the jungle.

Mojombo set up the SATCOM on the sturdy dock and turned the satellite dish until he picked up the orbiter and the set beeped.

"Mr. Vice President Adams, I believe the radio is ready for you to set the frequency for the White House and to start your broadcast. To be sure they are receiving you, it would be good to call them and ask for a response."

Marshall Adams took the microphone that Mojombo handed him, moved the dial to the correct numbers, and pushed the send button.

"Calling the White House. This is Vice President Adams calling the White House."

6

Washington, D.C.

Wally's frantic message from Air Force Two to the White House set off a near panic. President Randolph Edwards called his top advisors together at once, and they sat in the Oval Office staring at each other.

"It's a kidnapping pure and simple," Johnson from State said.

"But from what Wally said, the man was literate, spoke perfect English, and his gunmen did not harm any of the Vice President's party or the newspeople with them." The comment came from the CIA representative, Donaldson. "Doesn't sound like a terrorist to me. Terrorists would have killed everyone in the motorcade after they captured the Vice President."

"Wally said there were no ransom demands," the President said, reading from some papers. "That the man who spoke English was the leader of a group called the Bijimi Loyalist Party. Have we ever heard of them?" He turned to the man from the State Department.

"No, we've hardly heard of Sierra Bijimi," Johnson said.

"What's our course of action?" General Lawford, the president's National Defense Advisor, asked.

"Hell, what can we do? Damn near nothing," FBI Director Worthington said. "Somebody snatched the Vice President. We've never heard of the grabber. He's not with the government of that nation, so we have no clout and no target there. Damn little we can do now until we hear from the people who hold the Vice President."

Donaldson tapped his pen on his pad of paper. The CIA

man nodded grimly. "Got to admit it was a delicate and finely planned operation. Tree down across the road. The rigs all stopped. Snipers take out the twelve soldiers before they can fire a shot. Well-placed rounds that didn't even come close to the two cars in the middle. That takes disciplined, well-trained troops. Then their leader gets the drop on the Secret Service men and it's all over."

"You know that Wally is reliable as the Vice President's top aide," the President said. "They checked the limo after they found it at the end of the road at the river landing. Evidently the kidnappers took the Vice President upstream to their strong point. Wally says the group has vanished up there before after making a raid in the city or against the Army. He also said the SATCOM radio is missing from its spot in the limo. Maybe we'll be hearing directly from the kidnapper on the SATCOM. Make sure we keep an open channel for that set at all times."

"Taken care of that, Mr. President," Sage Billings said. He was the President's Chief of Staff.

"Goddamnit, Mr. President," General Lawford said. "We should send in a dozen of our river patrol boats and blast everything in sight until they give up the Vice President. We've got to show a strong hand or they'll try to bleed us dry."

"Easy, General. Easy. So far we don't know what is happening. We need to find out what these Loyalists want first, before we can decide anything."

Billings caught the President's attention. "Sir, what about our long-standing and well-voiced policy of never negotiating with terrorists? Does that include the people who are now holding the Vice President of our nation against his will?"

President Edwards shook his head, his lips a firm angry line. "I just don't know, Sage. I don't know. First we have to determine that these men who have Vice President Adams are terrorists. Perhaps this no-negotiating problem will just go away."

"Vietnam," General Lawford said. Everyone looked up. "Reminds me of how the SEALs worked the war in Vietnam. They made the rivers their highways, charged up and down them getting their jobs done neatly and swiftly. I'd suggest we send in our special platoon of SEALs to be on station there in Sierra City, even before we decide what we need to do. Anything we come up with, they probably would be involved with anyway."

Lawford looked around the table. "Mr. Donaldson, could you get your favorite SEAL platoon over to Sierra City in twenty-four hours?"

"We could." He looked at the head of the table. "Mr. President, I'm liking what General Lawford just said more and more. Fact is, we can put the SEALs on the scene, and use them for recon if nothing else. They can get in and out of a rat trap and not even bother the cheese."

The President looked around the table. He saw three of the men nod. Worthington bobbed his head. "Let's do it, then see what else we can do when we need to do it," he said.

"Are there any Naval units in that area?" the President asked.

"We utilized some of our assets last week up near Spain, which are the closest ones to this problem," Johnson said. "I remember the CNO saying he had no units south of there, so we would have to fly south off a carrier."

"Spain is how far from West Africa?" General Lawford asked.

Donaldson frowned. "Just a minute." He wrinkled his brow and rubbed his forehead. "Even with some flyovers, it would be over three thousand miles from the task force in place to that small country. We would do better to fly in some Rangers from Germany with a couple of stop-overs."

"Premature," the President said. "First we find out what this guy wants, and then we talk with him."

"We try to figure out a new policy about negotiating with terrorists?" the CIA man, Donaldson, asked.

"We're not negotiating, and we don't know that he's a terrorist," the FBI director said. "First we wait and see what we have here."

A knock sounded on a door, and an aide came in with some papers in his hand. He went to the President and whispered something to him, then gave him the papers.

The President put them on the table, adjusted his reading glasses, and went over the words carefully. Partway through he looked up.

"Well, this is good news. A SATCOM message directly from Adams. The Vice President says not to worry about him. He goes on:

" 'I'm being well treated and I am safe and in no danger. I already consider these men I'm with as friends, not enemies, and certainly not terrorists. I'm not sure why I am here, but Mojombo Washington, the leader of the Loyalist Party, told me that he would be making some demands on the United States soon.

" 'I don't feel like a hostage, and certainly not like a person who has been kidnapped, although technically, I guess I was. I'll be back in touch with you when I have more news. In the meantime, don't do anything sudden, rash, or bold. General Lawford, there is no reason for any massive military response, at least not right now. Mr. Washington has not told me what to say. He's listening to me and usually grinning. He says he's working on a list of demands that he will be sending to you soon.

" 'In the meantime, tell my wife and family that I am being treated well and that the food is remarkable, if a little different. We eat lots of fruits here. I'll be back in touch soon. Sign that: Marshall Adams, Vice President of the United States of America.' "

General Lawford snorted. "Hell, he would have to take a poke at me. Never has appreciated me." He looked around. "So, okay, no massive military strike. What the hell else can we do?"

"Simple," the President said. "We sit here and wait until we hear from this Washington or from Adams. There seems not to be the extreme emergency that we had thought."

"Seems like we should be doing something," the CIA man said. Donaldson scowled. "Hell, we at least could send the SEALs into the capital city and have them sit on their hands if they have to. Better to have some kind of presence there beside our twenty Marines at the embassy."

Billings, the Chief of Staff, nodded. "Yeah, sounds kosher to me. We send our favorite platoon down there, which certainly can't be labeled as a massive military response. How soon can they get there, Mr. Donaldson?"

"I'll check with the Chief of Naval Operations, but I'd say with the business jet it should take no more than twenty-four, maybe thirty-six hours at the most."

The advisors looked at the President. "Yes, I know some of these SEALs," he said. "We've used them before. Reliable. They won't go off half-cocked. Yes, Donaldson, let's get it in motion. Send the Third Platoon of SEAL Team Seven to Sierra City, Sierra Bijimi."

Sierra City, Sierra Bijimi

General Kiffa Assaba paced his office. He had just heard about the slaughter of twelve of his best Army Rangers and the capture of the American Vice President. This had to be the work of Mojombo Washington. His face turned red and he hurled the riding crop he always carried across the room. It hit a lamp, knocking it over and smashing the brittle shade. Assaba didn't react to the broken lamp. He continued pacing.

How could the terrorist have known where the convoy would be going? There had been some plans made, but certainly no announcement. The general public would have no idea of the motorcade itself or its direction or destination. So there had to be a spy within the top elements of the Army or the government. Which one?

He should take a thousand men, charge up the river, and kill everyone he found. Sooner or later he would run down Washington and his ragtag bunch of misfits. Yes, he must do that. He would talk to the President about it today. This new attack would be just cause. He could say they were going to rescue the kidnapped United States Vice President.

A knock came on the door. Then his aide, Major Kabala, came in. The tall soldier smiled wearily.

"General Assaba, sir. That matter we spoke of early this morning is ready. We have set up a court-martial in the old Supreme Court room. Everyone is there ready to proceed."

Assaba let out a tired sigh. He rubbed his hand over his

wolfish face and blinked large eyes. Then he nodded. "Yes, it must be done. I'm ready."

They walked out of the office, down the hall of the Government Building, and into a courtroom recently vacated by the Supreme court. Now it was military-oriented. Six officers sat on the high bench, with two tables in front of them. At one stood a prisoner dressed in a bright orange jumpsuit. He was handcuffed and his legs bound together with a short chain. He had not shaved recently, and his beard showed as dirty smears on his more brown than black face.

One man stood beside him, his Army-appointed defense counsel.

General Assaba marched up to the high bench, sat in the empty chair at the center of the six men, and rapped with a gavel that lay in front of him.

"This court-martial is now in session. Will the clerk read the indictment?"

A clerk rose and read a two-page charge against Private Tauba Kidira. General Assaba knew the crimes, which included desertion and stealing government property, namely a jeep. The man pleaded not guilty and the trial began.

The Army prosecutor brought two witnesses to the stand. One said that he saw the accused drive a jeep off the military post without authorization.

"I object," the defense counsel said. "It was dark at the time the alleged drive took place. The witness was more than thirty yards from the jeep. How could be identify Private Kidira as the driver in that darkness?"

General Assaba scowled at the lawyer. "The man is a second lieutenant in the Army. Officers don't lie. Objection overruled."

A second soldier testified that he had talked with Kidira the day he left and that Kidira had sworn that he would be a soldier no more. He would run as far away as he could.

"I object to this testimony, Your Honor," the defense counsel said, rising quickly.

"On what basis, Counselor?" the general asked.

"This is barracks talk. Every soldier who ever wore a uniform has cursed and yelled and sworn that he would desert. It's part of being a soldier. Almost none of the men ever do it. This is simply barracks-room talk that has no bearing on the truth of my client's action."

"Objection denied. The court will ignore what the counselor has said about the testimony."

The defense counsel tried to question the witnesses, but was denied the right. The defense counsel said he had no other witnesses. The prosecutor gave a one-minute summary and the trial was over. The officers on the bench stood and conferred briefly, than sat down.

"The finding of this court is that the accused is guilty of high treason, desertion, and stealing government property," one of the officers on the bench said. "The prisoner is sentenced to death. The sentence will be carried out immediately."

Two armed soldiers led Private Kidira out of the court. The judges and the general followed him. The condemned man walked to a stone wall just behind the courtroom, and turned to face the wall. When he was completely turned, General Assaba drew a .45-caliber automatic, put the muzzle against the back of Private Kidira's head, and fired one shot. The blast knocked Kidira down and killed him instantly. General Assaba moved up a step and fired three more times into the dead man's head as he lay on the ground, then holstered his weapon.

"No one deserts from my Army," he bellowed at the dozen witnesses. "No one. Any man who tries will wind up like this one did. Remember that." He turned and marched back into the building toward his office.

7

NAVSPECWARGRUP-ONE
Coronado, California
Platoon Three of SEAL Team Seven enjoyed its second
day of "camping out" on the beach just below the Kill
House on the Coronado Strand and just north of the Navy
antenna farm. Murdock thought about yesterday. They had
started with a full-operational-gear jog down the six miles
to the antennas in the loose sand. Then, after a five-minute
blow, they walked into the sparkling Pacific Ocean surf,
dove under the breakers, and swam out a mile due south,
then retraced their route. All of the SEALs now had the
new underwater Motorola personal radios, good for seven
miles underwater and five miles on land. It helped them
keep in touch with each other fifteen feet underwater even
on a moonless night. After the two-mile trek they worked
through the Kill House three times, taking names and times.
The new man, Omar Rafii, hadn't seen the new Kill House.

"Hey, I ain't been through one of these for over a year,"
he said. "We don't get out to the desert training much in
the other platoons."

"You'll have plenty of it here," Jaybird said. He had
taken an instant liking to Omar, and had been helping him
adjust to the new platoon.

"Just don't let Jaybird lead you astray," Senior Chief
Sadler told the young man. "You know why we call him
Jaybird, don't you? And it's got nothing to do with the little
bird legs he has."

"So tell me, Jaybird," Omar said.

"Hell, okay. We was in Austria, or Senegal or maybe

Paris, France—I don't remember that part too well—and there was this huge guy in this bar who was just itching to pick a fight with somebody. Everybody in the platoon knew I was the best street brawler in the outfit, so they started pushing me forward."

Somebody threw a brown MRE plastic pouch filled with sand at Jaybird.

"You're making that up, Jaybird, you asshole," Bradford yelled. "Tell him the real reason. About that four-story building in La Jolla that night about four years ago."

"Wasn't in La Jolla," Lam said. "He told me it was in San Francisco, down in Chinatown somewhere, and it was before he was even in this man's Navy."

That afternoon they worked a swim up to BUD/S and staged a mock attack on the grinder, then ran back to their campsite below the big antennas. That night they had a roaring campfire on the beach, and told war stories about some of the more hairy missions they had worked.

The next day had been a half hour of sit-ups and push-ups and stretching exercises before a six-mile run down to BUD/S and back.

When they came back, Murdock gave the men a fifteen-minute break. Then he lifted out of the dry sand and dusted off his cammies. "Break time is over, you ladies, time we get into some real workouts," Murdock called. They lined up in a column of ducks by squads. "We're going to run back to the grinder and check out some IBSs and get in some work. Let's move it. Omar, lead us out at a seven-minutes-to-the-mile pace. Out-a-here."

An hour later they had worked the IBSs twice coming in through the breakers, sliding up on the Coronado Strand, and rushing up through the water to create a beach landing. The next time they took the small inflatable boats out, Murdock made a change. "This time we get into the first wave and pretend that we dump the boat and everyone bails out in a simulated turnover. You all have that? We drop out of the boat into the breakers and swim and surf into shore, where we lay like logs for two minutes, before we charge up the beach to the dry sand with simulated firing. No live rounds. Let's do it."

The first boat motored into the surging Pacific swell just before it broke, and rode it halfway down before Lieutenant (j.g.) Gardner gave a yell and his squad dropped over the sides of the boat, let it surge forward, then surfaced and swam in behind the pounding roar of the big surf. All eight men made it to shore, and lay in the receding water as one wave after another half-covered them with foaming, sandy water.

Murdock headed his Alpha Squad's IBS into the wave. Jaybird was on the motor and he angled for the top of the big swell, then just before it broke he angled down the sliding wall of water. He was off by half a yard and the wave tumbled the twelve-foot-long boat upside down, spilling out the men and racing the floating craft toward the beach.

Murdock surfaced and began counting heads. The last time they had dumped an IBS this way, one of his squad had almost drowned. This time he found seven more heads bobbing in the water, and he signaled and all swam hard for shore, where they spread out and dove into the wet sand in a rough line facing the beach as the ocean waters flowed over them and then receded. After three minutes Murdock used the waterproof Motorolas.

"Charge the dry sand," he ordered, and the sixteen men lifted up and surged up through the water and wet sand and sprawled in the dry sand with weapons covering the thin strand of beach ahead of them.

"Jaybird, what happened?" Murdock asked.

"You said to dump the boat. So I dumped it. Not hard, just overplay the top of the wave by six or eight feet and you're going down."

"It was supposed to be a simulated dump, not a real one. Remember when we almost lost Canzoneri when the boat clobbered him in the head when it went over?"

"Oh, shit. Yeah. Sorry, Boss. Won't happen again."

Murdock gave them five minutes, then stood. "Okay, you hotshots, we have a swim. Know where the beacon is down on the point off the tip of the Naval Air Station? You've been there a dozen times. Lieutenant Gardner will lead us out on a three-mile swim to the beacon. Then we turn around and come back home to BUD/S. Take us down fifteen feet and keep in touch with each other. We'll use a long buddy line for each squad. Let's get wet."

Lieutenant (j.g.) Gardner took a compass reading on the point that he could see down the coast. He took the hand-held compass board, waded into the water, and checked the buddy line. The JG waved at Murdock, took the men down fifteen feet, and angled along his azimuth setting on the compass board toward the point.

Murdock swam in his position at the head of Alpha Squad. He loved the new Motorola radio, which worked better underwater than it did on the surface. The throat mike and earpiece made it an entirely hands-off operation, which would come in handy in a tough firefight situation.

Halfway there, Lieutenant Gardner called for a surfacing. The SEALs came up and the JG checked his course. He made a minor adjustment on his setting.

"Everyone okay?" he asked on the net. "We're about halfway. Let's do a mile on the surface. We're cutting across the water for the quickest route instead of following the curve of the land mass. Let's have a radio check. Alpha Squad first."

The men sounded off in squad field-marching order.

"Everyone accounted for. Let's take a swim."

They were crawl-stroking on the surface when their Motorolas sounded again.

"Murdock, lad, are you in range?" It was the Scottish-accented voice of Master Chief MacKenzie.

"Right, Master Chief. I read you loud."

"Bring the boys home, Commander. We've had a bit of a message from the CNO. Seems like he's needing your services again. What's your ETO BUD/S?"

"Thirty minutes if we push it. We're in the wet about two miles off. Heading your way now. Might take us a little longer. Keep the lights on."

"Copy that, Commander. Stop by and see me before you get dry."

"Roger, Master Chief."

Murdock waited a moment, then used the radio again. "Gardner, head us for home plate. Looks like we have a mission coming up."

It was thirty minutes before the SEALs ran up the beach in front of BUD/S and flopped on the sand. Gardner had set a pace that was ten strokes to the minute too fast, and the men were exhausted.

Murdock, Gardner, and Senior Chief Sadler hurried on to the Quarterdeck. Master Chief MacKenzie met them just outside.

"Have enough wet sand in my Quarterdeck already," he said. He handed Murdock a computer printout. It was in 16-point type and brief.

"Alert Third Platoon, SEAL Team Seven, to be ready to fly from North Island Naval Air Station at 1230 today. Bring all weapons, double supply of ammunition, full water gear, and tropical uniforms. Transport will be the Gulfstream II. Report to the embassy in Sierra Bijimi and await further orders."

"Where the hell is Sierra Bijimi?" Murdock asked.

"Looked it up, lad. It's on the west bulge of Africa. Small place with about four million people. Something must have happened down there we don't know about. 'Tis now 1015. Suggest you get your tails in motion. I'll have a bus here for your transport to North Island at 1215."

"Thanks, Master Chief. We're moving."

Murdock told the men all he knew about the mission as they walked over to their quarters, changed into clean dry tropical cammies, and got their gear ready to travel. Full combat vests and ammo and their weapons went into duffle bags, along with complete wet suits and all of their underwater gear. They had early chow at the Amphib base across the highway, and were in the parking lot next to the Quarterdeck by 1200.

Chris Gardner was grinning. "Damn, the second day I'm with the platoon we get activated. Yeah, this is my kind of duty. Glad to be on board."

"West coast of Africa?" Jaybird yelped. "Gonna take us a year just to fly over there. That's halfway round the fucking world. What does the Gulfstream II do? As I remember it goes five hundred miles an hour at forty thousand feet. Maybe stop in New York, then to Newfoundland, head southeast to the Azores, and then maybe Mauritania before we go south to that little country. We're talking some heavy sack time here, gents."

"How long, Jaybird?" Fernandez asked.

"Maybe twelve thousand miles at five hundred should come out to about twenty-four hours, not counting time stopped to refuel and the clearances and diplomatic shit. Say another six hours. Thirty hours. Then we'll also lose about eight or nine hours on the clock."

"Shut up, Jaybird, you're making my head hurt," Luke Howard thundered.

At the North Island Naval Air Station, the Gulfstream was warmed up and waiting for them. A slender, pretty woman in a khaki uniform met them at the door. Murdock spotted the lieutenant's bars on her shoulders and the silver wings on her blouse. She was Coast Guard.

"Lieutenant, some SEALs looking for a ride," he said. "You have any seats open?"

"Commander, we have nineteen. Also some good food just stowed. Glad to have you on board." She held out her hand. "I'm Sandra. I'm your bus driver for the trip."

"I'm Murdock. I hear we're heading for Sierra Bijimi."

"That's what my orders say. I've never been there before. If my flight plan works, we should find it."

They moved out of the doorway and let the men troop inside. Senior Chief Sadler claimed the first four seats for the officers and himself. "Don't crowd, we've got plenty of good seats," Sadler said.

Murdock and Gardner settled into their seats and strapped on their seat belts. Gardner shook his head. "These guys aren't going to be happy with thirty hours in the air. How about our taking a one-mile run on our second fueling stop? That could be Newfoundland. Then they'll be ready to sleep for about ten hours."

"Good idea," Murdock said. He liked this young man the more he saw of him. Yes, he would work out well in the platoon.

"Sierra Bijimi," Murdock said. "I didn't even have time to look it up on the Web. We don't know a thing about the country. I wonder what Uncle Sam wants us to do down there."

8

On Board the Gulfstream II
High over the United States

Just before the door had closed on the Gulfstream at North Island, a sailor had come boiling up in a Humvee waving a sheaf of papers. He ran to the door and pushed them at Senior Chief Sadler.

"Faxes just came in," the sailor said. "Master Chief told me to get here before you took off or I was toast."

"You made it," Sadler said. "Now drive slow going back." At once the crew chief closed and locked the cabin door.

Murdock and Lieutenant (j.g.) Gardner divided the stack of fax pages and began reading.

"Oh, yeah," Murdock said. Sadler and Gardner both looked at him. "Now we know why we're going to that little country. Some wild-eyed rebel down there kidnapped the Vice President and is holding him for ransom."

"No shit?" Sadler said.

"So all we have to do is track down this rebel band, kill all the bad guys, and rescue the VP," Gardner said. "Piece of cake."

"Yeah," Murdock said. "That's the what. Just how we do it will depend on a thousand different factors. Some of them must be in all this fax paper."

Then all three went back to reading. Quickly Murdock discovered that the tiny nation was only ten years old. It had been carved out from another all-black African country through a small revolution. It was near the west coast bulge of Africa, and had one good-sized river flowing through it.

The population was listed as being 3.8 million people in an area about twice the size of Delaware. The nation was a member of the United Nations, and had a questionably elected government that was reported to be totally corrupt, with most foreign aid ending up in the leaders' pockets.

It had been described as a "mess of a country" that deserved better. The standing Army of 4,000 was poorly trained and had old weapons, and the men were paid infrequently. Sierra City was the capital. The country's Navy consisted of six small riverboats and a few more than one hundred sailors.

Gardner looked up from his reading. "Sounds like a sorry outfit. Why was the Vice President there in the first place?"

Murdock grunted. "Yeah, here it is. He went there on a goodwill trip representing the President. This country was added to his tour only three weeks before he left when another nation backed out."

"So the rebels had to find out he was coming and then plan to capture him," Senior Chief Sadler said. "Just who is this Mojombo Washington character anyway?"

Murdock shook his head. "I don't see much about him. Evidently he's new to the ranks of the rebels. Here it says that the man speaks English and has attracted some support from the outlying villages. The police think he has a stronghold somewhere up the Amunbo River that runs through there. Eyewitnesses said that the Vice President was taken up that river in a boat."

"Who will we have to work with when we get there?" Gardner asked.

Murdock checked another page. "A small embassy has been established there and the new ambassador is in it. The President of Sierra Bijimi is Thom Kolda. We don't have much on him, but he evidently is the top bad guy in the place. Another bad guy probably is General Kiffa Assaba, who is the head of the Army and the National Police."

"Hey, look at this," Gardner said. "The only airport has one runway that's less than a mile long. The Vice President's Air Force Two had a narrow scrape landing there. It will be able to carry only half its normal load of fuel if it wants to take off."

• • •

Murdock was glad when they landed at Newfoundland. The JG took the men on a two-mile run without any weapons or equipment. Murdock used the Gulfstream's radio to try to contact Don Stroh in Washington, D.C. He got through to the right office, but the secretary there whom Murdock had talked with before, said Stroh had already boarded a commercial flight on his way to Africa. She couldn't say exactly when he would get there. Murdock thanked her and hung up.

He took out the fax orders and looked at them again. The SEALs were to report to the American Embassy in Sierra City and wait for further instructions. At least they could do a little looking around, get to know something about the situation. If it was as bad as the reports he had read, neither the Army nor the President would be of much help. Now he wondered how strong this rebel leader was.

A messenger from the airport office raced in a jeep to the refueling location and asked for Commander Murdock. He saluted smartly, then gave Murdock a large manila envelope and retreated. Inside were more fax pages. Murdock saw that they came from Stroh. He read:

"Murdock. This is the latest. We may not have such a panic as we first thought. We received a SATCOM message directly from Vice President Adams. I'll give you a word-for-word transcript. Here it is:

" 'Hello, Mr. President. Please don't worry about me. I'm being well treated and I am safe and in no danger. I already consider these men I'm with as friends. . . .' "

Murdock frowned, then read the rest of the Vice President's message. So he considered the kidnappers his friends, and he was being treated and fed well.

Stroh went on: "You'll land in Africa before I will. Get situated in the embassy or wherever they can house you and start nosing around to see what you can find out. This may turn out far differently than we first suspected. At least we stopped General Lawford from sending in a dozen F-18's to strafe the whole area up the river and follow up with a dozen riverboats to blast everything that wasn't dead already.

"Digest all of that local material and we'll talk as soon as I hook up with you in Sierra City."

The SEALs came back from their two-mile run. They had hardly broken a sweat. Lieutenant (j.g.) Gardner was sweating like a filly in August, Murdock thought. Gardner eased into his seat and shook his head.

"Hell, I thought I was in pretty good shape. Not so. I'm going to be on the three basics from now on, sit-ups, chin-ups, and pull-ups."

Murdock shuffled the Stroh faxes to him. Gardner read the first few pages and looked up in surprise. "Vice President Adams is already a friend of his kidnappers? What the fuck is going on?"

"That's what we'll find out after we land in Sierra City. Why don't you brief the men on Stroh's material and what we learned from the other faxes. I want all the men to know as much about this situation and about this country as we do."

"Aye, aye, sir," Gardner said. He wiped the sweat off his forehead and the back of his neck and stood up.

"Okay, men, listen up. We've had some more intel on our mission. Here's what we know so far."

Senior Chief Sadler followed the details of the situation, but he also kept thinking about the black girl back in San Diego who had been so full of life one minute, and an hour later dead in the alley behind the club where their Gaslamp Dixieland Jazz Band played. Had Shortchops given her an overdose, or was he just messing around with her? Sadler couldn't remember if the detective had told him not to leave town. Hell, he was a material witness in a murder case. He could be in one shit-pot full of trouble as soon as they got back to the States. He closed his eyes and took a deep breath. He'd have to worry about that when they finished this little job and reported across the Quarterdeck. Until then he had to concentrate on the problem at hand.

Near Camp Freedom, Sierra Bijimi

Mojombo Washington smiled when Vice President Adams finished his radio message to the White House.

"Excellent, Mr. Vice President. That was a fine report to your countrymen so they don't drop a nuclear bomb on our camp. I hope that they believed you. I realize it's a bit unusual for a man evidently kidnapped to give such a friendly report."

"They have to believe me. I hope to have more good news for them before long. You have a name for this camp we're going to?"

"Yes, it's Camp Freedom. We have about a half mile to walk up this trail to the camp. We didn't want it to be vulnerable to rifle fire from the river in case President Kolda sent some riverboats up this direction with soldiers in them."

The Vice President had been a bird watcher at one time, and now he enjoyed spotting various species in the thick jungle growth. He'd reached twelve species sightings when they emerged into a clearing beside a small stream they had been following. The camp was as rough as Adams figured it would be. There were two dozen tents that would hold six men each. He spotted a mess tent for cooking, but with no place to sit down and eat. There were a number of small fires burning around the area. He caught the gentle purr of a small gas motor, which could be running an electrical generator, so they might have lights.

He saw weapons everywhere. Each man evidently had to carry a personal weapon with him at all times. They were rifles, submachine guns, and a few carbines and pistols. A mix of guns that would be hard to provide ammunition for.

Mojombo led the Vice President to a tent and pointed in through the open flap. "This, Mr. Vice President Adams, is your tent. It isn't as fancy as a hotel room, but I hope you'll find it comfortable. It has the only real bed in the camp, and at night there will be electric lights if you want to read or write. I have a selection of books, fiction and non-fiction, and writing pens and paper."

"No bars on the flap?"

"Absolutely not. You're free to move around the camp. Of course it's about twenty-five miles through the jungle back to town if you want to hike it."

"I won't be doing that. I'm interested in your cause, in

getting this crooked, murdering President out of office." He
went into the tent and looked around. It was better than the
tents on some camping trips he'd been on. He sat down on
the bed. "Oh, yes, this is good." He looked up and frowned.
"Now, how is the revolution coming along? What can I do
to help? Right now there's no way I can bring in a battalion
of Marines with all of their firepower."

Mojombo stood just outside the tent.

"Come in, come in, sit down so we can talk," said Adams. "I did some Navy time. Maybe we can come up with
some ideas. How many men do you have with weapons?"

Mojombo stepped inside the tent and sat down in the one
straight-backed wooden chair. He made a fist with one hand
and rubbed it with the other hand. "I can put eighty men
on a march with weapons and enough ammo for a good
fight."

"The general has about four thousand, you said." Adams
scowled. "Probably reserves he can call up. Those are not
good odds."

"That's why we make surprise attacks and then run like
crazy. The traditional guerrilla operation."

"It's worked for you so far, but they will get wise to that
and keep out patrols, maybe put lookouts on the river at
night."

"You're right. I realize that with less than two hundred
men, I can never win an all-out battle with General Assaba's forces. That's why you are my guest."

Vice President Adams frowned slightly, then nodded.
"Yes, yes, I see. If I'm here, that would bring worldwide
attention to your cause, and to the atrocities and sacking of
the national treasury. But you need more than just publicity."

Mojombo stood and paced around the small tent. He
went back to the chair and sat. "Yes, more than publicity.
I can get maybe five thousand farmers and hunters and their
families to follow me down the river to the city. A citizens'
march against the federal government and the fraudulently
elected President. We might win, if more than half of the
military would swing over to our side and, with weapons,
march with us. I would need at least two thousand armed

men from General Assaba's camp in order to stage a real revolution. Until that happens, I'm merely a criminal rebel with a price on my head."

"I may have an idea that could help you, Mr. Washington. The American CIA calls it covert intervention."

Mojombo grinned. "That is beautiful, a wonderful idea. What you're saying is that some foreign nation, like the United States, sends in some troops on a highly secret basis. They help me win my revolution and slip out the back door before anyone spots them, and the whole thing is done covertly, and everyone but the bad guys wins."

Vice President Adams smiled. "Mojombo, you are an extremely bright and quick-thinking young man. Your English is better than mine."

"I had a well-to-do father who sent me to school in America."

"Why did you come back home? I'm sure you could have had a good job in the government somewhere."

"I finished graduate school at the same time my father took seriously ill. I came home to take care of him and my mother and because I love my country and want to help my people." They were both quiet for a short time. "Can you tell me more about this covert-intervention idea? Is it something that you could sell to your government?"

"I'm not sure. It would take a lot of investigation of the climate here, the whole situation, the criminal actions of the President and his Administration. Then you would have to prove that you have the support of the people, that they would be with you on an all-out assault on the capital."

"That would be the easy part. I can videotape fifty witnesses for you within a week. I can document the atrocities, the massive thefts of money and matériel, and the killings by the Army of many innocent farmers."

"Fifty witnesses to those crimes would be impressive. This all will take some time."

"If you could send in five hundred Marines with their firepower and a dozen helicopter gunships, we could reduce General Assaba's Army to a handful of wild-eyed hard cases in three or four days."

Vice President Adams stood, walked the short length of

the tent, and came back. A small boy slipped inside the tent with a wooden platter filled with several kinds of fruit, including a banana on top. Adams took the banana, peeled it down two inches, and had a bite.

"I'm afraid we couldn't be covert with five or six hundred men charging around your country. I was thinking more about twenty specialists to train and lead, perhaps carry out some swift silent strikes on their own."

Mojombo shook his head. "Mr. Vice President Adams. Frankly I don't see what twenty men could do to help us. I need men with rifles and machine guns and hand grenades to engage the enemy."

"You must have heard about the Army Rangers, the Marine Recon, and the Navy SEAL teams. These are Special Forces highly trained to do just this sort of work. I know of some of the work they have done around the world in the last five years, and it's truly amazing."

Mojombo took a small notebook from his Army-style cammy shirt pocket and began making notes. "Let's say for the sake of our discussion that we could get a team of specialists in here from the United States. What kind of a time element are we talking about? I had a timetable that already is behind schedule. This week I was supposed to be able to raise three hundred men. Most of my volunteers come from the outlying areas. I need many more from the capital."

"Time element. Yes, a problem. First I'd have to talk to them in Washington about the idea. Maybe we should fire up the SATCOM right now so I can talk with the President or his Chief of Staff. I know the frequency to get through on."

The Gulfstream II set down at the Sierra City airport at 1515. Murdock stood in the aisle and looked over his platoon. Most were awake after the long hop.

"We'll deplane in about five. Each man will take all of his own gear. The skycaps in this airport are hard to find. If we're lucky someone will meet us. Otherwise we send out scouts to find the embassy." There were a few grunts and hoo-has, and the men began gathering their gear.

A young Coast Guard flight chief came and stood by the door. When the brakes brought the plane to a stop, he opened the door and let down the stairs. Murdock moved off first. A yellow thirty-passenger school bus was parked fifty feet away across the tarmac. The driver came out and waved to them.

"Your limo's here," the American said.

A ten-minute ride in the bus, and it pulled into an enclosed compound of the U.S. embassy. The building was four stories, had bars on the windows on the ground floor and a ten-foot decorative steel fence around the outside of the property. A man wearing a slightly rumpled suit and white shirt and tie stood on the steps. Murdock walked up and met him as the troops lined up in squad order.

"Lieutenant Commander Murdock and the Third Platoon of SEAL Team Seven reporting as ordered, sir."

"At ease, Commander. I'm Ambassador Nance Oberholtzer. Still can't get used to that title. We're not nearly that formal here. Usually it's too damned hot. Hope you had a good ride. I have some faxes and radio signals for you to look at. I don't know how the hell we got in this jam. I didn't expect Mojombo would do anything while the Veep was here. I guess nobody calls the Vice President the Veep anymore. Who was it who popularized that term? Don't remember. I'll have to look it up."

"As I remember, Mr. Ambassador, that would be Harry Truman's Vice President, Alben Barkley. He was a real character."

"Yes, I think you're right. You must be a historian. Bring your boys in. I've got spots for them down on the second floor. Two to a room, but the beds are good. This will be your home for as long as you need it. Like I said, we're not all that formal here."

Two native men appeared and led the SEALs into the embassy and to the second floor, where they found the rooms and settled in.

One of the native men came up to Murdock. "Dining room on first floor end of long hall. We eat dinner at five-thirty. Okay?"

"Okay," Murdock said. He found the ambassador in his

office, which had been furnished recently and was still undergoing changes.

"Mr. Ambassador. I'd like a meeting as soon as possible with the top Army general here. Do you know his name?"

"Yes, that would be General Kiffa Assaba. A word of warning. He's not a real general. He has the rank and post because he's the hatchet man for the President. This is as near to an outlaw government as I've ever seen. But we have to live with it. I'll phone him at once and see when you can get together."

The general set it up for 6:30 that night at a downtown restaurant.

"That means he'll want you to buy him dinner," the ambassador said. "You know about money here? Probably not. Medium of exchange is mostly barter, but they also have paper currency called the dagnar. It's fifty of the suckers to one U.S. greenback. I'll give you a wad of five-hundred-dagnar notes. They are worth ten dollars each. Watch this sneaky little bastard. He'll see how he can use you and your men to help his cause."

"Be on my guard. Any more traffic on the SATCOM from the Vice President?"

"Yes, we did get a call he made to the White House. We have a recording of it on tape. Let me play it for you." He took out a tape recorder, put in a small tape, and hit the play button.

"Yes, this is Vice President Adams calling the White House. I'd like to talk to the President or to Walters."

"Mr. Walters will be right with you, Mr. Vice President."

"Good. I've got lots to say. Where is he?"

"Right here, Mr. Vice President. How are you holding up?"

"Fine. About this situation. You must know what a rotten gang we've got here in this Sierra Bijimi government. Rotten right down from the fraudulently elected President to the political general of the Army and the police. Mojombo Washington is trying to get it fixed and he can use some help. What we need to do is send in a battalion of Marines and wipe out the current officials, but I know you would frown on that. How about some Special Forces to come in covertly and do some work down here?"

"Good thinking, Mr. Vice President. Fact is, we shipped out a platoon of SEALs almost twenty-four hours ago. They should be in country by now."

"They are here on a covert basis?"

"As covert as hell."

"That could be a start. I really think this young man has a magnificent project here. I'm going to try to help him in any way that I can. Oh, do we have any Navy in this area?"

"We checked that, Mr. Vice President. The closest asset is a task force off Portugal. Take them several days to sail down within striking distance of you. The unit has been ordered to move in that direction."

"We aren't going to blow this little nation off the map. Tell everyone to relax. I'm in no danger. The SEALs are here. I've seen them work before. Now I'll try to send a runner to contact them. I think we're through here, Walter. You take care."

The ambassador turned off the tape recorder. "So, now you know as much about this situation as I do. The Vice President must be taken by this young man. Sounds like he wants to be one of the leaders in this battle coming up."

"What else do I need to know about this General Assaba?" Murdock asked.

"That's about it. He's a former night club owner who went broke. Later he helped the President get elected. When the top general in the Army refused some of the President's orders, Kolda had him tried and shot for treason. Then he moved Assaba into his place."

"Sounds cozy. We'll talk. Outside of that, I don't know what we'll do. Our CIA control should be arriving here today or tomorrow. After that we'll get to work."

The dinner meeting that evening went about as Murdock figured it would. General Assaba was a small man, slender, looked good in his uniform, had a wolfish face and overly large eyes that seemed to bore into everyone he looked at. Murdock tried an eye-to-eye contest one time, and lost quickly.

"My English," Assaba said. "Many years ago we were a

part of another country—we don't mention that it was a British colony. So the British taught everyone English along with our native Wolof. Now English is one of two official languages of our nation."

The restaurant was the most expensive in town, and the general ordered the highest-priced dinner and a bottle of wine.

"We know you are with the U.S. Navy SEALs, a Special Forces group, and we know that you are remarkably talented. Perhaps you can chase down this rebel Mojombo Washington. We have tried. We sent two gunboats up the Amunbo River to try to find him. The boats were heavily armed with machine guns and rifles. The men on the ship never saw a rebel. However, they took such heavy fire from the jungle cover that we lost ten men dead and six wounded, and had to turn around and power away before the boats had made it halfway to the suspected target."

"He owns the river. How close to Sierra City did the shooting start?"

"About fifteen miles upstream they took the first rounds."

"I'd like to talk to your G-2 man, your head of intelligence. Maybe by working together we can figure out a plan to move up the river at night, say, then hit the jungle and move around him and hit him from the rear."

General Assaba put down his fork, which had just dipped a bite of lobster into the melted butter, and smiled. "Oh, yes, I like the way you think, Commander. I'll set up a meet with our Colonel Dara for ten o'clock tomorrow morning at our headquarters in the Government Building."

A short time later the dinners and desserts were finished, and the men shook hands and left the restaurant.

Murdock took a taxi back to the embassy. He had a strange feeling about General Assaba. The man did not even sound like a military man, which he wasn't. His uniform fit, but any tailor could manage that. There was something about the man that hit Murdock the wrong way. Was he as corrupt as the ambassador said? If so, there might not be much value in helping him. What confused Murdock more than anything was the radio talk he had heard between the Vice President and the White House. Mr. Adams sounded like he had adopted Mojombo Washington and swung completely behind him in his try to overthrow the elected government and establish a real democracy.

If that were true, Murdock pondered, why should the SEALs do anything to help the forces of the fraudulently elected government?

9

Back at the embassy, Murdock, Gardner, Senior Chief Sadler, and Jaybird traded faxes as they again read everything they had about the country and the situation.

"Looks like we just stepped into a large pail of shit," Jaybird said. "No way we need to help these crooks steal more money."

"We're here to get the Vice President out of trouble," Lieutenant (j.g.) Gardner said. "If we have to help them a little to get the job done, then we do it."

"From what the Vice President himself said, he doesn't consider himself a captive," Murdock said. "He says he wants to help this rebel all he can. I wonder what he means by that."

They were in Murdock and Gardner's room, and they heard a commotion in the hall. Then a familiar voice came through the noise.

"Damnit, Murdock, come out of your hole. I've had enough trouble today without playing fucking hide-and-seek."

Murdock stepped into the hall grinning. "Well, if it isn't the wonder boy of the CIA, the next candidate for deputy director, your friend and mine, Mortimer J. Stroh."

"That's Snerd, Mortimer J. Snerd, and Edgar Bergen would sue you if he was still around. Murdock, you horse's heinie, how the hell is it hanging?"

"Long and lean. Glad you finally made it. You have lots of direction for us in this snake pit of a country?" Murdock saw the exhaustion showing in the CIA man's face. At forty-eight, he wasn't slowing down any. His brown hair was thinning a little, but his blue eyes still had a snap to them. His round face made his ears look too big for his face. Don Stroh was definitely not the fade-into-the-background type.

"Not a lot of direction for you. Our job is to rescue the Vice President without throwing a few million dollars to each side."

"Big-budget job, I'd say," Jaybird cracked.

Stroh grinned. "They still putting up with you around here?"

"Till death do us part."

"Might be sooner than you figure, Jaybird," Sadler growled.

"So what the hell we gonna do about the Vice President?" Stroh asked.

Murdock chuckled. "Great. No directives, we get to figure it out ourselves. The way it usually goes. We've found out this country is about ready to go down, from ignorance and bad government if nothing else. A bunch of official crooks and killers run the place."

"That's the way I hear it, too," Stroh said. "How do we get the second highest man in our government out of the jungle?"

"I'm talking to a colonel tomorrow and I should have some ideas after that. Off the top, it looks like a river cruise would be in order. A recon, done at night so we don't draw a lot of rebel fire. The river is theirs."

"What can we find out at night?" Gardner asked.

"Plenty," Jaybird said. "First we slip up on a village and grab a couple of men and ask them some questions. We can find out if the peasants out there in the boonies really like this guy the way some people say. If so, maybe he's not as bad as the government thinks. You hear Adams's last talk with the White House?"

Stroh hadn't. They let him read the transcript. He finished it and looked up. "Sounds like he's signed on as a rebel."

"Which means we can't go shooting up the rebel camps," Murdock said. "We have to contact them, but it has to be a soft contact, with no gunfire."

"We've already got contact," Gardner said. "He has a SATCOM, we have a SATCOM. Why don't we just talk to him?"

"Because we don't know when he might turn his set on," Murdock said. "Most embassies don't have SATCOMs. They have more sophisticated radio equipment. So we can't just ring him up like he had a phone. We can try, but don't expect much."

Ten minutes later Bill Bradford had the SATCOM antenna lined up with the satellite and Murdock made a call.

"Sierra City calling Vice President Adams. Do you read me? Sierra City calling Vice President Adams."

There was no response. The ambassador had been told of Stroh's arrival, and came onto the balcony where they had set up the dish antenna.

"We tried six times to call him, but evidently he had turned off the receiver," the ambassador said. "He'd probably worried about the life of his battery."

"We may have to send a man up there to contact them and get the radio signals worked out," Murdock said. He turned to the CIA man. "Now, Stroh, give us the rest of the dope on this strange little country and what the CIA and State has to say about it."

"State hardly knows it exists. The African desk has a thin file on this place, but nobody there has been here or knows much about it that isn't in the file. Basically stolen elections, bad people probably robbing the treasury and the country blind. Foreign intervention is their answer to every criticism. It's a small cancer on the world order. Nobody knows much about it or cares."

"Except our Vice President by the sound of him," Gardner said.

Sadler rubbed his chin. "Looks like our first job is to get upstream and make contact with this rebel. It might be a simple matter of promising him some covert guns and ammo for his little rebellion here. He'd probably shout hosanna for two hundred M-16's and five thousand rounds of ammo."

"Could be that simple, but Mojombo Washington could get that for any American he captured," Stroh said. "The

Agency feels that he has much bigger demands that will be coming. That should be the second thing we do, wait to see what those demands are."

Stroh stood. "I'm so damn tired I can't even see straight, let alone think in a straight line. Let's pick this up tomorrow right after breakfast. I hear the food here is great. I'm hitting the old feather bed."

"Dream on those feathers," Jaybird said.

"Hopefully."

"We're in no shape to do anything tonight," Murdock said. "Let's get some sleep and grab it by the balls first thing in the morning. Then maybe we can work up a mission for tomorrow night. No sense in going up that river and getting our skulls blown apart by friendly fire."

Breakfast was served from 0600 to 0900, and all the SEALs ate until they exploded. Six of them gathered around a conference table on the first floor and welcomed the ambassador. The general tone of the meeting was that they should get upriver and try to make contact. At the least they could talk to the villagers they found.

"Have to be a night mission," Murdock said. "I talk to Colonel Dara at 1000. He might help us without knowing it. We'll need a boat that can swim upstream. Dara might be our supply."

"We kept the SATCOM on all night, but the Vice President didn't transmit on the White House frequency," the ambassador said. "We're hoping he'll call this morning. If he does, we'll break in and let him know we can talk with him here and maybe help him."

Murdock checked his watch and headed for the Government Building, where the general said his G-2 would be. A young girl at a reception desk on the second floor took him to Colonel Dara's office. The man who held out his hand to Murdock looked like a soldier. He was five-ten, slender, with a firm grip and what looked to be a hard body toned by many workouts. His face was longish and he had a close-cropped haircut. He took off reading glasses as they met.

"Yes, the American SEAL. I know a lot about you people and your exploits. I'd like to get some Special Forces established here, but I'm having enough trouble holding together what Army we have left. It's my responsibility, General Assaba keeps telling me."

"Good to meet you, Colonel. We are an action-oriented force. Right now it looks like a trip up the Amunbo River would be the best move."

"We tried that. Got shot to pieces."

"I heard about that. I'd want to go up at night as quietly as possible. Then we could stop along the way at the villages and settlements and talk to them about the rebels. Someone might tell us where his stronghold is."

"We're pretty sure we know where it is. The trouble is, it's so far upstream and so well defended that we don't seem to be able to attack him with any success."

"I understand he's made some guerrilla raids lately."

"Yes, caught us by surprise both times. Night attacks. We haven't been on a wartime footing. Maybe it's time we go to that."

"Does he have any popular support?"

"Not much that we know of. Almost none here in the city. He's looked on as an educated outlaw by most people."

"Is he a real threat to your government here?"

"Not really. But we are concerned with the worldwide publicity that he's getting by kidnapping your Vice President. This is unforgivable. Because of that alone, we are obligated to put on a drive to eliminate him and, we hope, release the Vice President."

"Do you have any definite plans?"

"We hope your government will lend us five thousand Marines and helicopters so we can move in with them and wipe out the rebels, killing every man they have."

Murdock grinned. "We both know that isn't going to happen. Are there any roads up along the river?"

"The only jeep road goes up about ten miles. From there it's a horse trail that some two-wheeled carts can get by on to bring produce and crops into the city. There's quite a bit of boat traffic on the river. It's the best highway into the interior."

"Colonel, I need to do some recon. Could you supply me with a boat and crew to take a trip up the river tonight after dark? It would be a no-firefight-type situation. We'd go slow and easy and talk to as many of the local people we find as possible. This Mojombo might have set up a camp much closer to the city now that he feels he's getting stronger and has the Vice President as a hostage."

Colonel Dara frowned, then stood and paced his office for a minute. At last he sat down again and nodded. He made a phone call using the Wolof language. When the call ended he smiled.

"Yes, Commander Murdock. We'll have a boat and crew at your disposal at Dock Six, this afternoon at 1800. How many men will you take with you?"

"Alpha Squad will make the probe. Eight of us altogether. I'll try to bring your boat and crew back without taking a single enemy round."

"I'd appreciate it. Is there anything else? Weapons, ammunition?"

"We tend to travel with all our supplies so we can land and operate quickly. But thanks for the offer. I'll be back to make a full report on what I find upstream."

That afternoon Murdock sent his men and ten workers from the embassy into the city to interview the public and to take a poll about their feelings toward the government and Mojombo Washington.

They all came back early. When they tallied up their results they discovered that ninety percent had heard about the capture of the United States Vice President. Eighty percent had a favorable image of Mojombo Washington, calling him a patriot who was trying to help the common man. Only ten percent thought of him as a criminal and a kidnapper. The ambassador was surprised, and pleased.

Alpha Squad had an early supper at the embassy cafeteria, and then checked their equipment and weapons for the mission.

"Remember, we want this to be a silent operation," Murdock told them as they rode in the old school bus toward the river and Dock Six. The dock was made of wood and only forty feet long. The thirty-foot patrol boat was probably the largest craft ever to tie up there. The boat was adequate. It had a .50-caliber machine gun mounted on a pedestal on the short bow ahead of the cabin. Murdock could see where bullet holes had been patched in the sides of the boat and the cabin. He stashed his men on board and then went to the small cabin to talk to the captain, a full commander in the Sierra Bijimi Navy.

Murdock saluted him and the man returned the salute.

"Commander, I'm Lieutenant Commander Murdock reporting with my seven men for this recon."

"Welcome on board, Commander. I'm Martin London. Some of our people took British names when the British ruled our country. I hope this will be a quieter trip than my last one." London was about five-six and square-cut like an oak beam. He looked all military, and had deep-set eyes that almost were lost in his intensely black face. Murdock knew that this man was exactly what you saw. He would have no pretenses and would say precisely what he thought.

"You were shot up pretty good as I've heard," said Murdock. "We have no plans to draw any fire. In fact, we'll go without running lights. No lights showing of any kind except red interior ones if you use them. I need some personal input on the river, the land, and the people."

"I understand perfectly. I've seen films of your team's work. You are excellent at what you do. I commend you. I just hope that our forces will never have to come up against your men."

"I don't see how that would ever happen."

"Let's hope it doesn't, Commander. Strange things are going on in my country these days. Are you ready to shove off?"

"Ready, Commander."

They left the dock at 1815. Murdock had been assured that it would be totally dark at 1900 this time of year. The craft would make seven knots upstream, so they wouldn't be in the danger zone before darkness fell.

Murdock settled back along the rail and watched the river. It was slow-moving, and trees, plants, and vines grew almost to the water's edge. He wasn't sure how close they were to the equator, but it couldn't be far away. His cammies had been sticking to his back all day, and he looked forward to a slightly cooler time once the sun set.

There had to be fish in the water, but he didn't see any signs. Plenty of bugs swarmed around the water, but no fish was interested. Along the edge of the water he saw several people. One was carrying a load of firewood on his back. He could be walking into the city to sell it. Murdock spotted smoke from what could be cooking fires. The smoke lifted out of the trees and went straight into the air.

Once he saw three children splashing in the water. It was almost dark when he spotted an opening in the trees. A small stream came in from the side, and along each side were open spaces that had been planted with some type of row crops—vegetables, he guessed. Then the night closed in and he could see little.

The pilot of the craft moved out into the middle of the forty-yard-wide river. The speed of the water increased as the shores came closer together.

Murdock wasn't sure what he would find up here. There were few boats along the river. He could hire a fishing boat if he had to, but this worked better right now. It tied in the local military so they wouldn't get uptight about a foreign contingent barging into their territory. If it wasn't for the Vice President, the locals would never have agreed to the SEALs' visit. Now he had to make the best of it and get something accomplished. Like snatching the Vice President back from the rebels whether he wanted to come or not. That could be a problem later, but for now he was content to do his recon and see where they went from there.

The coxswain cut the forward speed as the night deepened. He had only a silver moon shining off the water to go by. Then a large fire blossomed on the left-hand shore. Murdock wondered what it was for.

"Spooky," Jaybird said from just behind Murdock. "Why are they having a bonfire?"

"Let's go over and see," Murdock said. Commander London appeared at Murdock's side.

"Must be a celebration of some kind. Our people go overboard with ceremonies and festivals. You want to come

in over there? As I remember, there is a small dock there
we could tie up to."

"Let's do it, Commander. SEALs front and center. Going
to take a walk. Bring your weapons, but keep the muzzles
pointing down. Everyone up to speed?" He heard soft re-
plies. He made a net check on the radio, and everyone
sounded off in sequence.

The boat nudged a used tire bumper tied to the dock,
and quick hands tied up the boat.

"I'll go with you," Colonel London said. "Might be able
to smooth the way some for you."

The fire now showed fifty yards away through some
trees. They took a well-used path, and slowed when they
came closer.

"Yes, it's a wedding," London said. "People out here go
all out on weddings. Sometimes the party lasts a week."

"Why don't we stay in the shadows here," Murdock said.
"Could you bring over two or three of the guests we could
talk to?"

"What we came to do, I guess," the boat captain said.
He walked away, and a short time later brought three men
back with him. One was so drunk he could hardly walk.
But he could talk.

"Have you heard of Mojombo Washington?" Murdock
asked him.

He looked at the boat captain and grinned. "Oh, sure.
Yes. Big man in the jungle. Wants to throw out the government. Hear him every time he goes past in his boat."

"Do you agree with him?" Murdock asked.

"Will this sailor shoot me?"

"No one will hurt you."

"Well, most of us like Mojombo. He's trying to help us.
We bring him food to help feed his soldiers."

"Most of the village people feel this way?" Murdock
asked.

"Most, except the spies for the Army. We hate the spies."

They talked to the other two men, and both said about
the same thing.

"Let's get back to the ship," Murdock said. He looked

at the Sierra Bijimi officer as they walked. "How far are we from Sierra City?"

"Eleven or twelve miles."

"Let's try the next village," Murdock said.

In the boat Murdock talked with the captain again. "You think that General Assaba knows how loyal these villagers are to Mojombo?"

"He doesn't want to know. He wants to hang on as long as he can. I have no respect for him. He isn't even a real general. He's never fired a gun except to kill someone in cold blood."

"You've seen him kill a person?"

"I was his Naval advisor until he realized he didn't need one. Yes, I saw him murder three men he suspected of plotting against him. All were good Army officers."

"Would you testify to that on a videotape for me?"

"No. Never. It would be my death warrant. I'll never go against the government. Not until someone shows me that he has the guts and skill and the manpower to win. Mojombo doesn't have it yet. He could. We'll just have to wait and see."

The next village was only fifteen minutes up the river. They came to a rickety dock, and Murdock, London, and the men got wet getting to shore. Commander London found two men they talked to. Both said about what the men at the first village did.

One looked closely at the boat captain. "Are we going to get in trouble with the Army?"

"No," Murdock said. "This man is our guide. No one will harm you for saying what you think."

On the walk back to the boat, Murdock turned to the commander. "I trust that none of this talk will be repeated to anyone in the military."

"I have no report to make out on this trip. I will tell no one. My only hope is that your and your men might hasten the day when we can have a truly democratic government and a strong military."

As the boat neared the dock in Sierra City after the fast downstream run, Commander London took Murdock aside.

"I'll do one thing for you, Navy SEAL. I'll report to Colonel Dara that the population we talked to were generally cool toward Mojombo, and still back the government."

"Thanks, Commander. That could be a great help."

10

Central Police Station
San Diego, California

The interrogation room was warmer than the rest of the air-conditioned station. Detective Petroff took off his suit jacket and fitted it over the back of a straight chair. He stared hard at the young black girl sitting across the empty table.

"Your name is Nancy, right?"

"Sure. I know ten girls named Nancy in a big town like this." She was about twenty, maybe less, Petroff figured. The word on the street was that she had been a good friend of Joisette Brown, the little black hooker who'd gone down with an OD of heroin.

"Your best friend in the whole world was Joisette, right?"

"Yeah, I knew her."

"You know where she stayed."

"Right. We met there sometimes to goof off and sober up."

"She stayed with a man named Shortchops Jackson. Isn't that right?"

"Never knew no last name. She called him Shortchops. He was a bass man. Played a wicked lick."

"How many times you been booked for hooking?"

"Two or three maybe."

"Wrong, Nancy. You've been picked up nine times now. Ten and you get six months in the slammer."

"Maybe I been in here four times."

"Nine, Nancy. All you have to do to walk is tell me where Joisette lived. That's all. You give us an address and

91

we drive out there and you show me which door to knock on. Hell of a lot better than doing six months hard time."

"Oh, shit. I wasn't even there when she died."

"We know. Now where did she live?"

"I can walk? No strings?"

"No strings."

The unmarked detective's car pulled up in front of a run-down four-unit apartment house on 27th Street off Imperial Avenue. It was the edge of Logan Heights, an intensely black and poor neighborhood. The building didn't look like it had been painted for ten years.

"Which apartment?" Petroff asked

"Upstairs on the left, number four. Can I go now?"

Petroff looked at the hooker where she sat in the secure rear seat of the police car.

Detective Lasiter had come along as backup for Petroff. He shook his head. "Missy, you stay put back there. We'll be back directly."

"You damn well better be here, Shortchops," Petroff said as he and Lasiter climbed to the second floor and looked at the apartment door. Petroff knocked three times, then three more. "Open up, police," he called. No response. Lasiter stepped back and slammed his foot and his 180 pounds against the door right beside the door lock. The old-fashioned lock popped loose and the door swung open.

With guns out, the detectives surged into the room. They found it scattered with garbage: take-out food containers, opened cans, dirty dishes, and unwashed clothes.

The detectives spent an hour in the apartment, searching everywhere including the spots where people often hid things. They came up with nothing. Not even the phone book helped. Lasiter dropped it, and it opened to a different page three times in a row. It didn't look like Shortchops Jackson had been home for a week, maybe not since the day Joisette had died.

"Another nail in the old bass player's coffin," Lasiter said. "If he didn't do it, why disappear?" They left, closing the door behind them even though it didn't quite latch.

At the unmarked car, Petroff opened the back door and

motioned the girl out. "He wasn't there. Anyplace else he might be? He ever say any friends he had he might be staying with?"

"He never talked much. Not while I was around. I don't know where he went off to."

"He's got to be somewhere. You know who Joisette was, who her father was?"

"No, she never said."

"You ever hear of Billy Ben Brown?"

"You kidding? Every cat knows about Billy Ben. He was the greatest jazz musician of all time. They had a big TV special about him when he died three or four months ago."

"Joisette was a late-life daughter of Billy Ben Brown."

"No shit? She never once said a word. Man, he was loaded. I mean he had more money than sense, somebody said. But jeez, could he wail with a jazz band."

Back at headquarters, Petroff had three phone messages. He put two of them down and called the last one, a good contact at the courthouse.

"Petroff, you owe me one," the clerk said. "The will of Joisette Brown has just been filed in probate. The girl finally came into her dad's money. Her estate is something like three-point-five million smackeroos."

"Good haul for a hooker."

"A damned rich hooker. I can't get you a copy of it, but I remember the beneficiary. One Shortchops William Jackson is the main heir. Then there are four others mentioned. Each to get fifty thousand. They are described as being the other members of the Gaslamp Quarter Jazz Band. Be in probate for about four months. Shortchops is also named executor of the will."

"When does he show up in court?"

"He doesn't. He hired a lawyer."

"Who is his lawyer?"

"Am I getting in trouble here?"

"Not a bit. Court filings are public records, open to the public and the cops. Give."

"Harlan J. Emmersome. Yeah. Around town he's also known as Loophole. If there's a loophole in the law he can find it."

"Thanks. He's my next courtesy call."

It took Petroff twenty minutes to look up the lawyer's address and find his building. It was a one-man law office in an uptown location not known for high rent. Emmersome was on the third floor, and the elevator worked. Petroff walked through the door and found a small outer office with a pert blonde, about twenty-five, working on her nails.

"Yes, sir, may I help you?"

After the preliminaries, she opened the door to the big man's office. He *was* a big man, just over seven feet, and yes, he had played basketball, and no, not in the pros.

"So, what can I do for the city's finest today?"

"One of your clients is in a sticky situation over the death of a girl and we need to clean it up. Problem is, we can't find him."

"Is there a name? That would help."

"You know the name, Shortchops Jackson."

"Yes, I know Mr. Jackson. But with the client-lawyer privilege, that's all I can tell you."

"One small item to consider. If I can prove that Shortchops had anything to do with Joisette Brown's death, he won't get a dime out of her estate, which means you won't collect your big fat fee for handling the probate. Let's see. My lawyer friends say that would come to something like a hundred and twenty-five thousand for your fee. More cash than you've seen in a whole good number of years."

"Sorry to disappoint you, Sergeant, but my fee is guaranteed, even if the client is found guilty and he gets nothing. Nice try, but it won't work this time. I know probate law."

"So, what if I tie you into the murder, make you an accessory to the crime, show that you helped in the OD? Then we've got you and you don't get a cent."

"You can't do that."

"You want to bet your future on it? I can manufacture witnesses who will say almost anything to stay out of the slammer. It would only take two."

The lawyer slumped in his chair. "Shit, you'd probably do it just to spite me. Okay, but I don't have an address on

Mr. Jackson. He calls in once a week to find out if he's needed. He won't be. It's all fairly routine."

"Unless I charge him and you with murder. Then I make one phone call to the probate judge and everything comes to a ridiculously fast and screeching stop."

"You wouldn't do that."

"Not if I can talk to him and he can clear himself. He was seen with the girl a half hour before she died. He was a heroin user. He was high on something when he was with her. It's entirely possible that he gave her the last shot of her life, and she went OD."

"What about the other four men in the will? Aren't they suspects too?"

"Could be, but I always go after the best one first, your client, Mr. Shortchops Jackson."

"Let me think about it."

"Think all you want. I've got enough now to bring charges and get a warrant. I'll be doing that tomorrow at noon. Give me a call before then, and I can put off the warrant a day or two."

Petroff walked to the door leading out of the office. "Now then, Mr. Emmersome, you have a nice day." He paused. "Emmersome, you have anything to do with the over-the-line tournament on Fiesta Island every summer?"

"No. Why?"

"Just wondered. The name sounds familiar."

Sierra City, Sierra Bijimi

Alpha Squad slept in until 1000 the next morning after the river trip. Murdock talked with Don Stroh over a late breakfast the kitchen fixed for the SEALs.

"The end result of our little trip was that the two villages we stopped at were fully behind Mojombo. The men were afraid of the Navy commander, and at first didn't want to talk in front of him. My guess is that villages farther upstream and more distant from Sierra City are also just as enthusiastic about Mojombo."

"So, where the hell does that leave us?"

"We need to contact Mr. Washington and have a sit-down," Murdock said. "We have to find him without getting our heads shot off. That's the first big job."

"Choppers. Do they have any helicopters in this runty little Army?"

"I didn't think to ask," Murdock said. He sent Jaybird to find out by phone or a visit to the Army headquarters.

"Say they do have a bird, even a small one that will fly," Murdock went on. "I can take a run upstream and try to find the location of the camp. The military says they think it's about twenty-five miles upstream. In the boat we weren't more than twelve."

"It's a government chopper, so why won't they shoot it out of the sky?"

"They will if it gets close enough. I ID the place and then we go in another way."

"How?"

"The road goes up ten miles, then there are horse trails. If horses can get through, a dirt motorcycle can too. I take another biker and we see how close we can get to their camp on the trails."

Jaybird came back to the conference room table. "They have two choppers and both are four-passenger types. Civilian models and with no weapons. I didn't ask if we could use one, but I'd bet the word would have to come from the general himself."

"Thanks, Jaybird," Stroh said. "I'll call the general and make the pitch. Maybe the CIA will have some clout with him."

He went across the room to the telephone, found a number, and called.

"Who's going?" Jaybird asked Murdock.

"You, Lam, and me. They'll want their own pilot. That's if we get a bird. Don't get your jockstrap on just yet."

Stroh came back looking as if somebody just stole his all-day sucker.

"Who ate your canary?" Jaybird asked.

"Fucking General Assaba. Says we have to talk. He hinted at the idea of our renting the damned chopper. I'm on my way over there right now."

"Going rate for that size bird is a hundred dollars an

hour," Jaybird said. "At least in civilized countries. Don't let him bleed you dry."

"We're doing this bastard a favor and he's trying to wheedle some cash out of us? Ridiculous. How bad do you want the bird?"

"I'd say up to a-hundred-fifty-an-hour bad," Murdock said.

"Only if that's the only way I can get it."

Stroh stormed out of the embassy, yelled for a car, and rode to the general's office thinking up all sorts of arguments for the general to be more than glad to lend them the chopper. The big man made him wait for ten minutes. Then a lieutenant let Stroh into the inner office.

It was huge, with game trophies on the wall along with large-caliber rifles, fishing rods, and pictures of the kills.

General Assaba remained seated when Stroh came in.

"Yes?"

"We just spoke on the phone about our making a recon trip for your Army, up the Amunbo River to tie down the exact location of your major enemy, Mojombo Washington."

"Yes. I'm not convinced that it would be helpful."

"Right now do you know exactly where his camp is?"

"No."

"Then how could it not be valuable information? With this intelligence we also plan on using the SEALs to make some kind of a move against the camp, but we need the data first."

"Our Army pilots argue against the flight."

"Your Army is democratic where the soldiers tell the officers what to do?"

"No. We command."

"Then it's your decision. We brought the SEALs here to help you with your permission. Our Vice President is in jeopardy every minute he's in that camp. We think it's in your best interests to help us get him out of there."

General Assaba turned and looked at the wall. When he turned back, he nodded. "Very well, we'll rent the helicopter to you, and our pilot will fly it and determine if he is in any danger of ground fire. You can use the chopper for one hundred twenty-five U.S. dollars an hour."

"That's not a diplomatic offer, General. We are here to help you and you want to charge us for using your equipment?"

"I'm not a diplomat, Mr. Stroh. I'm an Army officer. That's my first and final offer. Take it or stop blabbering."

"I'll take it, but our ambassador will also send a stern note to your President."

"Do what you wish. I'll need cash in advance for four hours. None is refundable."

Stroh felt his face turning red. He shot an angry glance at the small general, then turned quickly and hurried out of the room before he exploded.

An hour later the money had been delivered and the route chosen. They would move out from the river five miles and go upstream. Then when they were thirty miles away, they would start moving downstream and watching for an encampment.

Murdock inspected the craft before they took off. It looked as if it had been serviced and maintained properly. The last problem he needed was to crash the bird into the jungle.

They whipped north along the river for five miles. Then the pilot moved to the right of the river for five miles before turning north again, which would take them upstream.

"Sir," the pilot, a second lieutenant, said. "We're upstream about twenty-five miles."

"Good, do another five miles, then let's go find the river," Murdock said. He had been watching the jungle below, and was amazed how thick it was and what few clearings and signs of smoke he saw that could indicate habitation.

A few minutes later they swung to the left and back to the river. It was only a stream here, maybe ten to fifteen feet wide, and there were several stretches of rapids where the water raced downhill. There were no villages on this part of the river. But after three miles they began to find small settlements along both sides of the stream.

"Keep a sharp lookout," Murdock told his men. "Anything that moves, give us a yell."

"On the left," Jaybird chirped. "Looks like six men. Yes. A small puff of smoke, had to be a rifle shot."

At once the pilot wheeled away from the river and dove to get out of the line of fire.

"Stay close enough so we can see the river," Murdock shouted. "Go up another five thousand feet. Then get back to the river."

"Too dangerous," the pilot said.

Murdock put his KA-BAR blade against the young pilot's throat. "For now, I'll tell you when it's too dangerous. Now take us up to five thousand feet and get us back so we can see the fucking river."

The pilot's forehead beaded with sweat and he swallowed twice. "Yes, sir. Will do."

Higher in the sky gave them a wider view, but even so, they almost missed it. The pilot said they were twenty-five miles from the airport. In the distance, about a half mile from the river, they spotted a large clearing, and could see tents, many fires, and as they came closer, dozens of men.

"Get out of here," Murdock told the pilot when he saw some riflemen on the ground and figured they were about to fire. The bird pivoted to the left and dove a thousand feet, then leveled off.

"Take us back to town," Murdock said. "Make it the safest route you know. We've found out what we need to know."

Jaybird heard the shouted exchange with the pilot over the roar and clatter of the chopper.

"So, Commander, sir. Are we going to take a hike up to the rebel camp?"

"Not a hike, Jaybird. But some of us are going to pay them a visit."

11

Don Stroh raised his hands in a futile gesture. "What's a man to do? That's what the big brass in D.C. tells me, so I toe the mark. I tell you and you follow suit. The word again is: The U.S. Navy SEALs are not to engage in any firefights with the group of men headed by Mojombo Washington who call themselves the Bijimi Loyalist Party. The word is that we can probe, we can recon, but in no case can we fire at or near the camp or at any group of men from the Bijimi Loyalist Party."

Murdock slammed his hand down on the table. His open palm made a popping sound. "That puts a real crimp in our plans. I was figuring that maybe after we move up on the camp, we give them a show of massive firepower into the trees and brush overhead, and then use a bullhorn and tell them we're coming in to get the Vice President and any fire from their side would result in massive casualties."

"Good idea, but now it won't work," Stroh said. Murdock and his planning group sat around the table with Stroh working on coffee and soft drinks.

"So what the hell can we do?" Gardner asked.

"Quite a bit is left," Murdock said. "We know for sure where they are. We know they are lightly armed, mostly with the weapons they stole from the Army and police. We can still probe and recon. Jaybird, get Luke Howard in here. We're going to do another recon, one on the ground. We'll try to make contact with the Vice President. There is a horse-and-cart trail up the river. My guess is it goes all the way to the rebel camp. If it's wide enough for a horse, a dirt bike will roll over it like a superhighway."

Howard came in with Jaybird. "Howard, I want you and the senior chief to go out and get us a pair of motorcycle dirt bikes. Get the most cc's you can find. Rent them, buy them, or steal them. With first light Howard and I will be straddling those bikes and moving up the trail. We'll take our regular weapons, and food and water. I figure about thirty-five miles by land. We should be able to make thirty miles an hour if the trail is used much. We get as close to the camp as we can without attracting any attention. Then we try to move in on foot and make contact."

"What if the Vice President doesn't want to come out?" Gardner asked. "He sounded pretty convinced this Mojombo is the Second Coming."

"We fight that one if and when we get to it. The Vice President outranks us all to hell, but we can say we are operating under orders of the President, who outranks Adams. The President says for the Vice President to come out, so we pick him up and pack him out of there."

"That could turn out to be a nasty assignment," Stroh said.

Sadler agreed. "One hell of a mess if we had to do that. We'd have to reason with the man."

"Are you still here, Senior Chief?"

"Yes, sir. We need some cash, some dagnars, the old spondolics. Will Mr. Stroh provide the loot or will the ambassador?"

"Let's go talk to the ambassador," Stroh said, and the three left by the closest door.

"How far you think you'll get?" Jaybird asked. "I mean, they are bound to have some outposts along the river, and the cycles ain't gonna be easy to keep quiet out there in the jungle. Hear you coming for two miles."

"Yes, there could be some outposts," Murdock said, "but we'll have to figure out what to do when we get there. Did I see a report that the rebels stole a whole box full of personal radios on one of their raids? If so, they could have good communications between their outposts and the main camp."

"What are the rest of us lost souls going to do?" Jaybird asked.

Murdock grinned. "Jaybird, you and the JG and the rest of the men are going to do a fifteen-mile conditioning hike tomorrow with full gear. Get you acclimated a little bit better. I noticed you sweating like a pig yesterday."

"Thanks, Jaybird," Lam said. "We could have stayed here in the great air-conditioning. . . ."

"Not a chance," JG Gardner said. "We've had some training on the docket all along. In fact, the rest of the day is going to be devoted to an hour of PT and then a road run. Let's get everyone out of here and form up outside."

Murdock went with them and participated in the work-out. It was one of the mandates of the SEALs. All officers went through the same bash-and-smash six-month BUD/S training that the enlisted men did. They had no special priv-ileges. The only difference was all officers had to score ten percent higher than the EMs. Officers in the platoons also took all the conditioning runs, workouts, and swims the men did. It was a true togetherness operation and it worked. In the field there was no rank, only two squad leaders.

In the afternoon, Sadler and Howard rolled up to the embassy on a pair of motorcycles. One was an older Ka-wasaki. The second one was a Suzuki. Both were 500 cc's and had knobby, cross-country tires and shocks. Murdock grinned. He hadn't been on a bike for more than a year. He used to own three. He slid onto the Kawasaki that Sadler had ridden up, and led out with Howard right beside him. They did a cheap tour of the city, not riding fast, just getting the feel of the bikes and what they could do. When they came back nearly an hour later, both nodded.

"Should work," Howard said. "Mine is a little short on pickup, but we're not going to be in any races."

"Make sure the tanks are full of gas and park them in a protected place inside the garage," said Murdock. "We want to take off from here a half hour before light in the morn-ing."

"The bikes will be ready" Howard said. "We take our MP5s on our backs and no combat vests?"

"Sounds good. And plenty of water and some chow. We'll have the kitchen fix us something to travel."

"What's for tonight?" Howard asked.

"The ambassador has planned a special dinner. He wants all of us to attend. We won't be at the far end of the cafeteria this time. We put on clean cammies, our best manners, and we get a shot at the dining room."

"I understand there are several women here," Howard said. "We don't see much of them."

"For good reason," Murdock said. "Everyone will be on his best behavior tonight or there will be five hundred push-ups in the morning."

Howard chuckled. "I'll pass the word."

At six-thirty that night, the SEALs marched into the dining room in squad order. Mrs. Oberholtzer, the ambassador's wife and a matron of about forty with a generous waistline, immediately took charge.

"Young men, I don't want you to sit beside each other. Space out around the table. We have more than enough people here to separate you." She looked at some of the staff and five teenage girls, who stood at one side. "I want to remind you young ladies that you will show proper decorum and manners at all times. So, everyone please be seated."

Murdock sat beside the hostess, and soon they were into a discussion about Southern California. She had grown up in Escondido and then gone to college in Washington, D.C., where she'd met her husband.

"Are the avocado orchards still there?" she asked. "They were such a wonder and the fruit was so delicious. It's impossible down here to get any avocados. I would give twenty dollars a cup for a good supply of guacamole."

The conversation raced around the table as the first course came, and then the second. Most of the SEALs had no idea which of the eight knives, forks, and spoons to use. The men and women who sat beside them gently hinted at the right utensils.

Jaybird had been lucky to be seated beside the eldest daughter of the ambassador.

"I'm Cynthia," she said as soon as she sat down.

"Miss, I'm Jaybird, or David, I guess would be better. How come you're here at the embassy?"

"Oh, my father is the ambassador. I've lived in eight

different countries now, but I wish I could get back to school. Could you talk to my father about my going to San Diego State University? My mother always wanted to go there and she tells me such interesting stories about that area."

Jaybird was without words for the first time in his life. The young lady couldn't be more than eighteen, he decided, and had a soft white complexion that proved she didn't take much of the African sun. He tried to say something, and stumbled. Her eyes were so blue and her smile engaging. He shook his head and tried again.

"Sorry, Cynthia. I don't know what to say. I'm sure the ambassador wouldn't have time to talk to me. Why do you want to go to San Diego State?"

"The pictures of the campus are so great. I sent for a catalog last year and it is exquisite. Then the climate is so great and I want to learn to surf and dive in the ocean. I love the ocean, but we don't have one here."

"I noticed that."

They both laughed, drawing the attention of her mother. But the woman only smiled and went back to talking to Murdock about San Diego.

By the end of desert, Jaybird and Cynthia had gone through most of the ritual information exchange of a first-date dialogue, talking about where they'd grown up and what they liked and also about parents and family. Then the dinner was over. Jaybird tried to walk Cynthia back to her room, but a Sierra Bijimi guard at the stairway shook his head.

"Upstairs here is the private quarters of the ambassador," he said. "Entry is by written order of the ambassador only."

Jaybird caught her hand and held it a moment, then squeezed it and waved good-bye. He smiled broadly all the way back to his room, where Bill Bradford had just taken out his sketch pad.

"Have a whole potful of ideas I want to get down on paper before I forget them," he said. Jaybird shrugged and rolled onto his bunk. He was used to going to sleep with the lights on while Bradford worked on a painting or a sketch.

● ● ●

The next day, Howard and Murdock were on the road a half hour before sunrise. They had full tanks of gas, three canteens each, and a packet of food the kitchen had prepared. There were mostly sandwiches that would last all day and lots of fruit. They had been warned against drinking any of the water in the streams no matter how clean it looked.

They cleared the city and took off on the dirt road that led alongside the Amunbo River. They had the road to themselves until daylight. Then they spotted small tractors pulling loaded flatbeds that held fruits and vegetables and firewood. As the morning brightened, more and more rigs hit the road, and the motorcycles were slowed as the carts pulled by horses showed up and nearly clogged the road.

"Must be market day," Howard said. "We saw that big open market with stalls down at the edge of town yesterday. Lots of empty tables and booths. This must be the day."

By the time they hit the end of the dirt road, the farmers heading into town had dwindled to only a few. The SEALs kicked into the wide wagon trail along the river and made better time. Now and then a ditch cut across the path where a stream worked its way into the mother river.

It was after 0800 when Murdock held up his hand and pulled to the side of the trail. "Chow stop," he said. "I'm starved. Did we have breakfast before we left?"

"That we did, Commander. Bacon and eggs and hash browns with toast and jam and coffee. I ate until I almost popped my buttons. You did pretty well yourself with seconds."

They worked on sandwiches and the first canteen of water.

"Figure we've made about fifteen miles," Murdock said. "The going will be slower the fewer people travel this trail and the farther we get from the city."

"Right. When do you think we'll hit the first outpost? He's got to have one along this trail."

"My guess is about five miles from his main camp. If he's at the twenty-five-mile marker, we have another five miles before we have company."

"Will they be friendly?" Howard asked.

"Would you be?"

"Hell, no. Shoot first and talk later if anyone is still alive."

"So we move cautiously that last three or four miles to the twenty-mile mark. Maybe even ditch our bikes and take the rest of it on a hike so we can bypass the outpost."

"Sounds like a winner to me."

They rode again. The going was rough with washouts, potholes, and sometimes large tree roots exposed from the ground clogging the trail. Murdock doubted if they were making more than ten miles an hour.

A little after 0930, Howard held up his hand to stop. "Commander, figure we shouldn't make so much noise this far north. Maybe some hiking would be called for."

"Agreed. We stash the bikes where we can find them and nobody will steal them, then take one canteen and some sandwiches and take a stroll down a country lane."

A mile up the trail, Murdock paused. He was sniffing the air. "We haven't seen a village for the past mile or so. But I smell something that shouldn't be here."

Howard moved up beside the officer and grinned. "Skipper, sir, you must have led a sheltered life. That, my friend, is good old Mary Jane smoke, pot, the weed, marijuana. Somebody is puffing up a storm up here not more than a hundred yards ahead. Wind must be blowing our way."

Murdock chuckled. "Hell, you're right. I wasn't that sheltered. It's just been a few years. How about a detour?"

Howard pointed to the side of the trail away from the river, and they moved into the tropical-rain-forest tangle of vines, trees, brush, and creatures slithering along the moist jungle floor. Murdock took the lead using his best silent-movement approach as he went under, over, around, and through the growth, trying not to disturb a branch or step on anything that would screech in terror or break with a crack.

Fifty yards later, he angled back toward the trail and peered through the last foliage that screened him from the path. Twenty yards ahead, he saw a native hut that had been built almost on the trail. It was made of branches and some woven reeds or fronds for the sides and roof. It had a window and a doorway. In the window he could see a man resting his arms on it and looking down the trail. Twice Murdock saw the man sneak a puff on a nub of a cigarette. The man said something softly and passed the smoke to someone else. Howard slid in beside Murdock and saw the exchange. They nodded and headed back into the growth until they were fifty yards past the outpost, then returned to the path.

Now it was little more than a trail, nearly hidden by new plants and in some places vanishing completely, being taken over by the voracious growth of the greenery. Murdock decided it would be a great place to raise tomatoes. Think how fast they would grow. Of course you'd have to cut down some trees and brush so the sun could get in to ripen the fruit.

They hiked steadily for another half hour, and then Murdock held up his hand and they stopped. They listened.

"Rifle fire," Howard said. "Could be the flat crack of the old AK-47. Must still be a lot of them around."

"Right, and as deadly as ever. Good range, too. So what are they doing?"

"Target practice. We hear firing for a while, then all is quiet as they check the targets, then more firing. Ready on the right, ready on the left, ready on the firing line."

They both knew the routine. They moved with more caution now. The trail came closer to the river, which had shrunk in size as they'd climbed a gradual incline. Here and there they heard some rapids and saw a little white water. No boat was going up this stretch unless it was a jet-powered boat with no propeller.

"Will there be any more outposts?" Howard asked.

"I'd put in at least one more. From the rifle firing, my guess is his camp is on this side of the river. So we look for another outpost or at least a lookout along here anytime now."

"We go around him again?"

"Don't think so." Murdock said. "If it's handy, we capture him without harming him. Then we take him with us up where he can help us get through their defenses so we can talk with the good Mr. Washington."

"That just may be an idea whose time has come. You want me on point?"

They moved cautiously now. There was more rifle fire and it was getting closer, but it still sounded like target practice. They paused at each small turn in the trail and checked ahead. The fourth time they did it, they grinned. A lone cammy-clad soldier with a long gun over his shoulder walked from one side of a small clearing to the other side directly across the trail. Evidently this was his post and he had to walk it in a military manner.

Murdock signaled to the left and they faded into the jungle. Moving silently, they worked up to the far point of the guard's walking post. It was less than four feet from the jungle itself. Murdock eased up behind a huge tree and waited. The guard walked toward him, stopped, then did an about-face to go back in the other direction. That was when Murdock surged out of the jungle, took two steps, and hit the guard in the middle of his back, driving him forward and into the grass and weeds on his stomach. Murdock's hand went around the soldier's mouth holding it tightly.

Howard slid in beside them and fastened the guard's ankles with plastic riot cuffs, then caught his hands and brought them both behind him and manacled them. Murdock turned him over still holding his mouth closed.

"Now, young man, we don't want to hurt you. We're here to talk to your leader, Mojombo. Is he at this camp?"

The wild-eyed man mumbled something. Murdock took his hand away and the man screamed. Murdock's hand clamped back tight. Howard took a kerchief from his pocket and fashioned a gag around the man's head and through his mouth. He could breathe but couldn't yell. They sat him up and Murdock tried again.

"We're not here to harm you or you'd be dead already. Don't you agree?" The guard's eyes had lost their wild look and he nodded slowly. "We want to talk to Mr. Washington. Is he in this camp?"

The guard nodded again.

"How far is the camp? A mile?" The head shook no. "Two miles?" This time a nod.

"If I take off the gag, will you promise not to yell or scream, just talk to us?" The man frowned, evidently thought about it, then nodded. The gag came off.

"Now, Mr. Washington is at the camp close by. Can you take us there?"

"No, there are other guards."

"How many?"

"Three more. One every half mile."

"Can we go into the jungle and go around them?"

"No. A rocky wall on one side, the river on the other side. The guards would see us and shoot."

"Do you have a radio?"

"No, only officers have them."

"We could capture the other three guards," Howard said.

Murdock considered it. "Could, but a big risk factor. I have a notion that most of these conscripts are green and any little thing out of the ordinary, they're going to start shooting. We can't shoot back. Would put us in a dangerous position. So we go back." He dug into his cammy shirt pocket and took out a computer-printed message the ambassador had given Murdock before they left.

He unfolded it and showed it to the guard. "This is a message from the U.S. ambassador at Sierra City. He wants to help the Vice President. It tells him to turn on his SATCOM every day at noon and again at six in the evening so the ambassador can talk with him. Do you understand that?"

"Yes. Understand. Who are you?"

"Tell Mojombo Washington that we are U.S. Navy SEALs. We may wind up helping him instead of hunting him. The Vice President must talk to the ambassador every day. Do you understand that?"

"Yes sir." He frowned. "Are you an officer?"

"Yes, Lieutenant Commander Blake Murdock in the U.S. Navy. That's like a major in the Army. Can you take this to your commander?"

"When my guard duty is over in an hour. That way I won't get in trouble for leaving my post."

Murdock grinned. Somebody had trained this boy well. He looked no more than seventeen.

"All right. You do that. At the end of your shift you talk to your sergeant and tell him you have to see Mr. Washington. Here, give him this. It's one of the new U.S. gold-plated dollar coins. My good-luck charm. Give it to General Washington."

The guard looked at the coin, read the printing, and grinned. "Yes, I can do this. It will be good on my record." He frowned. "Can you untie me now?"

It took Murdock and Howard two hours to work back down the faint trail and around the first outpost. Then they jogged down the path toward their bikes. They stopped at the bikes and ate half the sandwiches and drank from the canteens.

"If we push it, we can get back to civilization in three hours," Murdock said. "I just hope that half the countryside isn't returning from market day and clogging up the road."

They were. Murdock groaned. They pulled into the embassy grounds slightly before 1700, just in time for chow at the cafeteria.

The ambassador welcomed the news of the contact. He checked his watch. Dinner was over. "Five minutes to six. Time for us to set up the SATCOM and try to talk to the Vice President. This could be the contact we need to turn round this difficult situation."

12

Camp Freedom
Sierra Bijimi

Vice President Adams turned on his SATCOM radio at five minutes until six and set it to receive on the same frequency he had used when talking with the White House.

It had been an interesting afternoon. The sentry had talked to his sergeant, who'd brought him at once to see Mojombo Washington. Adams had been in the leader's tent at the time. The soldier, in his new cammies, saluted smartly and handed a folded sheet of paper to his commander.

Mojombo took it and read it. He looked up and frowned, then read the words again.

"How did you get this message, Private?"

"Two men in uniforms almost like ours, but they had black marks on their faces like camouflage."

"Why didn't you shoot them?"

"They slipped up on me. I never heard them. Then they hit me in my back and knocked me down."

"Did they have weapons?"

"Yes, sir, some kind of submachine gun. Short ones tied over their backs."

Mojombo's voice softened. "Did they tell you who they were?"

"Yes, sir. One said he was Commander Blake Mur something. That he was a U.S. Navy SEAL."

"Be damned," Adams said. "They slipped past all of your security to get to this guy. They are experts at infiltration. They could do it."

"These men, did they hurt you?"

"No, sir. Tied my ankles and hands with plastic cuffs at first, then let me go. They mostly just talked to me."

"Did they kill any of our guards?"

"I don't think so, sir. All of our group of guards were present when we were relieved about half an hour ago."

"Thank you, Private. You did your duty well. You will get a special commendation and a promotion. You're now a corporal and you are dismissed."

The man turned, and a wave of relief washed over his face as he hurried out of the tent.

"What does it say?" Adams asked.

"Message to you from Ambassador Oberholtzer." He handed the message to the Vice President. He read it.

"Mr. Vice President. I hope this message gets to you. First, we must communicate. You have a SATCOM. So do I. It would be most helpful, sir, if you could turn your set on every day at twelve noon and again at six for any messages we have for you or that you might have for us. Leave it on the same frequency you used to talk to the President.

"We are aware of your solid support for the Bijimi Loyalist Party and Mojombo Washington. We are desperate to know more about him and his plans, and what you want to do in the next few days. The President is still concerned about your safety.

"Please let us know what we can do to help you. Two Navy SEALs have delivered this message. They have been instructed not to harm in any way any of the Mojombo forces. I trust they achieved this today and delivered the message.

"If you could confirm your receipt of this message at six o'clock this evening, we can talk.

"May you stay safe and in good health and spirits. I am respectfully your servant: Ambassador Nance Oberholtzer."

"What time is it?" The Vice President looked at his watch, a solar-tech one powered by the sun or any other light, which charged the batteries. "Good, only three-thirty. We'll talk with the ambassador tonight. Maybe we can get those SEALs to help us launch some attacks. They are good, fantastic. The best trained and most effective sea, land, or air combat forces ever assembled."

"How many of them?" Mojombo asked.

"That's the beauty of them. They work in platoons of sixteen men. Only two officers, but in the field every man is of equal rank. It's amazing what they can do. We send them all over the world on a covert basis to get our chest-nuts out of the fire."

"Who sent them here?" Mojombo asked.

"That's one question we'll have for the ambassador. Let's write down any more questions you have and we'll both talk to him."

The leader of the rebels stood up from the chair and paced around the tent. He sat down, got up again, and walked outside. Vice President Adams waited for him. When he came back he sat down and frowned, then gave a long sigh.

"Is this a good thing? This talking to the center of our enemy?"

"The ambassador is not your enemy. He's probably the best friend you have in Sierra City. This can only lead to help for you, benefits for you."

"I have no doubt that these SEALs are terrific. However, they are only sixteen. What can sixteen do against four thousand armed troops shooting at them?"

"Like you, Mojombo, they don't engage in pitched bat-tles except when they can assure surprise or a crushing blow with something other than manpower. Let's wait and see what the ambassador has to say."

"We will wait. In the meantime, we were working on some ideas for attacks on the corrupt politicians. We al-ready hit the main police station and the Army base. Should we burn down the Hall of Democracy, where the legislature meets?"

"Doesn't seem like a good idea. Maybe we should con-centrate on the military. Snipers could infiltrate far enough so you could shoot up the two small helicopters that the Army has. That would put their entire air force out of com-mission."

"Yes, good idea. We'll send a four-man team in tonight

to do that. Let me get the men started downstream on our smaller boat. The choppers are kept in the open at the Army camp just north of the capital. It will be a two-day mission. Now what else?"

"Electrical power. Where do you get it from?"

"Most of it comes across the border with Bijimi. We used to be part of that country. The British built the hydroelectric plant twenty years ago. Now it serves four different nations."

"So we leave the generators alone, and take down the lines that bring the power across the border. That would black out most of the nation and would cause an immediate uproar and problems for the Kolda government."

"I wonder about that. It would cause government turmoil, but the main losers would be the people, who would suffer the most. Let's get some better ideas."

"My Navy days didn't include a lot of G-2," Adams said. "The fact is I was a lowly lieutenant in the black-water boats that got shot up six different times in Vietnam."

"The police, the Army," Mojombo said. "Those have to be our targets. I hesitate to do anything that will kill civilians or make their lives any harder than they are right now."

"Yes, I get the picture. My next suggestion is that you're too far from the center of the action. You need to move closer to Sierra City."

"But wouldn't that put us in more danger from a raid by the Army? They could being in two thousand men with weapons and rout us in five minutes."

"Not if you move into an area and get the civilian population entirely on your side. Then if the Army tries to come in, your soldiers can fight or fade into the jungle and the civilians will come out in the street and totally swamp the soldiers. Civilians always inhibit a fighting force. You told me that the Army units won't chase you into the jungle. They proved that before."

"This idea of starting to enlist all the people in a town is good. I've thought of it, but haven't tried it. Say we moved down to the village called Tinglat. We would still be twenty miles from the city. There are over a thousand people in that village who raise some crops, cut wood, and harvest certain trees from the forest. I have friends there. Yes, I think they will support me. I'll go down there tomorrow with twenty of my men and we'll talk to them.

"They will be my people. I can protect them from the cheating tax collectors who routinely rob the workers in the villages. We'll strip the tax men and tar them and cover them with chicken feathers before we float them down the river on a small raft. Yes, I think we can do it. We'll start to claim territory and the population. When we get one area well protected, we'll get volunteers to swell our fighting ranks and then move to the next village as we make another jump closer to the city."

"Now, what about new targets for your night raiders? The government forces will soon be patrolling the river, so you might have to come in by land the last ten miles or so. Any more small Army units you could hit, or government warehouses stacked with foreign-aid food, say?"

"Oh, yes. At least one that I know about. It's in the north end of the city and is the President's personal cache of hard-to-get goods. I'd bet there is food enough there to feed my men for a year, if we just had some way to get it up here."

"You have a market day in town?"

"Yes. With our poor farmers, every day is market day, so they can scratch out a living from their small farms."

"Most of those wagons and trucks and carts go back up the trail empty, don't they?"

Mojombo jumped up and laughed. "Oh, you are so right. We can make a raid on the warehouse at night. Transport everything we want into another warehouse farther north in the city. Then the next day . . ." He laughed again. "Mr. Vice President, I'm tremendously glad that you are on my side."

Mojombo stood and nodded to himself. "Yes, I have much work to do and people to talk to before tomorrow morning. I will lead the raiders myself. We will need to steal trucks to move the matériel. Such a strike as this will not be extremely harmful to the President and his band of thieves, but it will put them on notice that we know more about him and his piracy than he thinks."

"I want to go along. I had four years in the Navy."

"No. It is too risky. You are still my key to the whole idea of a national revolution. I am working on the demands that I will make to the world. But first the talk with your ambassador at six, then the raid tonight and the exodus of the goods tomorrow." Mojombo paused. "Do I have your word as a gentleman that you will not try to join our force that marches out to the river shortly after dark?"

"I could be a great help. I can still shoot well. Mostly trapshooting now, but the rifle is an old friend who—"

"No. You can't go. It's too dangerous. Now, give me your word."

Vice President Adams scowled and muttered something under his breath while Mojombo grinned and waited.

"Hell, all right. I'll give you my word this time. But before this is over I want to be in the shooting war, you hear me?"

"I hear you, Mr. Vice President Adams. I'll be back in your tent in time for the six o'clock radio talk."

The leader of the Bijimi Loyalist Party slipped out the flap and Adams followed him, then went to his tent and took out the SATCOM. He had it set up and the small dish antenna aimed at the satellite an hour before it was time. He couldn't sit still. What would he say to the ambassador that he hadn't already told the President? He'd just tell him the truth. It was time the United States gave this regime a hard time, and helped out this struggling young party leader who wanted to return the government to the people. The U.S. told the world that it supported democracy, so it was time to stand up on this one and make its weight known. He hoped the Navy was sending a task force this way. They wouldn't even have to come all the way. The Navy jets could do a combat radius of almost 650 miles. At least the F-18 could, and it was an air-to-ground fighter. A couple of passes without any firing and these government troops would panic. He wondered how close the Navy was. Was there a carrier task force anywhere around?

They could pump up a destroyer with a C-53 chopper on it, scoot down this direction at thirty-three knots, and

beat the slow aircraft carriers here by a day or two. He'd
be sure to ask the ambassador about that.

Promptly at six o'clock the SATCOM just inside Vice President
Adams's tent came on with a call.

"This is Oberholtzer calling Adams. I say again, this is
Oberholtzer calling Adams."

The Vice President lifted the mike he had been holding
and pushed the send button. "Adams here waiting for your
call. This is all encrypted, isn't it, so no one else can know
what we're saying?"

"Right, Mr. Vice President. Only those U.S. units that
have SATCOMs that are tuned to this frequency at this
time. Which makes it tremendously secure. I'm glad to hear
from you. Despite your messages, Washington has become
increasingly concerned about your situation there. The President
doesn't want you running off on a fire mission somewhere
and getting your head blown off your shoulders."

"Don't worry. I tried, and Mojombo won't let me go
along. When are you going to send some help for these
men? They are fighting their hearts out and have only made
a dent in the corrupt Administration that Washington seems
to support. We need the Navy to send in some aircraft and
some surface craft and threaten the hell out of President
Kolda. We're only two hundred miles from the Atlantic,
for God's sakes. Navy jets can do that in ten minutes.
What's the matter with you people anyway?"

"Mr. Vice President, decisions like that are way out of
my hands. As you know, that has to be done in Washington.
There is a Navy task force on its way. I'm not sure where
it is, but they did say they would send a destroyer at flank
speed that will outrace the task force. I've had a signal from
the task force commander that the destroyer should be offshore
here sometime tomorrow. She has two helicopters
usually used for antisubmarine warfare, but they can be
slightly adapted."

"That's not going to help much, Oberholtzer. We need
about twenty F-18's to do a flyover of the Government
Building fifty feet over the roof and scare the shit out of
these crooks. Why not drop in six or seven platoons of

SEALs to grab the President and the head of the Army and do it up quickly?"

"Like I said . . ."

"Yeah, I know. Not your decision to make. So I'll call the President again. His set must always be on. What good news do you have for me? A pair of SEALs visited this area today. One was called Blake. A commander."

"Right, Mr. Vice President. Commander Blake Murdock and another SEAL moved up your way and delivered the message you must have received."

"So why don't you send me the whole platoon? What is it, sixteen men? Send them to me so we can get some real firefights going here."

"Now *that* we can talk about. The SEALs have guns free for any operation except against the Loyalist people. Maybe we can work out some kind of a joint attack. Hit them from both sides. The SEALs can lay down a devastating amount of gunfire once they get in position."

"Mr. Ambassador, Mojombo Washington wants to talk to you. He's right here."

"Mr. Ambassador, Washington here. We met once, but you wouldn't remember. What can you do to help us up here?"

"Not a lot, but we're talking with the President and the Navy. I'll let you know the minute we have any good news."

"That is sounding better," Washington said. "We have a small operation going down tonight, but if it works, it will happen without a shot being fired. Let you know how it comes out tomorrow. So when can you send the SEALs upriver?"

"Have to talk to the commander about that."

"Is he there? Give him the mike."

"Just a minute and I'll get him. What I'm wondering is, will the people follow you if you can get a full-scale revolution going? Can you get enough support for a mass march on the Government Building and throw President Kolda out of office?"

"Probably not without half of the Army coming over to my side. Then we'll have a chance. The Army is the big factor. A lot of the top officers are unhappy with the current command. I'm working on it."

"Mr. Washington, this is Lieutenant Commander Murdock."

"I hear you were almost in Camp Freedom today."

"Close enough, Mr. Washington. Glad you received the letter. I hope the sentry we gave it to was not punished. He did nothing wrong. He's a good soldier."

"Actually I promoted him to corporal. Now. When can you bring your platoon up here and help us plan some attacks and then help us to take down President Kolda?"

"I'd say as soon as you get the support of and control the countryside and half of Sierra City. Then we'd have a chance of taking down the government. A revolution is a tricky affair. The people and the Army are the keys. Like you just told the ambassador, you need half the Army to desert to your command."

"You're not very encouraging."

"There's a lot we can do from this end, or with your help. Hit at some strategic points that won't harm the civilians. If you want them on your side, you can't start by killing half of them."

"Right. One of my rules is that we will strike at no position where any civilians will be hurt or inconvenienced. For instance, we won't blow up the water-filtration plant in Sierra City."

"Good move. I'd like to meet you, Mr. Washington, and talk. You tell your outposts and lookouts that three motorcycles will be coming up the trail tomorrow and not to blow our heads off. We'll use the password of Harley Davidson."

Washington laughed. "Oh, yes, the Harley Hog. I rode one once. Then I wanted one for five years. Done. I may not be here by the time you get here, but talk with the Vice President and look over my men. Now, put the ambassador back on."

"Yes, Mr. Washington," Oberholtzer said.

"You contact the Navy. Tell them what we need. Also tell the President that tomorrow I'll be making my demands that the U.S. must meet in order for me to turn the Vice President over to the embassy there in Sierra City."

"Demands? I thought this was a non-kidnapping situation."

"I have demands. Quite a few and rather tough to meet, but the U.S. and the rest of the world can do it. I'll give my demands to the President on this frequency and on an international radio frequency tomorrow night at six."

13

SDPD Headquarters
San Diego, California

Detective Sergeant Petroff stared at the three piles of paper on his desk. He'd cleaned all the other cases off it. One stack detailed all of their interviews with the involved persons in the OD death of Joisette Brown. The second was Joisette's will and legal papers. The third pile was all they knew about Shortchops Arnold Jackson.

Petroff had an OD on a heroin victim, confirmed now by the autopsy. There were three other drugs in her system, but they hadn't killed her. However, the police had found no syringes at the scene. Neither of the women had a syringe or any drugs with them. The medical examiner hadn't indicated if death was due to a self-induced OD or to one induced by a person or persons unknown.

Then there were the legal papers, the legal and binding will the victim had left, and transcripts of the special interviews with three of the band members after Petroff found out they also were in the victim's will. The one he hadn't talked to a second time was the SEAL, Sadler, who the Navy said was on a mission "overseas." The SEAL master chief petty officer out on the Coronado Strand assured Petroff that he would be notified as soon as Senior Chief Sadler returned to the base. There was no estimate given when that might be.

Three of the members of the Gaslamp Quarter Dixieland Band said they knew nothing of the dead girl, had only seen her briefly that one time the night she died, and that they had no knowledge whatsoever that they had been named in the will each to get $50,000. They were stunned when he told them. There was no chance these three straight-laced dudes were lying. He didn't know yet about Chief Sadler.

The stack of goods on Jackson was mostly from the musicians' union and the Internet. His hometown paper in Cleveland had run a series of articles about him and his jazz work a year ago. Petroff had copies. They didn't help a bit. Well, a little. The man had been on chemo for a year to beat testicular cancer. It could come back at any time somewhere else in his body. He was seventy-eight years old. He was black, so he probably had prostate trouble. Petroff couldn't find any serious police records on Jackson. Busted twice in Cleveland for possession, but was cleared both times. That was it. Certainly no serious shit like murder. Had Shortchops given the girl the OD deliberately so he could collect his inheritance? He'd had the opportunity when he was alone with her. He'd had the means. He'd had the motive. But it all was shit-faced circumstantial, and not nearly enough to get a warrant for his arrest.

Two of the band members said that Chief Sadler had left the back room at the club just after Shortchops and the girl did. He was gone about five minutes. They figured it was a piss call.

Again circumstantial. Both Shortchops and Chief Sadler had the opportunity and the motive for killing the girl. He didn't know if Sadler had the means. The other band men said, as far as they knew, Sadler was straight-arrow when it came to drugs.

Which put Petroff right back in the vise, and the captain was squeezing it. Petroff had a week to get enough evidence for a warrant, or they would leave it open as an OD death with no suspects.

The 3.5-million-dollar estate kept bugging Petroff. A lot of men would do a lot for that kind of money. Had Shortchops waited for his chance and then hit Joisette with a huge OD? The medical examiner said there was enough heroin in her system to kill her two times over. Could the girl have taken a hit and forgotten it and had another one? Or had Shortchops given her a shot not knowing she'd already boosted? Or had Shortchops deliberately given her a double dose knowing that it would put her down and dead in the alley before anyone could get there to help her? There was a chance that Chief Sadler had provided the fatal pop of heroin so he could collect the fifty thousand. That was a pile of money for a hardworking enlisted Navy man.

A week. He had a week, and then the captain was closing the file and putting him on something else. What the hell could he do in a week? Easy. He had to find Shortchops. He put on his jacket and headed for the garage. He had some favors due in the black community. There had to be somebody down there who knew Jackson, and maybe how to find him. It came down to digging up Jackson for a long talk, or quitting the whole damned case.

An idea hit him squarely between the eyes. There was a chance he could phone Senior Chief Sadler. The Navy said they would cooperate in every way they could. He started the unmarked Ford and headed for Coronado. There was a chance. Maybe a good one.

A half hour later he shook hands with Master Chief MacKenzie in the Quarterdeck.

The master chief read from the card just presented. "So, Detective Sergeant Petroff, what can I do for you today?"

"I'm at a critical point in my investigation of a death I think was a homicide. Senior Chief Sadler is a material witness and I need to talk with him. I know he's overseas. I also know he usually is on covert missions. What I need is a telephone interview with him of about ten minutes. I don't want to know where he is or what he's doing. None of my business. Solving this murder is. Who do I have to see to get approval for you to use your radios or phone lines to get me in touch with Senior Chief Sadler?"

MacKenzie nodded at the detective and sat down behind his desk. "Sergeant Petroff, let me make a phone call. I realize that the Navy has no exclusion rights when the police ask for our cooperation. This is slightly different. If you could wait in the outer office for a few minutes, I'll get your answer."

"Fine, no problem. Oh, do you have any coffee?"

When the door closed, MacKenzie dialed Commander

Dean Masciareli. The boss of the SEAL complex was in and not busy. He took the call. After hearing the request in detail, the commander made an instant decision.

"I don't see how we can deny the sergeant a call. Just be sure it's covert as to area and activity. You might try SATCOM first. I have no idea what time it is in Africa. Carry on, Master Chief."

When the detective came back inside he expected to get a quick no. His face brightened with the good news.

"We'll try to contact the platoon by SATCOM," said MacKenzie. "It's a military radio that works off the satellite system. Usually we can contact any of our people anywhere in the world. I'll have it set up and get the antenna adjusted."

The master chief looked at his watch. "With the time differential it should be early evening there. Which means they might not have their set turned on. It could take us an hour to make contact."

"Fine, I'll wait. Just so the coffee holds out."

It was almost two hours later before the calls every fifteen minutes to Murdock's platoon brought an answer.

Master Chief MacKenzie explained the situation.

"I can have Senior Chief Sadler here in five minutes," Bill Bradford said. "Hey, there he is. Just a shake." There was some dead air, then a new voice came on.

"Petroff, you still bugging me? Hope you've got that case all wrapped up."

"Afraid not, Senior Chief. Have a few more questions for you. Did you know you were mentioned in the dead black girl's will?"

"Will? How would a down-and-out hooker have any money for a will?"

Petroff explained it to Sadler.

"You mean she was a kid of the Billy Ben Brown, one of the greatest jazz men who ever lived?"

"She was. She left to each of the men in your jazz band fifty thousand dollars."

"Now I know this is a prank call. Nobody ever left me anything. Who are you really?"

"Would the master chief play a trick on you, Senior Chief?"

"No, guess not. Wow. Well, all I can say is that I had no idea. I bet the other three guys didn't either, right? Hey, wait a minute. Are you implying that one of our band guys had anything to do with the girl's OD just because we were in her will?"

"Had crossed my mind. What I haven't told you is that Shortchops Jackson gets the balance, something over three-point-five-million dollars."

"That I don't believe."

"Believe it. Billy Ben earned millions and knew how to keep his cash."

"What does Shortchops say about this?"

"I'd like to find out. We haven't seen him or talked to him. He vanished the same night the girl had the overdose. You know where we can find him?"

"No idea. But you're crazy if you think any of the other four of us had anything to do with that OD."

"Where did you go during the break when you left the back room just after Shortchops and Joisette left?"

"So that's it. I had the opportunity and now the motive. Sorry to bust up your case, but I went to the john. People have to do that, you know. And no, I don't have any witnesses. I don't need any help quite yet to take care of my own basic bodily functions. Now, if you don't have any more sensible questions, I have work to do. We're getting busy here today, so I'm signing off."

The speaker on the SATCOM went dead.

"You must be through," the Master Chief said to Petroff.

"Evidently. Trouble is, I don't know a damned thing more now than when I came out here. Thanks, Master Chief MacKenzie. I still want to hear from you the minute Senior Chief Sadler hits your Quarterdeck."

Sierra Bijimi, Africa
Amunbo River

It was night. Mojombo Washington had twenty men crammed into the powerboat that had come down the river on low power to cut down on the noise. He pulled in at a

small village fifteen miles north of Sierra City, and almost
five miles upstream from where they usually landed with
the boats.

The men formed into a column, and Mojombo led them
out at an easy jog toward the city. At the first small village
they borrowed two trucks that they promised to bring back
before sunup. Both were small vans with twelve-foot-long
bodies, which would hold a lot of goods.

They rode the rest of the way to the northern part of
Sierra City, and left the trucks a block from their target. It
was a large warehouse in a section not far from the river.
Originally it had been used to keep merchandise and goods
coming into the country via the river on small boats. Now
it had been sealed, and there were two guards pacing in
front of the big truck door.

Mojombo and his best marksman settled in the grass in
the prone position and aimed their AK-47's. Both were
pleased with the field of fire and the one-hundred-yard distance.

"Do it," Mojombo said, and they both fired. The sharp
crack of the rifles jolted into the quiet night and stilled a
dozen nighttime insects and a nighthawk in mid-cry. They
waited a moment. Then a squad of six men rushed the
building, dragged the dead guards out of the light, and
opened the big door. The first truck was ready, and was
backed into the warehouse. Then the door was closed. Two
men took the place of the guards, using their weapons and
hats. In the poor light outside, they were hard to tell from
the government troops.

Inside the warehouse, the men turned on the lights, and
Mojombo whistled in amazement. "He's got everything
here. Food, TV sets, video players, and cases of liquor."

He did a quick survey and marked things to take. "All
of the canned food, the packaged food. Anything we can
eat," he told the workers. The eighteen men rushed around
loading the truck. To one side he found two new Honda
500cc motorcycles. He pushed them on board the truck
himself. Most of what he saw he couldn't use. Dozens of
pieces of furniture, recliners, dining-room sets, bedroom
sets. There was nothing perishable. He found a dozen five-

gallon cans of gasoline. He took those for the bikes and his generator at the camp.

When the first truck was filled, they drove it out and backed in the second. Just then a jeep rounded a corner a block away. They pulled the door closed and waited. The men in the military jeep evidently were checking on the guards. The rig didn't stop. The man in the front seat simply waved at the two soldiers in front of the warehouse walking their posts. Then the jeep drove on.

The men inside filled the second truck with more of the food.

"Should we burn it down?" Lieutenant Gabu asked Mojombo. The leader frowned. "No, all of this can be given to the people when we take over. Let's leave it here. Let's move out now."

Mojombo's second in command closed up the second truck. They looked outside, had a go from the two guards, and drove out, with the men inside and hanging on the sides and backs of the two trucks as they moved quietly through the dark streets north.

They drove to the end of the road at the ten-mile point from the city, and there the men began carrying the goods off the trail into the edge of the jungle, just out of sight. When everything was hidden, two men drove each truck back to the owners and thanked them with three cases of food each. Then they hiked back to the cache of food.

Mojombo took his men into the jungle another two hundred yards and let them go to sleep. They would be up at dawn to greet the people taking goods to market, telling them that when they came back there would be a surprise for them.

"It will be with the goodwill of the Bijimi Loyalist Party," Mojombo told the people who began streaming by with their carts and wagons loaded with goods to sell at the open market.

Just after midday, some of the farmers began moving back up the trail. Mojombo stopped them, and his men piled cases of food on their empty carts and wagons and one small truck. He told them they could have one case for every three they delivered as far north as possible. The farmers were delighted.

"We will remember you, Mojombo," one elderly farmer said. He had twelve cases of food on his horse cart. "We will help you however we can."

One of Mojombo's men went with every four groups taking food up the trail.

Just before nightfall, Mojombo's men had moved more than two hundred cases of food up the trail. The carts were used up to the twenty-mile mark. Then it was a walking trail. They hid most of the food off the trail and carried the rest to their camp. The hidden food would be used as needed, or it would be taken downstream to their next camp when they moved toward the city.

At Camp Freedom, Mojombo went at once to the Vice President's tent and found the strangers. All the men stood at once.

"I'm Lieutenant Commander Murdock," one man said. "You must be Mojombo Washington. I'm glad to meet you. This man is my good right hand, Jaybird, and over there is our motorcycle specialist, Luke Howard."

"Yes, I'm Washington, and I fully intend to lead my people out of this wilderness of graft, corruption, and murder the present government is riddled with. I want you and your SEALs to help me."

"Our primary mission is to aid and protect the Vice President. I don't imagine that you'd let us take him back down the trail tomorrow morning?"

"I can't let you do that. As you see, I have the guns and the men to stop you. No sense in your dying here in a foreign land. I want you to listen to me. Hear the plans I have for my people. You already know about the murdering, rotten, criminal element we have running our nation. I want you to help me with some ideas and strategies so I can move into Sierra City and take over the government and hold free and honest elections."

"Mr. Washington," Murdock said. "Do you remember your American history? It took our George Washington eight years to win his revolution. Are you ready to put in that kind of time here to win yours?"

"No. This is a much different situation. The government is holding on by its fingernails. They have used up all of their goodwill with the people. The Army is starting to become nervous and could break into pieces at any time. All we need is a few sparks and we can move this country into a new era."

"Do you have the support of the people?" Murdock asked.

"We did today." He told them how the people had done everything he'd asked them to do. "Today the party made a lot of new friends. All we have to do is show that we can lead them, and we'll have a grand march against the Government Building."

"With the Army cutting down half of them with a hail of lead," Jaybird said.

They talked until it grew dark. The generators began, and lights blossomed around the camp and in the Vice President's tent.

"I have some strategies that I believe will help push the President back and incite the Army to mutiny," Mojombo said. "What can you tell me that might help with new ideas or attacks or new ways to discredit the President and win over the people?"

"The Vice President told me about his idea for you to move closer to the capital, and to solidify your support by the people as you go," Murdock said. "You need to show control over half of the country and the villages. This way you can win new converts and men for your army.

"Staging your hit-and-run raids are tremendously effective. The Army will never know when the next might come and where you'll hit next. You could be shooting up the military installations every three or four days. Blow up facilities, barracks, burn down buildings, shoot up transport. Kill as few soldiers as possible and the Army brass will get the idea that you're not after them, but the Army power."

"Fine, until we run out of ammo," Mojombo said. "We don't have an unlimited supply."

"Raid more Army ammo bunkers," Luke Howard said.

Murdock watched Mojombo. He wasn't satisfied with the talk. "Mr. Washington. Let us confer here for a while to-

night, and tomorrow we'll have some ideas that might help
out your cause. We'll make them as practical as possible
and see if we can help set up and carry out some of the
attacks. May we have a green light on that, Mr. Vice President?"

"I can give you that authorization. The White House
might not agree, but they are one hell of a long way from
here. Where is that U.S. Navy task force?"

"Should be a destroyer offshore sometime tonight or tomorrow," Jaybird said. "Depends what choppers they have
on board. Probably the smaller ones, the SH-60B used for
sub-hunting, but we can adapt them."

"All right, gentlemen, I'll leave you to your conference,"
said Washington.

"Ten-hut," Murdock barked as the Bijimi Loyalist Party
leader stood to leave. The SEALs snapped to attention.

Mojombo grinned. "Hey, I couldn't even get into the
ROTC. But thanks anyway. See you tomorrow."

He left, and Vice President Adams motioned for the
SEALs to gather around. "Now we get down to work. This
great man needs our help. I'm convinced he can lead his
people out of this quagmire the current officials have
dumped the nation into. So, let's get our brains working
and come up with some great attack plans that will leave
old President Kolda reeling."

"You weren't kidding about our being able to get in a
few shots in anger against this bunch of crooks?" Howard
asked.

"I don't see why not. As long as none of you get
wounded, the brass back in Coronado will never know. At
least, I won't tell them. Now let's do some tall thinking
about this problem."

14

The next day at 1 P.M. the SATCOM stuttered out its bursts of electronics as the Vice President called Washington, D.C., and the embassy in Sierra City. When he had them both on the air, he gave them a report.

"Mojombo Washington is going to make his demands for my release at three o'clock today. Two hours from now. Ten A.M. your time. He wants the news media to listen to the demands in both D.C. and Sierra City. He says they will be detailed, and vital to his nation. He warns that he will also make a pitch for the world to swoop in on President Kolda and throw him and his criminal bunch of thugs out of office. Any questions?"

"I didn't think you were a hostage," the President's Chief of Staff said. "The President is at a power breakfast right now, but I'll have him here for the announcement. It will be recorded. Yes, we can open the transmission to the press. We'll set it up shortly in the press room. Any idea what Washington's going to say?"

"Not the slightest. We'll be back in touch with you in about two hours." They signed off.

"What's this demands business?" Murdock asked. "I thought you were his buddy and newfound friend."

"I thought so too. He did say one of the reasons for inviting me to be his guest here was to focus worldwide attention on his country and the sorry leadership it has now. That must be part of it. I'm sure millions of people now know what and where Sierra Bijimi is who never had heard of it before my. . . . visit. . . . here at Camp Freedom."

"Every news service in the world carried your story big-time when you were snatched," Jaybird said. "Right now there are about forty newspeople in Sierra City waiting for something to happen."

"Sounds like it's going to today."

Mojombo Washington said, "Knock, knock," at the tent flap and slipped inside. He carried a clipboard with some papers on it.

"I hope you gentlemen slept peacefully and had a good breakfast and lunch. I try to feed my men well."

"Yes, we've been treated fine," Murdock said. "You really going to make some demands for Mr. Adams' release?"

"Absolutely, big-time demands. How is our time?"

"Almost two hours."

"Radio all set up and the antenna checked?"

"All done, Mr. Washington," Howard said.

"Good, I'll be back later. Sometimes I like to surprise folks and start things a little early. But not this time. I'll be back."

At exactly 3 P.M., Mojombo Washington took the handset from the vice president and began:

"Good morning to the United States and to the world. Today we have some serious business to attend to. It's my pleasure to report that Vice President Adams is well and in good spirits, and working with me for the freedom of my country, Sierra Bijimi.

"To further those ends, I have some demands that must be met before the Vice President can be returned to you. These demands are:

"One. Send in ten thousand United Nations troops to throw out the current government at every level and run the country until free elections can be held.

"Two. With supervision and direction by the United States, hold free and open elections within six months to elect new government officials at all levels within the country.

"Three. Deliver with United Nations supervision one million tons of food to be distributed to our nation's poor by U.N. personnel.

"Four. Direct World Bank interest-free loans in the amount of ten billion dollars available to Sierra Bijimi industrial and business firms without involving any current government agencies.

"Five. Begin investigations by the World Court of all current government leaders on charges of bribery, theft, murder, and looting of the national treasury.

"Six. Begin an immediate airlift of small arms and ammunition sufficient to help the Bijimi Loyalist Party's armed forces to maintain order until the U.N. and U.S. forces are in place.

"These demands are not open to negotiation. A meeting of a high U.N. official and a high U.S. official and the leader of the Bijimi Loyalist Party should take place within three days.

"These demands are made on behalf of the downtrodden and exploited people of Sierra Bijimi, and not for the personal gain of any individual or group.

"I look forward to comments and action from the United Nations and the United States. Thank you."

He turned off the mike. "Gentlemen, I'll be in my tent waiting for a reply." He slipped out the flap and was gone.

"Wow," Jaybird said. He had written down the demands as Mojombo made them. "Too much," Jaybird said.

"He's asking the impossible," Murdock said. "The U.N. never has invaded a country and taken it over. Not a chance. The World Bank won't make a single loan knowing the monetary corruption in this country."

"So what you're saying is that if anything gets done down here to help Mojombo, it's up to us to do it. Me and your SEALs." The Vice President scowled as he said it.

Murdock looked out the tent flap and at last nodded. "Looks like that's about it. So, let's get the rest of these plans we were working on finished so we can get into some action. I feel like I'm rusting at the switch here."

"Now you're talking," Jaybird said. "First we turn on the SATCOM and see Don Stroh's reaction and what the newspeople said."

The moment he turned on the SATCOM, it spoke to him.

"Stroh calling Bull Pup. Stroh calling Bull Pup."

"Yes, Bull Pup here. What's the reaction down there to the demands."

"The press went wild. Every phone line out of here was jammed. Big news. Kolda must have heard about the demands coming and had a man with the newsies. From what we know now, he's launched eight to ten boats upriver loaded with troops. We have no count, but an estimation is there are about two hundred men on board. These are mostly small pleasure boats, but he's jammed lots of soldiers on them. Tell Mojombo that he probably can't stop this bunch with sniper fire from the river."

Howard went to bring the Loyalist Party leader back. When Mojombo heard the news about the troops coming up the river, he ran out to the small clearing and bellowed out a command.

Men poured out of tents and the edge of the jungle and from near the river. Each man had a weapon with him. They fell in what was evidently platoon and squad order.

The SEALs moved out so they could hear. ". . . and the word is that ten boats are coming upstream. We go to Plan B. I want a hundred men with rifles along the riverbank. Run down the trail until you see them coming. Then find good cover and fire when they are in range.

"First target the boat driver, try to knock him out. If there is a cabin, riddle it with gunfire. We have to stop them on the river. Once they get to the trail up here, we have to move and move quickly.

"I want every man to draw three hundred rounds to fit his weapon. Do it now. We move out in five minutes."

Murdock caught up with Mojombo in his tent digging out ammunition.

"We want to go with you. Three more rifles might help. We'll need AK-47's. You have any extras?"

Mojombo hesitated, then grinned. "Glad to have you aboard, Commander. I'll get you weapons. Bring your sub guns as well. We should be able to get about eight miles downstream before they show up. Then it will be target practice."

"If they break through?"

"Then we run back up here and move everything we can carry. We had to do it once before. Let's go."

•   •   •

Two hours later, the troops rested along the river. Murdock figured they had covered nearly ten miles. Murdock shifted the three hundred rounds of the 7.62mm in the small sack on his hip. The AK-47 he had was far from new, but it had been well taken care of. He had eight magazines for it with thirty rounds in each one. The Kalashnikov had two firing rates, full automatic at six hundred rounds per minute, or single-shot. He'd probably keep it on single-shot for any distance work.

They waited.

Twenty minutes later one of the lead scouts a half mile downstream called on one of the new handheld radios.

"They are coming," Mojombo told his men. They were all on one side of the river, and each one had good protection behind a tree or a rock or a mound of dirt, so he could still see the river plainly and with a good field of fire.

Murdock and the other two SEALs had trees with trunks two feet wide. He had no idea what kind of trees they were, but he was glad they were there. The men had strung out five yards apart covering almost five hundred yards of shoreline.

Murdock and the SEALs were in the middle of the line. "Fire when you see a target," Mojombo said on the radio, and the word was passed. "Let's put that first boat dead in the water and drifting back downstream."

As he said it, Murdock heard a stuttering fully automatic AK-47 blasting away downstream. There was return fire, and Murdock heard at least one machine gun. As the boats powered upstream, more and more rifles took up the hunt.

The first boat never made it to Murdock. The pilothouse of the thirty-footer was blasted away, and no man dared try for the controls. It slued to port, barely missed a thirty-five-footer, and drifted downstream.

The volume of fire continued to grow. The first boat Murdock saw was a fishing craft, maybe forty feet long. It looked like it was made of solid wooden planks, and had absorbed hundreds of rounds. There was no glass in the cabin windows. Murdock concentrated on the small pilot-house, grazing his shots just over the windowsills, trying for some instruments or a hand stretched up to steer the craft by a man sitting or lying on the floor. Murdock wished he'd brought a Bull Pup along on this run. They had five of them back at the embassy.

His rounds didn't faze the fishing boat. It kept laboring up the river at five knots. He moved his sights to the next boat, a smaller pleasure craft with no good protection built in. The small bridge had been cut with many rounds. Murdock saw a hand holding the wheel and another on what could be the throttle. He aimed at the wheel hand and sent six rounds into it. On the fourth round the hand jolted off the wheel, and Murdock gave it two more rounds for good measure. The small craft stalled against the current, then pivoted to the side and slammed into a twenty-foot fishing boat before it floated down the river with the current.

A swath of machine-gun rounds cut into the trees and leaves over the SEALs' heads, and Jaybird screeched in anger.

"Where's the fucking MG? Anybody see it?"

"Yeah, firing out of the steps down to the cabin on that blue and white boat," Howard said. "About time we welcome him to the party."

The boat was almost even with them and less than forty yards away on the far side of the river. Jaybird kicked his 47 into automatic, and sprayed the black hole of the steps area with the fifteen rounds left in his magazine. Then Howard picked away at the same spot with single shots. The machine gun didn't fire again from that position.

Only eight boats moved past Murdock. He heard men in the brush behind him evidently running upstream to have another shot at the boats. When the last one, a small pleasure craft with sheets of steel set inside the pilothouse, moved upstream past Murdock, he picked up and led twenty men into the jungle and north up the river. It was hard going through the trees, vines, and roots, but soon they could hear firing again. They went another hundred yards and moved toward the river. Now there were only six boats. That made fewer targets for the riflemen, and they slammed round after round into the boats as they came along. Another machine gun chattered, and it brought a surge in rifle fire that soon quieted the MG. The Loyalists kept pounding the boats, which had nowhere to hide and no protection. Jaybird wondered where the two hundred troops were.

Murdock saw only four boats left. He and his men moved north again. By the time they came to the river, there was only one boat left, the large fisher with the solid hardwood construction. As the SEALs watched, the boat turned toward the far shore, then turned again and surged downriver with the current. All shooting stopped.

"Rally round." The word came down the ranks, and they moved forward to a small clearing where Mojombo stood waiting for them.

"Good work, men. Excellent. We've turned around two hundred men at least hidden in those boats. Now, what about our own casualty report? Sergeants, check your men. I saw at least two wounded. Are there any more?"

Three more moved up with wounds. Two men carried a third man who had been hit in the head and died instantly.

"Get poles and make a litter. Use your shirts with the poles through the arms. Three shirts should do it. Carry our dead hero back to camp. Do we have our medic along? Check the wounds. We'll leave a six-man guard for you. The rest form up and move out. Time to get back to the camp. You men did magnificently well today. General Assaba is probably screaming and tearing out his hair. Another big defeat for him. Commander Murdock. Bring up the rear and keep up any stragglers. If any man needs the medic, have him wait on the trail. Let's chogie."

Mojombo looked over at Murdock. "Oh, yes, I know the word. From the Korean War. One of my roommates at college said his father used the word all the time. I got used to it. See you back at Camp Freedom."

An hour later at the camp, Murdock settled down to clean his adopted AK-47. Vice President Adams walked over and sat down on the ground beside him. The man holding the second-highest office in the United States of America had changed into cammies and they looked good on him, Murdock thought.

"You enlisted, Mr. Vice President?"

"I tried, but he wouldn't take me. I'm not even a citizen. I said I'd take dual citizenship, but he just laughed and said

I had a part to play, just be patient. I hear you turned back three hundred riflemen and twenty boats."

"Close. Tomorrow it will be five hundred. What do you hear from downtown?"

"The embassy has closed its gates and will admit no one. The ambassador is afraid that President Kolda will retaliate against the U.S. for Mojombo's position. He's glad the SEALs are there to beef up his protective force. He's only got twelve Marines and if a hundred soldiers decide to storm the gates . . ."

"He say anything about the destroyer coming in?"

"Said it's on station five miles off the coast and a hundred and sixty-two miles from Sierra City."

"Jaybird, what's the range of the SH-60?" Murdock asked.

"At least five hundred miles, Commander. That would be a mission radius of about two hundred and fifty."

"Let's see if Mr. Washington can carve us out an LZ here near the camp. If so, then we'll see if that destroyer captain will send us a Seahawk without its torpedoes and with two door gunners on some machine guns."

Jaybird was back within five minutes. "The camp already has an LZ. They carved it out when they thought they'd steal the two choppers the Army has. It's plenty big enough for a Seahawk to settle down in."

"Mr. Vice President, let's fire up the SATCOM and talk to the good Mr. CIA himself, Old Man Stroh."

"Think they'll do it?" Jaybird asked.

"They have two of the birds and they sure aren't going to be doing any antisubmarine work around here. We convince Don, he can twist some CIA tails and get the CNO to order the chopper to come in here."

Five minutes later Don Stroh was interested. "So we get one of the Seahawks in there, what will you do with it? I need something solid to use to sell the CNO."

"Lots of missions. For one, we can intimidate the hell out of the federal troops with the two .50-caliber machine guns. We can move a squad around the country quickly. We can hit and get away fast. We can take the Vice President for a trip to the destroyer to have a hot shower and some better food. All sorts of shit we can do to disrupt the current government here."

"I like that part about getting the Vice President out of there and back on U.S. soil, or steel. I'll see what tails I can twist."

"You do that, and make it snappy. Time's a-wasting here, big brother."

The Vice President looked at Murdock when he put down the handset. "You were joking about taking me out to that destroyer off the coast, weren't you?"

"I said take you out there to get a shower, nothing about your staying there. That's the only idea they will grab hold of. Once we get the chopper in here, we can do all sorts of good stuff. They can bring us more ammo, maybe some grenades and some good old C-5 plastique. Can be a real lifeline."

"Commander, do you think the Seahawk will fit inside the parking lot at the embassy?" Jaybird asked.

"I don't know. You're the encyclopedia on sizes of things. What's the rotor diameter on the Seahawk?"

"Fifty-four feet."

"Plenty of room in that side parking area. You thinking of taking a trip back to the embassy to see the ambassador's daughter?"

"Hey, she's way too young for me. I was just being polite."

"Good. Now even if that chopper doesn't come, we need a good mission for the Bijimi Loyalist Party for tomorrow. What's it going to be?"

15

On the Amunbo River

Luke Howard leaned over to Jaybird and whispered even though there was no need to. "You really think this is going to work?"

Jaybird shrugged. "Hell, I don't know. It looked pretty good on paper last night and this morning. We take this little boat and we plow downstream to the five-mile landing, five miles from the city center, where we hike inland about five hundred yards and we meet the rest of the SEALs. On a quirky deal like this a dozen things could go wrong. Like the bus could blow a tire or run out of gas or get stopped by the Army. So we play it as it goes and hope for the best."

"They bringing the Bull Pups?"

"You bet, all six of them, and one of the EARs. The idea here is to destroy property and not build up any kind of a kill count. We use the stun gun if we have to."

"These guys we have with us, can we rely on them? They didn't get much training, bunch of rebels."

"Loyalists, Howard. Remember they are the good guys. They know where the Army base is and how to get around town. We have four of them for good measure, and their long guns just might come in handy."

Murdock moved to the back of the thirty-foot boat and slid in beside his men. "We do this by the book. The fewest enemy casualties possible, the greatest physical plant destruction practical, and then we haul ass as fast as permissible."

A few minutes later the pilot of the boat slowed and

angled into the right-hand side, where a rickety dock survived yet another landing. Two shadows slid out of the darkness and tied up the boat, then motioned, and the three SEALs and four Loyalists left the craft. The two men untied the boat, and and it powered back upstream to the hiding spot chosen. It would come on a radio signal from Murdock, who now carried one of the Loyalist radios.

The three SEALs watched the dark, silent houses as they went past. It was the edge of the city, and most people were inside. Murdock checked his watch. A little after 2100. Right on schedule.

Ahead he could see the school bus. He'd have to ask why the embassy had a school bus. They stepped on board, and the driver moved out at once.

"About time you AWOL suckers showed up," Senior Chief Sadler growled. "Good to have the team together again. And some fucking action. We all ready?"

"You bring all the gear we need?" Murdock asked.

"We did. Six Bull Pups with plenty of rounds, and the EAR. Also thirteen eager and anxious SEALs ready to pop their britches if they don't get some action. Gardner has been training our asses off."

"Should be interesting tonight. First the motor pool on the edge of the base. Target practice really, from what the locals tell me. One of the rebels' top men, Lieutenant Gabu, is with us. He's our point man. Gabu, come meet JG Gardner and Senior Chief Sadler." They shook hands in the gloom of the rolling bus.

"How much longer?" Gardner asked.

Lieutenant Gabu looked out the window. "Almost there. Two minutes."

"Let's get up and get ready," Sadler called. The SEALs lifted out of the seats, adjusted their combat vests and weapons, and stood in the aisle ready to move out.

The bus stopped and Gabu looked at the men. "Alpha on me to the left, Bravo with Commander Murdock to the right. Let's go."

They ran out of the bus and spread out along a fence that wouldn't keep a stray cow out of the area. Ahead a hundred yards the motor pool spread out. It consisted of

three low buildings with a dozen trucks parked on this side
and three buses next to the second building. Each squad
had three Bull Pups. All of the men except the Loyalists
had Motorola radios.

Murdock touched his mike. "We'll go with the twenties.
Impact on the vehicles, then WP into the two buildings we
can see. As soon as we torch these two, Alpha Squad will
chogie down the fence to get shots at the third building
behind the big one. Bull Pups up and spread your rounds.
Fire when ready."

Two of the 20mm rifles fired almost at once. Murdock
sighted in his weapon and aimed at one of the trucks. The
round caught the front and tore the engine half out of the
hood, but the gas tank didn't explode. He fired again at
the back of the truck, and the fuel tank went up in a sun-
bright fireball that rained burning fuel on the two trucks
parked beside it. He heard another fuel tank explode, and
turned his weapon on the roof of the large building.

His first WP hit the side of the building and bounced off,
making a bright fireworks display of spraying white phosphorus near the trucks. His second round vanished over the
side of the building, and he soon saw the flames from the
burning roof. The other 20mm rounds blasted into the two
buildings, and quickly they were roaring blazes. Murdock
saw a few men running around the building, but nobody
looked like they were trying to put out the fire. Maybe the
base had no fire department.

Then he heard a siren that could be a fire engine. He
used the radio to get Alpha Squad moving to the third
building. His Bravo men lay in the grass watching the fire.
The bus had been driven a half mile away from the fence
so it wouldn't be involved. They waited as the buildings
burned and the buses and trucks melted into each other. If
there were any more vehicles inside the buildings, they
would be toast by now.

He heard the crack of the 20mms down the way, and
soon Gabu and Alpha Squad jogged back to the rest of
them.

"Enough here," Gabu said. "I love those twenties. When

can I order up about two hundred of them?" He grinned.
"Let's go find the bus."

It was parked on the side street where it was supposed
to be. Gabu was the last man on. He talked with the driver,
who circled back toward the base three miles from the burning motor pool. The bus eased up toward another fence not
much stronger than the first one. Gabu got the men outside
and pointed.

"Longer shooting this time. Six hundred yards to the administrative building on the right, then the post exchange
and the mess hall and theater. No show tonight. I checked.
On the other side are the officers' quarters. Houses and
barracks. We want all of them.

"Commander Murdock says the men who fired the twenties at the motor pool switch with a man who didn't fire.
Everyone gets in on the fun. Airbursts here won't do much
good, so let's stick to the impact fuses and WP. Spread out
again and fire when ready."

Murdock handed his Bull Pup to Howard, who grinned,
bellied down in the weeds, and pushed the muzzle through
a hole in the fence, then sighted in. His first round came
up short, but his next two hit the administrative building.
With the range established, Howard put in WP rounds in
his magazine and started the bonfires going.

Murdock looked up when he saw headlights along the
fence. An inside-the-fence jeep patrol. He brought his MP-5
up and sprayed the jeep with nine rounds. He watched it
come forward again, then hit it with nine more rounds from
the thirty-round magazine. The jeep spun to the left away
from the fence, hit a small ditch, and flipped over. One man
crawled away from the machine. Murdock let him go. It
wasn't hunting season on federal troops. Not yet.

The six Bull Pups fired for only four minutes, but in that
time they left twenty buildings burning furiously. The men
formed up and jogged away from the fence. A half mile
down a second road they came to the bus and piled on
board.

"Is the fun over for tonight?" Jaybird yelled.

"Not quite," Gabu said. "We've saved the best to last.
For this one we have to do some footwork. The target is at

the far end of the Army base, and carefully housed. We'll
have to move in, take out any guards, and then get to work.
We're going after the ammo dumps."

There were some cheers.

"There are three of the underground bunkers that are now
being used. I happen to know which ones they are. We
have a ten-minute bus ride, so relax, fill your magazines,
and get ready. We will probably run into some opposition
on this one."

It was fifteen minutes before the bus stopped along a road
that had no houses on the off-base side. Just fields and a
few cows. The men went through the fence and moved into
a combat formation as they worked through plowed ground
that was kept free of grass or weeds.

"Fire breaks," Gabu said as he walked near Murdock.
"They don't want a grass fire to blow up their ammo."

When they were a quarter of a mile off, Murdock, Lam,
and Gabu went up on point. The rest of the platoon and the
Loyalists spread out in a protective half circle behind the
point men. The three passed an unused bunker, and Gabu
pointed at two others just ahead. A guard with a submachine gun in his hands walked a beat outside the first bunker. A moment later they saw a second man walking his
beat at the second bunker.

Lam pointed to the EAR and Murdock nodded. He
waited until the two guards almost met at the far ends of
each of their posts.

The familiar whooshing sound slashed into the calm
night, and the two soldiers crumpled as if they had gone to
sleep. Which, Murdock knew, they had.

"Now," Murdock whispered, and the three ran to the
bunkers and checked the doors. Both had locks. Murdock
took a square of C-5 from his vest and cut it in half, then
gave half to Lam, who ran with it to the far bunker door.
Murdock and Lam pasted the puttylike explosive against
the locks and then inserted timer/detonators. They had
agreed on three minutes. They looked at each other through
the pale moonlight. Murdock lifted his arm and snapped it
down. They pushed the detonators to the on position, and
the three men ran behind the bunkers.

The cracking explosions rolled off the other bunkers and raced toward the base buildings, which they could see still burning. The men ran around the bunkers, and saw both doors swinging open. Murdock used his flashlight as they went inside the first one cautiously, not knowing what to expect. Lam had a flashlight as well.

"Looking for C-4, C-5, or dynamite," Murdock said. Lam found some to the side, and Murdock figured there must be two or three hundred of the quarter-pound bars. Lam and Gabu ran to the third active bunker and set a charge to blow its door off. Then Lam came back. They each took three pounds of the C-4.

"Timers set for ten minutes," Murdock said. "We need plenty of time to get away from these mothers."

Murdock stayed in the first bunker, put a timer/detonator into a quarter pound of the C-4, and set it on top of the three pounds of the explosive. He looked around. There were artillery shells, bombs, ammunition, rifles, more ammo, mortar rounds, and cases of dynamite. It should make an interesting bang when it all went off almost at the same time.

He set the timer for ten minutes, pushed it in to activate it, and ran out the bunker door. Lam stood there waiting for him. Together they hurried to the third bunker and saw Gabu coming out.

"Almost wish we could have stolen about half of these goods before tonight," he said. "What the hell, maybe this will break General Assaba's back and he'll take off for Tanzania." They ran back to where the rest of the SEALs and the Loyalists had held their defensive perimeter protecting the sappers' backs.

"About five minutes," Murdock said. "We should be hitting the bricks to get back to the bus." This time it hadn't moved once it let them off. There was no place to hide it.

The men hiked back toward the bus, then stopped and turned when Murdock called a halt. "About now," he said.

The first blast went off a minute later. The concrete roof of the ammo bunker, with three feet of dirt on top of it, simply lifted off and canted to one side as the tremendous explosion slashed into the midnight sky. It was followed

by a blast of air rushing into the spot where the air had
been sucked up and shot skyward. Then came the return of
the air in a hot blast that slammed half of the men to their
knees.

Then the second and third tremendous explosions ripped
through the night sky, lighting it like daytime for a half a
second. Then the blackness closed in and the rush of air
came and went again as the laws of physics held and the
roof of the second and third bunkers cracked, then blasted
skyward in a million bits of rock, dirt, and concrete. Most
of the rocky rain came down well away from the SEALs
and the Loyalists.

They all piled onto the bus and grinned and laughed and
shook their heads in wonder.

"I've seen some big Fourth of July fireworks," Miguel
Fernandez said, "but nothing ever like this."

The bus lurched forward, driving away from the Army
base, taking a fifteen-mile detour around the big reserva-
tion, and then swung north and worked toward the river.
They were twenty minutes ahead of schedule. The bus
parked a quarter of a mile from the landing, and Murdock
sent Lam ahead to check out the area. He took the Motorola, and five minutes later called back with a worried
voice.

"Skipper, we've got some real trouble up here. I'd say
there are at least forty, maybe more, Army regulars spaced
around the road and alley and in every possible firing position that looks out on the rickety dock we landed on. Not
a chance in hell we can get through there and on the boat
without about half of us hitting graves registration. Any
ideas?"

16

"Yeah, I've got an idea, Lam," Murdock said. "Get your ass back here pronto and don't make any contact. We go around them or something. Oh, yeah, the radio. Wondered why I've been carrying it." He took out the ten-inch-long radio, turned it on the way he had been told, and pushed the send button.

"Boatman, Murdock calling."

"Yes, Murdock. We've been wondering where you are. You're late."

"Don't go to the same dock you let us off at. Federals have an ambush set up there. Where else can we meet?"

"I was afraid of that. We've used that dock too often. Go about a half mile upstream. No dock, but I can get in to where the water is only about two feet deep. We'll board there. Okay?"

"Sounds good. Give us ten minutes."

Murdock told the men. Sadler and Gardner had kept their section of the SEALs on the bus.

"We better get back to town," Sadler said on the Motorola. "You guys get back on your little boat. Let's plan another raid as soon as we can. Best we stay down here and help protect the embassy."

Murdock agreed, and told Sadler on the radio. The three SEALS and four Loyalists pulled back silently away from the ambush, and then hiked upstream. Gabu knew the spot. "We've used it a couple of times before, but we better check for another ambush."

Lam did the honors, and reported no enemy in the area.

Ten minutes later the seven raiders were all on board the boat.

"Any casualties?" Murdock asked.

"We didn't take any enemy fire," Jaybird said.

One of the Loyalists had a sprained ankle, and the others teased him about it.

Gabu sat beside Murdock on the run up the river. "I'd say we did good work tonight. We destroyed General Assaba's entire motor pool and probably ninety percent of his trucks and buses. We ravaged his administration building, the PX, his theater, and most of the officers' living quarters. He's going to be hurting tomorrow morning."

"Plus he won't have much ammo or bombs or explosives now that those three ammo bunkers are blasted into rubble," Murdock said. "You're right. We did one hell of a lot of good work tonight."

The White House
Washington, D.C.
President Randolph Edwards studied the blowup map of Sierra Bijimi on the wall in the Situation Room on the first floor of the White House.

"This little pipsqueak of a country is causing us all this pain?" the President asked. "Fewer than four million people in a country twice the size of Delaware, and they are holding us captive? On these demands and the use of the helicopter off the destroyer by the SEALs, I'm open to suggestions."

The CNO, Admiral Burlington, spoke up first. "Mr. President, the use of the Seahawk helicopter off the destroyer *Benford* is acceptable to the Navy. Especially if it can help rescue the Vice President from that camp and get him on board the destroyer and then the carrier."

"Isn't that taking the risk of putting us in the middle of what looks like a civil war in an independent nation?" Johnson from State asked.

"We've already got sixteen SEALs there working behind the scenes, and in some combat situations, if I know this particular platoon of SEALs," Donaldson of the CIA said.

"I'd say get that chopper in there and see what good it can do, and then if it works, fly out the VP."

"Hell, yes, use the SH-60 in there," General Lawford, the National Defense Advisor, said. "Be a shame to have one so close and not use it. Keep the other one on the destroyer at least until the carrier arrives on station. Then maybe we should up the ante and use some of our F-18's to do some bombing and strafing of the Sierra Bijimi Army."

"Now you're getting us into a shooting war without any authorization by Congress," Sage Billings, the President's Chief of Staff, said. "You want another Vietnam here?"

"Enough," Edwards said. "Admiral Burlington, give a go to the chopper with guns free under the control of Commander Murdock. Now, what about these demands? Are they as hard to meet as they look?"

Johnson, from State, cleared his throat. "Mr. President, they all are contingent on the big one, that the U.N. go in with troops and take over the country. The U.N. has never done that. It has assisted revolutions in places, and stopped them in others, but I don't recall them ever moving in, in force, and defeating a soverign nation with troops."

"So where does that leave us?" the President asked. "State?"

"I would suggest a radio transmission to Mojombo Washington explaining our position, that we can do nothing until the U.N. takes over the country. At that time we will be delighted to help organize and run the elections, to help establish a police force, and to rebuild their Army. Until that time, we can do nothing for them.

"Oh, we should make this transmission available to the world press. They have been clamoring for some kind of a reply."

The rest of the men around the table nodded. "Not much else that we can do," Donaldson said. The National Defense Advisor gave a curt nod, as did Admiral Burlington.

"All right, gentlemen, looks like this meeting is over. Mr. Johnson, set up a broadcast to Mojombo and let the press in on it. What about that helicopter, the Seahawk?"

The Chief of Naval Operations smiled. "Mr. President, I

used my cell phone and the bird will be on its way within an hour. We have to notify the Loyalists that it's coming and get some directions from them. Consider it done."

The President watched the men rise and leave. He looked at his Chief of Staff. "Sage, would you stay a moment?"

Sage Billings followed the last man to the door, closed it, and came back and sat across from the President.

"Sage, what's your eval on Adams? What's he really doing down there?"

"Sir, I think he was caught up in a plot by Mojombo Washington to grab worldwide publicity for his cause. That part certainly has worked. The kidnapping and the subsequent stories have been all over the international airwaves and print media for four days now. Beyond that, he may be looking at the next Presidential nomination. You can't run for a third term. I think he is starting his drive for the nomination right now."

"Do you think that Adams will come out if he gets the chance?"

"No. From what I've heard of him talking on the air, he's dedicated to this young revolutionary, thinks of him as a cross between Thomas Paine and George Washington."

"I could order Murdock to grab him, put him on that chopper, and take him to the carrier whether he wanted to go or not."

"You could, and that would destroy a good friendship and make a political enemy for you for the rest of your life."

"You don't think I should remove him forcibly?"

"Absolutely not. He's enamored with this Mojombo. He thinks he can help him reclaim his nation. Maybe he can. Let's give him a little rope. Let's see if he's the man you want to back for your spot next year, since this is your second term in the White House."

"A little rope. Yes. He might hang himself, or he might lasso a bunch of black hoodlums down there and restore a small nation to honest and open government."

"You win in either case. The chopper is a good idea. It and the SEALs could make a huge difference in how many troops the local counterfeit general has at his command if a showdown comes."

Camp Freedom
Sierra Bijimi

The morning after the raid on the Army installations in Sierra City, Murdock, Lieutenant Gabu, the Vice President, and Mojombo had a conference. Both the men were delighted with Murdock's report on the mission and the huge amount of destruction the Bull Pups' 20mm rounds had caused.

"The ammo bunkers, too?" Mojombo asked.

Murdock pointed to Gabu, who gave a blow-by-blow description of the destruction of probably ninety percent of the Army's ammunition and ordnance.

"So where does that leave us?" Mojombo asked. "What else can we destroy to bring down President Kolda that won't harm any civilians, soldiers, or the government buildings?"

"Not a whole lot left," Gabu said. "We can hit the other Army camps around the city. Most are small and some specialized, but not much in size."

"Let's do it," Mojombo said. "You can go out tonight on another mission."

A soldier hurried up to the group and talked quietly to the Vice President.

"Well, it seems that Don Stroh has been calling us on the radio. Let's all go over to the SATCOM and see what he has to say about the raid last night."

A few moments later they gathered around the radio and the Vice President called Stroh in Sierra City.

"Yes, good to talk to you as well," said Adams. "How did General Assaba like the bit of action last night at his Army base?"

"He has denounced it as a murderous rampage by an outlaw band that has no conscience and no morals. He claims sixty-four civilians and ten soldiers were killed in the outrage. He says he's determined to track down the culprits and hang them all. After a fair trial, of course."

"Do most people believe him?" the Vice President asked.

"Almost no one I've talked to. My boys sure did the job with the Bull Pups. Now, we have a small development. The destroyer *Benford* is off the coast. The skipper has received official orders to send one of their Seahawks fully armed, minus the torpedoes, up to your Camp Freedom. They ask for an LZ. I told them the camp is about thirty miles up the Amunbo River and they can't miss it. You can expect the craft to land sometime within the hour."

"Great news, Mr. Stroh. Tell me, does the chopper have a guns-free order?"

"The bird will be under the command and orders of Commander Murdock. He is free to use it as he sees fit to accomplish our goals in Sierra Bijimi."

"Exactly what are those goals, Mr. Stroh?"

"To help Mr. Washington unseat the current regime and establish a democratic form of government for the people of the country."

"Is this still a covert action?"

"It is considered semi-covert. We aren't telling the press about our work, yet we don't have to hide it either."

"Ask him about key members of the Kolda Administration," Murdock said. "Could they be considered legitimate targets?"

The Vice President asked Stroh.

"Murdock must have asked that. He knows the U.S. government has a policy against the execution of any person. However, if there is no direct tie with any of our U.S. personnel, I'd think that it might slip under the rug somehow."

Murdock motioned that he wanted the handset. He hit the talk switch. "Stroh, is this frequency being monitored by Washington, D.C.?"

"I'm sure it is."

"Let's relieve them of that task. Remember the number of my apartment in Coronado?"

"Yes. I do."

"Let's go to that frequency now and continue."

Murdock looked at the dials and reset one. He waited a moment. Then he made a call.

"Murdock calling Big Don."

"Yes, yes, we've made the switch. Now what can we do?"

"Tell the ambassador we need the names, addresses, and any known habits of the six top officials in Kolda's Administration who are criminals and killers. We'd like all the data you can get on them by noon tomorrow."

"Yes, we'll get what we can."

"Then we want the rest of the platoon up here. When the Seahawk gets here, we'll see if we can drop in at your house in the side parking lot. Probably sometime tomorrow. Clear out all cars and the bus."

"Should I come too?" Stroh asked.

"You'll be more valuable as our eyes and ears down there. I hope they bring the chopper with side-door machine guns all mounted and ready to go."

"Sounds like you'll be busy. We'll check the tone of the city here and see what the sentiment of the people is. Your hit at the Army last night greatly reduces the Army's ability to fight from the standpoint of both matériel and morale."

"Good, now good-bye. We have some work to do."

Murdock hit the off switch on the powerful radio and looked at Washington. "Well, Mojombo, who is the first of Kolda's henchmen you'd like to see in an early grave?"

"General Assaba, no contest."

"Won't he be on the Army base?"

"Not after last night. We burned down his house as our first order of business. He often stays in the Presidential Palace, a big place with about forty rooms built especially for our first President."

"How do we get him out in the open?"

"He loves to eat at fancy restaurants, where he always dines on the house with his contingent. He has a big Cadillac he rides in. He almost without fail bets on the revolver-death game."

"How many people does he travel with?"

"Usually five or six, including three women."

Murdock frowned for a moment. "Okay, we take along a sniper rifle, a Bull Pup, and the EAR. If we can't get him alone, we hit his car with the EAR. Then when it stops, we move in, pull Assaba out, and he gets one in the back of the head."

"If he's in the open and fairly alone, we can take him down with the sniper rifle or the Bull Pup," Washington said. "We going down tonight?"

"Yes, you, me, and Luke Howard, our squad sniper. Let's use your small boat to get to the fifteen-mile dock. Then we go in the rest of the way by foot. We can pass for federal troops with our cammies. We may have to requisition some of those billed caps they wear."

"The Russian-roulette gambling club is the place we can count on Assaba going to. He could eat at one of ten or twelve different restaurants."

"Is there an open area around the club?"

"No, crowded, narrow streets. They'll keep a parking spot open for Assaba. We can get there early and set up."

"The EAR most likely first. How long to get down the river?"

Washington frowned. "Three hours. We can take fishing gear. The last stretch of the river is good for fishing. We can use civilian clothes there, and maybe on into town."

"After dark we won't have to hide the weapons. Let's get ready and do it."

They left at 1600 in the twelve-foot boat with motor. The second half of the trip they put on civilian shirts and hats and pretended to fish. They had no bait or hooks on their lines, only sinkers. After it was dark, they turned off the engine and drifted. Mojombo kept the small boat along the far shore. They heard rifle fire ahead on that side, and slanted to the other wooded shoreline.

On a hunch, Mojombo went past the fifteen-mile dock and angled into the shore down a quarter of a mile, where they hid the boat in some heavy vines. They changed back into their cammy shirts, and moved through the tangle of trees and brush to the one-lane dirt road that led south. Murdock brought his MP-5 up to port arms as he moved, just as a precaution. It was a fast-response weapon. They had walked fifty yards when a bright light snapped on not thirty feet from them and a voice barked out a command.

"Drop your weapons and put your hands into the air or we'll fire."

17

Murdock dove to the left as he triggered the MP-5, raking the searchlight and killing it, and then swinging the muzzle to where he figured the voice had come from. A moment later a wail of pain lanced into the night. Murdock rolled four times, stopped on his stomach, and lifted the MP-5. There were shadows ahead. Then two shots fired. He kicked out three three-shot bursts from the sub gun at the muzzle flashes he saw, then rolled three times in the grass and weeds. When he stopped, he fired another six rounds at one muzzle flash he saw ahead. Then all he heard was silence. He clicked his mike twice and heard two clicks back. Both the other men had Motorola personal radios. A moment later came another set of clicks.

"Anybody hit?" Murdock whispered into his throat mike.

"Negative," Howard said.

"Caught one in the arm," Mojombo said. "Not too bad. I think it went on through."

"Left side of the road," Murdock said. "Move over here if you can with no noise. Might be one of them still alive up there."

Murdock heard someone coming. Mojombo. Howard floated up without a sound. "Let's backtrack a hundred yards and move over to the next road," Mojombo said. "It's not this traveled. Maybe they don't have any blocking group there."

"We clean up on this bunch?" Howard asked.

"No, but first we look at that arm. Shield me, Howard, while I use my mini-light on Mojombo's arm. Over here." He saw the African leader push up his left sleeve. The bullet had lanced through the flesh on the lower side of his arm well away from the bone. Murdock used a kerchief and bound up the wound tightly. "Now it shouldn't bleed. Let's move."

They found the next road south in a few minutes and jogged toward the city. Twice Mojombo asked the time. It was 1920 the last time.

"The betting stops at 2200," Mojombo said. "Assaba will be there a half hour before then. He always bets."

"So we have time to get there and get set up?" Murdock asked.

"Yes, should have. Maybe five miles to go."

"We take him before he goes in or after he comes out?" Howard asked.

"Before," said Mojombo. "Fewer people on the street. Afterwards, hundreds of men are around the doorway."

They jogged down a dirt road that turned into a street with houses on both sides. Mojombo led them around the block to a less-traveled street, and they kept moving. Twice they stopped and let Army patrols move through the streets. The squads of four men were walking. No trucks, Murdock decided.

The last four blocks they moved cautiously, with Mojombo in the lead rushing from one shadow to the next. When he stopped them, they were half a block from the club in the downtown business area. They had come up an alley, and directly across the street was the club where the girls bet their lives on five-to-one odds. A parking spot had been left open right in front of the door.

"He'll get out on the far side away from us," Murdock said. "We have to use the EAR as soon as his car stops. You tell us that it's the right car and Howard will fire. Then we charge up at once to the car and open the door, and you confirm your ID of the general."

Mojombo nodded. They waited. It was just after 2120 when a big black Cadillac swept into the parking spot.

"Yes, that's his car. I know the license plate."

Howard fired the EAR. The familiar whooshing sound came, and Murdock and Mojombo leaped up and charged the fifty feet to the black car. Two men who had been ready to open the driver's-side door had fallen to the street. Three people beyond the car had also dropped to the sidewalk in a quick sleep. Murdock grabbed the driver's-side rear door and jerked it open. Two women almost fell out of the car. He pushed them back in. In the light from the dome bulb, Murdock saw a uniformed man on the far side. The door opened and Mojombo leaned in. He nodded. Then his hand came up and he fired twice with a .45 automatic at point-blank range into the general's forehead. Murdock slammed the door and took off running for the shadows. He heard feet pounding behind him. Mojombo caught him thirty yards up the alley. Behind them there were a few cries, then an uproar as men poured out of the gaming club.

Murdock and Mojombo ran past Howard, who jumped up and sprinted after them. Three blocks away the trio sagged into deep shadows and panted to catch their breaths.

When he could talk, Mojombo waved at Murdock. "It was my job to pull the trigger. I did. Now we get the hell out of here. They will throw every river patrol craft they have onto the water as soon as they get the word. Our small outboard couldn't compete."

"We have to leave the boat and jog back up the river trail," Murdock said. "Is it a good trade-off, the boat for Assaba?"

Mojombo laughed softly. "It is a wonderful trade. We can always steal another boat. Now we better get moving. We may have to split up. If we do, we meet at the ten-mile dock."

They stepped into the street, and Howard led them on an easy jog that would cover seven miles in an hour.

They saw no patrols, and didn't hear any whining motors on the river. It was slightly after 2300 when they came near the ten-mile dock.

"Break time," Murdock said. They sprawled in the grass under some trees and gulped in fresh air. Mojombo reached into a small backpack he had worn and took out six candy bars.

"Courtesy of President Kolda's warehouse," he said. "Quick energy for the rest of the trip."

They jogged for another two miles. Then the horse-cart

trail became too dangerous and they slowed to a walk.

"A thirty-mile hike," Howard said as they moved along the trail. "This is a little more than I signed on for, Skipper."

"We take ten-mile training hikes all the time," Murdock said. "Twice last month we did twenty-milers."

"Yeah, but not after combat," Howard said. "I used up a batch of nervous energy back there when you guys charged the car. I didn't know what was going to happen."

"We made it, and the President will have to look for a new hatchet man," Mojombo said. "The people of Sierra Bijimi owe you two a great debt of gratitude."

It was a little over four hours later when the trio walked into the tent area of Camp Freedom. Only one light was still on. Vice President Adams heard them arrive and stepped out to welcome them.

"How did it go?" he asked.

"We have one less villain on our list," Mojombo said. "I thought I was in fair shape. Not true. I had a tough time keeping up with your SEALs." He turned to Murdock. "You'll have to give me your physical training program before you leave. My men could use the added strength and stamina."

"Right now all I need is a cot to flake out on," Murdock said. Howard had already stumbled into his tent and dropped on the cot, sleeping before he could take off his clothes.

"Commander, just wanted to tell you that the Seahawk arrived," said Adams. "It's got door-mounted thirty-caliber machine guns and looks lean and mean. I do suggest that we find some paint and cover up the U.S. markings on it. No sense going out of our way to get in trouble."

"Glad they made it. We'll talk about it tomorrow."

The next morning, Murdock was up at 0600 and had chow at the mess tent, then went to look at the Seahawk. It was what he had seen before, only with no twin sub-killing torpedoes under the belly. The inside had been stripped of nonessentials, and a .30-caliber machine gun was mounted in each of the two open side doors. A friendly, redheaded, freckled-faced Navy man poked his head out of the cabin and grinned. "Hey, you must be the commander. I'm Josie Halstrom. This is my bucket. Hope we can do you some good. I usually have a copilot and a sensor operator. But we left the sensor man on the ship since we wouldn't be looking for any subs."

"Morning, Halstrom. I'm Murdock. How many men can you carry in this rig?"

"The sister Blackhawk calls for twelve, but with your SEAL gear we could probably stuff in sixteen, if nobody exhales. One of them on each of the thirties." The pilot frowned. "We really going to get in some shooting action?"

"That's the plan. My bet is you've never been shot at before."

"No, sir, and that's the truth."

"We'll try to keep it that way. We'll do the shooting. You had breakfast?"

"Yes, sir."

"I'll be in touch," Murdock said, and went toward the Vice President's tent. The Veep was working at doing sit-ups on his bed.

"Twenty-nine and thirty," Adams said. Then he sat up and wiped sweat off his forehead. Murdock stood just inside the flap, his floppy hat in his hand.

"Mr. Vice President, I know the President wants me to talk you into going out to the destroyer offshore. He's worried about you. How can you get the nomination for President if you're six feet under down here in Africa in an unmarked grave?"

Adams chuckled. "Now that's a new argument. I know that the President would like me to get out of this country, but I feel such a bond with these people. They are getting taken advantage of, and Mojombo Washington is their only hope. I'm going to stay and do whatever I can to help."

"You know that the President could order me to take you out to the destroyer, and I'd have to tie you up and carry you to the chopper."

"You wouldn't do that."

"You're right. But if you wind up with a bullet blowing

your head off over here, it will be the end of my Navy
career."

"Hadn't thought of it that way. I'll be careful, for both
of us."

"Any reports yet from Sierra City about the little general?"

"Let's ask Don Stroh."

They called him on the SATCOM, and he said the news
media was going wild. "You should hear the TV newsmen.
So far it's a two-hour special on local TV that may go on
all morning. The international press are wildmen. They
have interviews with the sleep victims, and with the women
in the car with him, and the bystanders who took a nap as
well. Nobody knows what kind of magic weapon it was.
Some are saying it's a ray gun, and others say it's an atomic
sleep pistol. The witnesses do say that two men in Army
uniforms charged the car and one of them shot the general,
then both ran into the darkness."

"Any comment from the President here?" Adams asked.

"Only a brief statement describing the general as a long-
time servant of the people of Sierra Bijimi and saying that
he would be missed."

Murdock took the mike. "Stroh, I'm trying to figure out
where the rest of the SEALs would do us the most good.
Down there in the middle of things, or up here? We have
to go down there anyway for the action. What do you
think?"

"Shorter trip from here to a target. I have some of the
data you need. Not sure if I should read it over the air."

"I figure we can send in the Seahawk once or twice before Kolda starts yelling at you. Want to ship the goods up
by chopper?"

"Sounds good. Hold on, some trouble at the gate."

Murdock waited. Two minutes later, Stroh was back.
"Trouble, big buddy. We've got about five hundred federal
troops at the front gate and a colonel who is demanding to
see the ambassador. Everybody has a gun. Our Marines
have set up a machine gun aimed out the front door at the
gate. If somebody starts shooting, we're not going to stand
a chance."

"Order all of our men not to be the first to fire. Nobody fires a round unless specifically ordered to by you or JG Gardner. The colonel may just want to talk."

"Then why did he bring five hundred guns?"

"Persuasion and insecurity. See what he wants. Keep in touch. We can't give you much support from here."

"I better get down there," Stroh said. "Later."

Sierra City

Don Stroh ran from his room at the rear of the building to the front, and down the steps to the first floor. He passed the machine gun in the entranceway with its ugly muzzle pointing toward the front gate. Ambassador Nance Oberholtzer was halfway to the barrier when Stroh caught up with him.

"What does this guy want?" Stroh asked.

"Not sure. So far I've only heard shouting. He wouldn't violate United State soil by crashing the gate and charging in here, would he?"

"Depends how serious he is, and what orders he got. Maybe as a colonel, he's now in charge of the Army. Keep calm, voice low and serious. You know the routine. The louder he shouts, the softer you talk."

The two men stopped six feet from the metal bars on the eight-foot-high gate.

"You the ambassador?" a man with silver leaves on his shoulders asked.

"Yes, I'm Ambassador Oberholtzer." His voice was controlled, just loud enough for the man to hear.

"The President demands that you come now to his office for an official reprimand."

"Of course, if President Kolda requests that I come to his office for a talk, I'll be more than happy to go." The ambassador paused in a studied ploy. "Did you think you needed five hundred troops to convince me to come?" His voice was soft, his words carefully enunciated without a trace of emotion.

"I do what the President tells me to do. You will come out and get in my car."

"No. Absolutely not. I am the ambassador, not one of

your cowering countrymen. I will drive to the Presidential
Palace in my own car with my honor guards. If you don't
allow me to do this, you will provoke an international incident. You don't need that right now."

He waved at the garage area, and a two-year-old black
Buick rolled out of the yard and toward the gate.

"Back up, make way," Stroh bellowed as the large metal
gate started to roll back on its track. The mass of riflemen
edged backward. Then, at a word from the colonel, they
turned and ran down the street, where they formed up into
columns.

Two armed Marines and Stroh stepped into the car with
the ambassador, and they pulled through the gate, which
closed quickly.

"You've been to see him before?" Stroh asked.

"Three times. Two of the visits I was chewed out for
stopping foreign aid after he stole what we sent him. The
Marines will stay in the lobby. I'll take you with me."

"Moral support?"

"About it. Don't say a word unless he asks you a question."

"Easy."

The car stopped in front of the Presidential Palace, and
they were escorted inside, where the Marines settled down
in chairs and Stroh and Oberholtzer were shown to a couch,
where they sat for thirty minutes before being admitted.

"The old make-him-wait ploy," Oberholtzer said. "I've
used it a time or two myself."

The President's office was large and elaborate, with the
main man's desk at the far side under the nation's flag. The
President did not rise as they walked in. He stared at Stroh.

"Who is this man?"

"My new special assistant. He came in three days ago."

"No matter. I think your Marine guards blew up my
Army camp and killed the commanding general last night."

"Mr. President, may I respond?" Oberholtzer asked. The
man sitting at the desk nodded. "All of our Marines were
in the compound each night this week from dark to daylight. It is our policy, and your suggestion. They had no
hand in the destruction at your Army base, or the death of

the general. From news reports it seemed like dissidents from the Army killed the general. The men were reported to wear your Army's jungle cammy uniforms."

The President leaped to his feet, his face red as he screamed out the words. "No, not my own men. Everyone knows the general was assassinated by foreign agents who used a new kind of ray gun to stun everyone in the area. Then the cowards ran to the car and shot General Assaba. Everyone knows it was foreign agents."

President Kolda leaned forward, balancing on his hands, his face blood-red now; his breath coming in gasps.

"Everyone knows," he said again, and slid into his chair. His hands covered his face a moment. Then he looked up.

"You and your complete embassy staff have twenty-four hours to get out of my country. I am expelling every one of your embassy people. As of six P.M. today, no Sierra Bijimi citizen will be allowed to enter your compound. You're through here. Now get out of my sight."

On the way out to the car, Stroh looked at the ambassador. "Can he do this?"

"Oh, yes, he can. We'll close up the embassy, hire some guards to patrol the walls outside, and scoot over to Zambia until this gets cleared up."

In the car Stroh frowned. "Easy for you diplomats to leave, but what about the SEALs? They don't have diplomatic passports. They don't have any passports at all."

18

As soon as Stroh hit the embassy parking lot, he ran up the steps to the second floor where the SEALs were quartered.

"Listen up," he called. "Moving day. President Kolda has closed down the embassy. You guys and I will be moving up to Camp Freedom as soon as the Skyhawk chopper can get here. I'm on my way to call in the bird now. Kolda is trying to play hardball. He doesn't know about our chopper yet. I'd guess we have about two hours before we fly out of here."

It took him an hour to raise the SATCOM at Camp Freedom.

"Yes, Stroh, this is Camp Freedom."

"Good. At last. Get Murdock."

"Aye, sir. Right away."

It was five minutes before the commander came on the radio.

"Murdock here. What can we do for you, Mr. Stroh?"

"You can get that chopper warmed up and send him down here as quickly as possible. Every U.S. citizen at the embassy has been kicked out of the country. The SEALs and I are coming to pay you a visit. Don't send anyone with the bird except the pilot and copilot. We'll have fourteen bodies to fill it up. Let me know when the bird takes off and his ETA. I'll leave this set on to receive with somebody monitoring it."

"That's a roger. I'm on my way."

Stroh packed his one airline rolling bag and took it down to the front door. He had learned to travel light. Sometimes he had to buy clothes wherever he was, but for him packing was never a problem.

The SEALs were wrapped up and ready to go in thirty minutes. They waited in their rooms, glad for a day off from training. Lieutenant (j.g.) Gardner and Senior Chief Sadler found Stroh in the cafeteria having a cup of coffee. They joined him.

"What will we be doing up at Camp Freedom?" Gardner asked.

"Probably getting in on some of the action," Stroh said. "Not sure just how far my orders go. I'll check with Washington when we hit the camp."

Bill Bradford, who had been baby-sitting the SATCOM, came running into the cafeteria.

"Hey, figured I'd find you in here. Murdock called. The chopper just left. He says it should have a flight time of about fifteen minutes. He said the pilot asked for two red flares on the LZ. It may take him a couple of circles to find us since he doesn't know where the embassy is."

"Everybody into the east parking lot," Gardner said. He took one last gulp of coffee and ran with the others to the second floor to pick up all of his gear.

The SEALs were waiting with their equipment when the Seahawk swept in from the north. It hesitated a moment. Then the pilot must have seen the two red flares. He raced in, slowed, kicked the nose up on the bird, and settled to the ground.

"Mount up, let's move," Gardner bellowed over the sound of the chopper. The SEALs ran to the helicopter in squad formation and climbed onboard.

Stroh had told the ambassador they would be leaving, and he waved at the man, who now stood on the steps. Then Stroh jumped on board, squeezed into a small opening, and at once the bird lifted off. The pilot climbed the little chopper as he slanted away from the center of town to get to the countryside. Then it was a straight run up the river.

Ten minutes later the Skyhawk settled down at the LZ at Camp Freedom, Murdock waited for them.

"About time you guys got here," he barked at the men. "No tents or cots left, but we've got plenty of good soft grass to sleep on. Chow here is good, and we'll get some action. Understand El Presidente didn't take kindly to his top man cashing in his chips."

"Madder than a bumblebee with a boil," Stroh said. "Got so mad he couldn't talk. That's when he threw us out. Whole damn embassy is packing up to fly to Zambia."

Murdock looked over his platoon. "Mahanani, I want you to take your kit over to the leader's tent and look at his arm. He picked up a round last night on the way in. A patrol surprised us with a searchlight in our faces. See how the in-and-out looks."

"Aye, Commander. I'm moving."

"Mojombo wants us to bunk down over in this section. He's not sure now long we'll be here. The word around camp is that we'll be going downstream to the first village about five miles away. The people there have asked for protection by the Loyalist Party. It's the first move to retake the outlying areas and gaining strength."

"When do we get into some action?" Canzoneri asked.

"As soon as we work out some details," Murdock said. "This first move is more important right now. If Mojombo doesn't have the people behind him, his cause will sputter and blow out."

That afternoon, Mojombo met the rest of the SEALs and welcomed them. "You got here just in time to move," he said. "We go downstream about five miles tomorrow morning. Most of the men will be living and eating with the villagers in their homes. This is going to cut down drastically on the supplies we need. We'll pick up that cache of canned food on our way past tomorrow. What we can't take with us, we'll come back for with some carts. So relax, you guys, and enjoy the wonders of the outdoors and nature herself."

That afternoon the soldiers began to take the camp apart. All of the tents came down, but the pole frames would be left. They had four carts that would be pulled and the motorcycle that they'd brought from the President's warehouse. The three SEALs would ride their bikes down as well.

By chow time that evening most of the camp had been dismantled. The word went out that the trek south would begin at 0600. Right after early chow at 0500.

Murdock and Stroh huddled with Mojombo.

"What can we do that will hasten Kolda's departure from office?" Murdock asked.

Mojombo thought about it. "Probably a hit at the police. We hurt the Central Police Station last week, but there are six more around town. The police here are not what you think of as police. They all are soldiers with blue uniforms. They all have the mentality of storm troopers. Some casualties in their ranks would bring cheers from the population. The police are the most hated group in the whole government system."

Gardner grinned. "Colonel, if you would tell us where these facilities are, we could do some work on them while you're getting in solid with the villagers."

Murdock nodded. "It would seem like a good choice. We could take out the buildings and anyone in them with our twenties. It would be a quick and simple hit and then we'd hustle back north."

"Why not use the Seahawk?" Jaybird said. "We could fly to an LZ three or four miles in the country so they wouldn't hear us coming. We chogie in to our targets and do our business, take a hike back to our protected transport, and be back to our grass shack before morning."

Stroh had been listening. He looked at Murdock. "I'd think the commander and Howard would like that chopper idea after they made that thirty-mile hike a couple of nights ago."

"Amen, brother, you have seen the light," Howard said.

"Oh, while I've almost got the floor, we were talking about some prime candidates for a visit," Stroh said. "We have details and locations on four so far. These would be two- or three-man missions strictly on a hit-and-run-like-hell basis."

"Tomorrow is moving day," Murdock said. "After we get situated there, and find a nearby LZ for our Seahawk, we'll get with Mojombo and detail our police targets. Then I want him to look over our four-man hit list to see if he agrees with the ambassador."

The pilot of the chopper and his copilot drifted up to the group. "For you who don't know these gentlemen, the red-head is Josie Halstrom, the Seahawk's pilot," Murdock said. "This must be the copilot."

"Yes sir, sir, Commander. I'm JG Hal Parcells."

"We going to have an LZ down below?" Halstrom asked. "We can lift out a good-sized load of whatever needs to be moved."

Mojombo gave the pilot a high five. "Now why didn't I think of that. Lieutenant? Why don't you and I fly down-stream first thing with daylight and we'll find a good LZ close to the village. As I remember, this one has a soccer field. We could use that. Can we check it out before we take a load down?"

"If you think it's close enough, we might as well take a load as we look," said Halstrom. "Save fuel. I brought extra tanks, but fuel is going to be a problem soon."

"Could you have the other sixty on the destroyer fly in three barrels of juice for you?" Lam asked. "All we'd need would be a hand pump and we could keep you gassed up."

"Good idea. I'll talk to my CO tonight on the chopper radio and set it up for tomorrow afternoon." Halstrom grinned. "Commander, where did you find these guys?"

"Lieutenant, we sifted through half the Navy before we picked our platoon. It's paid off."

They heard cheering, and looked down at the one flat area of the camp. Twenty men were in a hot soccer game.

"Yeah, most popular sport in our country," Mojombo said. "You call it soccer, we call it football."

"Thank God for soccer," Halstrom said. "That field down at the village will be an ideal LZ."

The meeting broke up. Bill Bradford took out his sketch pad and made drawings of the tents, the chow hall, and the soldiers in their new cammies looking stiff and unsure. "Man, I'm getting all this travel and places to sketch, and besides that, I'm getting my SEAL pay to do it. What a deal. I may re-up for about twenty more."

Paul Jefferson tried to get a chess game going, but he couldn't find anyone interested. At last he approached JG Gardner.

"Sir, how about a friendly little game of chess. I hear you played in college."

Gardner grinned. "Hey, you didn't hear that, Jefferson, because I didn't. It was the high school chess team and I was captain. You want black or white?"

In an hour it was dark. The generator had already been packed on the chopper along with most of the heavy kitchen equipment. When darkness hit, the troops went to bed. They had left up the Vice President's tent. He invited Murdock in to use the other cot. Murdock at first declined, then thinking about another night on the hard ground convinced him and he took it. He thought they might talk a while, but as soon as the VP hit his bunk he was asleep, snoring softly.

The next morning chow was simple, and then the move began. Murdock had never seen such mass confusion. There was no beach-master to move groups and items in an orderly process. The tents had been carefully folded and tied to ten-foot poles, and men shouldered each end of the poles and headed down the trail. Other soldiers carried goods in slings across their backs. Some had sacks and baskets filled with goods. Several shouldered cases of canned goods.

The chopper took off at first light, and and was back thirty minutes later empty and ready for a new load. Mojombo had stayed at the new location to talk to the people. He soon found twenty homes that would take two soldiers each. Two SEALs wound up on a pole carrying a tent. Murdock, Jaybird, and Howard rode their motorcycles down to the soccer field, then grabbed a chopper ride back up with ten others to make a second trip.

Three horse-pulled carts came down the trail from where Mojombo and his men had hidden the rest of the food they · took from the President's warehouse. It was stacked in a pile inside one of the tents that had been put up using freshly cut poles from the jungle.

Loads were potluck. Men took whatever they wanted to carry. Murdock and Jaybird grabbed twenty-four-can cases of vegetables and headed down the trail. They met fifty men coming back up for another load.

By afternoon everything had been transferred. A dozen tents were set up around the edge of the soccer field so there was still room for a game. Men had been assigned to the homes, and the rest took to their bunks in the tents. The SEALs had tents now too, and cots.

"We going out tonight?" Jaybird asked.

"Haven't you had enough action for one day?" Murdock asked.

"Hell, no. Just getting warmed up. How about us hitting two cop stations at the same time. One squad on each one. We could ask Mojombo where two of them are the closest together."

Murdock had been feeling uneasy, as if the SEALs were a fifth wheel here. "Check with the chopper pilot and see how his fuel is. He said he'd get in fuel via the other bird tomorrow. Then we'll decide."

Murdock went to talk to Mojombo. He was hosting a group of local village leaders. They were delighted to meet one of the SEALs. When Murdock found a minute, he asked Mojombo about two police stations near each other that they could hit at the same time.

"Yes, there are two. I'll get back with you in about an hour. Still plenty of time. I need to do some fence-mending here about our using some of the soccer field."

In two hours it was set. The whole platoon would jam into the chopper for the quick flight. The targets were on the south side of the city, so they would fly around it and then come back. They would need to take two local men to guide them to the right spots.

Murdock called the SEALs together and told them it was a go for that night. They would leave just after 2300. "Anybody feeling the effects of the native food? Any diarrhea, upset stomachs, or vomiting?"

Tracy Donegan held up his hand. "Been heaving for the past two hours. Don't know why. Doc gave me some pills."

"Anyone else?" No one else responded. "Okay, you

guys. We need to take two guides with us and that over-loads the bird. So Donegan and Howard will keep the campfires burning for us tonight. Howard, you had enough work the other night.

"Get a nap if you want one. We'll suit up with all weapons and normal ammo and load out of the LZ at 2300. Any questions?"

"We have guns free on the police, or just the building?"

"Mojombo says the police are only soldiers in blue uniforms and most of them are sadistic bastards. The population hates the cops. Yes, we have open season on police in blue uniforms." There were no more questions. "Check your squads and I'll see you at 2250 at the LZ."

The Skyhawk had plenty of fuel. The pilot said they still had just a little over half their load, which would be good for about 250 miles. Murdock had met the two guides earlier and assigned one to each squad. His man was named Tehabo, and he had been a taxi driver in Sierra City up to a year ago.

"I could find that police station blindfolded and with one leg broken," Tahabo said. He spoke good English along with a native tongue.

They were crammed into the Seahawk like overlapping feathers on a hawk's wing, but eager to get on to the job. It wouldn't be more than a twenty-minute flight, the pilot assured them. It took twenty-two minutes. They landed at the midpoint between the two targets. Each squad formed up, and the guides moved out through the fields headed for the edges of the city, and then into the streets where the police stations were situated.

Murdock's man set a steady pace, and the SEALs followed him. It was an hour-and-a-half hike into the city and to the alley across from the police station. Lam went up to the end of the alley in the heavy shadows and did a quick recon. He used his radio.

"Nobody outside. Flag over the second story. Building looks like wood and it's about fifty feet square, maybe less. Windows across the second story. Heavy door leading inside. What I'd guess are no-parking signs around the front.

No vehicles there. Hold it. A black unmarked sedan just pulled up. Two men in blue uniforms with pistols on their hips left the car and went inside. They didn't use a key or knock, just opened the door and walked in."

"Any people on the street?" Murdock asked.

"Negative."

"Can you walk around to one side of the building and get a picture of it from there? Any cover that direction?"

"A pair of old trucks half a block down. I'll waltz along like I belong here. I have a Bull Pup and could use it on those second-story windows if they have any down the side."

"Wait. I'm sending Jaybird down with his MP-5 to go with you. Let me know when you're in place. Wait for an order to fire."

Jaybird lifted off the dirt and ran to the end of the alley. He and Lam vanished around the corner. "We're moving up," Murdock told the rest of his squad. The alley was twenty feet wide. Murdock put one Bull Pup on each side, and the rest of the men in between.

They waited.

Two men in blue uniforms came out of the police station, got into the car, and drove away.

"We missed those two," Ken Ching said on the net.

"Maybe they'll be back," Vinnie Van Dyke said.

"Skipper," Lam said on the radio. "We're in place. Four windows back here. Ready when you are, C.B."

Murdock grinned. "Let's get the party going. Two rounds each Bull Pups into the windows, all HEs. Fire when ready."

Murdock and Bill Bradford angled their weapons at the two windows on the front of the police station and fired. They saw the immediate effect. One exploding 20mm round went through a window; the other blasted beside the second glass pane and smashed a three-foot section of wall inward. They both fired again. These rounds both went inside and exploded. Murdock heard the other rounds going off at the side.

"One round WP each weapon," Murdock said. The fast-burning white phosphorus shells hit inside the structure, and moments later they could see smoke coming out of the building.

"Watch for rats off the sinking ship," Murdock said. "Only blue uniforms. No civilians. I've got two." He let the men between the 20mm guns take out the runners. Two died at the edge of the sidewalk. A third made it to the side of the building before he screamed and dove to the concrete.

"We've got two window jumpers," Jaybird said. "When they land they are gonna be toast."

Murdock heard a siren in the distance. "Chicks come home," Murdock said. "All hold fire. Move it, Jaybird."

Thirty seconds later the two SEALs raced down the sidewalk and into the alley. "Let's get out of here," Murdock said. "Tehabo, can you find that spot where the chopper let us off?"

"Easy," he said, and started jogging back down the alley. The siren sounds increased until it seemed like a dozen patrol cars were heading toward them. They were halfway up the alley toward the next street when Tehabo yelled, "Down!" The SEALs hit the deck and Murdock stared at a Sierra City police car that had driven into the alley. Its siren whined to a sudden stop and its bright lights turned the alley into a daytime shooting gallery with Alpha Squad the targets of choice.

19

Nobody had to give an order. The fraction of a second after the SEALs hit the ground, their weapons were up spitting lead at the car. The barrage of shots shattered the headlights in a second and a half, and the windshield at almost the same time. In the darkness the SEALs leaped to their feet and kept firing as they charged forward.

The driver and anyone inside the car must have been so surprised to see seven armed men coming at them when their headlights first hit them that they didn't reach for weapons. Or if they they did, they were too late.

In ten seconds the SEALs had charged past the dead in the car and sprinted for the end of the alley. There they checked outside, saw the street clear, and ran across it and down half a block, then straight ahead for two more blocks, before they slowed and stopped in some deep shadows.

"That was a surprise," Murdock said softly on the net. "Any casualties?" No one spoke. "Okay, you guys, we better be moving. Going to be all sorts of cops in this area in a few minutes. Which way to our magic carpet, Tahabo?"

The man stood there with glazed eyes, his breath ragged, his hands holding the MP-5 like he would never let go of it.

"Tahabo? Snap out of it, Tahabo. We're in the clear, they didn't even get a shot off." Murdock scowled. Even in the faint light of a street lamp half a block away, Murdock could see the man was in shock. Murdock slapped him hard on the cheek. His head jolted to the side and then back.

"Oh, God. Oh, God. Did you see them? They had us dead, all of us dead. Oh, God. What happened?"

Murdock shook him. Tahabo moved his head, then turned toward Murdock. "How did we get out? I remember the lights nailing us in that narrow alley. I thought I was going to die right there."

"We shot before they did. You did too. We ran past them and out. We made it. You're not dead, believe me."

The guide took a deep breath. "My tooth still hurts, so I guess I'm not dead."

"We need you to take us back to the chopper pad," Murdock said.

"Oh, yes. Right. Sorry. Yes, I know this area. We came through here. We need to work to the left out of here."

"You ready to move?"

"Yes, sir."

"Let's go."

Tahabo looked up the block, then the other way, then headed straight south down a street, which soon turned into a trail. They went across two fields, then came to a pair of trees at the edge of a field.

"This is where we got off," Tahabo said. "See the two trees? Not many in fields out here."

"Time?" Murdock asked.

"0112, Skipper," Jaybird said.

"Was he going to stay here or come back?" Lam asked.

"Supposed to stay here unless he saw trouble," Murdock said. "Now we have no timetable. Can he find this place again?"

"Let me take Tehabo and scout down toward the other target," Lam said. "If we find Bravo, we come right back here. Then we'll try a couple of flares to attract our flyboy's attention."

"Go," Murdock said.

The rest of the SEALs flaked out in the grass. Some of them pulled magazines from their weapons and put in fresh ones, then charged a round into the chamber to be ready.

"Take it easy," Murdock said. "We may be here a while."

It was just over an hour before Lam gave a bobwhite call and came in leading Bravo. They carried one man. Murdock ran to meet them, and took over carrying Frank Victor.

"He got cut up pretty bad, Skipper," Mahanani said. "They were waiting for us outside, caught us setting up. We've got three wounded. The other two not so bad."

"How is Victor?"

"He took a round in his chest and one in his neck. The neck shot was lucky, went between the carotid and the jugular and missed his spine. Bled like a stuck shoat. Got it stopped. Worried about his chest. He can't walk. Might be bleeding inside."

They eased Victor off at the assembly point and Mahanani worked on him again.

"Jaybird, one red flare in the air, now," Murdock said.

Gardner came up with his arm in a sling. "Bastards caught us setting up," Gardner said. "We beat them back, then burned down their fucking building. We must have nailed about ten of the blue shirts. Carrying Victor slowed us down."

"How's the arm?" Murdock asked.

"Not bad. Mahanani thought the bone might be broken. Sling and splint just precautions."

"You did good, Gardner. You brought back your squad and you burned down your target. Now if that fucking chopper would get here . . ."

When the red flare burst high overhead, the SEALs went motionless. It drifted in a gentle breeze away from town. When its twenty long seconds were over, it sputtered and the sky went dark again.

Murdock turned to Lam. "Hear anything?"

The scout with the best ears in the platoon shook his head.

"If he saw it we should get some sound by now. Wait five minutes, Jaybird, then one more red flare."

Murdock waited. He turned, but couldn't see Bradford. He used the radio. "Bradford, you have that SATCOM?"

"Aye, sir. Strapped on my back like a second damn skin."

"Good. If that chopper doesn't show up, we'll have to

try to contact Stroh. I told him to keep his set on receive while we're out on a mission just in case."

The second red flare jolted into the air, burst, and floated slowly toward the ground on its small parachute.

It drifted faster this time, and was halfway down when Lam used his Motorola. "Yes, Cap, I've got some sound. A chopper for damned sure, coming from the west. What's it doing out there?"

"You sure, Lam?"

"I'd bet my last sputnik on it."

"Sputnik isn't money," Fernandez said.

"So it won't cost me much. He's headed this way. You want a ground flare, Skipper?"

"Wait until he's closer. Any way to ID him?"

"Not a one, other than he should be the only helicopter in the whole nation right now."

They waited. Soon they all could hear the *whup-whup-whup* of the rotor blades as the craft moved toward them.

"Light sticks," Murdock said. The SEALs took out the plastic tubes with chemicals in them, broke the seals inside, and the mixed chemicals gave off a pink or green light. They held the cool sticks high over their heads.

"He's turning our way, not chasing the flare," Lam said.

Two minutes later the chopper slanted over the light sticks, did a fast turn, and set down in the open field thirty yards from the troops.

Gardner carried Victor on his back. The SEALs stepped on board and made room to lay Victor on the floor. Mahanani shook his head when Murdock looked at him.

"Not the best, Skipper. He's unconscious. Has lost a lot of blood. He needs a doctor and a hospital."

Murdock went forward and talked with the pilot.

"Halstrom, how far to your destroyer?"

"From here about two-fifteen."

"You have a doctor on board?"

"Yes, sir. Three of them, and a small operating room."

"How close is the carrier?"

"She's about ten miles to sea from us."

"You have juice enough to reach the carrier?"

"Yes, sir."

"Let's get off here and head directly for the carrier. Tell them we're bringing in a wounded man, shot in the chest and the neck. He's unconscious, breathing is ragged. Pulse is slow and weak. Let's move, Lieutenant."

When they were in the air, the copilot called the carrier and gave his report the way Murdock had told him. The response came on earphones, and he turned to Murdock.

"We have clearance for a direct flight. Our time to the carrier deck is eighty-eight minutes. We can cut that some, but we're pretty heavily loaded. Tell the men to hang on, we're moving up to four thousand."

Murdock told the men where they were going.

"Victor woke up for a minute, said it hurt like hell, then passed out again," the medic said. "His pulse is a little stronger now and his breathing is better. An hour and a half. Damn. Wish we could do better. He's got a chance of making it."

Murdock went back to the pilots. The copilot turned to him. "Need to tell you why we weren't there when you got back. We stayed on the ground for a half hour. Then a jeep or something with a searchlight came looking for us. We lifted off and led him off to the west, where we quickly lost him. Then we worked back a couple of miles at a time watching for a flare. We figured you had some. How many did you fire?"

"Two. You must have been close enough to see the second one. Glad you got here. Can you go to max cruise and still have enough fuel to get to the carrier?"

Halstrom nodded. "We're on forty-nine percent now. We can go at least halfway on max. That should cut our time down by ten minutes."

"Do it. That ten minutes could save my man's life."

They landed on the carrier after a flight of seventy-two minutes. A dozen men waited with a gurney, and they ran to the chopper before the blades stopped spinning. SEALs dropped out of the craft to make way for the medics. They lifted Victor gently onto the gurney, and a doctor began examining him as they rolled toward some doors. A commander poked his head in the side door of the chopper. "SEALs?"

"Yes, sir," Murdock said. "Can you bunk these men down for the night? Then we'd like to get this bird refueled and ready to take off about 0900. I'd like to go to the hospital and be with my man."

The officer pointed at a sailor nearby. "Take the commander to the hospital."

They caught up with the gurney at an elevator, and Murdock saw the doctor taking Victor's vitals as they went into the lift.

Two hours and three cups of coffee later, Murdock still waited in a small compartment off the operating rooms. He stood and paced the area again, and then looked up as a man in scrubs and a mask came out of the OR.

"Commander?"

"Yes, how is my boy?"

"He's in pretty bad shape, but he's past the critical stage and he's going to make it, unless something we can't see now develops. The round he took in the chest shattered on a bone and did all sorts of damage. One small fragment went into his heart. We retrieved that with no real damage. His lungs caught most of it. But we're satisfied with what we did in there. The round to his throat was the easiest. It went through the fleshy part of the neck, missing the vital veins and arteries and his spinal column. We'll need to keep him here for at least two weeks. You from San Diego?"

"Yes, sir."

"Then when he's ready to travel, we'll send him by air to Balboa Hospital."

"Thank you, Doctor."

"Entirely welcome." He paused. "You're in Sierra Bijimi?"

"Yes, sir."

"We don't get many bullet wounds these days. We patched up two of your other men as well. A JG Gardner with a shot arm and an Omar Rafii. He had a grenade fragment in his leg. Dug it out and he's on light duty for a week. Now, you need a bunk. I'll have one of the men find you some quarters for the night."

"One more thing, Doctor. I need to talk to your communications people. How do I do that?"

The doctor led him to a phone and dialed.

"Yes, sir, Communications," came over the phone.

"This is Lieutenant Commander Murdock. Do you have SATCOM frequencies?"

"Sir, that would be the portable SATCOM units?"

"Yes. Can you send and receive to them?"

"If we had the right frequencies."

Murdock gave him the numbers. "I just arrived on board on a medical emergency for one of my men. I need to report in to my CIA control on Sierra Bijimi where we are. Use that frequency and call for Don Stroh. Tell him we're on board, all of us, and we have one serious wounded but he's going to make it."

"Sir, I should have some authorization."

"Sailor, we're the reason your whole damn task force came all the way down here. I'm sure if you want to wake up the captain, he can verify that I'm authorized to use the SATCOM frequencies. Why don't you just go ahead and try to contact Stroh? I'll stay on this phone while you try."

"Yes, sir. I'll try that. If I get burned I'm going to call on you for some backup."

"I'll be there, Sailor. Give Don Stroh a call."

Murdock waited. He checked his watch. It took almost five minutes. Then the sailor was back on the line.

"Yes, sir, I made contact and gave him your message. He said he can get to sleep now. He said he'll see you tomorrow, or later today. He was a little sleepy, sir."

"Good. I'll pass along a commendation to your boss. Right now I'm going to try to find a bunk."

"Good night, sir."

By that time it was 0528, and Murdock took an offered empty hospital room and dove onto the bed. He didn't even take his boots off.

A nurse awoke him at 0900, and he growled at her.

"Commander, did you know that you're officially lost? Nobody on board knew where you were. Lieutenant Gardner finally tracked you down. He says he's scheduled a flight for 1300 and figures you and the men need another three hours of sleep. Shall I get you up at 1200?"

Murdock saw someone had spread a blanket over him. He tried to get his eyes open. They refused.

"Yes, ma'am, 1200 will be fine." He was asleep again before she shut the door.

Murdock woke up by himself at 1130. Washed up, combed his hair, and had a quick breakfast at the dirty shirt mess. Then he tried to find his men. He didn't even know who to ask. He shrugged and called the ship's captain. He got a full commander, who laughed at Murdock's question.

"You want to know where your fourteen SEALs and two Sierra Bijimi nationals are?"

"Yes, sir. We came in about 0300 and they were bunked down somewhere."

"Commander, give me five minutes and I'll find them. Call me back."

"Aye, aye, sir."

Murdock hung up and had another cup of coffee. He called back after four minutes by his countdown watch.

"Commander, we didn't lose them after all. They were tucked into some transient bunks. Right now they are all on the flight deck waiting for you for their 1300 flight time in a Seahawk."

"Thanks, sir, I appreciate it." He went into the corridor, nailed the first enlisted man he saw, and had him act as a guide to take him to the flight deck. There a white shirt took him in tow and walked him down the long deck to the chopper operations center, where he found Third Platoon chomping away on box lunches.

"Saved you one," Senior Chief Sadler said. "Did you know that you've been lost?"

20

Sierra Bijimi
Village of Tinglat

The Seahawk arrived at the new village before noon, and Mahanani checked out the two wounded. JG Gardner's right arm was responding to the treatment. The carrier doctors had said the bone had not been damaged, and had taken off the splint. It should heal completely in two to three weeks. Until then, no rope-climbing or arm exercises like push-ups or pull-ups. Omar Rafii's shrapnel wound in the leg was not serious. He limped a little, but could keep up on anything but a twenty-mile hike.

Mojombo had been organizing the village. It now had a council and a mayor. They sent a delegation with Mojombo and six soldiers to the next village downstream, Salal, where there were over two thousand people. It was another ten miles downstream where a good-sized river had carved out a small valley used for growing vegetables. Mojombo would be back by nightfall.

"What are we going to do?" Senior Chief Sadler asked.

Murdock motioned to Vinnie Van Dyke. "Go find our guide from last night, Tehabo. Tell him to hang with us from now on."

"What will we do?" Sadler asked again. "Plan out the next hit on a police station? If we do it, we'll be ready."

"Next time we need to keep the chopper farther from the city," JG Gardner said. "Somebody heard it and reported it. The nearest police station was ready. Almost cost us a KIA."

"Agree," Murdock said. "When Tehabo gets here we'll

figure out the next two stations to hit. Until then double-check and clean your weapons and work over your gear. After we have some native chow, we'll take a hike. Anybody having trouble with the food? We can always go to MREs."

"What's not to like?" Jaybird asked. "Lots of vegetables, some chicken, and now and then some delicious dog roast."

Three of the SEALs pretended to throw up.

The Vice President and Stroh joined the group. "Nothing new from Washington," the Veep said. "Not a thing the U.S. can do on the demands until the U.N. acts, and they haven't even scheduled an emergency meeting on it. The kidnapping and demands may be put down to public relations and attracting worldwide coverage for Mojombo's cause."

"What kind of defense has Mojombo put up around here?" Murdock asked.

Stroh shook his head. "Not much. He figures his outposts downriver will be able to give adequate warning. Looks like his plan is to fade into the jungle with his fighting men. He says not even the federal Army would slaughter the villagers."

"He does have outposts down the river trail then?" Murdock asked.

Tehabo had arrived with Van Dyke, and he spoke up. "Yes, sir, Commander. We have four levels of lookouts down the trail almost to the ten-mile dock."

"Good, then I don't see any problem doing some conditioning work with my men."

After noon chow, the SEALs took an hour break. Then Gardner put them into squad formations and took them into the valley created by the tributary to the Amunbo River. The flat land was half a mile wide and laced with small plots filled with growing and harvested crops. Murdock brought up the rear. He wanted to watch Gardner in action with the men. He still had to prove himself to them. Working with them with his wounded arm would be a plus.

It was just after 1500 when Murdock and the men heard the first shots. They came from the village. The SEALs turned and raced down a trail toward the village. Murdock figured they were two miles away. The shooting continued from Tinglat, then tapered off. Murdock was more worried when the quiet settled in. Lam charged ahead of the pack to report on the situation. A quarter mile from the village, Gardner put the SEALs into the brush and waited for Lam's radio recon report. It came quickly.

"Sir. The village is quiet. There is some wailing, which must mean dead villagers. I see no government troops. Moving in closer. People are coming out of the jungle and out of the huts and houses. Two buildings are burning and there's no way to douse the fire. I'd say the bad guys have left. I don't see any of the Loyalist troops."

The SEALs charged into the village at a run. The mayor came out with tears streaming down his face.

"They attacked without warning," he said. "They killed three men in the open, then searched every building. They found the two Americans and tied their hands behind them and hustled them downriver."

"They took the Vice President and Don Stroh?"

"Yes, both unhurt, but both gone."

"How big a force?" Gardner asked.

"Not large, maybe thirty."

"We're going after them," Murdock said. "If they harm the Vice President, all of us might as well resign from the Navy and start digging ditches. Let's move. Alpha out front. We're on double time down the trail. Lam, sprint out front a quarter and keep your eyes on."

Within a minute the SEALs had formed up and jogged out of the village and down the jungle trail along the river. It wasn't wide enough for side by side, so they went single file with five yards between them.

Lam moved out a half mile ahead, then slowed. He worked a gentle jog that would eat up six miles an hour. He had every sense on top alert. Every fifty yards he stopped and listened. The fourth time, he heard a rifle or machine-gun bolt slam forward somewhere ahead. He slowed and worked into the jungle out of sight, then moved forward without making a sound. It took him ten minutes to spot the rear guard. Three of them and a machine gun set up to command fifty yards of open trail.

"Skipper, we've got a rear guard. I've got my twenty. Should I wipe them out?"

"That's a go, Lam. One round should do it. How far ahead are you?"

"In front of you probably less than a half mile. I've lost ten minutes moving up, so you're closer now. No sound of the main body."

"Do it, Lam."

Lam moved a small branch, leveled in the 20mm sights, and triggered the weapon. From thirty yards the round exploded on target at almost at the same time the report came. Two of the federal soldiers were blown into the air, their bodies laced with shrapnel from the twenty. The third man sat on the bank of the river a moment, then pivoted over and slid into the river without a splash. He sank immediately.

"All clear," Lam reported. "I'm moving out at a six-mile trot."

"Don't get too far ahead of us. We're moving faster now. Watch it."

Lam kept up his pace, his eyes and ears straining to pick up any sound out of the ordinary. He blocked out the calls of native birds, dulled the buzz of insects, and ignored the wind whispering through the trees. His total concentration was downtrail for any foreign sound whatever.

He went another mile before he sensed the danger. He stepped into the brush and behind a large tree just before a machine gun chattered off twelve rounds that slammed into the tree and cut brush and leaves from the vines and brush around him. He dropped to the ground and slithered deeper into the jungle, then worked ahead slowly.

"Found another MG," Lam said on the Motorola. "This time they saw me first, but I avoided their hot lead. I'm working downstream toward them. Must be camouflaged well and have a good field of fire. Later."

It took him twenty minutes to probe downstream. Twice he edged up to the trail itself without exposing himself. On the third look he saw the target. Three soldiers with a machine gun poking out over a fallen tree. The men behind it had total cover and concealment from the front. Only the muzzle of the MG and the gunner's head showed over the tree.

Lam was thirty yards away. He could take out the man behind the MG. Or he could put an airburst into the tree over the federal soldiers' heads. Would an airburst work this close? He wasn't sure. No way he could take down all three of them silently. He wasn't that much of a knife man.

Lam settled in and aimed at the tree a dozen feet over their heads. He checked his aim again, and fired. As soon as the Bull Pup went off, he rolled away from the edge of the trail and crawled deeper into the woods.

He heard no reaction from the machine gunners. Slowly he worked back to the trail and peered around a large tree trunk. The MG still rested on top of the log. He could see no one behind it. He hurried through the brushy jungle until he could see behind the fallen tree without exposing himself. Without a sound he lifted and looked over some brush at the fallen tree.

Two men lay sprawled on the ground. A third man tried to lift his arm, then let it drop. He shook his head and tried to stand. He fell face-down in the jungle floor. Lam watched him for five minutes. He didn't move. Lam rushed into the spot and checked all three. Dead now. He took the MG and threw it into the brush, then settled down and called Murdock.

"One more MG cleared," he said. "You all can come on down."

"Moving," Murdock said.

"I'm back to checking down front."

Lam went to the trail and listened. Nothing. He moved slower now, wondering if the federals had continued to hike toward home, or if they had slowed or even set up another ambush. They had to know someone was following them. The MG rounds and then the two 20mm shots would tell them that much. If they were listening.

"If you catch them, Lam, remember we can't fire into the group. We don't know if Stroh and the Vice President are with them or if they took them down by boat. Caution."

"Roger that."

He slowed again. Lam was almost at the point where the

trail widened into a wagon-sized road. He paused in the brush checking it out. Something didn't seem right. What was it?

He grinned. Yes. No birds calling or singing, no insects chirping. Too many men around. He could see smoke coming from the next village's cooking fires, but they were a mile away. Where were the soldiers? He sectioned the scene before him, both sides of the trail, all the way to the river, twenty yards. Nobody.

Unless they were as good as the SEALs.

Where were they?

He faded into the jungle more and hit his Motorola. "Cap, some trouble up here. Too damn quiet. They must have laid a grand ambush. Suggestions?"

"Let's ambush the ambush," Gardner said. "Lam, you hold there and keep the major ambush locale under observation so they don't move it. Alpha can join you. Bravo will go into the green a quarter mile, go around your position, come back to the trail well beyond the federals, and move up until we find them. Then we hit them from both sides at once. Skipper, what do you think?"

"Yes, let's do it. Time element?"

"Cap, you're probably about a half mile behind me on the trail," said Lam. "This jungle is the pits. It'll take the JG an hour to circle around a quarter and come up behind them. He'll need to be a mile downstream from me. He should come about to the next village, and cut for the trail."

"Roger that, Lam. We're moving."

Lam waited.

An hour later Lam had faded back twenty yards from his OP and watched for Alpha. Murdock materialized beside him without a sound, and Lam almost shot him.

"Damn, Skipper, you're getting good," he whispered. "We move twenty straight ahead but keep the men in the woods. The JG has had an hour and twenty by now. He should be in position."

"He isn't," the Motorola chirped. "We're at the trail well downstream from them. Ran into some nasty vines. We'll move up cautiously and watch for any sign of the ambush.

They won't be so careful on this side. Give me ten."

Another wait.

"Yes, now this is better," Gardner said. "We're in position. I have an officer and two men with their boots off and wading in the edge of the river. Their weapons are on the bank, if you can believe. We're taking them out with silenced shots, then moving up until we can see somebody else."

"Good, JG." Murdock said. "When we start our little party, I want everyone on the jungle side of the trail so we don't shoot each other. Copy?"

"Roger that, Commander. Who makes first contact?"

"After your threesome in the river, I'd guess that we should. Maybe bug them out back toward you."

"Copy that, Commander. We're ready to begin."

There was dead air. Murdock looked at Lam, who shrugged.

"Sometimes it takes a minute or two."

They heard nothing from downstream. Then the Motorola came on. "Three down and dead. We're moving up cautiously. Can't be more than a hundred yards from you. Fernandez is on point. We're all on the side of the trail away from the river. Fernandez just froze."

"Hold there. We'll put some twenties into the area that looks like it could be their positions. Hold. Everyone fire into the area we pinpointed," Murdock said. "Twenties, I want two airbursts in those trees just over the trail. Do it now."

Alpha Squad's eight guns spat out lead. The twenties barked and then the airbursts exploded. A few seconds later Murdock saw two cammy-clad soldiers jump away from a tree near the trail and race downstream. They were around a bend in the trail almost at once. Two more federals tried to run for it, but were cut down by MP-5 rounds. Vinnie Van Dyke had set up his machine gun, and was puncturing every hiding spot he could find with the NATO 7.62 rounds.

Murdock heard weapons firing from down the trail. Now he saw that the bend in the trail meant there could be no danger from friendly fire.

"Hold your fire," he said into the Motorola. The wave of hot led stopped in a second. "Ching, Jaybird, check them out. Be careful."

The two SEALs slipped from tree to tree until they were behind where the ambush had been staged. Jaybird fired three rounds from an MP-5, and then all was quiet.

"We've got eight down and dirty. No survivors. We take back the weapons?"

"Roger that, Jaybird. Gardner, what happened?"

"We met four trying to escape this way. They are down and out. We're collecting weapons and ammo. Seven on this side. The rest of the force must have left these here as a final blocking force. We found some tire tracks down about a hundred. Looks like they were met by at least three vehicles. The two captives must be in Sierra City by now."

"What happened to Mojombo's lookouts?" Murdock asked.

"We found two bodies down here that had been tortured and then took a bullet in the back of the head. Probably two of the outpost guys."

"The others are probably in the jungle somewhere," Senior Chief Sadler said.

"Let's clean up the weapons and ammo and get moving. Meet us here, JG."

"Roger that."

For Murdock it was a long walk home. He had to report to Washington, D.C., that Stroh and the Vice President had been captured by the federal troops. He couldn't decide how to tell what had happened. In the end, he forgot about strategy. He'd just tell it the way it was.

Mojombo was not back from his political campaign when Murdock and his men arrived back at Tinglat. The mayor came out and welcomed them. They put the stack of enemy weapons in front of Mojombo's tent. The mayor grinned when Murdock told him about the federal troops that had died.

"How did they strike so fast with the Loyalist soldiers here?" Murdock asked.

"Almost all of the soldiers were on a training hike up the trail," the mayor said. "Mojombo told Lieutenant Gabu to work them hard. All gone but three injured ones."

"I thought Mojombo had security out."

"He did, but the federal soldiers must have killed them. It is a sad day. We have found two more dead. They killed five men in our village."

"I just hope that they didn't take the SATCOM," Murdock said. "Then they could listen in on our broadcasts." Murdock found one SATCOM in the leader's tent and another one in Stroh's tent. Murdock had two of his own. He called Bradford to set up the SATCOM and aim the dish antenna. When it beeped, he picked up the handset and made the call.

"D.C., this is Murdock."

There was no immediate response. He made the call again and on the second try, he made contact.

"Murdock, this is Don Stroh's friend."

"I have some bad news. Don and the Vice President have been captured during a military attack on a village north of Sierra City. It came as a complete surprise. We had no idea the military knew that the Mojombo forces had moved south ten miles. We followed them, but they put up rearguard actions until the captured men were taken into the city. We don't know where they are. But we're sure that the Sierra Bijimi federal troops captured them."

"This is what we have been afraid of. Any way to get them back?"

"We're working on it. Might take some time. You have no diplomatic contact in Sierra City. Who do you protest through?"

"I'm not sure. I'll let State take care of that. Stand by while I spread the word. Keep your SATCOM on at all times. We'll figure out something and send you some orders. This is going to cause a crisis situation back here."

"Yes, sir."

"I'll call you back."

Murdock took Sadler, Lam, Jaybird, Gardner, and Miguel Fernandez to a meeting at his tent. "You know the problem. We're going to get orders in a few hours to go into the city and get the men back, especially the Vice President. I want suggestions how we do that."

JG Gardner spoke first. "Your guide the other night, Tehabo, knows the town well. I'd put him on one of our motorcycles and send him into town to use his contacts to find out where the men are being held. It can't be the Army base. Maybe the Government Building, a locked basement room perhaps."

"I like it," Jaybird said. "Only, let's send in at least two men in case one gets compromised or captured. One of the Loyalist troopers or somebody from this village."

"A villager would never have enough money to buy a motorcycle," Fernandez said. "Send in two Loyalist men. In the meantime we can stir up the pot by taking out two more police stations. Keep them on the run."

Murdock pointed at Jaybird. "The Loyalist troops are back from training. Find Tehabo and get him over here. Have him pick out another man who can ride a motorcycle and can do some nosing around in town without getting shot." Jaybird left at once on a jog toward the Loyalist troops' tents.

"We'll use Gardner's Loyalist trooper guide for the next police station, but let's just do one. I don't like the idea of splitting up our men for what could be a heavy firefight. Fernandez, go find the guide you used the other night. Bring him back here. Tell him he'll get some extra pay for his help."

Murdock looked back at the three men left. "Any more ideas about finding the Veep?"

"My guess would be he's in the Government Building," Lam said. "It must have some secure rooms in there."

The SATCOM radio sounded. Bradford gave the handset to Murdock.

"Murdock, this is the office of the President calling. I'm Sage Billings, Chief of Staff. Are you there?"

"Yes, Mr. Billings. We read you loud and clear."

"Good. We've had an emergency meeting here and everyone is upset about this development. We thought you had better protection for the two men. Now to cases. Your orders are to go into Sierra City, find the two men who are held captive, and bring them back under U.S. control. Tie them up if you have to and put them on the chopper and fly them out to the aircraft carrier just offshore."

21

"Roger that, Mr. Billings. We're working on plans now to find where the men are being held. It may take us a day or two to find them. Then we'll figure out how to extract them. Remember that down here the federal troop strength is a little over four thousand men."

"I hear you, Murdock. The bottom line is the President wants Adams out of their clutches and onto that carrier where he'll be safe."

"Roger that, Mr. Billings. We'll keep you informed."

Murdock put down the handset and turned to his men. "Now it's official. We get them out of there as fast as we can. First we get the two men off on their motorcycles. Gardner, you coordinate a hit at the next police station tonight. We'll leave at 0100. Cover all the bases. Now where are those motorcycle guys?"

Jaybird brought his two men back. "You both can ride the motorcycles we have?" They nodded. "Did Jaybird tell you what we want you to do? You'll be spies in the enemy camp. You'll have to find federal troop hats; otherwise your uniforms are the same as theirs. Look for special guards, lots of guards. Check out the Government Building if you can. We suspect they might be holding the two men in there. Any questions?"

"Do we take our weapons?"

"Do federal troops around the city carry weapons?"

"No, sir, usually not," Tehabo said.

"Then keep only concealed weapons. Be as inconspicuous as possible. Don't drink anything, don't get in a fight,

and don't challenge anyone. Move with confidence but not
like you're a spy. Okay?"

"Okay," Tehabo said. "We will work together since
many of the federal troops work in pairs around the city."

Murdock dug into a case in his tent and brought back
two stacks of dagnar bills. "You may need some money.
Act as any other pair of soldiers would. But no drinking.
Now, get on your bikes and get out of here. Oh, it might
be good to ride round the outskirts of town and come in
from the south."

The men saluted smartly, turned, and hurried to the motorcycles.

Gardner came back and sat on the grass outside Murdock's tent. "We have our target. The guide is here and
ready to go. We have alerted Lieutenant Halstrom, the pilot.
They will have the bird ready to fly at 0100. We're working
on resupply of ammunition now. Most of our men are down
a little. We'll get up to full normal load after I talk with
the sergeant in charge of the armory tent. Right after chow
I'm putting the men down for a five-hour sleep period. We
need to be awake and ready for anything tonight. I expect
there will be outside lookouts at all of the police stations."

Murdock nodded. "Good work, Gardner. Give us a year
and we'll rub that JG off your rank."

"That would be good, Commander. My father has been
chiding me about that."

"He's the admiral?"

"Yes, sir, two stars. He expects me to get three."

"Bummer."

As they talked, Mojombo came into camp with his ten
men. They heard about the raid on the village as they arrived, and Mojombo came directly to Murdock.

"It's true?"

"Afraid so. The SEALs were on a march up the valley,
and your men were on a training run up the trail north. The
federals hit us at exactly the wrong time. I'm afraid they
killed your outpost men. We found two of them."

Mojombo slumped to the ground. "It was going so well.
We are to send a platoon of soldiers and an officer down

to Salal tomorrow to protect them. They are completely on our side. Now this."

"Mojombo, may I make a suggestion?"

The distraught leader nodded.

"Your outposts and lookouts must be hidden so no one on the trail can see them but they can see everything. Each of your lookouts must have a radio. If they see anything, they should report it at once. I can send Lam with your men to help them find positions and conceal themselves if you wish. You should get new lookouts in place before darkness."

"Yes, good suggestions. We'll accept Lam's help. We have the radios. I was overconfident. I won't be again. But you have a problem now as well. How will you get your two men back?"

Murdock outlined the plans. The Loyalist leader nodded. "Yes, if your men can find out the location where they are held, you will have your hardest part done."

He stood and let out a long sigh. "It seemed so easy at first. Now it is becoming harder and harder. I need to get the lookouts in place."

Lam stood. "I'll be ready whenever you call me."

Mojombo waved at him and walked toward where many of his men had congregated around the tents.

Murdock went into his tent and dropped on his cot. What else could he be doing? How else could he try to get the Vice President returned to them? Now he knew that he should have put the Vice President on the Skyhawk as soon as it landed and accompanied him out to the carrier. The damn barn door. He laced his fingers together behind his head and tried another angle. What would Kolda be doing with the two men? Some propaganda story to the world press? Neither man would have a passport. They had diplomatic status, but that did them no good if they couldn't prove it. What in hell would Kolda do?

He gave up and closed his eyes. Let go of it. Just forget about the damn problem. Maybe his subconscious would come up with something. A small nap. Yeah.

• • •

It seemed like only seconds later when somebody pushed his shoulder.

"Hey, Cap. You almost missed chow. Not the best, but my guess it's some kind of dog-meat stew. Not bad. Some good bread made out of something. No flour around here. Got me. You can still make the end of the chow line."

Murdock sat up and wiped his eyes. "Yeah, thanks." He figured out it was Senior Chief Sadler talking. "Thanks, Senior Chief, I owe you one."

On the way to the mess tent, Murdock remembered the problem. His subconscious had let him down. Not a hint of an idea about Stroh and the Veep.

That night at 0100 they took off in the Skyhawk on their way to Sierra City. Gardner and his guide, Gamba, had selected the site for their attack. It was a larger police station than the other two and would for sure have security out. Gardner had redlined Omar Rafii.

"Rafii's limp was worse, and when we checked the wound it had broken open. Mahanani said it could get infected. He pulled it together and dosed it with medication and wrapped it up tight. He's supposed to stay on his bunk until tomorrow noon at least.

"The rest of the men are ready. We don't have Lam for our point, so I suggest we use Fernandez."

"Your ball game, Gardner. I'm just along for the fun of it."

Then the noise of the chopper made talking too hard and they settled in for the ride. They circled around the city ten miles out from the last lights, and came in from the south. They were about ten miles from the first lights of the city when they let down. Gamba jumped from the bird and looked around.

"Want to know where we are, so I can get back to this spot," he said. A small stream worked its way across the gently sloping farmland. At last he nodded.

"Okay, we go now," Gamba said.

"This time the pilot has one of our Motorolas," Gardner said. "With him at two thousand feet, the little radios should be good for eight miles. I told the pilot to stay here unless he started taking enemy fire. Then to memorize this spot and get back here every hour on the hour after the first three hours."

They jogged across the fields, found a road going their direction, and kept up the pace, moving at a little better than seven miles an hour. That was about a nine-minute mile, and they could keep it up for four hours if they had to. Murdock remembered once or twice on past missions when they had been forced to go that long.

Gamba worked the point with Fernandez.

"We're coming into some of the city now," Fernandez said. "Looks like almost every house and building is dark. No streetlights out here. Just downtown is my guess. We're home free along here."

They slowed their jog to a fast walk and kept three yards apart in a column of ducks.

After twenty minutes of hiking, the streets became more commercial, and soon there were business sections, then residential, and sometimes mixed. Gamba called a halt ten minutes later. They were in an alley, and the darkness was complete as two-story buildings loomed over them.

Gamba talked to Murdock and Gardner on the radio. "Now I need to do some looking around. We're two blocks from the police station. They could have guards out this far. If I find one, there will be more. Smoking will give them away. Everyone here wants to smoke. I don't understand that. I'll take Fernandez with me for support."

"Be back in fifteen minutes," Gardner said.

The SEALs slumped on the alley dirt. The front man automatically went out as security, and Murdock, who was at the tail end of Alpha Squad, went back twenty yards as rear security.

After twenty minutes, Gardner called on the Motorola. "Fernandez. Where the hell are you?"

The whispered voice came back. "Just watched Gamba eliminate a guard with his knife. He can play on my team anytime. He said there are no more guards between us and the station. We can move down to the end of this block and have open fields of fire at the front and side. I'm coming back to lead you here."

In five minutes he keyed his radio again. "Move it, SEALs, to the end of the block you're on. I'm at the first cross street."

Ten minutes later JG Gardner had the men in the positions he wanted them to be. Half would fire at the police station. This one was made of concrete block, so they would have to hit windows with the twenties and maybe blow off a door. He put three SEALs behind them for security, and put two more on each side in a square perimeter.

"All units in position?" he asked on the Motorola. The four groups checked in. Murdock had worked forward to the eight men who would put fire into the police station. He had his Bull Pup and figured he could help.

"Four rounds each with the twenties," Gardner said. "The three twenties on the left of center hit the doors and windows on the front of the building. The other three fire at the side windows. Your weapons are free."

Murdock had knelt down, and now aimed at the large door on the front of the building and fired. The sound of the six Bull Pups going off created a crescendo of sound that kept increasing until the twenties stopped.

Reaction inside and outside the police station was quick. Ten men lifted up from the left side of the station and charged across the open street toward the street mouth where the SEALs had fired from. The two SEALs on that side cut down three of them with the MP-5's. A twenty-round burst just in front of them blasted four more dead, dumping them on the concrete street. The other five dove behind cars and an old truck, and began firing at muzzle flashes.

"Cover," Gardner barked into the Motorola. The SEALs in the street mouth rushed to the near side of the building, which came to the sidewalk.

Then three Army men pushed sandbags off their weapon and fired a machine gun from an emplacement near the left side of the police station. Murdock targeted it with a twenty, and the impact fuse detonated on the side of the weapon and destroyed it and the three men manning it.

MP-5 fire kept down the heads of the men who had hidden behind the cars on the street. Two twenty rounds hit one of the cars, exploding it and igniting the gasoline in both rigs in a second spectacular blast. Now men ran out the front door of the police building, one of them slapping at his burning shirt. Two 5.56 rounds cut him down.

"Let's use two rounds each on the twenties with WP," Gardner said. The rounds soon slammed into the building, some falling harmless as they missed the blown-out windows. Half of them penetrated the building, and soon smoke billowed out of the front of the structure and windows on the near side.

Gardner surveyed the scene. No more opposition. He was ready to give the order to pull back when they heard a racing motor and saw a tanklike vehicle roll around the near side of the station and move directly at them. A heavy machine gun chattered on its front roof mount as the rig rolled toward them. They could hear the tread as it worked over rollers.

"Light tank or armored personnel carrier," Murdock said on the net. "Everyone take cover, cease fire. Our rounds won't hurt him, not even the twenties. Get your C-4 out and make it into quarter-pound bombs. Insert a timer detonator, but don't set it yet. We'll see what he does. We should spread out along here. Ten yards between men. Find any cover you can. He's stopped firing. He can see no targets."

"Any casualties from that last action?" Gardner asked.

"Caught some shrapnel or a ricochet in my left arm," Senior Chief Sadler said on the net. "It's okay, I wrapped it up. Ready for duty."

"Here he comes," Gardner said. "He's got no headlights, maybe a nightscope. He must have viewing slots up there in front. Anybody know where they should be?"

Jaybird sputtered a moment. "Oh, yeah, viewing ports on both sides of most of these rigs. I can get on top of him and work down to the slots, push half of a quarter of C-4 into it, and set the timer/detonator. Half is inside, half outside."

"No way," Murdock said. "Too dangerous."

"We move up and try for the tracks?" Mahanani said.

"Best bet."

They watched the rig crawling toward them. They could see it better now in the soft moonlight. It was a half-track with tires in front where the body of the rig slanted sharply up to the top, six feet off the ground.

"Hold fire," Gardner said. "Two men on each side of him when he gets closer. It'll take a sprint across the street."

"Who the hell?" Murdock asked as a shadow eased away from a building closest to the police station, then charged across the open street and slammed against the side of the station. The half-track had just passed that point. Then the figure raced up to the back of the slow-moving machine, jumped on board, and crawled over the bare metal toward the front.

"Jaybird, if that's you I'm gonna kill you," Murdock said on the net. There was no response. "Figured," Murdock said.

The machine moved slowly forward. The figure crawled under the roof-mounted machine gun and angled down to the slanting front. He eased forward and down. Then his arm came out and it worked over what must be the viewing port, Murdock decided. He could imagine Jaybird jamming the inch-thick puttylike C-4 into the half-inch-wide viewing port, then punching in the timer detonator and pushing the timer.

A few seconds later the figure retraced his climb to the top and then jumped off to the street, did a shoulder roll, and came up running for the safety of the buildings across the street.

The small tanklike vehicle slowed, then stopped. They heard metal on metal as one of the side doors opened. Before anyone could leave, the C-4 went off half inside the armored personnel carrier. The sides of the rig bulged for a second. The unlatched door blasted off its hinges and flew into the street. Smoke billowed from the open doorway, the viewing ports, and the off-side door, which had also blown open and sagged on one hinge.

"Move to the center street, form up, we're out of here," Gardner barked into the Motorola. The fourteen SEALs and one Loyalist guide raced to the middle street and quickly jogged away from the now-burning half-track. A moment later an explosion ripped through the rig as flames found the fuel tank.

Ten blocks away from the police station, Gardner eased the men to a walk. "Any more casualties?"

Nobody spoke up, then a strange voice said, "Hey, I shit my pants when that fucking Jaybird . . ."

"Jaybird, I'm at the end of the line. Get your little ass back here, now." Everyone knew it was Murdock's voice.

Jaybird waited at the side of the street for the rest of the detail to pass him. He fell into step beside Murdock.

"Sorry, Cap. It just seemed like a good idea at the time. Hey, no harm, no foul."

"Against a direct order is something of a foul." Murdock shook his head. He grabbed the smaller man and gave him a hug and lifted him off the ground. "Jaybird, you little bastard. Don't you never die, you motherfucker. Not never. Don't even think about it." It was the traditional best tribute one SEAL could give to another. He put Jaybird down and they jogged to catch up with the rest of the platoon.

"Wonder what the driver thought when he saw that putty coming in through his view port?" Jaybird asked.

"I'd let you go back and interview him, but it's my guess he's in no condition to answer any questions."

They both laughed and caught up with the rest of the platoon.

Two miles past the last house, Gardner called a halt. Mahanani found Sadler and checked him out using his small flashlight.

"Not good, Senior Chief. Tore up your forearm. Had to be a ricochet. It's a furrow three inches long. Still bleeding like a bastard. I can stop it with enough pressure. You want a morphine?"

Sadler, sitting on the ground, nodded and leaned back until he was lying down. "Damn, not supposed to hurt this much."

Mahanani took the MP-5 from him and handed it to the closest man, Jefferson. Then he spent five minutes sterilizing and then medicating the wound. He wrapped it tightly and then put another bandage over that. He pushed one more ampoule of morphine into Sadler's right arm and helped him stand up.

"Hey, Chief, what day is this?"

"Who the hell knows? The only easy day was yesterday. Let's get out of this stinking town."

"We're ready to march, JG," Mahanani said.

An hour later they found the Skyhawk where they had left it, and thirty-five minutes later after a roundabout route, they settled down on the edge of the soccer field at Tinglat. It was a half hour to dawn when the SEALs hit their cots. Most went to sleep instantly.

That morning Murdock came alive at 0730, had chow, and reported to Mojombo's tent. "One more cop station down and dirty," Murdock said. "We picked up one slightly wounded. What's with our spies in the capital city?"

"We set up a relay radioman down near ten-mile dock. These radios we took from the police are good for well over ten miles, so we can get reports. We changed the frequency on them so the cops can't hear us. Tehabo reported in late last night. So far they have found no large number of guards around any of the police or military buildings. They did pick up one important statement that Kolda made to the newspapers. He said if the violence, the attacks by the Loyalist Army, do not stop, the American, Don Stroh, will be publicly executed tomorrow morning by a firing squad."

22

Murdock gathered all the SEALs around him just outside his tent. He told them about the threat to Stroh. "So what are we going to do about it?"

"We find out where public executions are held," Jaybird said.

Murdock pointed at Jaybird. "Go ask Mojombo and any of the Loyalists soldiers who might know. Move."

"When we find out, we move out tonight, chopper down to the five-mile line, and infiltrate the area they will use for the execution," JG Gardner said.

"Agreed. We'll work out an exact time."

"We take one Loyalist with us for each of us," Lam said. "They have some good people."

"Sounds reasonable. Go check with Mojombo."

"We try to cut down the force protecting the area before any civilians or the death party comes," Sadler said. "Which might postpone the deed."

"Sounds good. Depends how and where they plan to do it." Murdock frowned. "Hope it won't be six riflemen with Stroh against a block wall on some downtown street."

"Either we go in blackface and gloves, or we have to be totally hidden by daylight," Jefferson said. "Hell, Howard and me will be okay. You honkies gonna be up a crick."

"Trouble is, we're a foot taller than most of these natives," Howard said. "Hard to hide that."

"Bradford, check with Mojombo to see if he's heard anything from our spies. Maybe we could snatch him tonight before daylight and before they start the walk to the wall."

Ching scowled. "Say it takes us twenty minutes to chopper to the five-mile zone. Then we infiltrate to the downtown area we want in another hour. We recon the potential lockups, pick out our hide-holes, and go to ground. Another half hour. We've burned up two hours to target. Unless the spies can pinpoint the holding cell."

If we left here at 0100 we'd have some time to play with," Donegan said. "Like if there was no good places to hide. We might have to pull back a ways. I like the blackface-and-gloves idea myself."

Jaybird came back. "Mojombo says there is a wall just in back of the open market that was once used for executions. That could be the site. It would give us a lot of cover in the market stalls. He said the other spot could be the Central Police Station. It has a concrete-block wall on one side. It's also been used before."

"Great, we have two execution locales," Vinnie Van Dyke said. "I don't like the idea of splitting up our platoon."

Lam came back, and everyone looked at him. "Mojombo says he knows what we're thinking of doing. He'll be over shortly to advise us. He says a one-on-one wouldn't work with his men. But he could send along a squad of twelve men with a sergeant to be under the control of Commander Murdock. He's talking to D.C. and will be here when he's finished."

Murdock drummed his fingers on his knee where he sat on the ground in front of his tent. "Kolda doesn't have to be brilliant to know that us SEALs are still in his country. He can also figure out that his threat is going to pull us into his house. All he has to do is tell one of his Army colonels to provide him the firepower he needs for a good ambush, then try to lead us into the trap.

"We have two possible incarceration spots for the men. One would be the Government House, the other the Central Police Station. He knows that Mojombo has riddled the Central Station once before. So it must be vulnerable. So would he choose the Government Building? It could have more soldier guards, a greater number of rooms and places to hide the prisoners."

Mojombo had walked up and listened to Murdock.

"Yes, I quite agree that he knows that we will try to outguess him. That still leaves the two spots where the men are held. I just heard from our men in the city. Tehabo has infiltrated the units at both spots. From what he says, the men at the police station are secretive but gloating in a way. They say if anyone tries to shoot their way into that area, they will be met with a total surprise. Nobody will say what it is, and Tehabo was run out twice when he tried to walk into the restricted area. It could mean they have a deadly ambush set up even though the men are not held there. Or it could mean the ambush is to protect the prisoners."

"What about the Government Building?" Gardner asked.

"Tehabo gives me another story. He says it all looks calm and normal at the Government Building. There are always a lot of soldiers around it as regular guards. He wandered a lot of halls and even got into the basement, and he found no spot that had any more guards than any other. No part had been restricted. But he says that could be a low-key way of hiding the men."

"So, we're still snookered," Murdock said. "I like the idea of trying to free the two men tonight, before they parade them down to some block wall. That will be a much safer operation. Should mean fewer federal rifles around. So let's consider the rescue by darkness instead of at the hanging."

"I might have a solution," Mojombo said. "Don't split your forces. Let me take twenty men and borrow two of your SEALs with the Bull Pups. We'll take the Central Station because from our intel it has the most danger and probably the best possibility of housing the two captives. You take your SEALs and investigate the Government Building."

"Done," Murdock said. "What about timing?"

"You'll be flying down. The chopper could come back and take us down as a second load to a different area. Save a lot of hiking that way. The pilot and copilot will have one of our radios and one of your Motorolas. He should have a specific pickup spot for both of us to come in on call."

"We could leave at midnight and your men could get out of here at 0100. I'd suggest you cut your squad to sixteen men including two SEALs. Any more and the chopper is going to split a seam."

Murdock looked over his men. "Any comments or questions?"

Jaybird cleared his throat. "Skipper, is there anyone in the Loyalist camp who might have worked in the Government Building, or knows the layout of the two floors, and is there a basement?"

Mojombo grinned. "Bingo. I have two men. Both worked in the Government Building for five years. One was a janitor. He knows every nook and cranny in the place. I'll detach both men to you as soon as I can find them."

"Now, it's almost 1100," Murdock said. "Let's check weapons again, clean them up, and get your ammo ration from wherever you got it. We need a count on how many twenties we have left. Each man give me a count. Anything else?"

Mahanani held up his hand. "Sir. I've been watching the senior chief. His wound is deeper than I first thought. I think he should take a ride out to the medics on the carrier. I'd feel a lot better about it."

"Do it. Take him with you. While you're on the carrier, see if you can requisition two hundred rounds of 20mm HE. I don't see why their rounds won't fire in our weapons. We won't have the airburst potential, but the HE effect will do for now in case we run out. Get the senior chief moving." Murdock paused. "We need two Bull Pups to go with Mojombo. Let's make it Howard and Jefferson. Mojombo, that way your squad will be all black. Its not racist, it's color-coding." That brought a laugh. "Howard, you take my Bull Pup and I'll pack your MG. Jefferson, you already have a Bull Pup. You two find out when to report to Mojombo."

Murdock called Bill Bradford. The big man responded at once. "Bring your sketch pad and some sharp pencils. I want you to make a drawing for us."

Ten minutes later the two Loyalist soldiers came packing

their AK-47's. They reported to Murdock. Their names
were Kaedi and Sandari.

"Do you men know if the Government Building has a
basement?"

"Yes, sir," Kaedi said. "It does. I was a janitor there. I
know the whole building."

"Good. This is Bill Bradford, he's an artist. Tell him
about how long and how wide each floor is. He'll make an
outline, and then you show him how to fill in the rooms so
we can label them. It might take two or three sheets for
each floor."

Kaedi nodded and they began. Murdock looked at Sandari. "What did you do at the Government Building when
you worked for them?"

"I worked as an accountant on the second floor for three
years."

"Did you get around the building a lot?"

"Yes, but mostly on the second floor."

"Is there a basement?"

"Yes, under about half of the building. The newer section
does not have any underground."

"Could our two men be locked up in the basement?"

"Oh, yes. There are storage vaults down there. One for
the nation's gold supply, one for paper money, one for
valuable documents."

"Are they airtight?"

"Oh, no. Once a clerk was locked in overnight and it
didn't hurt anything except his pride."

"How do we get to these vaults?"

"From the main back door there is a hallway to the left.
Halfway down it is another door marked 'Basement.' Stairs
go down, but no elevator. Twenty steps. No security doors
or guards when I was there."

"You are going to show us the way once we get inside,
Sandari. Why did you join the Loyalists?"

"The government accused my brother of being a spy for
a foreign country. They had a quick, illegal trial and then
they shot him. I want to kill fifty of them."

"Good, Sandari. Good to have you with us. You go find
Jaybird and tell him to stick to you like glue. Thanks for

your help. You'll be flying out with us tonight. Stay with the SEALs until then. Okay?"

"Okay, Commander," Sandari said. He saluted. Murdock returned his salute.

He heard the chopper take off. It was a calculated risk letting it fly out to the carrier and back. But they could use the 20mm rounds, and he didn't want to take a chance on the senior chief losing his arm to some tropical infection.

Bradford finished the sketches of the two floors and the basement. Kaedi said the best place to hold prisoners would be in the documents room in the basement. They would check that first when they got inside. If the prisoners weren't there, the SEALs would work through the rest of the building.

Noon chow turned out to be a corn-and-rice mixture with baked fish and a side of sliced carrots. The surprise of the day was coffee. They had found five five-gallon cans of ground coffee in the loot from the President's warehouse.

Just after noon, a runner came to Murdock's tent. He was wanted on the SATCOM. Murdock went to the leader's tent and took the offered handset.

"Murdock here."

"Billings, Commander. What to report about the Vice President and Mr. Stroh?"

"Nothing yet. We're trying to pinpoint their location. We think we have it down to two spots. We'll raid both those places tonight. It's about 1300 here now. We should be on site in twelve hours. We will take all precautions to keep the two men safe, and as soon as we have them in our hands, they will, I say again, sir, they *will* be transported directly to the aircraft carrier."

"Good. The President said you were a good man. Good luck on your mission. Oh, one word from Cliff Donaldson, the CIA director. He said if there is no way to rescue Don Stroh alive, he is to be terminated. He's a storehouse of CIA data and can't be allowed to be kept by a rogue leader who could sell him to any one of four or five interested parties. Do you understand, Commander Murdock?"

"Yes, sir. If Mr. Stroh can't be rescued, he must be terminated. Understood. Will comply. Wilco."

"That's it then. The President sends his best and wishes you success in your mission."

"Thank him for the men. We'll report in when the mission is over no matter what time it is. Are we five hours ahead of you?"

"I think that's it, Commander. Signing off."

Murdock put down the handset and stared at Mojombo. "You heard the orders. They are binding on you too, since we're both looking for the same prize."

"I understand, Commander. If we draw the prize, we will make every effort to bring out both men. If it is impossible to rescue them and we have the ability, Mr. Stroh will be terminated, but not the Vice President. Right?"

"Correct. It won't come to that. I have a good feeling about this raid. We're going to bring them back. One of us. Right now I couldn't guess which one of us it will be."

Murdock called Gardner into their tent and dropped the flap. "Let's have a little critique of the mission last night," Murdock said. "First, your evaluation."

"Yes, sir. First I appreciate the chance to run the operation. On top, we accomplished our purpose. The police station was burned out and they lost at least a dozen men, maybe more. We had only one casualty, and that's not life-threatening. Our movement to the objective went well. Our guide did his job. Lam was as efficient as ever and brought us to the right spot. The actual firefight could have gone better. The men coming from outside and attacking us was a surprise. I should have expected something like that. We did reduce them, and scared off the five who escaped from the car fire.

"The armored personnel carrier was another surprise. I didn't know their Army had any such rigs, let alone the police. Frankly it stumped me. I've never met anything like that before."

"That's why Jaybird took it on," Murdock said. "We've busted up a dozen or more of them. Almost always with C-4 or TNAZ in the tracks. Stops them dead. Jaybird was showing off a little. He likes to do that. I just hope one of these days it doesn't get him or some other SEAL killed."

"That was about it. We formed up and moved out. Mahanani took care of the wound and we hit the takeoff spot and got home."

"Want to rate yourself from one to a hundred?"

Gardner rubbed the back of his head. "Damn, well, I guess a ninety. Five off for the squad outside the station and another five on the personnel carrier."

Murdock watched the junior-grade lieutenant. He'd done well, and would soon have his own platoon. He was good. How had he stayed a JG so long? "I disagree with your figure. It should be a ninety-five. The squad of shooters outside didn't surprise me. The personnel carrier did. So, Lieutenant, put a big eagle's feather in your floppy. You did good."

"Thanks. I appreciate that. I better get over to the ammo tent and see that our boys get their pockets filled. I have a count on twenties in my squad. We have five left per man."

"We have four per man. No more mass firings. We'll use them carefully unless we get some new stock from the carrier. Have you set up a sleep period?"

"Early chow at 1600, then sleep period from 1630 to 2300. We on the first chopper run or the second?"

"Let's take the first. Tell Mojombo he has the second trip."

"That's a roger."

The rest of the afternoon, Murdock sweated out the chopper. It came in just after 1700 with both SEALs and two cases of a hundred rounds of HE 20mm.

"Their ordnance man said these twenties should work in our weapons," Mahanani said. "He told me to compare them for weight and size and extractor operation. Then if there was any question, not to use them."

"Do it," Murdock said. "If they check out, get some sandbags to protect yourself and place the weapon through them with the trigger behind them, and fire off one of the new rounds. My bet is that they will work fine for HE contact."

Josie Halstrom, the chopper pilot, walked up and waited to talk to Murdock. "I've got a new copilot. My other one didn't like getting shot at and developed a serious stomach problem. No guts is my guess. Anyway, we're ready to do a double run tonight whenever you're ready."

"Good. First run about 0100. You better get some sack time yourself before then."

Halstrom nodded, and headed back to his bird on the edge of the soccer field.

Mojombo called from his tent three down, and Murdock went over to the African leader.

"SATCOM and they're asking for you. They asked me if you ever had your own set turned on."

Murdock took the handset. "Murdock here."

"Yes, Commander. Billings. We've just had a message from State. They have received a radio demand through a third country from Sierra Bijimi President Kolda. He says he has liberated our Vice President from the criminal rebel terrorists and is ready to return him to United States authorities. Kolda says his nation has suffered seriously in military action to rescue the two men, and he needs payment of three billion U.S. dollars. The money will help to cover the terrible death and destruction to his capital during the fight to rescue the Vice President and another diplomat, Don Stroh."

"The bastard. Our orders still stand?"

"Yes."

"We've planned an operation. I'm not sure that Kolda doesn't have a SATCOM. If he does, he could be listening in. He didn't make any threats against our men, did he?"

"No, but he did say that he expected quick cooperation by the U.S. since the Vice President is seriously ill and needs the best medical care possible. It can't be provided for the Vice President here in Sierra Bijimi."

"The bastard," Murdock said. "I'll report back to you in eighteen hours."

"Good luck."

"Thanks, Mr. Billings. We'll need it."

23

Mahanani, Lam, and Howard picked a spot well away from the village to test the 20mm rounds brought back from the carrier.

"Look exactly the same," Lam said. "The grooves, the markings, only thing different is the fuse, and we can't even see that."

"Weigh about the same," Mahanani said, hefting one in each hand.

Howard laughed. "Sure, Old Weights and Measures himself here. Let's give it a try."

They set up the Bull Pup with a heavy wooden box filled with dirt on each side. The trigger was just behind the boxes, and the round in the chamber. If it blew inside the weapon, the boxes of dirt should take up the impact.

"Who gets to pull the trigger?" Lam asked.

"Hey, it's Howard's Bull Pup," Mahanani said. "He gets the honor."

Howard reached down, lay flat on the ground behind the weapon, and curled his finger around the trigger.

"Get back thirty yards," he told the other two. "No sense in all of us getting killed." They grinned and moved back.

When they were to the rear and behind tree trunks, Lam called out. "Ready on the firing line." It was the age-old military order that all was safe to begin target practice.

Howard shut his eyes, ducked down, and pulled the trigger. They heard the familiar loud crack of the round going off. Then fifty yards downrange a huge tree took the round in the center of its trunk with a smashing explosion as the HE round detonated.

Howard sat up and smiled.

"Hey, you chickens, these rounds work fine. Pass the word." Howard pulled back the lever and checked. A new round from the magazine had moved up into the firing chamber after the first shell casing had been ejected. *Yes.*

The Skyhawk with the thirteen SEALs and one Loyalist soldier had kept a minimum altitude of fifty feet over the water as it raced downstream, pulling in sharply at the five-mile dock, and found the LZ a quarter of a mile from the river beside a tributary. The small open field had been harvested. The SEALs and the Loyalist soldier, Sandari, jumped out of the helicopter and ran at once for the cover of the jungle growth. The chopper lifted off at once and powered north over the heavy greenery on its way by a new course back to Tinglat.

The SEALs lay in the jungle growth for two minutes listening for any reaction around them. Gradually the insects began to sound again with their mating calls and operational buzzing and clicking. A bird sang, then another. Murdock licked his lips and stood.

"Move," he said into the Motorola. The squad walked out of the growth to the riverbank and trotted down it to the road along the river. They were in the outskirts of Sierra City now, and moved quickly from shadow to shadow as they worked down the main road to a less-traveled street. Sandari led them. He told them he had grown up a short distance from the five-mile dock. They threaded through dark alleys, past shuttered houses and buildings, and along narrow streets that looked like cattle trails at times.

Murdock checked his watch. They had taken off precisely at 1200 and flown for twenty minutes. Now it was almost 0100 and they were not at their target.

"How much farther?" he asked Sandari.

"The Government Building is this side of the main business district," Sandari said. "Maybe ten more minutes."

They came up to the rear entrance of the large Government Building. It was only two stories high, but spread out over most of the square block. The near half of the block held an empty parking lot.

"Guards?" Murdock asked.

Sandari pointed to the far right corner of the building, then to the central rear door and again to the far left.

"Jaybird, guard to the far right. You and I will do him. Then move to the central rear door. The guard on the left can't see the back door. Let's move."

The two ran down the block and came out less than forty yards from the lookout post. They leaned against a wooden building and watched the guard. He walked a short post and came back. Then he put his rifle on the ground and dug into his pockets. A moment later they saw a flare of light.

"Smoker," Murdock said. "Good, his night vision will be seriously impaired for five minutes." Murdock and Jaybird crept around the building, and then walked naturally across the open space toward the guard. They would act as if they belonged there. They had their weapons slung and were talking when the guard looked their way. He looked again, then waved. The two SEALs waved back, then slanted toward the man.

"Hey, got a smoke?" Jaybird asked from ten feet away. The guard snorted.

"Damn moochers. Buy some of your own smokes sometime." He had just reached in his pocket, when Jaybird's KA-BAR knife lanced through his shirt and drove deep into the soldier's heart killing him instantly. Jaybird caught him and dragged him into the building's shadow. The rest of Alpha Squad rushed across the open space. Ken Ching picked up the dead guard's AK-47, slung it over his shoulder, and manned the guard post.

Murdock led the rest of the squad close to the building and out of sight of the guards on the rear entrance at the center. Bravo Squad followed, and soon the SEALs were within twenty feet of the two men on guard. Murdock and Jaybird slung their MP-5's, drew their KA-BAR knives, and held them in their right hands with the blades hidden behind their arms.

They walked out into the open and toward the two federal soldiers. One guard called out in a conversational tone, "Hey there, you lost?"

"Shortcut," Jaybird said.

"Anybody got a smoke?" Murdock asked. "I'm dying for a smoke." By that time they were within ten feet of the two guards. The guards frowned, and one started to pull up his slung rifle. Jaybird swung up his silenced MP-5 and put two of three rounds into the man's chest. The other guard froze for a second, and it was long enough for Murdock to jolt forward and ram his fighting knife into the man's lung. He went down. Murdock pulled out the KA-BAR and slashed it across the guard's throat. They dragged both guards into the shadows next to the building. Then Donegan and Rafii walked up and took the place of the guards, using their AK-47 rifles as props.

Murdock ran to the rear door. Locked. He fired six rounds from the silenced MP-5 at the lock. Metal and lead flew, then the door unlocked and drifted open. The ten SEALs rushed inside leaving the three outside who had replaced the guards.

Sandari led the group. He walked quickly down the central hall to the left and pointed to the basement door. Locked. Jaybird used his silenced MP-5 and fired one three-round burst at the lock. He pulled on the handle and the door opened. Sandari went through first, turned on two light switches, and then went down the steps. Murdock was right behind him.

"Second door to the right," Sandari said. "That used to be documents." The door was unlocked. Sandari turned on the room lights to find the space empty. He shrugged, and they went to the next door. This one was locked. Murdock fired twice with the MP-5 and broke the lock. Murdock heard a muffled cry from inside the room. Sandari opened the door and turned on the lights.

"Thank God," Don Stroh said. He was tied to a bunk in the otherwise empty room. He wore the same clothes, had a shadowy beard, and his hair was rumpled.

"Where's the Vice President?" Murdock asked.

"Next room. We tap on the wall now and then. No code, just to know we're alive."

Jaybird cut the thin nylon ropes that held Stroh to the cot. He stood and his knees gave way, then held, and he walked around a little. "Damn, good to be moving."

Murdock had left with Sandari. They ran to the last door. It also was locked. This time it took six rounds to break the lock. Murdock opened the door and rushed inside. The lights were on. The Vice President sat at a low desk with a pen and paper. He threw down the pen and jumped up. For a moment he looked confused. Then he must have recognized Murdock. His face broke and he began sobbing. He rushed to Murdock, threw his arms around him, and wouldn't let go.

"It's all right, Mr. Vice President. We're here. We're going to take you home. Don't worry. The worst is over. We're going to get you out of here."

It took several minutes before the Vice President would let go of Murdock. Tears still washed down his cheeks. "They put a loaded gun to my head three times. They tried to get me to sign all sorts of confessions. I kicked one of them in the balls and he beat me with a club. God, I want to get home."

Jaybird ran back up the steps and checked in the main hall. He saw no sign of any federal troops. He hurried down the hall toward the rear entrance, then jolted into a doorway as a detail of ten armed federal soldiers marched into the hall from a room and turned away from him. When they were gone, Jaybird rushed back to the basement stairway.

Murdock and the platoon waited for him. He motioned, and they ran down the hall toward the rear door. Three federal soldiers came out of a room and stared at them, then lifted their rifles. Jaybird and Bradford cut them down with a dozen rounds. The SEALs ran faster, the Vice President and Don Stroh keeping up with them. The two men were in the middle of the group. They made it to the rear door. Jaybird opened it a crack and looked out. He shut it quickly.

"Skipper. There's a vehicle out there and two men have guns trained on our guys."

"Can you nail them with silent rounds?" Murdock asked. Jaybird nodded. Van Dyke and Fernandez moved up to the door and when Jaybird opened it a foot, they both fired. The bullets hit the two federal officers in the chests and knocked them down. The SEALs, along with the Vice President and Stroh, poured out the door, picked up Donegan and Rafii, and stormed for the far side of the building. They took fire from the vehicle that was parked near the entrance.

Bill Bradford stopped, turned, and fired one round from his Bull Pup. The 20mm hit the half-ton truck and exploded, silencing the guns there.

The SEALs picked up Ching at his guard post and sprinted for the nearby building. A machine gun cut through the silence. The lead splattered just to the side of the SEALs as they crowded behind a wooden building.

"Where is he?" Gardner yelled. Nobody knew. Then Gardner saw the flashes and aimed a 20mm round at them. He hit the laser button, and the round exploded over the heads of the machine-gun crew. Two of them went down dead. The third man crawled back to the .30-caliber weapon and continued to fire.

Fernandez zeroed in on the flashes with his sniper rifle and fired six carefully aimed shots. The machine gun ceased to function.

"Let's move," Murdock said. Sandari led them down the block at a trot, angled away from the Government Building, and they were halfway down a narrow street with shuttered businesses on both sides when a seven-man squad of federal soldiers blocked their way and at once began firing.

The SEALs took cover wherever they could find it. Three old cars were the best to be had. The SEALs returned fire. Two twenties exploded in airbursts over the soldiers. One lifted up to run toward the corner, but Fernandez nailed him with two rounds from his sniper rifle.

The firing from ahead fell off. Another airburst twenty silenced it. Two federals lifted up and raced to the shelter of a building at the corner. They made it.

"Canzoneri, Mahanani, go check for survivors," Gardner said. The two ran forward on a zigzag course, then stopped and kicked the corpses. One man lifted his rifle, but a round from Mahanani's MP-5 ended the threat.

"All clear," Canzoneri said on the Motorola. The platoon ran forward, stepped over the bodies, and hurried up another block. Murdock had assigned Lam and Bradford to take care of the Vice President. One of them was always near him. When the firing started in the street, Bradford had pushed the Vice President behind the car and held him there. On the march they stayed beside him. He struggled now to keep up, and Lam was on the Motorola.

"Skipper, we're having trouble staying with you. Cut the damn pace."

"That's a roger, Lam. We're slowing down. How's he doing?"

"We'll make it if we go slower. Remember, he's a civilian and probably fifty-five years old."

They walked from there on. Murdock didn't worry about Don Stroh. He could take care of himself and keep up. They were almost out of the splash of houses near the four- or five-mile line when Sandari dropped to the ground. The rest of the SEALs went down as well. Sandari didn't have a Motorola. Murdock crawled up beside him.

"A truck and soldiers in the road ahead," Sandari said.

Murdock looked it over. A roadblock. They might have roadblocks up every night. This one had one truck and five or six men. The SEALs could take it out or go around it. If the SEALs splattered the soldiers, it would pinpoint their location. He didn't like that.

"Lam, how's the Veep doing?" Murdock asked.

"He's tired, but he says he can make it. He should be behind a desk somewhere, not out here."

"Seen Stroh?"

"He's around. He picked up an AK-47 at that last set-to. He thinks he's a SEAL now."

"Good. He'll have some practice. All hands. We have a roadblock ahead. We're going into the field to the left. We need to move that direction to find our chopper. Absolutely no noise. We'll keep ten yards apart. Follow our path."

Murdock motioned, and Sandari walked off the dirt road into a field, and went out a quarter of a mile before he turned north again. They hiked for another thirty minutes through fields and along some roads, and then turned back to the right.

"Twenty minutes and we should be at the chopper," Sandari said. Murdock had kept close tabs on the Vice President. He would hold up well as long as they just kept walking, Lam told him. Stroh had come by, and had been disappointed they hadn't had another firefight now that he had a weapon.

The Motorolas picked up a transmission.

"Calling Murdock. This is Halstrom. Come in, Murdock. I've got some trouble."

"Halstrom. Murdock here. Just barely hear you. Where are you?"

"Almost five miles north of the drop-off point. I waited there after the second run with Mojombo. He said wait there. An hour later a bunch of gunmen started shooting. I had to lift off. Took some rounds and some damage. I flew out a ways and set down so I could inspect the ship for any real problems. I found some. They cut up my bird pretty bad. Three rounds into the engine. I have a cut oil line, a messed-up fuel line, and control-surface damage. Just no way I can put this bird in the air. Afraid I can't ferry you guys back to the village."

24

The Night Joisette Died
San Diego, California

Shortchops Jackson waited for the white cop to come up to his rolled-down window.

"What's the problem, Officer?"

"Will you please get out of the car and put your hands on the roof?"

"Sure." Shortchops did as he was told. He was frisked quickly and then told to turn around.

"So what's the problem?"

"Your left taillight is out. With a nice car like this, I figured you'd want to know. Can I see your registration and license?"

"Registration is in the glove box."

"I'll get it," the cop said. He sat in the Caddy and pushed over so he could open the glove box. He took out an owner's manual with the registration paper clipped to the first page. He took it out and read it with his flashlight.

"Are you Arnold Jackson?"

"Yes, sir."

"Your license says Arnold S. Jackson."

"Right, I don't always use my middle initial."

"Okay, sit down in the car. I'm going to give you an equipment violation. You get it repaired within thirty days and send in a receipt with the signed ticket, and you'll be square."

"Yes, sir."

Five minutes later the cop pulled away from Shortchops and the thin black man gave a sigh of relief. He changed his mind about going to Las Vegas. Hell, the cops would find him sooner or later. Maybe he should just go down to the Central Police Station and say he'd heard they wanted to talk to him about Joisette. Yeah, maybe, maybe not. For now he'd go home and get some sleep. If he was going to clean up and get straight, this was the time to start. He had to get clean; he had to get a lawyer. A new shirt and some good slacks wouldn't hurt. Some nice ones. Even new shoes. Shortchops grinned. He was feeling like a rich man already.

The cops worried him. How do you prove that you didn't do something? Tough. They had to prove that you did. Tougher when you didn't do it. He drove carefully back to Southeast San Diego, and parked down the street from his apartment. It was the worst place he had ever lived. Maybe in a few months he'd have lots of money. Or maybe he'd be in jail waiting trial for murder. First thing he had to do was vanish. Leave everything in the apartment and get the hell out and find a new place. Yeah, move. All he'd take would be his fiddle. That's why he liked the Caddy. It had room enough to tote the bass wherever he went. That was the problem. Where did he go? The cops could be down at his place right now waiting for him. They were smart, had contacts. He did know quite a few people in town, especially around his apartment. He grinned. And he knew a few hookers. So where this time of night?

He decided. He'd have to sleep in the car tonight. In the morning he'd find a cheap apartment somewhere. He could even stay at one of the missions downtown. Pray and sing a little and you could bunk there for a week at a time. Yeah. Praise the Lord.

Back to the Veep Rescue
Near the five-mile dock
Sierra City, Bijimi

Murdock knew that everyone in the platoon had heard the word from the chopper that it couldn't ferry them back to their camp at Tinglat. Conference time.

"Lam, Sadler, Jaybird, JG, Mahanani, Sandari, and Stroh, front and center for a powwow. Now."

They gathered under some tall trees at the edge of a field where the chopper was supposed to land.

"Sonofabitch, they did it to us again," Jaybird said.

"Somebody said if you get raped enough times, it doesn't hurt anymore," Mahanani said. "This must be our tenth time."

"Enough," Murdock said. "Our concern now is how we get out of here and up north. Evidently the federal folks have patrols or blocking units or something in this area. They may have been expecting some reaction from the Loyalists or us.

"First, our main package. Mahanani, how is the Vice President holding up?"

"He's tired, but delighted to be out of prison, as he put it. He can walk and looks to be in good shape. What do we have, about fifteen miles yet?"

"Close to it," Jaybird said. "Do we have any energy bars, chocolate, anything that might give him an energy boost?"

"Tried chocolate bars, but they melted and ran out of my vest," Mahanani said. "We have something else that I don't remember the name of. We'll give him a bar every hour."

"Good. Lam, about how far are we from the trail north and should we take it?"

"Not the one along the river. The federals will have that zeroed in. They know we go north. It's a no-brainer for them."

"So, do we crash jungle for fifteen miles?" JG Gardner asked.

Sandari shook his head. "No jungle. There are dozens of trails that go to the north. Some move away from the river a mile. The federals can't cover them all."

"Can you find them for us?" Murdock asked.

"I know the trails, but I can't guarantee that they will be safe."

"Pick out what looks like the safest one. You and Lam recon it for a mile, then come back. Go, now."

Murdock looked at the other men. "Okay, you guys. We've got ourselves a little problem here. Put on the other uniform. In their place what would you do about us?"

Senior Chief Sadler took the lead. "Patrol forces squad

size so they could cover more trails. Then in back of them, I'd put a blocking force for a surprise. Say we blast through a seven-man squad and think we're home free. The blocking force hears the firefight, moves up and establishes an ambush, and catches us in a deadly crossfire with their AK-47s, MGs, and sub guns.

"They would have a good-sized force at the five- and ten-mile docks, knowing that we've used river transport before. It wouldn't make any difference if there was no boat there. We could call it in when we arrived and they could blow us out of the water and off the dock."

Lieutenant (j.g.) Gardner took the floor. "Why not go out three miles from the five-mile bridge and set out two-man patrols walking six or eight of the main trails north out of town? Cover them all. Walk these men back and forth from the eight- to ten-mile marks. These men would be expendable, but if they made contact with the enemy, it would pinpoint the location of the Loyalists. Then we rush in massive forces and overwhelm the bad guys, in this case us."

Murdock held up his hand. "So when we move, we go slow and easy. If we run into any enemy, we reduce them with the EAR if possible to keep from giving away our position. Then hope to squeeze through their dragnet and move up the trail toward the village. How far will we need to move north before we're out of the danger zone?"

Jaybird looked up. "They want us bad, Skipper. I'd say they'll have troops out at least fifteen miles."

"Mahanani, how are our two tenderfeet?" the commander asked.

Mahanani slapped Stroh on the back. "This gung-ho, shit-kicking CIA desk man who never thought he'd be in the field has actually fired a few shots in anger. Him and his trusty AK-47. He's now a genuine, imitation, ersatz SEAL. He'll make it fine if he doesn't try to be a hero and learns to keep his head down.

"Our other man could be a problem. He's showing some signs of stress. His pace has slowed, but there doesn't seem to be any physical impairment, except one small limp. Hey, damn big word for me. I don't think we'll get to the point where we have to carry him. I've thought about a horse cart if Sandari could scare up one. Most of the trails are good for another five miles before they close in. One of those motorcycles would have been great. I'd suggest the cart if possible, and that would give him a rest, and then maybe we can put him on the horse for the last ten miles."

"Can you saddle a cart horse?" Jaybird asked.

"Most horses over here would probably go either way," JG Gardner said.

"To find a horse and a cart, we'll need a village," Murdock said.

"Lam told me he smelled cooking fires a while ago," Jaybird said. "He figured there was a small village about a mile ahead. We're downwind."

Ten minutes later Lam and Sandari came back. Both were sweating from the run back down the trail.

"We found a trail looks good," Lam said. "No sign of any military."

"How close are we to a village?" Murdock asked Sandari. "We hope to buy, rent, or steal a horse and a cart that the Vice President can ride in."

"Half mile straight ahead to a village," Sandari said. "For cash dagnars I can find a renter."

"Go now and meet us on the trail. We'll be moving ahead at once."

He took the stack of bills Murdock gave him and left.

"Lam, take the point. We're walking, and keep it reasonable so the Veep can stay with us. Let's keep five yards apart. Move out."

The Vice President was hurting. He had developed a slight limp, and now it became worse. It took them ten minutes to do the half mile to the village, Murdock realized. He was glad when he saw a cart with cushions in it and a sturdy-looking horse hitched to it.

"I don't need no stinking horse cart," Adams shrilled when Murdock asked him to step on board.

"You might not need it, Mr. Vice President, but the rest of us do so we can make better time. The quicker we get out of the danger zone out about fifteen miles, the better off we'll be. Doesn't that make sense?"

Adams wilted as he stepped onto the cart and settled into

the cushions. "Yeah, you're right, Murdock. I'm being bitchy. Sorry. I want my AK-47 back just in case. Hell, I can still shoot."

After that they made better time. Murdock put the horse cart in the middle of the line of march, and Lam had them at a seven-miles-an-hour pace. It was an easy jog that they could keep up for miles. Even the horse liked it at somewhere between a walk and a canter. One of the SEALs led the horse by a line.

They had hiked another three miles before Lam used the Motorola. "Better hold it in place, troops. We have a small problem up here."

It was the simplest kind of roadblock Murdock and Gardner saw as they worked their way up to take a look through the murky night air.

"Damn log across the trail. We can get over it easy, but the cart will have trouble."

"Anybody defending behind it?" Gardner asked Lam.

"I smelled some cigarette smoke but it's gone now. Not sure if it came from there or some nearby village." Lam shrugged. "Odds are there's at least a squad behind the log. They must have cut down a tree to get it in place."

Murdock called up Rafii. "That leg wound hurt your knife-throwing arm?"

"Not a bit, Skipper."

"Good. We may have visitors up front. I want you, Lam, and the JG to work up on the right-hand side of the trail. Go through the brush and vines and be as quiet as Lam is. If it's only two or three, see if you can get them with thrown knives. Any more, Lam, take the rest out with silenced shots. Take MP-5s."

The three men faded into the jungle, and Murdock tried to hear them moving forward but he couldn't. He was sure Lam was showing the others how to get through, around, under, or over the vines and trees and plants that luxuriated in the tropical rain forest.

Murdock tried to watch ahead. The platoon had moved up to within thirty yards of the roadblock. They couldn't hear anything. Murdock watched, but saw no flare of a match that might be used to light a smoke. They waited.

Twice Murdock thought he heard the short grunt of a silenced shot, but he wasn't sure.

Lam led the two men, showing them how to move without making noise. They penetrated ten yards into the thickets away from the trail, then moved forward paralleling it for thirty yards. Then Lam headed them back to the trail. They stopped just behind the fallen tree. The top of it extended far into the jungle, where it had created a sweeping path as it came down. Lam eased through the brush until he could see along the heavy trunk lying on the ground. Nothing.

He closed his eyes and concentrated. When he opened them he sectionalized the area, looking at one small section at a time, before moving on. He had left the other two men ten yards behind him. In the third section he found a cammy-clad soldier holding a weapon and leaning against the tree. He could be sleeping. Lam kept looking. He found the second man three feet behind the log lying on the edge of the trail. Also could be sleeping. At last Lam found the third man, sitting upright against the two-foot-thick tree trunk, rifle in his hands, peering over the top of the log.

Lam clicked his Motorola twice, and the two men behind him worked up silently. He pointed out the alert soldier, and Rafii nodded. He worked closer until he was ten feet away, then lifted up and his right hand came down sharply. Lam couldn't see the knife flying through the air, but he heard the groan from the man it hit. He fell forward and moaned as he rolled over. He tried to shout, but the sound came out as a gurgle. The noise was enough to awaken both the other men. They waved their rifles. Lam shot one of them with his silenced MP-5, and Gardner nailed the other one with a three-shot burst. Then all was quiet.

Lam motioned for the others to stay put, and he worked ahead without a sound to check on the three and see if there were any more defenders. He paused at the edge of the trail. He couldn't see or hear anyone down the trail. The three bodies in front of him hadn't moved since the attack. He surged out and checked all three. Lam touched his Motorola.

"We've got a clear field here, Skipper. Three down and out. But the damn tree is a problem."

The rest of the platoon came up, and Sandari grinned. "No big worry," he said. "Trees fall down over trails all the time. We unhitch the cart and ten men lift it over the log and put it down. Then I talk to the horse and lead him around the end of the log through the trees. Happens all the time."

Fifteen minutes later the Vice President was back in the cart, and they moved up the trail, which was becoming increasingly rough and narrow.

They stopped after a half hour of marching. The trail was too narrow now for the horse cart.

"Mr. Vice President, have you ever ridden a horse?"

"You're kidding. This plow horse can be ridden?"

"We're going to find out. That knee of yours isn't going to hold up for eight or ten more miles. Sandari is getting on the horse's back now to see how he performs. My guess he's as gentle as a puppy."

He was, Murdock was glad to see. They boosted the Vice President onto the horse, where one of the cart pillows served as a make-do saddle. Then they moved again. Sandari told Murdock it was not more than eight miles to the village. He would be surprised if the federal troops were out this far.

"I'll believe that when we hit the Loyalist outposts," Lam said.

Ten minutes later, Lam put the platoon down. "Skipper, up here, quickly. I don't know what the hell is going on. Sounds like a bunch is having late chow or early chow. I smell cooking fires and meat and all sorts of food up here. Noise like it's the Fourth of July."

Murdock, Jaybird, and Gardner hurried up the trail to where Lam lay in the brush at the edge of the path. They all heard the noise.

"How far off our route?" Gardner asked.

"Must be a clearing up there. Maybe fifty yards ahead and off the trail by not more than a dozen yards. No way we can get past them and not be seen."

"Then let's hold a celebration in their honor," Murdock said. "We move up as close as we can to get open fields of fire and we test out those new 20mm rounds to see how well they work."

25

Lam came back from his scouting mission. "Oh, yeah, Skipper. They are just starting to chow down. I counted twenty of them and what looks like a field kitchen. I couldn't tell if any of them were officers. We've got some good fields of fire. It's near a small stream that goes toward the river. They're on this side of it in a small field somebody has carved out of the jungle. Those farmers must spend half their time beating back the growth of vines and small trees."

"Can we get all of our Bull Pups on line?" Gardner asked.

"Plenty of space."

Murdock left Mahanani with the horse and the Vice President, and took the rest of the men forward. Lam edged into the heavy growth beside the trail and worked across to the other side of the opening that spread out to the left. They would have forty feet of space in the edge of the jungle to set up. It took five minutes to get the fifteen men placed. Then Murdock used his Motorola.

"If you have airburst rounds left, use them. First shots from the twenties, then everyone open up. Twenties go to 5.56 after the first round. No reason to be quiet on this one. Check it out. Twenties we fire in ten seconds." He waited, then counted down from four. At one the Bull Pups roared and at once the rounds exploded. Two were airbursts, and the others hit the field kitchen and the line of soldiers. More than half went down with the first rounds. Then the rest of the weapons fired, picking off the survivors and those trying to escape. In twenty seconds it was all over. Two men crawled toward the jungle. They were quickly nailed with two rounds each. All else was quiet.

"Gardner and Rafii, go in and make sure everyone is down," Murdock said.

The two men sprinted for the death scene. Murdock heard one round fired, then all was quiet.

"Their weapons are the newer AK-74's," Gardner said. "We better scoop up all of them we can find. I need four more men in here."

Murdock pointed to four men near him, and they ran into the carnage and retrieved weapons and ammo. Each man brought back four of the big rifles. They spread them out among the men. Then Murdock brought up the horse and they headed up the trail. Lam and Sandari were out ahead a quarter of a mile. Murdock expected no more federals. Those out on patrol must have reported back for a late midnight supper. Or their last supper, however you looked at it.

Mahanani pulled up beside Murdock and fell in step with him. "The Veep is looking better. He was so tired before he could hardly spit. Now he's going to make it okay."

"Good. We've got maybe two hours left. We should hit some of the Loyalists' outposts before long."

Jaybird used the Motorola. "Hey, Skipper, we haven't heard or seen anything of Mojombo and his men. Where in hell are they?"

"My guess they swung deeper into the jungle, farther away from the river to get away from any federal troops. He'll probably beat us back to the village."

It was dawn before Murdock and his platoon hiked into Tinglat. Mojombo welcomed them.

"You found them. Great. We came up empty at the station, but we took it down and wasted a lot of their soldiers. They had a bomb they had rigged as a booby trap just outside the station. We watched them setting it up after we got there. It was no problem. We caught the same message you did from the pilot. We found him, and left half of our men there to give him some security for the rest of the night. With daylight there are supposed to be F-18's flying air cover for him, and three choppers bringing in repair parts and mechanics and twenty-five Marines for a perimeter defense. The pilot had been in touch with the carrier on his radio. He estimated an hour of work before he'd be ready to fly out. He's going back to the carrier, and they'll leave one of the Skyhawks for us to use here. Does Washington, D.C., know about the men being rescued?"

"We just got here. I'll let Stroh do his own reporting to his friends in Washington. As for me and the men and the Vice President, it's sack time."

Stroh had gone directly to his tent. He took out the SAT-COM and adjusted the antenna, then made his call.

"Right, Chief," he said. "We're both free, out of there, and hale and hearty. Well, the Vice President has a bit of a limp, but outside of that . . ."

"Get him on a chopper and out to the carrier as soon as possible. We've been sweating branding irons back here. When can you get a chopper in?"

"One is supposed to come to replace the one that got shot up after it dropped us off. Maybe a couple of hours."

"If it doesn't come, you call the carrier and have them get another one in there. That's the carrier captain's primary mission, to rescue the Vice President. He better do it as quickly as possible."

"Chief, I'd think a call from the CNO would be more productive. He can get the captain on line in minutes."

"Yes, all right, I'll tell the CNO to do that. Now that the important stuff is out of the way, how are you?"

"Just tired as hell after hiking for about thirty miles. I'm finding my cot and cutting you off and getting some sleep time."

"Good night, Stroh."

"Yeah, good night, Chief."

Stroh went over to the Vice President's tent, and saw the second-highest official in the U.S. government snoring away peacefully. Stroh woke him up.

"Mr. Adams, sorry to wake you, but I just wanted you to know that a helicopter will be coming in soon and you will be put on board for a flight back to the carrier. Presi-

dent's orders, nothing I can do about it. Are you about
ready to head back?"

"Oh, hell, yes. I've seen enough now to really twist some
tails when I get back to Washington. That chopper can't
get here too soon to suit me. Thanks, Stroh, you've been a
real help to me. I won't forget it."

"Good to be able to help, Mr. Vice President. Now I'm
going to find my bunk."

The Skyhawk sliding into the soccer field an hour later
awoke Murdock and half the camp. He remembered the
edict about getting the Veep out to the carrier. He hoped
the Vice President didn't give them a hard time.

Marshall Adams was the first man to the chopper after
it landed. He shook hands with the pilot, told him who he
was, and the pilot nearly fell down trying to find a good
place for the Vice President to sit on the trip. At last he
found some packing blankets and made a seat on the floor.

Murdock, Stroh, and Mojombo all stood in the doorway
as the pilot radioed the carrier and told them he had his
package and was about to take off.

"You're not coming, Mr. Stroh?" Adams asked.

"Not yet. We have a couple more things to take care of
here."

"Good. Try not to get shot."

"Oh, that reminds me," Stroh said. "I better have Mahanani take a look at this arm." He held up his left forearm,
which had a bloody bandage around it about halfway up.

"You're shot," Murdock said. "Why didn't you tell
somebody?"

"We had bigger worries about then," Stroh said. "Besides, it builds up my macho image."

Murdock grabbed him by his good arm and pulled him
away from the chopper as the pilot wound up the engine.
"Come on, you desk jockey, you've yet to experience the
wonders of field first aid."

By noon that day Mojombo had set up a screen of sentries,
guard posts, and clusters of twenty-man emergency forces
on all the major trails down five miles below the village.

That still left ten miles on down to the ten-mile boat dock as no-man's-land.

"We're controlling everything north of that line," Mojombo said when Murdock wandered up to his tent about 1300. "If federals want to come north of that, they have to fight their way in."

"How's your campaign to enlist the other villages going?" Murdock asked.

"My top lieutenant made calls on three villages yesterday and we have their support. There are about twenty villages up here beyond the city. We want them all. Then we can move downstream."

An hour later they heard a burst of rifle fire to the south. "About a mile away, maybe less," Murdock said. Mojombo sent a runner to see what the firefight was about. He came back quickly with a man with his hands tied in front of him. He wore the cammies and the billed cap of a federal soldier.

They hurried the prisoner to the commander's tent, and he stood ramrod straight, and would have saluted except for the tied wrists.

"Sir, I am Second Lieutenant Rozolo with a message for you from Colonel Ronald Amosa."

Mojombo frowned. "Is that the same Amosa who is commander of a regiment?"

"Yes, sir. The message is not written down. I memorized it on the colonel's orders."

Before he could go on, there was a disturbance at the side of the soccer field and a man hurried away from a half-dozen soldiers who were heckling him. He looked around, then came directly to Mojombo's tent.

He braced at attention and saluted. "Sir, I am Captain Markala, of the Second Regiment of federal troops commanded by Colonel Amosa. I'm glad that Lieutenant Rozolo got through. The colonel sent two of us so one for sure would survive. The colonel has a proposition for you. Can we speak privately?"

Murdock and Stroh excused themselves and walked away toward the soccer field. A dozen kids were hard at a game.

"The enemy has a proposition?" Stroh asked.

"It wasn't from some general, from a colonel who commands a regiment." Murdock nodded. "That could be good news."

"Like a defection?" Stroh asked. "How many men in a regiment?"

"Depends on the army. Usually from one to four thousand."

"Well, now, that would change the odds all over the map," Stroh said.

"Right now it's speculation."

"Oh, sure. The colonel sends out a captain in civilian clothes to move north, and he sends a lieutenant to infiltrate, both trying to get to Mojombo. Both with a proposition. That's a deal, that's a defection of a thousand men to Mojombo's side of the war."

"Let's hope so," Murdock said. "This tropical paradise, with all the snakes and bugs and flies, is starting to get me down."

The three men conferred in Mojombo's closed tent for an hour. Then the captain went to a tent at the edge of the camp, and came back dressed in cammies with captain's bars on his shoulders and a billed cap.

A runner found Murdock and Stroh in their tents and told them they were wanted at the leader's tent.

Mojombo grinned when they came in. He introduced them to the captain and lieutenant, then had them sit down.

"Captain Markala brings us good news. Colonel Amosa is ready to defect to our side and bring his one thousand soldiers with him. All he asks is that he can retain his rank, lead his troops, and have the chance to head the new Army of Sierra Bijimi after our revolution is won. All of these conditions are acceptable to me. The captain and the lieutenant will be moving back south as soon as we feed them and form up a security patrol to go with them as far as the ten-mile bridge."

"How soon will the defection take place?" Stroh asked.

"Within two days the colonel will head a task force that will bring his regiment to the ten-mile dock, supposedly to establish a line there and sweep north eliminating all of our

Loyalist opposition," he said. "He'll bring his own transportation, his supplies, field kitchens, a medic aid station, and quantities of arms and food to last his troops for two weeks.

"Only instead of sweeping north, he will establish an iron line across the area and begin to move south, dislodging any federal troops he finds and winning over the civilians to our Loyalist cause."

"Congratulations," Stroh said. "Are there any more units like his that might defect?"

"He thinks there is one. If he can bring that regiment with him, that would cut the federal troops in half."

"What can we do to help?" Murdock asked. "We're here. We might as well be earning our keep."

Stroh lifted his brows at that, but said nothing.

"The colonel suggested two strikes that we might consider just after his defection is made known. One would be to shut down the electrical power to the city. We get all of our electrical power from an international grid. The power is hydroelectric generated by our neighbor. The colonel suggested if we simply unplugged the relay station where the entire power for the nation comes in, it would have a staggering effect. All business would shut down, the government would come to a standstill. Most of the military would be affected.

"If we could keep the power off for twenty-four to forty-eight hours, it would have a telling effect on the civilian population. The colonel figured that we could hold the relay station until the federals launch a good-sized attack against us there. We cut and run and let the federals turn on the lights. By then the damage would have been done to the federal cause.

"The second job would be to lead our unit on a strike at the municipal water plant. We have a filtration plant and a pumping a station that supplies high-quality drinking water to our city. If we shut that down for twenty-four hours, we could cause a big uproar and then turn on the spigots again."

"Be glad to send our men with yours on both jobs," Murdock said.

"Good. You, Captain Markala, Lieutenant Rozolo, and I will ride motorcycles down the trail to the ten-mile bridge. We meet Colonel Amosa there at dusk to work out any final arrangements."

Murdock looked at the federal soldier. "Captain, is this a trap to wipe out me and Mojombo? You realize without him the revolution would sputter and stop."

The captain nodded. "I understand your concern. This is not a trap. If it were, I'd be dead as well, since the soldiers would attack the four of us. It's no trap. We can ride down within a mile of the bridge, and then leave the bikes and hike through the jungle to the site, if you would be more comfortable with that."

"Sounds like a good plan. The careful soldier is an old soldier," Murdock said.

"I agree with you," the captain said.

Mojombo smiled. "Good. I don't think it's a trap, but the caution is prudent. I served under the colonel when I was in the Army. He's the most honest officer I've ever met. He's straight and dedicated and will live up to his word." He looked at Stroh. "Does the U.S. Government have any objections to this defection?"

"Not at the moment," said Stroh. "But, if it turns out to be a trap, and you two men are killed, I can promise the federal troops that they will be hit time and time and time again with missiles from the air launched by our F-18 aircraft. When the eighteens are done, there won't be enough left of the federal Army to guard a goat herd."

"I'll be ready an hour before dark," Murdock said.

On their way back to their tents, Stroh kept scowling. "It could so easily be a trap," he said.

"You indicated that. If it is, I'll smell it out and get Mojombo out of there fast. For now, we just have to wait and see."

26

Murdock watched the other two men test-ride the motorcycles, then put Captain Markala first in line and Mojombo next. Murdock brought up the rear with the lieutenant on back. The most inexperienced rider went first. They left at 1700, which gave them two hours to make the destination before dusk. Murdock wanted to recon the area after they got there early.

They hid the cycles a mile from the ten-mile dock and hiked through the jungle. Mojombo led the way now. Murdock had seen nothing to suggest a trap. When they were two hundred yards from the dock, they stopped, and Murdock went on ahead silently, deep in cover, to check out the area. There was no one on or near the dock. He moved closer and checked the wooded growth beyond the dock. The closer he looked, the more evidence he found of men in waiting.

Why were they there? Were they simply early and had decided to wait out of sight until the appointed time? Maybe. Murdock chewed it over again and again. They could have a dozen non-lethal reasons for staying out of sight. *He* was staying out of sight as well. Murdock went back to the other two men and told them what he had found.

"Typical," Captain Markala said. "The colonel is a good soldier and a cautious one. It's my opinion that he would hide himself if he arrived early. Why don't we wait until just before dusk. Then I'll walk out of the jungle and onto the dock. If all is well, the colonel and his men will come out. Then I'll wave at you that it's clear and you and Mojombo can come to the dock."

"Sounds reasonable," Murdock said. "Only let's change the plan a little. You go and contact the federals. If it's a real meet, you bring the colonel and one of his men with him and come into the jungle to this spot, where we'll have our talk. We're not going to walk out there with twenty or thirty guns on us from the brush. How do you react to that idea?"

Captain Markala grinned. "Just about what I would have suggested if I had been in your place. Yes. Good idea. We have nothing to hide. No plans to kill you. I'll do as you suggest."

A half hour later, just before dusk, the three men moved silently through the jungle. Murdock and Mojombo stopped ten yards from the edge of the clearing. Captain Markala waved at them. "We'll be back soon." He walked out of the jungle and went quickly to the dock. He stood there for a minute or two watching the water. Then two men came from the other side of the dock and met him. They talked. A moment later all three turned and walked toward where Mojombo and Murdock waited.

"Keep your hands away from your weapons and come inside here slowly," Murdock said loud enough so the three men could hear him. They did as he directed. Just inside the line of trees and brush the men stopped.

It felt right to Murdock. The colonel was armed only with a heavy pistol on his belt. He wore a cammy uniform with silver eagles on his collar. He was a half a head taller than either of the other Africans.

"Colonel Amosa, excuse the precautions, but I felt they were needed. I'm Lieutenant Commander Blake Murdock of the United States Navy SEALs."

"Commander, I have heard of your group. You are extraordinary fighting men. I admire that. We come in peace. Our intentions are exactly as my captain has outlined to you. We will be moving into this area in twenty-four hours, but not to do what the general has ordered us to do. We will come self-contained to be on duty for two weeks. We'll establish a solid defensive line across this northern area and start moving toward Sierra City. No federal troops will be allowed past us, and if they don't surrender and join us, they will be wiped out."

"How many men do you bring, Colonel?"

"Our regiments are small, only about a thousand men instead of four thousand. We are battalion-size by American standards. But we are tested fighting men. I have trained them. We have food, ammunition, supplies, and transport to handle our operation."

"Why are you defecting, Colonel Amosa?"

"For the good of my country. For two years, I have hated what the government is doing. Now the Army must step up and support Mojombo Washington and his Loyalist Party, and hold honest elections to return the government to the people."

"How many more regiments are there?"

"Two more and the support units and headquarters elements."

"Can you get another regiment to come over?" Murdock asked.

I'm working on Colonel Massad of the First. But he's a little timid. Not my choice for a regimental leader, but not a bad man. I'll work on him. But for now, tomorrow, just me and my thousand men."

"We're bowled over by your help, Colonel," Mojombo said. "Is there anything we need to do to get ready?"

"Just be sure not to fire on us if you see us. We'll be about ten miles below your strong points. But there shouldn't be any federal troops within that area. As we move south toward the city, we'll do it in your name. If you want to detach fifty men with us, I'll integrate them into my forces."

"Good. I'll send them down in the morning under the command of Lieutenant Gabu."

"Have them contact Captain Markala." The colonel nodded. "Good. This has gone well. We will be moving by truck to this area early tomorrow morning, so I better get back. Yes, we have transport. We'll coordinate our work starting tomorrow."

"Colonel, we have a plan that could swing public sentiment to the Loyalist side," Murdock said. "We want to shut down the power station for twenty-four hours. Not blow it up, just take it off-line and kill the electric power to the nation for that long. Do you approve?"

The colonel frowned. "It will be an inconvenience to many people, especially the computer people. But they can stand a one-day vacation. Yes, and when it goes back on line we'll trumpet the news to the people through the radio and newspapers that their power is courtesy of the Loyalist Party. I have high-level contacts with the press."

"We had also considered shutting down the water pumping plants," Mojombo said.

The colonel shook his head. "Doesn't sound good to me. Too dangerous. People could die. Water is absolutely essential. I'd say don't do the water plant."

"You're right. We won't. I'd like to attach most of my men to your command," Mojombo said. "A separate company and under your direction. I'm not a general by any means."

"We'll talk about that as soon as we get our line built here and start moving south. My hope is we can liberate at least half of Sierra City within a week."

They talked a moment more, then said good-bye, and the colonel and his men left the jungle and vanished into the night. The two others moved out to a trail and headed north a mile to where they had left their motorcycles.

It took them most of an hour to ride the ten miles up the crooked, root-filled trail to Tinglat.

Before he went to his tent, Murdock checked to see if the Skyhawk was in its nesting place. It was. The pilot sat in the cockpit reading a book by a flashlight. Murdock said hi, and Josie Halstrom looked up and grinned.

"Hey, man, good to see you. I hear we're picking up some support from the local Army lads."

Murdock chuckled. "Right, we are, a thousand men and support. How did you hear about it?"

"Rumors all over camp."

"Why are you back here?"

"Talked my boss into letting me come back in a different ship. He told me not get this one shot up. We up for any short-haul trips anywhere?"

"Could be tomorrow night. I'll let you know. Right now my bunk is looking better and better."

They said good night, and Murdock headed for his tent and found JG Gardner snoring softly on his side of the space. Murdock figured that was a good idea. The defection of one regiment of the federal Army was a huge windfall for the Loyalists. It could spell a quick end to the revolution. Especially if Colonel Amosa could bring over another regiment. That night Murdock knew he was going to go to sleep smiling.

The next morning, Murdock talked with Mojombo before he decided which of his men to send south to hook up with Colonel Amosa.

"This electrical substation or power station—do you have anyone who is an electrician or has worked at this place?" Murdock asked.

Mojombo frowned, and then called in a runner and told him to ask for any electricians or anyone who had worked at the South Substation.

"Yes, I see," he said. "It would be helpful if we knew exactly what we can disable at the plant that will be quick and easy to replace. Not exactly throwing a switch, but something like that. We don't want to blow it up."

"Amen to that, Washington. I'd suggest that we send out our group tonight. Where is it located?"

"The substation is about twenty miles south of Sierra City. We'll need to take the helicopter. It is a handy gadget. I'm planning on getting some for the government as soon as we get a new one elected."

"Will you be running for President?"

"I hope so. I'm more politician than general. But that will have to wait. I do suggest we go at night to cut down on any ground fire against the chopper."

"Agreed. This pilot is ready for anything. Let me know how many men we'll need and if we need to take any electricians with us."

Don Stroh scowled at Murdock as soon as the SEAL came out of the headman's tent.

"Been looking for you, Commander. Just how in hell did you get me in trouble this time?"

"Trouble?"

"Yeah, my boss called me on the SATCOM and told me to get my ass out of here and back on the carrier at the first opportune moment."

"I swear, Stroh, I didn't say a word to anyone on the SATCOM. I don't even know who your boss is. Maybe it's routine."

"He even knew I got shot in my arm. Now somebody has been talking with somebody."

"The fun here is winding down, Stroh. I'd guess the President has about a week left in office."

"Bradford. He's your top SATCOM man. It had to be him talking to somebody on the air. Wait until I find him."

Murdock grinned. "Stroh, maybe you better calm down. As I remember, Bill Bradford is six-two and runs about two-twenty or so after a good meal. You gonna take him on with bare knuckles?"

Stroh grinned and slammed his fist into his hand. "Yeah, I sort of forgot how big he is. Uh-oh, yeah. Well, at least I can talk to him."

"Stroh, little buddy, I need a favor."

"Is it going to cost me?"

"Not a penny. We'll be going out on another action tonight. I want you to stay in camp."

"Just when the fun begins? How can I really prove myself to your platoon guys if I can't trade shots with the damn federal troops?"

"You did already, and you're wounded. So you're medically grounded. Now, take care of that arm and use the medication and do whatever else Mahanani told you to do. If you don't obey orders like a good little CIA desk man, I'll ship you back to the carrier."

"Okay, okay. I'll stay in camp. I don't know why. No good booze here and no women at all. Well, some black ones over there in the village. But I've never been partial to black."

"Good. Now, I've got to talk to the men and then to Mojombo."

An hour later, Murdock knocked on the center post of the tent, and Mojombo waved him inside.

"I've had three men report to me about the electricity plant," said Mojombo. "One of them worked for a time at the substation. He says it's on the top of a small mountain with the big towers leading the wires in and then out of it."

"Did he know how we could disable it without ruining the whole thing?"

"He had some ideas, but he'll need to look at it again. We'll take him along. Him and me and all of your SEALs."

"Sounds good. Daylight or dark?"

"The electrician said they used to have two men on night duty, and neither one was armed. Might be different now. Especially after our raids, the federals might have eight or ten men there defending the place."

"Then let's go after dark and slip up on them. Hike in the last mile. All we have to do is follow the power lines."

"About seventy miles down there. If we leave at dusk we should be in good shape. Your SEALs all in fighting shape?"

"All except Stroh, who I ordered to stay here."

"Best for him. I'll see you this afternoon to set up our time schedule."

That afternoon, the SEALs were told about the mission. The senior chief and the JG gave them details about the raid and when it would lift off.

"I like it," Rafii said. "No hiking."

"Maybe," Jaybird said. "Remember our last round trip on a helicopter? We walked home."

All of the walking wounded made it to the flight. Gardner had the bullet wound in his right arm, but it was healing. Rafii's wounded leg was not bothering him. Sadler's left arm wasn't as bad as they'd thought at first.

The fifteen SEALs and two Africans in the Seahawk lifted off the soccer field promptly at 1930, and made a wide swing around Sierra City. They found the power lines and followed them for twenty miles before the pilot saw the hilltop substation ahead. He pulled out a mile from it before he hunted an LZ. He found one beside a moderate-sized stream where flooding had choked out the jungle and left a small clearing that had been farmed.

"Stay right here unless we tell you to come get us," Murdock told Lieutenant Halstrom. He had one of their Motorolas, and it was tuned and checked. He waved at them and went into the edge of the encroaching jungle to be a defensive force of one.

Lam led the hike to the mountain. It was higher than it had looked from the chopper. They were near the top when Lam called a halt.

"Somebody up there, Cap. Not sure how many, but some. Must be an outpost. Should I take a closer look?"

"That's why you get the big pay, Sailor. Scope it out."

Five minutes later, the SEALs heard Lam on the Motorolas.

"Skipper, I've got a two-man lookout position. No bunker or protection. Both are sitting on a log beside a sort of trail up from a stream. Must use it for getting water. Both men are soldiers and armed with long guns. Want me to take both down with my MP-5?"

"How far to the substation?"

"About a hundred yards, up an easy slope. I don't see anyone around the high-fenced area."

"I'm coming up to take a look."

When Murdock squirmed up beside Lam in the thick growth, he saw a problem. They could see the big transformers and electrical grids and power cables, but anyone in the small control building on this side of all the electrical equipment could also see the two guards. If they went down, someone inside would know it.

"This gives us a big problem," Murdock whispered to Lam. The two soldiers sat on the log thirty feet out front. "How are we going to take out these two and hit the control shack up there at the same time and not damage any delicate instruments and controls?"

27

Lam looked at the scene again, then grinned. "Hey, Cap, you joshing me or what? This is a piece of cake. We take out the people inside the control shack first. Put one EAR blast into that substation window, and a second or two later we take out the two guards with silenced MP-5s."

"You're right," Murdock said. "Remember the Bishop Museum in Hawaii? The EAR shots didn't hurt any of the artifacts in there, so we should be okay here." He hit the Motorola. "Get the EAR up here pronto," he said. "Lam, just after the EAR shot, you take out the sentry on the right, I'll take the man on the left."

Kenneth Ching came charging up with the EAR, and settled in for a shot after Murdock pointed out the target.

"Right through the window, Ching. Make it a good one." On the Motorola he told the platoon to move up where he was and stay out of sight. "We're going to use the EAR through the window, then take out the two sentries. When they are down, we charge up the last hundred to the control room and see what we have to work with."

Murdock looked at Ching in the darkness. "Whenever you're ready, Ken."

A second later Ching triggered off the highly charged burst of enhanced air that slammed through the distance and shattered the pane-glass window as it burst inside the small shack. For a moment Murdock wondered if the sides of the structure would explode outward. They didn't. He heard Lam fire, and he refined his sight on the second guard and pulled the trigger on single-shot. Murdock's chest hit was a little off center. He fired again where the guard had fallen, and the soldier didn't move anymore.

"Let's go," Murdock said into his mike, and the seventeen men lifted up and charged silently up the slope. There was a high fence around the substation itself, but the ten-foot-by-ten-foot shack stood outside the fence.

Murdock tested the door. Unlocked. He jerked it open and stared inside around the doorjamb. In the lighted room he saw two men lying on the floor. Murdock motioned the Loyalist soldier forward, and he looked around the shack.

"Nothing here to hurt the substation," the Loyalist soldier said. "We have to get inside the fence."

"No wire cutters for a fence this heavy," Jaybird said.

"Blow it," Murdock ordered.

Canzoneri, their resident explosives expert, ran forward and looked at the fence gate.

"Easiest way to get in is to blow the hinges off," he said. As he talked, he pasted two one-inch squares of TNAZ plastic explosive on the hinges and inserted twin timer/detonators. "Get back thirty," he said. Then he set the timers for twenty seconds, pushed them both to activate the timers, and sprinted to the side and behind the control shack.

The sharp crack of the explosives sounded like twin rolls of thunder in the carpet of green jungle that covered the hills.

"Everyone down and dirty," Murdock barked in the radio. "There has to be a small force up here and they will be on the run. Keep your eyes on."

"I've got noise coming up the back of the hill," Tracy Donegan said. "Sounds like company."

"Spread out, find cover," Gardner said on the Motorola.

Donegan saw them first. "I've got a dozen coming up a trail, bunched. We have weapons free?"

"Wait until we can see them all," Murdock said. "Fire on my MP-5 rounds."

Donegan was closest to them. He counted eleven as they came up the trail and then spread out as they entered the cleared space around the far side of the electrical substation.

"Now," Murdock said, and chattered off six rounds from his MP-5. At once the rest of the men fired. The rattle of the MP-5s was covered with the heavier rounds coming from the sniper rifles and the machine gun. Then the 5.56 rounds shrilled into the fight, and the eleven federal soldiers caught in the open with no cover went down.

Two surged up and darted for some trees at the edge of the clearing. One took a round in the leg, but both made it into the brush and tangle of the jungle growth. JG Gardner was closest to them.

"Donegan on me, let's go get those last two." The SEALs' fire cut off as all the enemy were down. Donegan and Gardner sprinted twenty yards to the edge of the forest, where Gardner held up his hand and they both stopped. He pointed to his ear and then into the growth and both listened.

They heard sounds of movement even through the lush tropical growth. Gardner took the lead, running where possible, ducking under and around trees, skirting patches of thick growth, and every fifty feet stopping to listen.

"Getting closer," Gardner whispered on the last stop. They had worked down the back side of the mountain, and now a small ridge showed to the left that bordered a tiny ravine no more than fifty feet across. The two SEALs paused to look. Gardner lifted his Bull Pup and fired a 20mm round into the valley. The round went off with a snarling roar, and Gardner waved them forward.

"Saw one of them beside a tree down there," he said. "Hope I nailed the little bastard. Let's go take a look."

They worked through the jungle growth faster now. Up here on the slopes the ground was relatively dry. The almost daily rain could run off toward the drainage downstream.

The SEALs moved up on the target tree carefully, supporting each other as they leapfrogged the last fifty yards. At the tree they found one man slumped against some brush. He lifted a pistol and was about to shoot at point-blank range when Donegan swung up his H & K G-11 caseless-bullet rifle and sprayed ten rounds into the surprised federal soldier. There was no sign of the other one.

"We wasted one of them, but there's no sign of the other

one, Skipper," Gardner said on the radio. "The second man must be long gone."

"Bring the dead man's weapon and ammo and return," Murdock said. He had just finished a tour of the substation with the Loyalist soldier/electrician.

"If we just blow up the place, we run the risk of blacking out the whole grid back up through four countries," the soldier/electrician said. "It would be easy if there was a transformer we could knock out, but the juice comes in high voltage and goes out as high voltage."

"So what do we tear up?" Murdock asked. "No switches we could throw and black it out?"

The electrician laughed. "Not that easy. No switch that strong. We need to hit it at the output. We could blow down that first steel tower, or cut the lines that it carries."

"The lines would be easiest to repair. Let's work on them. How many do we need to cut?"

It took the electrician a half hour to decide where to set the charges. Canzoneri helped him set up the TNAZ and place it on supports that got the lines started south. The blasts would knock down the supports, overstress the thick cables, and tear them apart. When they dropped into the jungle they would be dead and harmless.

The electrician figured the repair time would be about a week, with the facilities and equipment that the federal troops and the substation's manpower could raise. Then he shook his head. "No, there is a way to do it quicker. They can put in bypass cables to send the juice south, then build permanent supports and finish the job. The bypass could be done in two days."

Murdock nodded. "Good, let's go ahead and set the timers for two minute. Then we get everyone back down the hill a ways."

Canzoneri and the electrician coordinated their work, then pushed in the timers to activate them. Then the two men rushed down the trail fifty yards from the substation.

The explosions were not large, and they came in a succession of snarling blasts that were followed by huge showers of sparks as the power lines parted and the dead ones fell into the Sierra Bijimi jungle waiting to be repaired.

Murdock, the JG, Mojombo, and the electrician ran up to the substation and looked over the results of the blasts.

Mojombo was pleased. "Yes, that will make a statement to the general population. The federal Army will rush workers up here to fix the damage. We have struck a blow for liberty."

Murdock watched the black man. There was no doubt about his sincerity. He was dedicated to his nation and his plans to rip it out of the hands of the despots who ruled it now. Murdock's big problem was trying to figure out how he and the SEALs could help him do that without getting in a batch of serious international trouble. He shrugged. First they had to find the chopper and get the hell out of there before more troops came in.

Murdock used the Motorola. "Load them up and move them out," he said. "Column of ducks. JG, you take the lead with Lam out front on point. I'll ride drag. If you Easterners don't know what that means, it has nothing to do with how I dress. In the Old West on a cattle drive, the worst possible spot was to ride drag or the last man on the drive. The drag rider had to chase strays back into the herd, prod along the loafers, and in the process eat all the dirt that four thousand hooves could dig up and swirl around in a huge dust cloud that always drifted back over the drag rider. Enough? Let's move."

Fifteen minutes later they were almost down the mountain when the Motorola warning stopped them.

"Skipper, looks like we have a situation here. From what I can tell in the dark there is a whole piss-pot full of troops heading our way. My estimate is about forty to fifty. Suggestions?"

"How far off, Lam?"

"Skipper, I'd say maybe a half mile. Some of them are even singing. Not a care in the world."

"We'll go to ground. I want everyone to take a hard-right-flank march and move fifty yards into the jungle cover. Keep the man next to you in sight at all times so we don't get split up. Move it right now."

It was more than twenty minutes later that they heard the federal troops go by. They didn't march exactly, and there were some more songs. It sounded more like a summer camp outing than an Army movement. Murdock waited ten minutes after the men passed before he called for his troops to move back to the trail and get on down the mountain.

After they left the trail, Lam angled them toward where the chopper should be. They were within a mile of the bird when Lam went on the net again.

"Skipper, I'm not sure what the hell is going on up here. You better come take a look. Near as I can tell from this distance, the federal bohunks have set up what looks like a permanent facility up here. Nothing like this when we came in earlier tonight."

"I'm coming, Lam. Could it be that we're on a slightly different course than the one we went in on and we just missed this installation?"

"From the looks of it, you're right. It's been here for some time. We were lucky to miss it when we came in. Now we need to take a small detour. Must be a hundred men and tents and even some four-wheel-drive rigs."

"Any activity like they heard the blasts up on top?"

"Doesn't look like it. I'll wait for you here."

Murdock and Gardner took a look.

"Too many of them, unless we want to hit them with all of our twenties," Gardner said.

"Then the survivors would chase us all the way to the chopper and might shoot it down," Murdock said. "Let's slip around them and find the chopper and get out of here. We don't need a body count on this run."

They backtracked half a mile, then charged into the jungle. Murdock used the Motorola. "Halstrom, you still wide awake?"

There was a moment's dead air. Then: "Oh, yeah. Had a wake-up call about an hour ago. Heard a patrol of some kind, but it never got within sight of the chopper or me. But they left to the south and west if I'm oriented."

"Yeah, we found their camp. Almost went in for a dog-steak dinner, but declined. We went around them. Any landmarks around there we can zero in on?"

"Not much. Just the little tributary stream. It's not huge, as you know."

"We'll put our bloodhound noses on and see if we can find you. Darker out here than an old maid's bedroom at midnight."

Murdock found Lam. "So which and where?"

"He's got to be north of us. I worked too far down the trail before I turned west and north. Let's give it another try. Wish these Motorolas had a built-in homing device."

"We can suggest it."

After a twenty-minute hike, Lam came on the net. "Oh, yeah, troops, we're on the right track. We're at the little creek we passed before, the one the chopper should be on. We turn upstream and should nail him in about ten."

They did.

Once everyone was on board, Gardner asked for a casualty report. They had one turned ankle that wasn't all that bad, and nothing else. They flew a more direct course this time back to their camp north of Sierra City, and landed well before dawn.

As they walked to their tents, Lam saw three shadowy forms in front of Mojombo's tent. He warned the others. They advanced slowly. One of the forms sat up.

"Mojombo?"

"Yes."

"Good, you're back. I'm Captain Kintay from Colonel Amosa's regiment. There have been some changes and we need to talk with you right now."

28

Kintay and his two fellow officers, along with Mojombo, Murdock, and Gardner, all went inside the leader's tent, where Mojombo lit three candles.

"My men don't get to use electric lights here, so neither do I," Mojombo said. "Now, what is so important that it needs a nighttime meeting?"

Captain Kintay looked up. "Time is indeed important. Matters are changing rapidly in Sierra City and with the government of President Kolda. Three of his cabinet members have resigned. Colonel Amosa has confirmation that Colonel Massad, who commands the First Regiment of eleven hundred men, has agreed to defect with Colonel Amosa's regiment. Instead of coming up country tomorrow, they will seize the Central Army Base and put the whole thing under our control. That means by tomorrow night we should have under our command two thirds of the armed forces. We will send delegations to the other regiment and the various smaller units demanding that they come to our side or they will be annihilated. It is our opinion that by day after tomorrow, we will control over ninety percent of the Sierra Bijimi Army."

"This indeed is good news," Mojombo said. "Will there be any move to take President Kolda out of office?"

"We wanted your advice on that matter. We have no plans to stage a coup and set up a military government. We wish your suggestions."

Mojombo looked suddenly serious, as if he had the weight of the whole world on his shoulders. He blinked twice, cleared his throat, and then looked up. "Captain Kintay, it is my suggestion that after you have the military power, you send tanks and a massive number of armed men to the front of the Government Building and demand the resignation of the President and the Vice President. Give them four hours. If they do not resign and leave the capital, you should move in and carry them out by force.

"With these resignations, an interim government would be run by the Speaker of the House. The Speaker should then call for new elections to be supervised by the United Nations and the United States. Nominations would be made within a month, and elections would be held, closely supervised by the United Nations and the United States, within three months."

The two other federal officers had been writing quickly on pads of paper they had produced.

Captain Kintay smiled. "Good. Good. It is as we had hoped and wished and prayed for. Can you and your top lieutenant ride motorcycles?"

"Yes, Lieutenant Gabu and I both can ride, and we have motorcycles here. Did you come on motorcycles?"

"We did. Colonel Amosa suggests that we ride out tonight to the ten-mile bridge, where we will find truck transport to take us to the Army camp before daylight. It will be safer that way."

Mojombo looked at Murdock. He had tears in his eyes. "It seems that we have won, that the honest, loyal citizens and the soldiers of Sierra Bijimi will at last have a chance for a freely elected government."

"Then it looks like our job here is about done," Murdock said.

"Please stay for two more days until we see what happens in the city. I'll send a messenger up here every day to let you know how it's going. Give us two days to be sure we can oust the President."

Murdock nodded. "Two or three days, we can do that. Yes, we'll be on standby here in case there's something we can help you with."

Murdock and Gardner went back to their tent.

"So, it looks like this is about wrapped up," Gardner said.

"Maybe. You never can tell about a dictator like Kolda.

He might have some contingency plans. He must have known that Amosa was about ready to defect. He could be in Ghana or Nigeria by now. He might even be on his way to his Swiss bank account."

"True, but he also might be tucked into some fortress with a hundred guards, and they'll have to dig him out with bombs and bullets. I hope that's the case."

"Let's talk to Stroh. We'll wake him up and let him know what's happening." Murdock grinned. "Yeah, about time we get to wake him up in the middle of the night for a change. Where's his tent?"

Stroh came out of a deep sleep snorting and yawning. When they turned on the light he blinked, and at last saw who was there.

"You guys crazy? It's still dark out."

"Thought you might like to know the latest developments."

"Better be important. I was in this dream with this woman who was . . ." He blinked. "What's going on?"

They told him.

Stroh grabbed his SATCOM and fired it up. Before he made his connection in Washington, D.C., the two SEALs vanished out of his tent and dove into their cots. It had been a long day.

Stroh let the SEALs sleep in until noon. Then he roused Murdock from his slumbers.

"Hey, buddy, you awake yet?"

Murdock kicked his feet onto the canvas floor of the tent and groaned. "It better be important, Government Agent, or I'm gonna tear your arms off and beat you silly."

"Yes, important. The President, is that important enough for you?"

"I knew I shouldn't have been so friendly with that guy. He can really get a person into a lot of trouble."

"Like now, rookie. The President has ordered you to go into Sierra City with two men and a SATCOM and give State a blow-by-blow description of what's going on. They want to know if the coup takes place, if there will be democratic elections, when the embassy can be reopened. Shit like that."

"And if we're in the wrong place and we get shot up into pieces by either side . . ."

"You'll get a medal and a nice letter from the President to your survivors."

"Thanks a bunch. When are we supposed to get into town?"

"No rush. You should have been there by now. You're to take the motorcycles and move in this morning, or afternoon as it is now."

Murdock growled, pulled on his boots, and took one last look at Stroh. "Hey hotshot, you want to come along? Maybe I can get you killed on this one."

"Thanks, but no, thanks. One bullet hole in my hide is enough. I'll leave the tough stuff to you young bucks."

Murdock found Lam and Jaybird and told them their new assignment.

"At least we'll see the end of it," Jaybird said. "What weapons?"

There were two motorcycles left in camp. Murdock rode one and Jaybird and Lam the other one. They were surprised to get all the way to the ten-mile dock before they ran into any military. They moved up cautiously, and Murdock called from cover to a lone sentry near the dock.

"Hello, sentry. Are you with Colonel Amosa's regiment?"

The soldier pointed his rifle at the sound. "Who's asking? Show yourself."

"Are you in the Second Regiment under Colonel Amosa?"

"Yes. Who are you?"

"U.S. Navy SEALs. We've been helping the colonel and Mojombo. We're supposed to report to him down in the city."

"We control all of this area now. My captain didn't say anything about any SEALs coming."

"He didn't know. We need to get through and find the colonel's headquarters. Don't shoot, we're coming out."

They rolled the two motorcycles out. The soldier was surprised.

"Wow, motorcycles. Can I take a ride?"

"No time. We need a guide from your unit to get us through the city and into the Central Army Base."

An hour later they were near the center of the city when they came to a roadblock in the middle of a street that had buildings on both sides. There was no way around it. The two guides from the Second Regiment shook their heads.

"We'll have to go back a half mile and go around them," the corporal with them said.

"What's behind them?" Murdock asked.

"It's just a pocket of resistance. We control most of the city now."

"Twenties," Lam said.

Murdock nodded. The roadblock was a six-by-six truck parked sideways, with a jeep on each side closing down the narrow street. The SEALs divided up the targets, and each fired two rounds from the Bull Pups. Lam's second round into the truck hit the fuel tank, and it exploded in a mass of flames engulfing both jeeps as well. Two men ran away from the flames. The SEALs let them go.

Ten minutes later the fire was burned down enough that the SEALs and the Loyalist men could jump over the last of it and rush on down the street.

Mojombo laughed when the three SEALs marched into his room in the command post of the big Army base.

"Well, you came quicker than I figured you would. I'll bet Washington wants to know what's going on. You can send your first report. We have more than ninety-five percent of the armed forces under our command. I've promoted Colonel Amosa to brigadier general in command of all the nation's armed forces. We have two teams repairing the power lines at the substation. They should be done before dark today. We have three tanks and five hundred men in front of the Government Building awaiting the resignation of the President and his entire executive department."

"Will he do that, knowing that he'll face trial for graft, corruption, and murder?" Murdock asked.

"We expect him to give up. He has no place to go. He has no airplane or helicopter. Even his cars have been reduced to two. We expect him to give up soon."

"He'll run," Jaybird said. "How many men does he have with him?"

"He has about fifty of his interior guards."

"You have all the doors covered?" Lam asked.

"We do. He can't get out."

"Are there any tunnels, secret stairways, anything you don't know about?"

"I hope not," Mojombo said.

"What about civilian workers in the building?" Murdock asked. "Are they still inside or have they left?"

"We will be allowing them to leave ten at a time. The evacuation will begin shortly."

"That's how he'll get out," Lam said. "Disguised as a waiter or gardener. He'll slip past your sentries, who won't be checking the civilians."

Mojombo frowned. "Possible."

"Describe him for us," Lam said.

"He's about five-eight, heavy, a hundred and eighty pounds. Slow on his feet. He's losing his hair. Usually wears glasses. Walks with a slight limp."

Murdock looked at his two men. They nodded. "Get us transport to the Government Building," Murdock said.

"You think . . ." Mojombo stopped. "Yes, right away. Oh, I will be installed by the military in the Government Building as Caretaker President until elections can be held." He smiled. "Right this way for some jeeps and backup."

Two hours later, Murdock, Lam, and Jaybird kept in touch on their Motorolas. So far they had seen dozens of civilians come out the three doors being used for their evacuation. All wore civilian clothes. A few had on their work uniforms. Two were cooks, one a driver with hat and uniform. None had matched the description of the President.

Jaybird hit the net. "Hold it. I have four men coming. All are tall, young, with military-type haircuts. Their clothes don't really fit. Give you any ideas?"

"Have the soldiers pull them to one side and hold them,"

Murdock said. "Even a President needs four or five guards to help him walk to freedom."

"Bingo, I've got six men about the same type and dress," Lam said. "And just behind them is a fat little cook, with his white shirt and grease-stained pants and white chef's hat. He's got a mustache and beard that I bet I can pull right off."

"Move your squad of soldiers up and take them," Murdock said. "I'm on my way."

Murdock heard the weapons firing before he got around the corner from the side door of the big building. He saw dozens of people flat on the ground. Fifty yards away six men in civvies ran toward a row of houses. Two dropped from rifle fire. Murdock heard a twenty fire, but the men had slid around the corner of a building unhurt. He spotted Lam chasing them. The commander put on a burst of speed, and sprinted down a street, and caught Lam looking around the corner of a building.

"Skipper. They surprised us. The bastards had Uzis under their shirts and blasted the four soldiers without warning. Then they ran. By the time I got here they had made it to the buildings."

"They couldn't have planned it," Murdock said. "It had to be a spur-of-the-moment move. So probably no transport."

As he said it, a big car jolted out of a building halfway down the block and raced toward the corner thirty yards away. Lam came down on it with his Bull Pup and fired. The round impacted the rear of the vehicle and exploded. Murdock and Lam ran toward it. The car slued into a building and crashed. Smoke but no fire came from the wreckage. Three men struggled out of the front of the car. One was the fat cook still wearing his hat. Murdock took down the two tall men with a pair of shots for each from his 5.56. They still carried their weapons. The fat man turned. He had blood on his arm and face.

The SEALs moved up to the wreck slowly. Jaybird charged into the scene and checked the car. "No live ones," he reported.

Murdock stared at the man who would be king. "President Kolda?" he asked.

The fat man in the cook's clothes looked up out of half-open eyes. He wiped blood from his face and tried to stand straighter.

"Yes, I am President Kolda, and I demand to be treated with respect."

"The respect you showed the innocent people you killed? The respect you showed by closing the schools and stealing the money? The respect you showed the United States by stealing most of the twelve million dollars we sent you for agricultural reform? Sure we will. You bastard. I should kill you right here, but I'll let you live so you can be tried for treason, for murder, fraud, grand theft, and a dozen other crimes. If I can, I'll be here in time to see you be executed by a firing squad. Until then, you can think about this."

Murdock switched his Bull Pup to single-round on the 5.56 and shot ex-President Kolda in the right knee, shattering his kneecap and exploding the whole joint. The man crumpled into the street with a scream of agony and despair.

By the time Murdock and his men had commandeered a car and transported ex-President Kolda back to the Army base, the resistance was over. The remaining guards in the Government Building had come out with their weapons held over their heads. The Loyalist troops occupied the Government Building and brought Mojombo to the President's office, and there he waited for the electrical power to come on. The moment it came on, he gave a talk to the country on TV and radio.

At the Army base, Lam set up the SATCOM and Murdock made his report directly to the State Department in Washington. When he was through, he looked up to find that Jaybird had appropriated a jeep, and they piled in and headed for the ten-mile dock and their motorcycles.

Back in the tent in Tinglat, Murdock made a complete report to Stroh and asked him to get orders for the SEALs. Stroh repeated to his boss on the SATCOM what Murdock had told him, and ten minutes later the SEALs had their marching orders.

"Back to the carrier at first light in the morning," Stroh said. "From there you will be checked out by the medics, then flown to the airport at Dakar in Senegal, where a Navy Gulfstream II will meet you for transport back to San Diego."

"Oh, yeah," Murdock said, and headed to his bunk for a few hours of sleep. Next stop, the Quarterdeck in Coronado.

29

NAVSPECWARGRUP-ONE
Coronado, California

Murdock checked his desk calendar. Third Platoon, SEAL Team Seven, had been home for a week. The walking wounded had been checked over at Balboa Navy Hospital in San Diego's Balboa Park, and returned to duty. Frank Victor was the only worry. His neck wound was not serious, but the doctors were worried about his chest. The bullet had fragmented, and they still weren't sure they had it all out. Victor would be out of the platoon for at least two months, probably three.

Murdock put in a call for a temporary replacement in case they were yanked out for a mission before Victor was duty-ready. Master Chief MacKenzie had sent over three candidates. The man would go into JG Gardner's squad. He didn't like any of the three, and three more came the next day. He picked one, a wiry little Vietnamese who was tough as old leather, could swim like a fish, and had been on top of the rung through his tadpole training. He'd been a SEAL for two years and both Murdock and Gardner liked him. His infectious grin played a big part. His name was a small problem, Vinh Lai. It was pronounced Vin Lie. They'd get used to it.

Murdock stretched and looked at the training schedule. JG Gardner had pushed the men once they came back from their three-day leaves. They needed it. The days in Africa with little action had taken a toll. Now they started every day at 0730 with the three ups: pull-ups, push-ups, and sit-ups. They had started with twenty-five of each and now were up to sixty-five. They were on schedule to go up five more every day.

The phone rang, and Murdock picked it up. "Third Platoon, SEAL Team Seven. Murdock."

"Yes, I figured it would be you." It was the master chief on the Quarterdeck. "I've had two requests from the San Diego Police to talk to Senior Chief Sadler. It's about a murder case that he was somewhat involved in before you went to Africa."

"A murder case?"

"He was a witness to what the police say happened before the death. They want to talk to him again. It was at that jazz club where he plays his horn."

"The cops want to see him today?"

"As soon as possible. They suggest that he come down to the Central Police Station and ask for Detective Petroff. Tell him to call first and set up a time."

"Consider it done, Master Chief. Thanks."

Murdock hung up and called on the Motorola for the senior chief to come into the office.

Two hours later, Senior Chief Sadler parked on 14th Street, fed two quarters into the meter, and walked over to the Central Police Station. At the big desk he asked for Detective Petroff and gave his name. A woman in uniform told him the detective would be right down, and pointed to some chairs in the small lobby.

Sadler had started to flip through the San Diego *Union-Tribune* when Petroff loomed over him.

"Ah, yes, the globe-hopping senior chief. How is the trumpet sounding these days?"

"Not the best when I don't practice every day. A trumpet player can lose his lip in a rush. Have you found out if the girl died of an accidental OD?"

"Not yet. We were hoping that you could help us find your buddy Shortchops Jackson."

"By now you know much more about him than I do. I just did the gigs with him once a week. I've never been to his apartment, if he has one, or his house. I don't know where he hangs out when he isn't with us. I know little more about him than some of his history and the great music he's played. He has out six different albums, did you realize that?"

The tall, slender detective dropped into a chair next to Sadler and stared at him from his almost black eyes. "Did you know that you're considered a suspect in the OD murder of Joisette Brown? Why? As I told you before on the phone, you were named in her will with an inheritance of fifty thousand dollars. I know a lot of men who would do a lot of things to get their hands on fifty big ones."

"I'm not one of them. I never knew anything about that until that day you called. It's not a motive for me."

"You did leave the rehearsal room while Joisette was still alive."

"When?"

"We figured you went to the bathroom. Did you?"

"Yes, I usually do. I told you that. My prostate isn't all that it should be."

"Did anyone see you there?"

"Of course, two cooks, three waitresses, and the cocktail girl with the big boobs."

Petroff stood and walked around his chair. "Snide remarks won't help the situation. I could put you under arrest."

"And I would sue you for twenty million dollars. Now if you don't have anything of importance to ask me, I am still on duty with a lot of work to get done."

"Afraid I'm not quite finished yet. Do you know the name of the hooker who Joisette was with that night?"

"No. I never saw her that night or before or after that night."

Petroff rubbed his chin. "A definitive answer."

"Have you talked to her about what Joisette did in that alley? Did she see Joisette take a hit with a needle?"

"That's police business. I can tell you we have talked to her. She wasn't what you would call a solid witness. She'd been on drugs that night as well."

"Didn't you pick up any drug paraphernalia at the scene?"

"Of course."

"Did any of it have the dead girl's prints on it?"

"I can't tell you that."

"In other words what you found didn't have her prints, or you would have closed this case out a week ago. Sorry, I wasn't out at the death scene, I didn't see Joisette and Shortchops shooting up in the hall or outside. If Shortchops knew who Joisette was, I'm almost positive that he wouldn't provide her with any drugs."

"She lived with him for almost six months on and off."

"So you've got a simple OD self-inflicted."

"Not without that syringe."

"Wish I could help you. Anything else?"

The cop shook his head. "Thanks for stopping by. If you think of anything that might clear Shortchops, give me a call." He held out a white card.

Five minutes later, Senior chief Sadler sat in his car thinking about it. Did he know where Shortchops lived? He did take him home one night. It was raining and the man didn't have a car. Yeah. Where did they go? Like he had told the cop, he didn't know where Shortchops lived. But could he piece it together now? Exactly where had Shortchops directed him? Could he find the place again?"

Not the best part of town. Where? Grant Hill. Yeah, right beside Logan Heights. They had driven straight out Broadway to 28th Street. Turned right, but how far?

He gunned the engine, pulled out of the parking spot, and found Broadway and turned east. It took him a few minutes to get to 28th. He turned right and watched the houses and small apartments. Mostly large houses turned into four or five units. But he had driven here six months ago, just after Shortchops had joined them. He could have moved two or three times since then. Or maybe moved back. Sadler drove under Freeway 94 on 28th and kept watching.

At K Street he hung a right and slowed. Yes, it felt familiar. But was it right? The first cross street was Langley. It only went to the right. Halfway up he stopped again. The house he was hunting had been purple and green. He had seen the unusual paint job even in the rain at night. They had laughed about it. Shortchops had said the owner was drunk when he bought the paint, then couldn't afford to buy any more. It had been mixed to order so he couldn't take it back. He used it.

Sadler stopped in the street in front of a house painted purple with green trim. Four units. He remembered he had waited until Shortchops dashed through the rain and went in a door on the left. Hell, why not? The area was predominately black. He felt out of place as he passed four black kids playing on the sidewalk and moved up the concrete to the door, then around to the left to the next entrance. He knocked.

A black woman about forty-five opened the door a foot. She scowled. "What you'all want?"

"Looking for a friend. Shortchops Jackson used to live here." She started to close the door, but his big Navy shoe wedged in and stopped it.

"Hey, I'm not the cops, I play jazz with the man every week. I want to help him."

The woman frowned. "You got a name?" He told her. She turned and shouted something, then waited. After what seemed to Sadler to be five minutes, she slowly eased away from the door. It swung open, and Sadler stared at the man he had known as Shortchops Jackson. He looked twenty years older, ancient. He had a week's growth of beard showing white on his black skin. His cheeks had sunk in and his eyes seemed to bulge.

"Be damned, the horn." He stepped back and waved for Sadler to come in. Shortchops grabbed a chair at once and sat down. His knees gave way and he barely made it.

"What'n hell you doing here?" he asked.

"Looking for you. Hey, the cops are hunting you. They need some answers."

"Can't. They'll throw me in jail and I'll never get out."

"Not if you had nothing to do with Joisette's OD."

Shortchops closed his eyes and tears seeped out around his lids and wound across wrinkles down his cheeks.

"Oh, yeah, my baby, my wonderful little adopted daughter. Tried to keep her off that shit. Did for a while. She went back. Said she was gonna be a porn queen soon as she got a wardrobe and met the right producer. She even went to Hollywood twice. Got stoned and called me."

"Tell me what happened that night."

"Yeah." He sighed, and for a minute Sadler thought he had gone to sleep or died. He snorted and sat up straighter. "That night. Yeah. Showed her off to you guys, then we went back outside. She gave me a small hit, a quickie, so I could still play, then she wanted one herself. I saw her fill the damn syringe. Way too much. Way too much. I tried to stop her, but I was too late. Then she smiled and told me how great she felt, and almost at once she fell down. I found the syringe and picked it up with my handkerchief and put it in my pocket. The cops would never believe me."

He opened his eyes and stared at Sadler. "I ain't exactly been a church choirboy. Got me a record. Done good lately. Just too much shit for my own body. Got me a woman helps me. Gonna get some money if I ever kick this damn murder rap."

"Maybe I can help."

"Nobody can help but Joisette or that hooker, Nancy. Who was so stoned she didn't even know if it was day or night."

"You still have that syringe wrapped in your handkerchief."

"Oh, yeah. Didn't want the cops to find it."

"You have it now, here?"

Shortchops frowned. "Have it?"

"Do you still have the syringe that Joisette used to shoot up that night she died?"

"Oh, hell, yes. In my drawer." He motioned to the woman, who had hovered in the background holding an iron frying pan. Sadler figured she wasn't doing the dishes.

"Get the handkerchief and the syringe," Shortchops said, sounding more straight than he had all night. The woman frowned, looked at Sadler.

"Sure you ain't a cop?"

"I'm in the Navy, and I play horn with Shortchops."

She nodded after staring hard at him, then went into another room. She came back a few moments later holding a white handkerchief. She started to hand it to Shortchops, but his hands shook so much she gave it to Sadler. He pushed back the edges of the white cloth to see the syringe. Carefully he folded the cloth over it again.

"Shortchops. I'm going to take this downtown to the police. If it has Joisette's fingerprints on it, you'll be in the clear. It will be a simple self-inflicted OD."

"No," he said. "No cops."

The woman walked in front of him and slapped him gently on the cheek. He looked up in surprise.

"Yes. The police. This man can help. You can stop hiding. You can get your money and we can live in a respectable house."

His eyes went wide, his head sagged, and the woman caught him before he fell off the chair. Sadler helped her carry him to the sofa and stretch him out.

"No more heroin for Shortchops," he told her. "This should clear him. You get him dried out and we'll be playing jazz again in two weeks."

Sadler left the room and hurried down to his car. He had put the handkerchief in his civilian jacket pocket and reached for his keys. Three teenage boys sat on the hood of his car. He stopped and stared at them. Two stood and walked toward him.

"Your car, mister?" the one just over six feet asked.

"Yes."

"You did shit by not paying us to protect it. Man, this is our turf. Don't nobody park here without protection." They moved up within three feet of him.

The third boy came up beside the other two. "I have protection," Sadler said. "It's right over there, that unmarked police car." Two of the boys turned to look. He kicked viciously out with his right foot at the boy in the middle who didn't look away. He felt his hard shoe skid off the youth's thigh and land hard into his crotch, smashing penis and testicles upward against his pelvic bones and bringing a wail of agony. The kid slumped to the ground and rolled into a ball.

One of the kids looked back quickly. Sadler slammed a hard right fist into the boy's jaw, and at the same time spun and caught the third boy with a back-kick in the kidney putting him on the ground. The only one standing backed up and lifted his fists, then thought better of it and turned and ran.

"See, I told you guys I had all the protection I need." He walked around them, stepped into his car, and drove away.

Detective Petroff was not in the Central Station when Sadler arrived. The dispatcher put in a call to him, and a half hour later he came in the door and spotted Sadler.

"So, you remembered something?"

Sadler told him the story that Shortchops had told him. The detective held out his hand. "Give," he said.

Sadler frowned. "Shortchops is a friend. I'd hate to see this evidence get lost and you continue to hound him. I'll give you the syringe, but I go with it to your lab and see if they can find prints on it and then find out whose prints they are."

Petroff nodded. "No problem. Right this way."

It only took fifteen minutes. There were plenty of good prints. Detective Petroff had a copy of a full set of prints of the dead girl.

"Match a hundred percent," the print technician said. "No doubt those prints on the syringe are those and only those of Joisette Brown."

Senior Chief Sadler came into the Third Platoon's office just as the SEALs marched back from the afternoon swim. He dropped into the chair beside Murdock's desk and told him the whole story.

"So, Shortchops is free and clear. His woman promised me that she'll dry him out and get the probate under way. There should be no problem with him collecting his three and a half million dollars or whatever it is."

"And you and the other members of the band will each get your fifty thousand?"

"Who knows, Skipper? I'll believe that much money when I see the check. Until then, what's on the Bunsen for tomorrow?"

* * *

Murdock checked out across the Quarterdeck at five and headed home. Next week he would have something to come home to every night. Ardith would be there. She had quit her job in Washington, D.C., and was in the process of closing up her apartment and moving to San Diego. Some of her things had already arrived by truck, and he had stuffed them into the apartment. They would have to find something larger.

She had taken the job there in San Diego's own Silicone Valley. She would be working on problem-solving and client applications for a whole range of computer problems. Nothing had been said about marriage, not yet. He had been considering it for the past month since she had agreed to take the new job in San Diego.

He parked in front of his apartment and took the steps two at a time. Only then did he notice that the front door was open and the security screen door was in place. Had he left it open?

A moment later he charged into the living room and heard a familiar voice from the kitchen.

"Dinner won't be ready for another half hour," Ardith Manchester said. "I figured I'd fly in and surprise you." She came around the door into the living room, where he stood staring.

"Hey, did I get the wrong apartment?" she asked with a grin.

He saw her lovely slender body, her sweeping froth of blonde hair down around her shoulders framing her beautiful face. Soft blue eyes drew him closer, and he stepped forward and pulled her into his arms.

"I like these kind of surprises, young lady. I really do. Are you here for good, and if so, when are the rest of your household things due to arrive?"

She reached up and kissed him tenderly, then with more ardor, before she eased away. "Those special stuffed pork chops have to be watched." She pulled him into the kitchen. "Yes, I'm here to stay. My roommate took over the lease in D.C. All my things are on a truck that will be here within a week. I go to work on Monday morning, and until then we can play house, make love, and house-hunt."

"Sounds good," Murdock said. "Which first?"

Ardith grinned. "Pork chops first, and this special dinner I've been slaving over for two hours. Then we'll see what develops." For a moment panic hit her face. "Oh, dear, this isn't football season yet, is it?"

"Not nearly. Now where are those pork chops? I'm starved." As Murdock worked on the dinner he watched the woman he would marry someday. But even with that kind of distraction, he couldn't help but wonder what was next for the SEALs. Where would they fly off to? What job would they be given to do, either in the open or covertly? What dirty little project would they get next? He took a bite of pork chop, watched Ardith, and grinned. He couldn't wait for the SEALs' next assignment.

SEAL TALK

MILITARY GLOSSARY

Aalvin: Small U.S. two-man submarine.

Admin: Short for administration.

Aegis: Advanced Naval air defense radar system.

AH-1W Super Cobra: Has M179 undernose turret with 20mm Gatling gun.

AK-47: 7.63-round Russian Kalashnikov automatic rifle. Most widely used assault rifle in the world.

AK-74: New, improved version of the Kalashnikov. Fires the 5.45mm round. Has 30-round magazine. Rate of fire: 600 rounds per minute. Many slight variations made for many different nations.

AN/PRC-117D: Radio, also called SATCOM. Works with Milstar satellite in 22,300-mile equatorial orbit for instant worldwide radio, voice, or video communications. Size: 15 inches high, 3 inches wide, 3 inches deep. Weighs 15 pounds. Microphone and voice output. Has encrypter, capable of burst transmissions of less than a second.

AN/PUS-7: Night-vision goggles. Weighs 1.5 pounds.

ANVIS-6: Night-vision goggles on air crewmen's helmets.

APC: Armored Personnel Carrier.

ASROC: Nuclear-tipped antisubmarine rocket torpedoes launched by Navy ships.

Assault Vest: Combat vest with full loadouts of ammo, gear.

ASW: Anti-Submarine Warfare.

Attack Board: Molded plastic with two handgrips with bubble compass on it. Also depth gauge and Cyalume

271

chemical lights with twist knob to regulate amount of light. Used for underwater guidance on long swim.

Aurora: Air Force recon plane. Can circle at 90,000 feet. Can't be seen or heard from ground. Used for thermal imaging.

AWACS: Airborne Warning And Control System. Radar units in high-flying aircraft to scan for planes at any altitude out 200 miles. Controls air-to-air engagements with enemy forces. Planes have a mass of communication and electronic equipment.

Balaclavas: Headgear worn by some SEALs.

Bent Spear: Less serious nuclear violation of safety.

BKA, Bundeskriminant: Germany's federal investigation unit.

Black Talon: Lethal hollow-point ammunition made by Winchester. Outlawed some places.

Blivet: A collapsible fuel container. SEALs sometimes use it.

BLU-43B: Antipersonnel mine used by SEALs.

BLU-96: A fuel-air explosive bomb. It disperses a fuel oil into the air, then explodes the cloud. Many times more powerful than conventional bombs because it doesn't carry its own chemical oxidizers.

BMP-1: Soviet armored fighting vehicle (AFV), low, boxy, crew of 3 and 8 combat troops. Has tracks and a 73mm cannon. Also an AT-3 Sagger antitank missile and coaxial machine gun.

Body Armor: Far too heavy for SEAL use in the water.

Bogey: Pilots' word for an unidentified aircraft.

Boghammar Boat: Long, narrow, low dagger boat; high-speed patrol craft. Swedish make. Iran had 40 of them in 1993.

Boomer: A nuclear-powered missile submarine.

Bought It: A man has been killed. Also "bought the farm."

Bow Cat: The bow catapult on a carrier to launch jets.

Broken Arrow: Any accident with nuclear weapons, or any incident of nuclear material lost, shot down, crashed, stolen, hijacked.

Browning 9mm High Power: A Belgium 9mm pistol, 13 rounds in magazine. First made 1935.

Buddy Line: 6 feet long, ties 2 SEALs together in the water for control and help if needed.

BUD/S: Coronado, California, nickname for SEAL training facility for six months' course.

Bull Pup. Still in testing; new soldier's rifle. SEALs have a dozen of them for regular use. Army gets them in 2005. Has a 5.56 kinetic round, 30-shot clip. Also 20mm high-explosive round and 5-shot magazine. Twenties can be fused for proximity airbursts with use of video camera, laser range finder, and laser targeting. Fuses by number of turns the round needs to reach laser spot. Max range: 1200 yards. Twenty round can also detonate on contact, and has delay fuse. Weapon weighs 14 pounds. SEALs love it. Can in effect "shoot around corners" with the airburst feature.

BUPERS: BUreau of PERSonnel.

C-2A Greyhound: 2-engine turboprop cargo plane that lands on carriers. Also called COD, Carrier Onboard Delivery. Two pilots and engineer. Rear fuselage loading ramp. Cruise speed 300 mph, range 1,000 miles. Will hold 39 combat troops. Lands on CVN carriers at sea.

C-4: Plastic explosive. A claylike explosive that can be molded and shaped. It will burn. Fairly stable.

C-6 Plastique: Plastic explosive. Developed from C-4 and C-5. Is often used in bombs with radio detonator or digital timer.

C-9 Nightingale: Douglas DC-9 fitted as a medical-evacuation transport plane.

C-130 Hercules: Air Force transporter for long haul. 4 engines.

C-141 Starlifter: Airlift transport for cargo, paratroops, evac for long distances. Top speed 566 mph. Range with payload 2,935 miles. Ceiling 41,600 feet.

Caltrops: Small four-pointed spikes used to flatten tires. Used in the Crusades to disable horses.

Camel Back: Used with drinking tube for 70 ounces of water attached to vest.

Cammies: Working camouflaged wear for SEALs. Two different patterns and colors. Jungle and desert.

Cannon Fodder: Old term for soldiers in line of fire destined to die in the grand scheme of warfare.

Capped: Killed, shot, or otherwise snuffed.

CAR-15: The Colt M-4Al. Sliding-stock carbine with grenade launcher under barrel. Knight sound-suppressor. Can have AN/PAQ-4 laser aiming light under the carrying handle. .223 round. 20- or 30-round magazine. Rate of fire: 700 to 1,000 rounds per minute.

Cascade Radiation: U-235 triggers secondary radiation in other dense materials.

Castle Keep: The main tower in any castle.

Cast Off: Leave a dock, port, land. Get lost. Navy: long, then short signal of horn, whistle, or light.

Caving Ladder: Roll-up ladder that can be let down to climb.

CH-46E: Sea Knight chopper. Twin rotors, transport. Can carry 25 combat troops. Has a crew of 3. Cruise speed 154 mph. Range 420 miles.

CH-53D Sea Stallion: Big Chopper. Not used much anymore.

Chaff: A small cloud of thin pieces of metal, such as tinsel, that can be picked up by enemy radar and that can attract a radar-guided missile away from the plane to hit the chaff.

Charlie-Mike: Code words for continue the mission.

Chief to Chief: Bad conduct by EM handled by chiefs so no record shows or is passed up the chain of command.

Chocolate Mountains: Land training center for SEALs near these mountains in the California desert.

Christians In Action: SEAL talk for not-always-friendly CIA.

CIA: Central Intelligence Agency.

CIC: Combat Information Center. The place on a ship where communications and control areas are situated to open and control combat fire.

CINC: Commander IN Chief.

CINCLANT: Navy Commander-IN-Chief, atLANTtic.

CINCPAC: Commander-IN-Chief, PACific.

Class of 1978: Not a single man finished BUD/S training in this class. All-time record.

Claymore: An antipersonnel mine carried by SEALs on many of their missions.

Cluster Bombs: A canister bomb that explodes and spreads small bomblets over a great area. Used against parked aircraft, massed troops, and unarmored vehicles.

CNO: Chief of Naval Operations.

CO-2 Poisoning: During deep dives. Abort dive at once and surface.

COD: Carrier Onboard Delivery plane.

Cold Pack Rations: Food carried by SEALs to use if needed.

Combat Harness: American Body Armor nylon-mesh special-operations vest. 6 2-magazine pouches for drum-fed belts, other pouches for other weapons, waterproof pouch for Motorola.

CONUS: The Continental United States.

Corfams: Dress shoes for SEALs.

Covert Action Staff: A CIA group that handles all covert action by the SEALs.

CQB house: Close Quarters Battle house. Training facility near Nyland in the desert training area. Also called the Kill House.

CQB: Close Quarters Battle. A fight that's up close, hand-to-hand, whites-of-his-eyes, blood all over you.

CRRC Bundle: Roll it off plane, sub, boat. The assault boat for 8 SEALs. Also the IBS, Inflatable Boat Small.

Cutting Charge: Lead-sheathed explosive. Triangular strip of high-velocity explosive sheathed in metal. Point of the triangle focuses a shaped-charge effect. Cuts a pencil-line-wide hole to slice a steel girder in half.

CVN: A U.S. aircraft carrier with nuclear power. Largest that we have in fleet.

CYA: Cover Your Ass, protect yourself from friendlies or officers above you and JAG people.

Damfino: Damned if I know. SEAL talk.

DDS: Dry Dock Shelter. A clamshell unit on subs to deliver SEALs and SDVs to a mission.

DEFCON: DEFense CONdition. How serious is the threat?

Delta Forces: Army special forces, much like SEALs.

Desert Cammies: Three-color, desert tan and pale green with streaks of pink. For use on land.

DIA: Defense Intelligence Agency.

Dilos Class Patrol Boat: Greek, 29 feet long, 75 tons displacement.

Dirty Shirt Mess: Officers can eat there in flying suits on board a carrier.

DNS: Doppler Navigation System.

Draegr LAR V: Rebreather that SEALs use. No bubbles.

DREC: Digitally Reconnoiterable Electronic Component. Top-secret computer chip from NSA that lets it decipher any U.S. military electronic code.

E-2C Hawkeye: Navy, carrier-based, Airborne Early Warning craft for long-range early warning and threat-assessment and fighter-direction. Has a 24-foot saucer-like rotodome over the wing. Crew 5, max speed 326 knots, ceiling 30,800 feet, radius 175 nautical miles with 4 hours on station.

E-3A Skywarrior: Old electronic intelligence craft. Replaced by the newer ES-3A.

E-4B NEACP: Called Kneecap. National Emergency Airborne Command Post. A greatly modified Boeing 747 used as a communications base for the President of the United States and other high-ranking officials in an emergency and in wartime.

E & E: SEAL talk for escape and evasion.

EA-6B Prowler: Navy plane with electronic countermeasures. Crew of 4, max speed 566 knots, ceiling 41,200 feet, range with max load 955 nautical miles.

EAR: Enhanced Acoustic Rifle. Fires not bullets, but a high-impact blast of sound that puts the target down and unconscious for up to six hours. Leaves him with almost no aftereffects. Used as a non-lethal weapon. The sound blast will bounce around inside a building, vehicle, or ship and knock out anyone who is within range. Ten shots before the weapon must be electrically charged. Range: about 200 yards.

Easy: The only easy day was yesterday. SEAL talk.

Ejection seat: The seat is powered by a CAD, a shotgun-like shell that is activated when the pilot triggers the ejection. The shell is fired into a solid rocket, sets it off and propels the whole ejection seat and pilot into the air. No electronics are involved.

ELINT: ELectronic INTelligence. Often from satellite in orbit, picture-taker, or other electronic communications.

EMP: ElectroMagnetic Pulse: The result of an E-bomb detonation. One type E-bomb is the Flux Compression Generator or FCG. Can be built for $400 and is relatively simple to make. Emits a rampaging electromagnetic pulse that destroys anything electronic in a 100 mile diameter circle. Blows out and fries all computers, telephone systems, TV broadcasts, radio, streetlights, and sends the area back into the stone age with no communications whatsoever. Stops all cars with electronic ignitions, drops jet planes out of the air including airliners, fighters and bombers, and stalls ships with electronic guidance and steering systems. When such a bomb is detonated the explosion is small but sounds like a giant lightning strike.

EOD: Navy experts in nuclear material and radioactivity who do Explosive Ordnance Disposal.

Equatorial Satellite Pointing Guide: To aim antenna for radio to pick up satellite signals.

ES-3A: Electronic Intelligence (ELINT) intercept craft. The platform for the battle group Passive Horizon Extension System. Stays up for long patrol periods, has comprehensive set of sensors, lands and takes off from a carrier. Has 63 antennas.

ETA: Estimated Time of Arrival.

Executive Order 12333: By President Reagan authorizing Special Warfare units such as the SEALs.

Exfil: Exfiltrate, to get out of an area.

F/A-18 Hornet: Carrier-based interceptor that can change from air-to-air to air-to-ground attack mode while in flight.

Fitrep: Fitness Report.

Flashbang Grenade: Non-lethal grenade that gives off a series of piercing explosive sounds and a series of brilliant strobe-type lights to disable an enemy.

Flotation Bag: To hold equipment, ammo, gear on a wet operation.

Fort Fumble: SEALs' name for the Pentagon.

Forty-mm Rifle Grenade: The M576 multipurpose round, contains 20 large lead balls. SEALs use on Colt M-4A1.

Four-Striper: A Navy captain.

Fox Three: In air warfare, a code phrase showing that a Navy F-14 has launched a Phoenix air-to-air missile.

FUBAR: SEAL talk. Fucked Up Beyond All Repair.

Full Helmet Masks: For high-altitude jumps. Oxygen in mask.

G-3: German-made assault rifle.

Gloves: SEALs wear sage-green, fire-resistant Nomex flight gloves.

GMT: Greenwich Mean Time. Where it's all measured from.

GPS: Global Positioning System. A program with satellites around Earth to pinpoint precisely aircraft, ships, vehicles, and ground troops. Position information is to plus or minus ten feet. Also can give speed of a plane or ship to one quarter of a mile per hour.

GPSL: A radio antenna with floating wire that pops to the surface. Antenna picks up positioning from the closest 4 global positioning satellites and gives an exact position within 10 feet.

Green Tape: Green sticky ordnance tape that has a hundred uses for a SEAL.

GSG-9: Flashbang grenade developed by Germans. A cardboard tube filled with 5 separate charges timed to burst in rapid succession. Blinding and giving concussion to enemy, leaving targets stunned, easy to kill or capture. Usually non-lethal.

GSG9: Grenzschutzgruppe Nine. Germany's best special warfare unit, counterterrorist group.

Gulfstream II (VCII): Large executive jet used by services for transport of small groups quickly. Crew of 3 and 18 passengers. Maximum cruise speed 581 mph. Maximum range 4,275 miles.

H & K 21A1: Machine gun with 7.62 NATO round. Replaces the older, more fragile M-60 E3. Fires 900 rounds per minute. Range 1,100 meters. All types of NATO rounds, ball, incendiary, tracer.

H & K G-11: Automatic rifle, new type. 4.7mm caseless ammunition. 50-round magazine. The bullet is in a sleeve of solid propellant with a special thin plastic coating around it. Fires 600 rounds per minute. Single-shot, three-round burst, or fully automatic.

H & K MP-5SD: 9mm submachine gun with integral silenced barrel, single-shot, three-shot, or fully automatic. Rate 800 rds/min.

H & K P9S: Heckler & Koch's 9mm Parabellum double-action semiauto pistol with 9-round magazine.

H & K PSG1: 7.62 NATO round. High-precision, bolt-action, sniping rifle. 5- to 20-round magazine. Roller lock delayed blowback breech system. Fully adjustable stock. 6 × 42 telescopic sights. Sound suppressor.

HAHO: High Altitude jump, High Opening. From 30,000 feet, open chute for glide up to 15 miles to ground. Up to 75 minutes in glide. To enter enemy territory or enemy position unheard.

Half-Track: Military vehicle with tracked rear drive and wheels in front, usually armed and armored.

HALO: High Altitude jump, Low Opening. From 30,000 feet. Free fall in 2 minutes to 2,000 feet and open chute. Little forward movement. Get to ground quickly, silently.

Hamburgers: Often called sliders on a Navy carrier.

Handie-Talkie: Small, handheld personal radio. Short range.

HELO: SEAL talk for helicopter.

Herky Bird: C-130 Hercules transport. Most-flown military transport in the world. For cargo or passengers, paratroops, aerial refueling, search and rescue, communications, and as a gunship. Has flown from a Navy carrier deck without use of catapult. Four turboprop engines, max speed 325 knots, range at max payload 2,356 miles.

Hezbollah: Lebanese Shiite Moslem militia. Party of God.

HMMWV: The Humvee, U.S. light utility truck, replaced the honored jeep. Multipurpose wheeled vehicle, 4 × 4, automatic transmission, power steering. Engine: Detroit Diesel 150-hp diesel V-8 air-cooled. Top speed 65 mph. Range 300 miles.

Hotels: SEAL talk for hostages.

Humint: Human Intelligence. Acquired on the ground; a person as opposed to satellite or photo recon.

Hydra-Shock: Lethal hollow-point ammunition made by Federal Cartridge Company. Outlawed in some areas.

Hypothermia: Danger to SEALs. A drop in body temperature that can be fatal.

IBS: Inflatable Boat Small. 12 × 6 feet. Carries 8 men and 1,000 pounds of weapons and gear. Hard to sink. Quiet motor. Used for silent beach, bay, lake landings.

IR Beacon: Infrared beacon. For silent nighttime signaling.

IR Goggles: "Sees" heat instead of light.

Islamic Jihad: Arab holy war.

Isothermal layer: A colder layer of ocean water that deflects sonar rays. Submarines can hide below it, but then are also blind to what's going on above them since their sonar will not penetrate the layer.

IV Pack: Intravenous fluid that you can drink if out of water.

JAG: Judge Advocate General. The Navy's legal investigating arm that is independent of any Navy command.

JNA: Yugoslav National Army.

JP-4: Normal military jet fuel.

JSOC: Joint Special Operations Command.

JSOCCOMCENT: Joint Special Operations Command Center in the Pentagon.

KA-BAR: SEALs' combat, fighting knife.

KATN: Kick Ass and Take Names. SEAL talk, get the mission in gear.

KH-11: Spy satellite, takes pictures of ground, IR photos, etc.

KIA: Killed In Action.

KISS: Keep It Simple, Stupid. SEAL talk for streamlined operations.

Klick: A kilometer of distance. Often used as a mile. From Vietnam era, but still widely used in military.

Krytrons: Complicated, intricate timers used in making nuclear explosive detonators.

KV-57: Encoder for messages, scrambles.

Laser Pistol: The SIW pinpoint of ruby light emitted on any pistol for aiming. Usually a silenced weapon.

Left Behind: In 30 years SEALs have seldom left behind a dead comrade, never a wounded one. Never been taken prisoner.

Let's Get the Hell out of Dodge: SEAL talk for leaving a place, bugging out, hauling ass.

Liaison: Close-connection, cooperating person from one unit or service to another. Military liaison.

Light Sticks: Chemical units that make light after twisting to release chemicals that phosphoresce.

Loot & Shoot: SEAL talk for getting into action on a mission.

LT: Short for lieutenant in SEAL talk.

LZ: Landing Zone.

M1-8: Russian Chopper.

M1A1 M-14: Match rifle upgraded for SEAL snipers.

M-3 Submachine Gun: WWII grease gun, .45-caliber. Cheap. Introduced in 1942.

M-16: Automatic U.S. rifle. 5.56 round. Magazine 20 or 30, rate of fire 700 to 950 rds/min. Can attach M203 40mm grenade launcher under barrel.

M-18 Claymore: Antipersonnel mine. A slab of C-4 with 200 small ball bearings. Set off electrically or by trip wire. Can be positioned and aimed. Sprays out a cloud of balls. Kill zone 50 meters.

M60 Machine Gun: Can use 100-round ammo box snapped onto the gun's receiver. Not used much now by SEALs.

M-60E3: Lightweight handheld machine gun. Not used now by the SEALs.

M61A1: The usual 20mm cannon used on many American fighter planes.

M61(j): Machine Pistol. Yugoslav make.

M662: A red flare for signaling.

M-86: Pursuit Deterrent Munitions. Various types of

mines, grenades, trip-wire explosives, and other devices in antipersonnel use.

M-203: A 40mm grenade launcher fitted under an M-16 or the M-4A1 Commando. Can fire a variety of grenade types up to 200 yards.

MagSafe: Lethal ammunition that fragments in human body and does not exit. Favored by some police units to cut down on second kill from regular ammunition exiting a body.

Make a Peek: A quick look, usually out of the water, to check your position or tactical situation.

Mark 23 Mod O: Special operations offensive handgun system. Double-action, 12-round magazine. Ambidextrous safety and mag-release catches. Knight screw-on suppressor. Snap-on laser for sighting. .45-caliber. Weighs 4 pounds loaded. 9.5 inches long; with silencer, 16.5 inches long.

Mark II Knife: Navy-issue combat knife.

Mark VIII SDV: Swimmer Delivery Vehicle. A bus, SEAL talk. 21 feet long, beam and draft 4 feet, 6 knots for 6 hours.

Master-at-Arms: Military police commander on board a ship.

MAVRIC Lance: A nuclear alert for stolen nukes or radioactive goods.

MC-130 Combat Talon: A specially equipped Hercules for covert missions in enemy or unfriendly territory.

McMillan M87R: Bolt-action sniper rifle. .50-caliber. 53 inches long. Bipod, fixed 5- or 10-round magazine. Bulbous muzzle brake on end of barrel. Deadly up to a mile. All types .50-caliber ammo.

MGS: Modified Grooming Standards. So SEALs don't all look like military, to enable them to do undercover work in mufti.

MH-53J: Chopper, updated CH053 from Nam days. 200 mph, called the Pave Low III.

MH-60K Black Hawk: Navy chopper. Forward infrared system for low-level night flight. Radar for terra follow/ avoidance. Crew of 3, takes 12 troops. Top speed 225 mph. Ceiling 4,000 feet. Range radius 230 miles. Arms: two 12.7mm machine guns.

MI-15: British domestic intelligence agency.

MI-16: British foreign intelligence and espionage.

MIDEASTFOR: Middle East Force.

MiG: Russian-built fighter, many versions, used in many nations around the world.

Mike Boat: Liberty boat off a large ship.

Mike-Mike: Short for mm, millimeter, as 9 mike-mike.

Milstar: Communications satellite for pickup and bouncing from SATCOM and other radio transmitters. Used by SEALs.

Minigun: In choppers. Can fire 2,000 rounds per minute. Gatling gun-type.

Mitrajez M80: Machine gun from Yugoslavia.

Mocha: Food energy bar SEALs carry in vest pockets.

Mossberg: Pump-action, pistol-grip, 5-round magazine. SEALs use it for close-in work.

Motorola Radio: Personal radio, short range, lip mike, earpiece, belt pack.

MRE: Meals Ready to Eat. Field rations used by most of U.S. Armed Forces and the SEALs as well. Long-lasting.

MSPF: Maritime Special Purpose Force.

Mugger: MUGR, Miniature Underwater Global locator device. Sends up antenna for pickup on positioning satellites. Works under water or above. Gives location within 10 feet.

Mujahideen: A soldier of Allah in Muslim nations.

NAVAIR: NAVy AIR command.

NAVSPECWARGRUP-ONE: Naval Special Warfare Group One based on Coronado, CA. SEALs are in this command.

NAVSPECWARGRUP-TWO: Naval Special Warfare Group Two based at Little Creek, VA.

NCIS: Naval Criminal Investigative Service. A civilian operation not reporting to any Navy authority to make it more responsible and responsive. Replaces the old NIS, Naval Investigation Service, that did report to the closest admiral.

NEST: Nuclear Energy Search Team. Non-military unit that reports at once to any spill, problem, or Broken Arrow to determine the extent of the radiation problem.

NEWBIE: A new man, officer, or commander of an established military unit.

NKSF: North Korean Special Forces.

NLA: Iranian National Liberation Army. About 4,500 men in South Iraq, helped by Iraq for possible use against Iran.

Nomex: The type of material used for flight suits and hoods.

NPIC: National Photographic Interpretation Center in D.C.

NRO: National Reconnaissance Office. To run and coordinate satellite development and operations for the intelligence community.

NSA: National Security Agency.

NSC: National Security Council. Meets in Situation Room, support facility in the Executive Office Building in D.C. Main security group in the nation.

NSVHURAWN: Iranian Marines.

NUCFLASH: An alert for any nuclear problem.

NVG One Eye: Litton single-eyepiece Night-Vision Goggles. Prevents NVG blindness in both eyes if a flare goes off.

NVGs: Night-Vision Goggles. One eye or two. Give good night vision in the dark with a greenish view.

OAS: Obstacle Avoidance Sonar. Used on many low-flying attack aircraft.

OIC: Officer In Charge.

Oil Tanker: One is: 885 feet long, 140 foot beam, 121,000 tons, 13 cargo tanks that hold 35.8 million gallons of fuel, oil, or gas. 24 in the crew. This is a regular-sized tanker. Not a supertanker.

OOD: Officer Of the Deck.

Orion P-3: Navy's long-range patrol and antisub aircraft. Some adapted to ELINT roles. Crew of 10. Max speed loaded 473 mph. Ceiling 28,300 feet. Arms: internal weapons bay and 10 external weapons stations for a mix of torpedoes, mines, rockets, and bombs.

Passive Sonar: Listening for engine noise of a ship or sub.

It doesn't give away the hunter's presence as an active sonar would.

Pave Low III: A Navy chopper.

PBR: Patrol Boat River. U.S. has many shapes, sizes, and with various types of armament.

PC-170: Patrol Coastal-Class 170-foot SEAL delivery vehicle. Powered by four 3,350 hp diesel engines, beam of 25 feet and draft of 7.8 feet. Top speed 35 knots, range 2,000 nautical miles. Fixed swimmer platform on stern. Crew of 4 officers and 24 EM, carries 8 SEALs.

Plank Owners: Original men in the start-up of a new military unit.

Polycarbonate material: Bullet-proof glass.

PRF: People's Revolutionary Front. Fictional group in *NUCFLASH,* a SEAL Team Seven book.

Prowl & Growl: SEAL talk for moving into a combat mission.

Quitting Bell: In BUD/S training. Ring it and you quit the SEAL unit. Helmets of men who quit the class are lined up below the bell in Coronado. (Recently they have stopped ringing the bell. Dropouts simply place their helmet below the bell and go.)

RAF: Red Army Faction. A once-powerful German terrorist group, not so active now.

Remington 200: Sniper Rifle. Not used by SEALs now.

Remington 700: Sniper rifle with Starlight Scope. Can extend night vision to 400 meters.

RIB: Rigid Inflatable Boat. 3 sizes, one 10 meters, 40 knots.

Ring Knocker: An Annapolis graduate with the ring.

RIO: Radar Intercept Officer. The officer who sits in the backseat of an F-14 Tomcat off a carrier. The job: find enemy targets in the air and on the sea.

Roger That: A yes, an affirmative, a go answer to a command or statement.

RPG: Rocket Propelled Grenade. Quick and easy, shoulder-fired. Favorite weapon of terrorists, insurgents.

SAS: British Special Air Service. Commandos. Special warfare men. Best that Britain has. Works with SEALs.

SATCOM: Satellite-based communications system for instant contact with anyone anywhere in the world. SEALs rely on it.

SAW: Squad's Automatic Weapon. Usually a machine gun or automatic rifle.

SBS: Special Boat Squadron. On-site Navy unit that transports SEALs to many of their missions. Located across the street from the SEALs' Coronado, California, headquarters.

SD3: Sound-suppression system on the H & K MP5 weapon.

SDV: Swimmer Delivery Vehicle. SEALs use a variety of them.

Seahawk SH-60: Navy chopper for ASW and SAR. Top speed 180 knots, ceiling 13,800 feet, range 503 miles, arms: 2 Mark 46 torpedoes.

SEAL Headgear: Boonie hat, wool balaclava, green scarf, watch cap, bandanna roll.

Second in Command: Also 2IC for short in SEAL talk.

SERE: Survival, Evasion, Resistance, and Escape training.

Shipped for Six: Enlisted for six more years in the Navy.

Shit City: Coronado SEALs' name for Norfolk.

Show Colors: In combat put U.S. flag or other identification on back for easy identification by friendly air or ground units.

Sierra Charlie: SEAL talk for everything on schedule.

Simunition: Canadian product for training that uses paint balls instead of lead for bullets.

Sixteen-Man Platoon: Basic SEAL combat force. Up from 14 men a few years ago.

Sked: SEAL talk for schedule.

Sonobuoy: Small underwater device that detects sounds and transmits them by radio to plane or ship.

Space Blanket: Green foil blanket to keep troops warm. Vacuum-packed and folded to a cigarette-sized package.

SPIE: Special Purpose Insertion and Extraction rig. Essentially a long rope dangled from a chopper with hardware on it that is attached to each SEAL's chest right on his lift harness. Set up to lift six or eight men out of harm's way quickly by a chopper.

Sprayers and Prayers: Not the SEAL way. These men

spray bullets all over the place hoping for hits. SEALs do more aimed firing for sure kills.

SS-19: Russian ICBM missile.

STABO: Use harness and lines under chopper to get down to the ground.

STAR: Surface To Air Recovery operation.

Starflash Round: Shotgun round that shoots out sparkling fireballs that ricochet wildly around a room, confusing and terrifying the occupants. Non-lethal.

Stasi: Old-time East German secret police.

Stick: British terminology: 2 4-man SAS teams.

Stokes: A kind of Navy stretcher. Open coffin shaped of wire mesh and white canvas for emergency patient transport.

STOL: Short TakeOff and Landing. Aircraft with high-lift wings and vectored-thrust engines to produce extremely short takeoffs and landings.

Sub Gun: Submachine gun, often the suppressed H & K MP5.

Suits: Civilians, usually government officials wearing suits.

Sweat: The more SEALs sweat in peacetime, the less they bleed in war.

Sykes-Fairbairn: A commando fighting knife.

Syrette: Small syringe for field administration often filled with morphine. Can be self-administered.

Tango: SEAL talk for a terrorist.

TDY: Temporary duty assigned outside of normal job designation.

Terr: Another term for terrorist. Shorthand SEAL talk.

Tetrahedral reflectors: Show up on multi-mode radar like tiny suns.

Thermal Imager: Device to detect warmth, as a human body, at night or through light cover.

Thermal Tape: ID for night-vision-goggle user to see. Used on friendlies.

TNAZ: Trinittroaze Tidine. Explosive to replace C-4. 15% stronger than C-4 and 20% lighter.

TO&E: Table showing organization and equipment of a military unit.

Top SEAL Tribute: "You sweet motherfucker, don't you never die!"

Trailing Array: A group of antennas for sonar pickup trailed out of a submarine.

Train: For contact in smoke, no light, fog, etc. Men directly behind each other. Right hand on weapon, left hand on shoulder of man ahead. Squeeze shoulder to signal.

Trident: SEALs' emblem. An eagle with talons clutching a Revolutionary War pistol, and Neptune's trident superimposed on the Navy's traditional anchor.

TRW: A camera's digital record that is sent by SATCOM.

TT33: Tokarev, a Russian pistol.

UAZ: A Soviet 1-ton truck.

UBA Mark XV: Underwater life support with computer to regulate the rebreather's gas mixture.

UGS: Unmanned Ground Sensors. Can be used to explode booby traps and claymore mines.

UNODIR: Unless otherwise directed. The unit will start the operation unless they are told not to.

VBSS: Orders to "visit, board, search, and seize."

Wadi: A gully or ravine, usually in a desert.

White Shirt: Man responsible for safety on carrier deck as he leads around civilians and personnel unfamiliar with the flight deck.

WIA: Wounded In Action.

Zodiac: Also called an IBS, Inflatable Boat Small. 15 × 6 feet, weighs 265 pounds. The "rubber duck" can carry 8 fully equipped SEALs. Can do 18 knots with a range of 65 nautical miles.

Zulu: Means Greenwich Mean Time, GMT. Used in all formal military communications.

From the author of
Marine Sniper
CHARLES HENDERSON

The Marine Sniper's Vietnam story continues in

SILENT WARRIOR

Available in paperback
in January 2003
from Berkley
0-425-18864-7

Also look for Henderson's
—THE FALL OF SAIGON—

The story of the fall of South Vietnam
and the evacuation of the last American Marines
from that country

Coming soon in hardcover from Berkley
0-425-18846-9